FLIGHT FOR TRUTH

CORRUPTION RUNS DEEP within the airline industry when Captain Darby Bradshaw is grounded and forced into a psychiatric evaluation in response to reporting safety concerns to senior leadership at Global Air Lines. What she doesn't know is that her removal is nothing short of a conspiracy to silence her safety concerns. Privatization of ATC, approval of drone operated commercial aircraft, short-cutting training, and the untimely crash of a Boeing 737 MAX are all tied to Darby's report. Her resultant research is about to uncover the truth. How high does this go? All the way to the White House. Not even her friends FAA Manager Kathryn Jacobs, DOT Secretary John McAllister, or Psychiatrist Linda Madden, can do anything to help her. The question is—can she save herself?

This is the fifth in the Fight For Series where truth is scarier than fiction. Flight For Justice coming soon, where it's not about truth and justice, but what you can prove in court.

Inspiration. Motivation. Plane Stuff.

"Sometimes truth is scarier than fiction"

By Karlene K. Petitt

at

Flight To Success

www.KarlenePetitt.com

FLIGHT FOR TRUTH

KARLENE K. PETITT

JET STAR PUBLISHING INC.
SEATAC WA

"It's no wonder that truth is stranger than fiction. Fiction has to make sense"

Mark Twain

DEDICATION

FLIGHT FOR TRUTH is dedicated to all those people who have faced an atrocity due to the abuse of power. Losing control of your life due to the unethical decisions of others feels like a passenger in a plane that is going down. But remember one thing—as long as you survive, your life is not over, it will just be different. Make that difference count and fight for truth.

FLIGHT
FOR
TRUTH

PROLOGUE

JACKSON RETURNED FROM his break, popping a couple antacid tablets into his mouth as he did. As the supervisor on duty in the SeaTac control tower, his responsibilities ran deep. He understood all too well that one misdirection could destroy many lives, including his.

Today the visibility was low, tensions were high, and the airspace was busy. Not unusual for Seattle. Days like this enhanced his appreciation for a clear day when he could see forever. He thought about forever as he sipped from his fourth cup of coffee of the day. He sighed. Nothing lasted forever.

Jackson had been working this tower just short of nine months since his transfer from the easy pace of Yakima, Washington. He had no idea what he was getting into at the time. He quickly learned, and each day he regretted his decision just a little bit more.

Stepping behind one of his controllers, he glanced at the screen. Global 32 had just been cleared to land on runway 16L. Alaska was arriving on 16R a half-mile behind. They were lined up five deep on the left, four deep on the right and multiple aircraft were on various arrivals. The center runway was closed for construction. God, he hoped they would open it soon.

The visibility was 4000 meters and light drizzle.

Jackson watched the arrivals as landing lights cut through the clouds—a beacon of warning that they were here, and would be landing shortly thereafter. Then the next aircraft would arrive. Then another, and another. One missed approach would mess up his perfectly choreographed play. One crash and the show would be over.

"What the hell?" he said. Setting his cup on the desk, Jackson darted his attention from the aircraft that broke through the mist toward Tom's screen. "Is Global lined up on the taxiway?"

"Shit!" Tom said, and called the aircraft. "Global 32, check your course."

Jackson's heart rate accelerated as he grabbed a headset to listen to the communications.

"Global 32 is correcting," one of the pilots stated.

They were not correcting. They appeared to be headed toward the tower. Jackson lifted binoculars and assessed the position and direction. Within seconds, warnings in the control tower screamed and lights flashed. Global was not correcting their course. They were aligned with the taxiway, but drifting his direction. *How the hell could they not see that they weren't aligned with the runway?*

Hell, they were a few degrees from heading directly toward the tower. He glanced at the wind velocity. A twenty-two knot crosswind wasn't helping.

"Global 32 go around!" Tom yelled. There was no response. The plane continued on its path. "Global 32 go around!" Tom shouted again. This time there was panic in his voice. He was a man screaming for his life.

Jackson contemplated evacuating the tower, but that thought was short lived. There wasn't time. Even if they landed on the aircraft taxiing below, they were done. The explosion would take them out regardless.

He reached over to sound the disaster alert and engage the fire department, but before he pressed the button the Global 737 began to climb.

"Global 32 is on the missed," one of the pilots stated.

Jackson wasn't going to die today. At least not in the next few minutes. But that knowledge did nothing to reduce his heart rate. He breathed deeply and closed his eyes, and then he said a silent prayer.

He hadn't realized how easily his life could be taken in the tower until now. Pilots were responsible for more than the lives of their passengers, but also the lives of everyone on the ground, including those in the tower. Death by airplane impacted thousands.

Now he understood why his predecessor had retired early. Months earlier, a mechanic had stolen an airplane from Alaska Airlines. He had taken a joy ride and then crashed it on Ketron Island. Only the pilot died in that accident, but he could have crashed it anywhere. That event opened the door to Jackson moving to Seattle.

Wondering if the stress was worth it, he watched the plane fly over the taxiway not more than 50 feet above a KLM 747 and three Alaska 737's. He lifted the binoculars once again, and watched the aircraft continue its climb. He then lowered his view from the aircraft to the FAA building just below. The government had built this facility just blocks south of the airport, directly under the flight path.

What the hell were they thinking placing that building off the end of a runway? he wondered. All it took was one pilot pissed off at the FAA, crashing into that facility, and all the pilot's problems would go away in seconds. There would be absolutely nothing anyone could do.

He lowered his glasses to where Global Flight 85 had crashed with the drugged pilot. That plane would have barreled through the heart of the FAA building if it had existed at the time.

The stories of Captain Bill Jacobs were still alive in the SeaTac control tower. Jacobs was not only behind the crash of Flight 85 but others as well. Then he had intentionally landed his plane in Puget Sound. *There are crazy people everywhere*, he thought.

"Tom," Jackson said, as he set the binoculars on the desk. "Brian's got your station, come with me."

They stepped away from the desk after Brian took over. He needed Tom to not only write up the event, but also to decompress. Jackson needed to assess if Tom could continue for the day. An event like this was not taken lightly.

"Write this up while it's still fresh." He worked to lower his voice. "Add to your report that they were off course and did not correct, despite your command and their statements of compliance. Make sure you include that you ordered them to go around twice. Not until your second command, did they comply."

Global was growing quickly in the Seattle market, and trying to push out Alaska. But Jackson would be damned if corporate political power and money would jeopardize the safety of his airspace. As far as he was concerned Global had far too many incidents in his backyard, beyond Bill Jacob's efforts.

Rapid growth led to instability, but this was getting to the point of ridiculousness. How long could an airline ride on the wings of luck? He only hoped they would get their shit together before it was too late.

Global Air Lines may have placed first in customer service for the quarter, but they sat in 15th place for safety. Jackson was astounded that passengers took their safety for granted. But then again, he supposed ignorant bliss was a way of life for many. As long as customers were treated well, nobody thought about safety. He placed two fingers to his wrist to check his heart rate. Better.

"Hey, you okay boss?" Don asked as he walked by. Don was one of the most senior controllers and Jackson was glad to have him on his team. He was also grateful to have him as a friend.

Jackson nodded and said, "Yep. But it looks like I picked the wrong week to stop sniffing glue."

"Welcome to my world," Don said with a grin. "And it only gets better."

CHAPTER 1

YAWNING, DARBY LAY in her bed and stared at the ceiling. There was one way to drive pilots nuts—ground them. She had thought about filing an on the job injury with her first signs of depression, but they would use that against her and call her crazy. Oh wait—they already had. She closed her eyes, wanting to fall back asleep and start her entire life over.

It had been nine months since Darby had flown an airplane. She'd gone from captain of a Boeing 757 to flying a couch—if she hadn't been crazy before, she was certainly working toward that reality now. Sucking in a deep breath, she threw back the covers and dropped her feet to the floor.

With a sigh, she pulled on her robe but didn't bother with her slippers. She left her robe hanging open, and headed down the stairs with a mission. Coffee.

Global Air Lines had grounded Darby on December 19, 2016, and she had been counting the days until her return. The truth was, she didn't know if she would ever get back. Fortunately, the company's delay had not killed her determination. She still had a little fight left in her regardless of some really hard days. Her friend Linda had told her depression was normal.

Darby wandered into her kitchen and opened the blinds. The streets were silent, but it was early. She glanced toward the sky. It would be a beautiful day in Seattle. If only she could fly. Technically she could fly small planes because they never pulled her medical or her license. But she didn't. She wasn't quite sure why not. Maybe that was a reminder of what she'd lost.

Despite Global's allegations, and her union advising her not to get her medical because she didn't need it, Darby had applied for her first class medical certificate and had gotten it. Once the union knew she was applying for her medical certificate, they advised her to not name the doctors she had been forced to see. They didn't want her to state she was going to psychiatric evaluations. She didn't listen to that advice either. Instead, she wrote on the medical form the names of all the doctors and the number of visits.

The reason that she gave to the FAA—"Labor dispute. AIR 21 filed." Apparently, the FAA knew what that meant. It appeared the FAA also knew that airlines used this tactic as a weapon, and therefore did not question her statement. Otherwise they would most certainly have denied it. The FAA allowed Darby to retain her medical, yet Global would not allow her to fly.

She opened her dishwasher and retrieved a cup. Her chief pilot had the nerve to compare her to the Germanwings pilot who had flown into a mountain and killed everyone on his plane. It was a lame ass statement that created nothing but fear, making it easy for the public to accept the removal of any pilot. Those accusations made management look like a hero because the public didn't understand or know the truth.

The truth was, a pilot who loves flying, loves people and life… no matter what mental health issue that befalls them, would not do such a thing. Sadly, many pilots have killed themselves, but not in an airplane. That was sacred. Only a sociopath would commit mass murder in the process.

Depression takes your own life. A sociopath takes the lives of others. Which made sense as to why Global management was trying to take Darby's life. There were definitive, clear signs of sociopathic behavior in upper management at Global Air Lines that could not be ignored.

Placing her cup into position, she dropped a pod of chocolate raspberry coffee into the Keurig dispenser. She closed the lid and pressed the button for the biggest cup. A ritual she did each morning. Sometimes more than once.

She glanced at her phone—55 minutes until show time. Darby opened the fridge and grabbed a carton of cream. After her cup was filled, she added a dollop. *Cold cream.* There was a time that she only added hot cream.

Being grounded sucked. Being grounded for no reason was unconscionable. Being grounded for reporting safety was criminal. All she had done was give Wyatt and Clark, the two top managers in flight operations, an internal report to improve operational safety. Hell, they could have thrown it away. They didn't have to kill the messenger. She ripped open a package of stevia and dumped the contents into her mug.

Darby wandered into the living room and sunk into her leather couch, glancing at her phone once again. She held her coffee cup with one hand and sipped, while setting an alarm on her phone with the other.

The oddity of time not moving, but then disappearing without warning was something that caught her off guard these days. Alarms were her friend. She set her phone down, stared into her cup for a long moment, and then sipped.

Global said they pulled her from duty because of something she had said to a manager. Then someone else said it was her behavior. The hell if she knew what the reason was, because they wouldn't tell her. She and some woman had sat in the middle of a hotel lobby discussing her safety report for over three hours, and then a week later Darby had a mental health problem.

That meeting was something she had revisited many times over the previous nine months, but she could not figure out what she could have said to give that impression. All she had done was talk about the report, training, and safety. She had actually liked the woman when they first met, albeit she had had absolutely no clue about safety. Ah hell, Darby was being too polite. The woman was an idiot. However, at the time she didn't know she'd been talking to the manager of the pass travel complaint department. Rich Clark, *the little bastard*, had passed Ms. Abbott off as an HR Safety Investigator.

Darby didn't know if she was naïve, or she simply wanted to believe the best in people. Either way it didn't matter. She stepped into their game and they won the first round.

"Get over it, Darby," she said. This was not the day to feel sorry for herself. It was outbursts like this that made her thankful to be living alone.

Darby hid her feelings well, pretending everything was okay when it wasn't. She had been unjustly grounded and may never fly again. Linda had told her Global may get away with this, but her life would not be over—just different. She knew her life wouldn't be over, but she also never believed they'd pull this off. However, the longer they kept her out the more she doubted herself.

Pushing those thoughts away she knew her fate could have been worse. She had no right to feel sorry for herself, not today.

Today was the anniversary when thousands died in the attack on America in New York. It was also the birthday of one of her favorite captains. She wondered how it felt to celebrate your birth on the day of death. Maybe none of it really mattered. *Maybe we really are just ants scrambling around, building something that can be squashed with a foot.* She fully understood how insignificant she was. But also, how fleeting time could be. Within a second it could all be over.

September 11th was the day that changed the world of aviation. An airplane had proven to be a weapon of mass destruction. Lives were lost. Freedoms of passengers and pilots alike were taken. If that wasn't bad enough, the world took note of another atrocity when a mentally unstable pilot flew into a mountain, not more than three months ago, killing everyone on his aircraft, thus destroying the lives of everyone connected to them. God, what was the world coming to?

Darby warmed her hands on her coffee mug thinking about the deaths of those she didn't know. She said a silent prayer. Then she thought about the deaths of those she'd lost. Tears filled her eyes. She looked toward the ceiling and willed herself to be strong. She forced her mind into the future. She wondered if she would be part of it. She wondered if they would ever control commercial airliners from the ground. She knew they were headed that way, but would they do it?

They had the technology, but if they used it for passenger aircraft or freighters—God forbid. If that day became the reality, the next level of terrorism would be underway. Then she thought about her report that had gotten her into all this trouble.

It had been many months since she'd mentally revisited her report. But something bothered her. Each day there was a new thought trying to break in. Something she was missing. Why the hell they did this to her was still a puzzle. It made absolutely no sense.

Most of the report was based on training issues. Why wouldn't they want to improve training? Everyone says it's because of money, but that wasn't the truth. Her airline was making billions, and there were many improvements that wouldn't cost anything. She even provided those suggestions in her report. It actually appeared as if Global was intentionally creating pilots who lacked knowledge and thus were losing confidence to fly, and in the process, these pilots were also losing their flight skills. But why were they doing this?

This questioned bugged her. The why. She had to shift from focusing on her plight to stepping outside the box to understand. But being in limbo waiting for a doctor to determine the outcome of her life was something difficult to ignore. It was as if they'd locked the lid to that box with her inside.

Her friend Kathryn Jacobs, a top FAA inspector, had designed a research project to address manual flight issues and pilot error based upon Darby's safety report. The FAA, however, did everything they could to stop Kathryn from conducting the research. The woman who had been trying to stop her had ended up in an untimely death, as had Kathryn's boss. But then the FAA promoted Kathryn to a position that sucked all her time. Between her career and being a single mom with twin teenage daughters, she had no time to do anything. Darby wondered if that promotion was nothing but another method of blocking her research.

Her friends cautioned her from being a conspiracy theorist. But nothing made sense. There was a truth in the facts, but she had yet to find that truth.

Fact one, Global knew their pilots were having difficulty flying because they had thousands of air safety reports. A Global captain, the director of human factors no less, had declared an emergency in flight because he'd lost the auto flight system. So Global knew there were manual flight problems, but they were not fixing them. Fact two, the FAA induced a pilot shortage by implementing a 1500 hour flight rule. Fact three, airplane orders were at an all-time high, so who would fly those planes with a pilot shortage? More than that, who would have the skills to fly them due to shitty training? Fact four, Darby had presented her training concerns and they'd compared her to the Germanwings pilot. Fact five, NextGen technology was knocking at the door.

Could they actually be intentionally shortchanging training to induce pilot error? With a pilot shortage, and nobody to fly those aircraft, would that be justification for the FAA to approve passenger drones? Aircraft controlled from the ground would be flying the public… a nightmare she did not want to believe would come true. But it simply might, unless something was done. She shuddered at the thought and took a sip of her coffee. Cold.

Darby headed for the kitchen, and stuck her cup into the microwave. Her 30 second button had become worn. The number was undistinguishable. Only she and her closest friends knew the meaning of that button.

The seconds counted down. Darby always came out of her depression, and when she did, she worked on her novel. She'd also learned workarounds and set alarms if she needed to do something or be someplace. Today, she needed to do something.

Her nerves were raw and seemed to be getting worse each day. No amount of time at the gym seemed to help her long term. There was no question as to the health benefits of a workout, so she forced herself to go. She had to force herself to do many things. To get up. Make coffee. Get through her day. She hoped a new normal would take hold and she could find joy again. But that had yet to happen.

Darby needed to get back to work flying airplanes. The microwave beeped and she jumped.

Opening the microwave to retrieve her cup, she smirked. Nobody was forcing her to make coffee. That stuff just sucked her in. She yawned again as she picked up her cup and her alarm rang, startling her. This time she laughed at herself.

"God help me," she exclaimed to the universe.

Darby carried her cup upstairs. She needed a shower to splash herself awake for what she was about to do. The irony of it all.

CHAPTER 2

AFTER A QUICK shower and a second cup of coffee, Darby was ready. She logged onto her computer and connected to Skype. She checked in with Tim Brandon from News Media, and they conducted the sound bite.

Yesterday she had received a surprise request from Tim, who was one of her Twitter followers—*Hey Darby, we are going live at 0640 Seattle time. Talking with Doctor Roan about mental health. Could you join us? Sorry for the last minute notice.*

Darby had typed—*I would love to.*

Within minutes of checking in, Tim's voice broadcasted live.

"We are here to discuss mental health in light of the Germanwings crash, where a pilot intentionally flew his commercial airliner into a mountain, killing everyone onboard," Tim said. "This event created quite a concern about the mental health of commercial airline pilots. Should passengers worry? Should we have tighter screening? Is stress pushing pilots in a direction to do this again?"

Darby wondered if Captain Clark was listening to the show. He may think he could silence her pursuit of safety, but the truth was—she would never quit. Grounding her just gave more time in her fight. She would kick depression's butt and then go after Clark's.

"Please welcome international pilot, Captain Darby Bradshaw, author of *Inside the Iron Bubble*, and Forensic Psychiatrist, Doctor Roan. I thank you both for being here today. We're going to focus on the FAA group that says they are going to review the mental health screenings for pilots. Darby, I come to you first, because we know there are unions and pilots that are not happy with this, saying this is a knee jerk and unnecessary reaction. What's your take?"

"I don't think having meetings and discussions is a knee jerk reaction," Darby began. "Some discussion should be had, but the reality of being able to test pilots for screening during our annual medical exams may not be a possibility. It's difficult, as Doctor Roan will probably attest, to do an analysis of somebody to that extent in such a short amount of time."

What Darby did not tell him was she had taken those tests, and they were not indicative of a pilot's performance or mental health. She also suspected if they became an FAA mandate, thousands of pilots worldwide would lose their jobs. As it was now, airlines could utilize these tests to legally remove pilots who didn't have a problem.

"Darby makes a good point. So, how much time do you need, Doctor Roan?"

"Well, the irony is… we don't actually do very good mental health screening for the general population as it is. But I agree with Darby, and the problem is that you can't really predict behavior at any given time. The problem with requiring pilots to be screened is that screening creates a situation where they become stigmatized, and they want to hide their symptoms."

"Doctor Roan, would pilots actually hide symptoms? And if so, what could you do about it?"

"What you need to do is create a screening system that doesn't penalize the pilot if they suffer, for example, from depression. They must be allowed to seek treatment so they won't lose their job," Dr. Roan said. "You need to create a judgment-free environment, where they can actually get treatment without fear of losing their job."

"Darby, let's discuss the job itself. In your experience, do you find that there's a lot of depression... a lot of stress that could lead to something like what happened with Germanwings?"

"Stress, depression, and the extent to which that young man flew the airplane into the mountain are three different situations," Darby said. "There are things, however, we could do to enable pilots to help eliminate the stress, so it doesn't build into something worse."

"What would those be?" Tim asked.

"The simplest thing would be to allow pilots mental health days. If pilots are sick, they don't go to work. Why not allow those sick days for mental health, too?" Darby asked. "If somebody's having a really bad week, and they're dealing with issues at home, be it children, finances, anything... they should have the ability to say, "Hey, I need a mental health break."

"Makes sense," Tim said.

"I agree," Dr. Roan added.

"Another thing we could do is create an educational model in the recurrent training program so that pilots understand symptoms of severe depression. I mean, we're often flying with the same guys for twelve-day patterns. If we had the tools and understanding, there might be some signs we could watch for."

"I think you've just brought up a great point here," Tim said. "You have two or three people there, and they're watching each other. You want to be able to tell people what to look for. But Dr. Roan, how difficult is it to train somebody who's not a professional to be able to look across, even to say that person's tired, or that person's depressed, and that person may do something stupid?"

"It's not as hard as you think," Dr. Roan said. "There are programs in this country right now for police officers to screen people for mental illness. Darby is correct in that if you're spending twelve days with someone, you are going to kind of know their baseline. You're going to know when something's off… if they're fatigued, or if they're irritable, or if they're depressed. You probably will get to know their personal life pretty well. Know if they're having marital problems, or relationship issues, so I think that there's definitely something to be said for that. But again, it has to be done in an environment where the person can receive treatment and is not judged or stigmatized for it."

"Darby," Tim began. "Knowing full well that commercial airline pilots have the lives of people in their hands, several times during a day, could be thousands of lives a day… from your experience and looking to what has happened with Germanwings, and the stress of just that… what *can* we do?"

"Like Doctor Roan said, we need to not make mental health a stigma. We need to enable pilots to be able to step forward without fearing that they're going to lose their jobs," Darby hesitated. "But also, opening up the doors for communication, and letting pilots know that it's okay, should help pilots to come forward. Mental health isn't and shouldn't be a black mark on the person."

"Darby, should the doctors be liable?" Tim asked.

"I think they should have some liability and responsibility. If a doctor thinks a pilot has a problem, there should be a built-in avenue that they contact the FAA. If a pilot doesn't have the mental capacity to know they have a problem to pull themselves out of the cockpit, they need help." Darby added, "Someone needs to help them, because they're not going to do it themselves."

"Doctor Roan, we have 30 seconds left. Would you agree with that?"

"Yes, I agree with that statement. I think the doctor has a responsibility to protect the public, and we see things like this, like, in California with what's called the Tarasoff Law, where there's a duty to protect, and a duty to warn. So, if a doctor is treating a pilot and they know that pilot's a potential danger to themselves or to the public, they do have a responsibility to protect public safety."

"I think we've said it very well here, too," Tim said. "People have issues and we should not make it a stigma. They need to be able to go to their bosses, their airlines, whatever it is, and say, *I need the time*, not fearing they are going to lose their job. It will keep everybody safer in the long run. Well put, indeed."

Background music began to play and Tim Brandon said, "Captain Darby Bradshaw, Dr. Michael Roan, it was a pleasure to have you both on the show. Thank you for joining us."

CHAPTER 3

DARBY LEANED BACK in her chair with a smile. This was probably the best thing she could have done to start her day. Apparently, there was nothing like discussing the mental health of others when yours was being challenged. Obviously, Dr. Roan and Tim Brandon didn't think she had a problem.

Her wheels were spinning fast enough for departure. She raised her arms overhead and did a little woo-hoo! This was the first time in months that her smile had felt real. So much so, it worked all the way into her soul. A spark of inspiration had hit with each sentence during the interview that had begun or ended with, "I agree with Darby." There was finally hope.

The doorbell rang. She jumped out of her chair and ran toward the window, peeking out to see who the heck was visiting her at 0730 in the morning. A car she didn't recognize was parked in her driveway, but she couldn't see who was at the front door.

Darby ran down the stairs and opened the door. "Oh, my god," she said. She didn't know if she should laugh or cry. She wrapped her arms around Ray and held him tight. "I missed you." *Could this day get any better?*

When they'd first met, Darby had been a pilot for Global and Ray had been a mechanic for the same company. They'd fallen in love. He'd all but moved in with her. Ray was also a licensed pilot with his own airplane, and one of the best pilots she'd ever met. Then everything changed. Ray became a Global pilot and Darby was grounded.

Darby stepped back, and she grabbed Ray's hand and pulled him toward the kitchen. It was early and he needed coffee. "Why didn't you use your key?" She asked. "Why didn't you tell me you were coming?"

"I felt funny barging in on you."

"What happened to the days when you would sneak into my bed and wake me up appropriately?" Darby asked, pulling a cup out of the dishwasher. "They're clean," she said, over her shoulder, knowing exactly what he was thinking.

"I was afraid you might shoot me."

"Only if you deserved it," she said, putting his cup into position. She placed a french roast pod into the socket.

"What happened to the days you would have pulled me upstairs instead of into the kitchen?" he asked as he typed something on his phone.

"Touché," she said. "You'll never guess what I did this morning."

Ray set his phone down. "I'm afraid to ask." His eyes smiled when he spoke.

"Ha. Ha," Darby said, handing him his black coffee. Damn, it was good to see him. She noticed his phone was face down. "Want to sit in the living room?"

"I'm good here," he said. "Unless you want to."

"Here's fine." She stuck her coffee pod in the machine, then opened the cupboard, removed a plate of cookies, and pulled off the foil. She set them on the table. "Chocolate chip."

"You baked?"

Darby grinned. "Nope. Jackie did."

"How's she doing?" Ray asked, reaching for a cookie.

"Fine. She's loving being a mom. Baby JJ is nine months old, crawling and driving her nuts getting into everything. John's been spending a lot of time in DC. Too much time."

Darby removed the cream from the fridge. She poured some into a cup and microwaved it with a push of the worn button, still thinking about her interview. After the beep, she dumped the hot cream into her mug. She took a seat across the table from Ray, not taking her eyes off of him. Man, he looked good. Pulling him upstairs would happen after he finished his coffee.

"I was on a live radio interview this morning with a forensic psychiatrist talking about mental health," she said. "We were talking about the Germanwings pilot, depression, testing and such, and the doctor kept saying he agreed with me."

"About what?"

"Mental health assessment measures. How there isn't enough time available for an AME to actually assess a pilot's mental health. How it would be easier for crew members who fly long trips to identify problems. That we should have mental health days. Stuff like that." She reached for a cookie.

"You're happy he agreed with you?" Ray asked. "If I knew that's what made you happy, I might have tried that a long time ago."

She threw her cookie at him, he leaned left and it went flying across the kitchen, hitting the wall. "The hell you would have," she said with a smirk.

"You're going to have to sweep."

"I'll work that into my busy schedule," she said with a wink.

Ray took a bite of his cookie, his eyes widened in approval. Then he said, with a mouthful, "So the psychiatrist agreed with you. That doesn't change anything, does it?"

"It changes everything." Darby said. "We spoke for 45 minutes. That's longer than I spend with my AME during my exam. If I was crazy, and *this* psychiatrist did not identify abnormal thought patterns, it proves two things… there isn't time during the AME examination, but more than that, a forensic psychiatrist did not think I had a problem."

"Yeah, but you never see something you're not looking for."

"Regardless, he's a forensic psychiatrist." Ray's expression was still one of question, so she clarified. "Forensic means he can testify in court. We had an adult, professional conversation. He's an expert on mental health and he agreed with me, meaning that I'm not a nutcase. That has to prove something."

"Huh." Ray said. "You know you don't need to prove anything. They can't label you something you aren't."

"But they did. They labeled me crazy and didn't even have the courtesy to tell me why." This was nothing short of putting someone in jail without telling them why. She lifted her mug, hoping a sip would lower her blood pressure which had suddenly spiked. A sip might have worked, but the cup never made it to her lips. "You and I both know that they fucking grounded me for no reason."

"But you don't have to be burying yourself in a hole because of it."

"What the fuck?" Darby set her cup down, pushed back from the table, and stood.

"Babe…"

She placed her hands on her hips. "Don't babe me. I didn't bury myself in a hole," she said, drumming her fingers on her hips. "Clark threw me into that hole and he's paying people to pile dirt on top of me." She fought the tears she feared would break free at any moment. Something she did not want to happen.

Ray stood quickly and wrapped her in his arms. He pulled her close.

Don't cry. Don't cry. Don't cry. Her internal mantra. She had not shed a tear in six months over this situation. She had closed up and buried her emotions. Denial perhaps. But the reality was, they might very well get away with throwing her away and she didn't know what she could do about it. Her only choice was to be strong.

Yet, Darby had never felt so helpless. Ray was drifting away a little more each day, with his newly found career. She should be by his side, flying as his captain. She would have been, if Global hadn't done this to her. But she also understood what he was going through, too. Tragedy never impacted just one person.

Ray released his embrace. "Give up this fight and marry me," he said holding her at arm's length. "Quit."

"What?" Darby said, pulling from him, shocked. She had so many things to say, but nothing found its way out of her lips. Instead, she reached for a napkin to wipe her eyes.

"I want a family." Ray walked to the window and stared out. He took a deep breath, then turned and looked directly at her and said, "You don't need this career. I can take care of you."

Darby's mouth opened and she stared, dumbfounded. They had talked about marriage before, but it had never been tied to a condition of quitting her job and staying home. It had always been when the time was right.

"Take care of me?"

"You know what I meant."

"The doctor hasn't even made his diagnosis yet."

"Then what? When he says you're crazy, you spend the next five years fighting? When will this ever end?" He returned to his chair and said, "Attorney bills will wipe you out. The stress will kill us."

"You think they're going to pull my medical?"

Ray sighed and looked down. Darby pulled out the chair and sat beside him. She touched his arm and he lifted his eyes to hers. They were filled with pain.

"What's really going on?" she asked. "What do you know?"

"I'm just tired of the fight." He ran a finger around the rim of his cup. "I want a normal life."

"You've never wanted a normal life before," Darby said, taking his hand. "Why now?"

"Life's too short."

"Do you think I would enjoy my life more by giving up?"

"No. I don't." Ray locked eyes with her. "But you don't have to view quitting and marrying me as giving up. That's your choice."

"That's not a choice."

"It could be."

Darby pulled her hand back and folded her arms. She closed her eyes trying to find the words to explain her feelings. But the truth was, Ray didn't need an explanation. He knew the truth. He knew what they were doing to her. He knew she wasn't crazy. He knew what her career meant to her. How could he possibly ask her to give up?

"Do we really need to have this conversation now?" she finally asked, opening her eyes. She stood and walked across the kitchen, then turned and leaned against the counter. She needed the distance or she might reach out and strangle him. How could he be so dumb?

"I love you. I would love to marry you. I would love to have your baby. But…"

"But?"

"Your love comes with a condition that I'm not willing to negotiate."

"No it doesn't," he retorted.

"What do you think 'give up flying, quit your job, and then I'll marry you' means?"

"That's not what I meant."

"I'm not dumb, Ray. I noticed you placed your phone upside down after your texting. Something more is going on here. Who were you texting? Clark? Is it time to pay your debt?"

"Goddammit, Darby!" He stood and faced her, placing his hands on his hips.

Ray had been a Global mechanic until Clark had personally invited him to interview as a pilot, with the condition Ray would keep eyes on Darby. She knew the plan, but she also knew it was a great opportunity for Ray. Until now, his deal had never compromised their relationship. This was not the first time someone had paid a man to fake a relationship. But marriage?

"Let me see your phone," Darby demanded.

"I'm not playing this game." He grabbed his phone from the table and shoved into his jacket pocket.

"So I just quit?" Darby said, looking from his pocket to his eyes. "What if the doctor's report says that I'm fine, and I quit for nothing?"

"He's not going to say you're fine."

"How the hell do you know?"

Ray pulled his keys from his other pocket and said, "I need to move forward. This perpetual holding pattern of fighting with the company sucks."

"You're preaching to the choir on that."

"Then why are you doing it?"

Was he kidding? "I gave an internal report to Wyatt and Clark to help the company to move toward SMS. They could have fucking thrown it away. Instead, they forced me into a psychiatric evaluation!"

"But you can end it. We could have a life."

"By walking away?"

"We could get married, and have a different kind of life."

"What message would that send to our kids?"

"You could get a different job."

"I don't want a new job. I would have to give up over twenty years of seniority. How the hell could I have a family never being home if I was junior on the seniority list?"

"I meant a job that allowed you to be home every night."

"Give up flying?"

"It's an option." He jingled his keys and impatiently said, "I need to go. Think about it. But please know that this is not going to end well with Global. It would be better to leave now."

"Tell me what you know," Darby demanded. "Please, I need to know."

Ray turned his back to her and opened the kitchen door.

Darby wanted to rush forward and yank him back into the house and slam the door shut. She wanted to undo time and meet him at the front door all over again, and drag him upstairs instead of into the kitchen. They could have made love. She wanted this all to end. But she couldn't move. She was watching the other half of her life walk away. First flying. Now Ray.

He hesitated halfway out the door, and then looked back at her. "I love you. Think about what I said. We can talk later."

Darby simply stared.

Chapter 4

WALTER CROFT'S STEEPLED fingers touched his forehead as he leaned back in his chair. Eyes closed, he was deep in thought. He'd come too far for anything or anyone to get in his way. He also knew they could not keep Darby Bradshaw in purgatory forever. *Shit.* They needed to end this. He should have stopped it when he could have.

Dropping his hands, he leaned forward to read the email again. He should have simply had lunch with her. To the hell with their advice.

The company wrote off $60,000 for his one-hour lunch donation to the cancer auction, his standard speaking fee. If the IRS got wind that Global did not honor this donation, an entire new can of worms would be opened. It would lead to a microscope on all Global write-offs.

It was his idea when he was the CFO, to donate type-ratings to the Women in Aviation International conference. A profitable marketing ploy. Global had to employ pilots. The aviation community was coercing them into employing women. Global trailed in that effort by last place. The brilliance of Global donating $45,000 for a type-rating, which would cost them a mere $5,000 if they followed through, was enhanced when they never gave the type-rating to the pilot. Instead, they gave the woman a job.

The winning pilots never complained. Working for Global was a much more valuable prize. It wasn't much money, but ten type-ratings annually added up. They also paid $10,000 for each of those type-rating recipients to stand on stage at the conference, showing the world they were supporting female pilots. That, too, came back into Global's pockets in many ways.

For the life of him, he could not understand why the boys in flight operations had such heartburn with women. Then he glanced at an email—Darby Bradshaw. He sighed.

Walter Croft had been appointed as Global Air Line's CEO after Lawrence Patrick's untimely death nine months earlier. Patrick driving off the bridge had been one of the most fortuitous events of Croft's life. Shortly thereafter he'd found Darby Bradshaw's paper titled *SMS and Safety Culture, an Ethnographic Study on Global Air Lines,* buried in Patrick's paperwork.

Darby was anything but crazy. They should have put her to work, and kept her busy. At the time he'd been furious at Clark for his actions. He could have simply thanked her and she would have gone away. No attention. No drama.

As manager of flight operations, Rich Clark controlled everything, despite George Wyatt being one level above him as a director. However, they were always cleaning up after Clark's temper tantrums, which were not unlike a two-year-old's emotional outbursts. *What power did that man wield?* One day Walt would find Clark's skeletons.

For some reason, the board wanted Clark to remain on staff. His predecessor, Patrick, had attempted to remove Clark after he'd gotten his assistant pregnant. Yet, she ended up out of the office and Clark remained. No harm, no foul. She was also a pilot for Global and Clark moved her into pilot hiring, where nobody questioned her multiple sick leave calls. She was happy and Clark proceeded unscathed.

When Clark overreacted with Bradshaw, Wyatt took action and mitigated the damages.

Wyatt, as director of flight operations, suggested they run an external audit based upon Darby's report, which was nothing but a partial audit they financed and they controlled. They conducted some high-altitude surveys. His rationale—if Bradshaw leaked the report to someone who cared—they may have received an actual, full audit, which was something that nobody wanted to happen. He doubted the FAA would go there, but until they controlled the administration there were no assurances.

Ordering their own audit was a stroke of brilliance. Controlling who, where, and what the auditors were looking at, gave Global control. The money they invested was nothing compared to what they would lose if someone dug too deep. After the audit there were suggested changes, but nothing serious was uncovered and nobody was the wiser. That audit was also supposed to protect them from any legal action.

The knock at the door was expected. Walt dropped his hands. "Come in."

Captain Rich Clark entered, and then closed the door.

"Thank you for joining me on such short notice," Walt said flatly. "Have you heard from Wyatt?"

"He's still in D.C. At least for the next few days."

"Fine." He stared for a moment and then asked, "What's happening with Bradshaw?"

"The doctor made his diagnosis."

"Has she been notified?"

"Not yet." Clark shifted his weight. "But she won't be returning to Global, or have the ability to fly anywhere else."

Walt raised an eyebrow. He was about to ask how, but decided he would rather not know. Plausible deniability was a central theme at Global that he honored. Leaning back in his chair, he folded his arms and assessed Clark. "You'd better be right on this."

"Nobody has ever come back from a Section 8."

Section 8 was a section in the contract enabling the company to pull a pilot from duty if the company believed the pilot could not hold a first class medical certificate. Clark had explained how they used that section to rid themselves of pilots they could not otherwise get rid of.

"Being a woman, does she have grounds to sue us?" Walt asked.

"The gender ship has sailed," Clark said. "What we're doing is a better guarantee."

"If she's off property, what will stop her from writing about this?"

"It won't matter," Clark said. "She's about to lose all credibility. Nobody will be listening to anything Bradshaw has to say for a very long time, if ever."

"What about her AIR 21 case?" Walt asked.

"OSHA is in our pocket. The investigator is… let's just say we own him." Clark pulled up a chair and sat in front of Walt's desk. "We'll have another year until he rules. She'll be long gone by then."

"What if this goes to court?"

"Two years on half-pay. She won't be able to afford an attorney without a paycheck."

"And if she does?" Walt asked, still not sure if they could count on Darby walking away from her career without a fight.

"We've got a law firm." He smirked. "She'll have an attorney that will suck any and all savings she may have had. We have time and resources. We'll delay."

"What if she holds out and makes it the full game?"

Clark rubbed the back of his neck and said, "Any judge will see we had an obligation to the public's safety due to Germanwings."

Because of Germanwings, airlines were able to claim a pilot was crazy and nobody questioned it. The public was relieved crazy pilots were grounded. Why would an airline do that if they didn't have a reason? The rationale was, they wouldn't.

In the aftermath of Germanwings, the Aviation Rule Making Committee for mental health was formed. The question had been whether or not to give a mental health evaluation to each pilot. That would have been a million dollar process, with a high probability that 90% of the pilots worldwide would not perform to standards. That testing could shut down Global, not to mention most airlines, overnight.

Negotiations with the chairman of the Aviation Rule Making Committee brought results to benefit airlines worldwide. No testing. He also happened to be the FAA administrator, and was offered a very lucrative position with Global upon his retirement.

The AIR 21 was the whistleblower law. Walt knew very little about it, but he'd been told there was no law protecting a pilot who was perceived as crazy. Conducting the audit further protected them. Darby had filed an AIR 21.

"Does she have a case?" Walt finally asked the million dollar question.

"Corporate legal says not a chance in hell."

Walt assessed Captain Clark for a moment and then said, "I hope they're right." Walt pushed back from his desk and stood. He walked to the window and glanced at the poverty below. With his back to Clark he said, "Legal also said she did not have protected activity and could meet with you. They were wrong."

Corporate legal had advised Clark it was okay to meet with Darby because she had no safety information, just safety culture. However, safety culture was an FAA mandate making it protected from retaliation, but unfortunately nobody in his company knew that at the time.

"We've just hired another law firm," Clark said.

"The third?" Walt asked turning.

Clark nodded. "At $3,000 an hour they *will* get the job done."

CAPTAIN CLARK WALKED out of Walt's office and headed towards the elevators. Who the hell cared if Darby had a case or not? Nobody would challenge him or his authority. Besides, Global Air Lines had the power to get away with murder if they chose to. He'd thought about that action at one point. But killing Darby would be far too easy on her. Besides, an administrative law judge would be nothing but putty in his hands. He relished the idea of taking everything away from Darby.

The elevator doors opened and he stepped on board. He stabbed the button for the second floor twice. He would do everything in his power to ensure she would never fly again, nor would she haunt his hallways. He would also financially drain her. He had learned early that if you allow one mole to pop up, anarchy would prevail. The mallet was the only way to control the problem.

CHAPTER 5

ONE OF THE best things about a crisis is it creates an opportunity for a date night with girlfriends.

Darby was sitting with her friends in a booth at 13 Coins. This was one of their favorite restaurants, geographically close to everyone's home and located across from SeaTac airport. Kathryn's teenage twin daughters and Jackie's teenage son were babysitting the baby. "What could go wrong?" Darby had asked Jackie with a grin.

While they had freedom for the evening, there would be no strip poker or drunkenness. Those were the good ol' days. Tonight was therapy for Darby. Which was probably a good thing. She had spent many hours on the phone with each of her friends over the previous six weeks, all of them giving her suggestions about Ray, and encouraging her not to go postal on Global. She smiled now at how diverse they were, and was thankful every day they were in her life.

Kathryn had ordered wine for the table. She could take control of any situation. But that hadn't always been the case. Her psychopathic husband, Bill Jacobs, had forced her to resign from the NTSB seventeen years earlier, despite her wanting to do it all—family and work. At the end of the day, hundreds of people were dead, Bill was in prison, and Kathryn Jacobs was a single mom, working in a top-level job at the FAA.

Linda was sitting across the table from Darby, sipping her wine, clearly assessing Darby's demeanor. Darby winked, and she smiled back without looking away. Linda had lost her husband when he'd crashed his airplane as part of Bill's scheme. As a single mom of a teenager she didn't roll over, but returned to school and became a psychiatrist. She had helped Darby through many dark nights.

Jackie had also lost the love of her life when her husband's plane crashed. Greg had been a friend to all of them, but was another by-product of Bill. Jackie had ended up marrying Kathryn's old boss from the NTSB, John McAllister. Together, they were raising Jackie's teenage son and their ten-month old baby girl. Jackie had been a flight attendant, but all she'd wanted to do was be a stay-at-home mom. Now she could. However, with every dream came sacrifice.

John became Secretary of the Department of Transportation and now worked in D.C., while Jackie lived in Seattle. His schedule was similar to a pilot's and they made it work. John spent a lot of time on an airplane.

This was the first time the four friends could all get together since Ray's ultimatum, and they were there to help. After dinner orders were placed, the ladies lifted their glasses and Darby made the toast. "To friends."

They all said, 'To friends' and clinked their glasses.

"What are you going to tell Ray?" Kathryn asked.

"Marry him!" Jackie exclaimed. "We would have so much fun playing with our kids together. We could be sister moms."

"Darby can't give up her career for a man," Kathryn said. "You want a relationship because you want to be with someone, not because you have to."

"But she wants to be with Ray," Jackie said. "Don't you?"

"No man should ever tell you what to do." Kathryn said.

"What feels right to *you*?" Linda asked.

"Nothing feels right," Darby said. "I can't explain what it feels like to be accused of being crazy for reasons unknown, and not be able to do anything about it. Then Ray gives me that ultimatum to give up on all I've ever worked for, or he's gone. I felt like my life was over again, the moment he told me."

"Your life is not over," Kathryn said. She reached across the table and touched Darby's hand.

Darby looked into her glass, and said, "When your career is more than a paycheck, but a passion… and it's gone… by no choice of your own, that's enough to push you over the edge. For survival, you find something to hang on to. My life preserver was Ray." Darby hesitated a moment and then added, "I'm alone. No career. No relationship."

"You have us," Jackie said.

"It took six weeks to get together," Darby said, immediately regretting having said that. "I so much appreciate all the calls, but you guys are busy. I need to figure out how to survive this on my own."

"Darby's right," Kathryn said. "We've been consumed with our lives, work, and schedules." She touched Darby's hand again. "I'm sorry."

"No. Don't be sorry. If I were flying, I would have limited ability to help you, too."

"Not true," Kathryn said. "You put your career on hold to help me with the girls when Bill went away. I would not have survived without you."

"I'd do it again." Darby lifted her glass, air toasted to Kathryn, and sipped. "But there's nothing you all can do for me aside from just listening. And you have."

"Then why not be there for Ray?" Jackie asked Darby.

"Ray doesn't need my help," Darby said. "He also didn't get ripped away like Greg. Ray is *choosing* to walk away."

"He's asking you to walk away with him," Jackie said.

"BS," Kathryn said. "Nobody should tell you to give up your dreams."

"He's doing what he thinks is best," Linda said. "I'm not defending him, but he thinks Darby quitting and marrying him is his way of giving her a solution that will fix everything."

"Darby doesn't need fixing," Kathryn said.

"Thanks, Kat," Darby said. "But it's more than that. He told me they were going to find me crazy. He knows I wouldn't give up the fight, a fight which would consume our lives. I think this solution was to save him from years of pain. Not me."

"Do you blame him?" Linda asked.

Darby stared Linda's way before she answered. "Not at all. I actually understand. But it doesn't make it any easier."

"Do you think he knows something more than he's letting on?" Kathryn asked.

"I have no doubt he does. But he won't tell me."

"I would be very surprised if they could manufacture a mental illness," Linda said. "The only thing would be if your psych tests were substandard."

"Do you mean the tests the FAA administrator claimed wouldn't be used on pilots?" Darby asked sarcastically.

"They weren't supposed to be used on pilots?" Linda asked. "Since when?"

"Since two weeks before they forced Darby to take the test," Kathryn said. "The FAA administrator ruled they would not be useful."

"Then why did they make Darby take it?" Jackie asked.

"They're using those tests to get rid of pilots," Darby said, as the waitress approached the table. She placed a double bucket of clams and a bowl of bread in front of them. After the waitress was gone, Darby continued, "Those tests have nothing to do with flying planes. Nothing to do with motor skills or ability to manage an aircraft. It really was kind of a joke."

"How did you do?" Jackie asked.

"They won't let me see the results." Darby grabbed a clam and dipped it into butter. "I think pretty good. Except... Well, I was given this random drawing. Nothing that made sense, just lines, boxes, patterns, etcetera. So the lady told me to draw it. I replicated it with precision. Then after nine hours of rushing me from one test to the next, she gave me a blank paper and told me to draw that picture again, this time from memory."

"Are you kidding?" Jackie said, eyes wide.

"I'm not kidding. I would have done better if she had told me I would be required to draw it later. I could have memorized it while doing it the first time. However, I think I got it relatively close."

"I can definitely see how that impacts the level of safety on an aircraft," Kathryn said with a chuckle.

"And your level of sanity, too," Linda added.

"I would have gone crazy just taking it," Jackie said. "I think I would have cried. Or simply drawn smiley faces."

"I still can't figure out why the hell they are doing this to you," Linda said. "Niman and I have spent many hours discussing this."

Niman was Linda's second husband, a surgeon who had done everything he could to save Greg. Darby was glad Linda had found him. Niman and Linda were both lucky to have each other.

Darby finally said, "I still think it has everything to do with the safety report I gave them."

"That doesn't make sense," Jackie said. The ladies had beaten this to death as to why they had done this to Darby, but nothing had ever made sense. Darby doubted it ever would.

"All I did was give them training concerns, along with an analysis of Global's safety culture and why it would not support the FAA's 2018 SMS mandate. I had been warned not to give it to them. Maybe they were mad I didn't heed the warnings," Darby said, reaching for another clam.

"Kill the messenger," Linda said. "But why? This is so puzzling."

"Who the hell knows? The situation is such that Global's training program and safety culture suck. The fix could be easy, but they are not doing anything to make the effort. I simply pointed out what they already knew, and then they attempt to silence me." She stuck the clam into her mouth.

"This is simply medieval," Linda said.

"No kidding. I think Kat's research could force the fix of their training inadequacies. More than that, the results might prove my sanity." Darby glanced at Kathryn, hoping to guilt her into pressing forward and finishing the research.

"I simply don't have time," Kathryn said. "They're running me ragged since my promotion."

"John's in the same position," Jackie added. "He's hardly ever home."

"Think about this," Darby said. "Kat was promoted after her boss was murdered. John received the DOT position after his competition was murdered, both of whom were working together. The CEO of Global drove off a bridge, or was pushed. The President of the United States was placed in prison. My friend was murdered after trying to take the plane from a crazy Global captain trying to crash it. Don't get me started on Bill. Then I bring forth all the training issues to Global's attention and get placed into a psychiatric evaluation."

Darby let this hang in the air for a moment as she sipped her wine. Then she said, "This is a puzzle and all those events are the pieces. I suspect if we put them together, we'll see the big picture."

"Sounds like you have already put those pieces together," Jackie said.

"I tried."

"What do you see so far?" Jackie asked.

"That our world is fucked up. Other than that, I'm still working on it," Darby said. "I think I'm missing a piece or two."

Their meals arrived and they discussed Kathryn's research proposal, based on Darby's assessment of Global's safety culture. Kathryn wanted to know why pilots were not manually flying their aircraft, which appeared to be a contributing factor to pilot error. These issues were flagged by the Office of the Inspector General, and despite the FAA's recommendation to airlines encouraging manual flight, the problems continued and they blamed the pilots.

Darby's report had identified many problems within Global, and Kathryn had wondered if they were worldwide issues. Kathryn designed the research and, sure enough, her job had been threatened if she were to have continued. After her boss had died, and she had been promoted to his position, she'd intended on gathering the data with government approval. However, there was never time. They kept her hopping. Darby was beginning to think they had never intended to allow her to do it.

"Why don't you have Darby gather the data?" Linda asked, wiping the corner of her mouth with her napkin. "She could analyze the data and write the results. Perhaps write a book."

"She has the time," Jackie added, laying her napkin beside her plate.

"That is exactly what she needs," Linda said. "Focusing on her passion and doing something constructive would shift her mind away from everything that she has no control over to something that she does."

"Therapy, with results at the end. I like it," Kathryn said. "Darby, what do you think?"

"Oh, my god. Are you kidding me?" Darby said. The moment Linda had suggested the idea her heart sped up. "That would be amazing. I'm actually going nuts trying to find an answer to a puzzle that can't be solved at this time. Maybe this is the missing piece."

"Well, there is nobody more intimate with the research than you. You identified the problems," Kathryn said. "Plus, nobody has more knowledge about the subject matter. I'm just kicking myself that I didn't think of this myself, six months ago."

"Everything happens at the right time," Linda said. "Had she been in the middle of research when Ray dumped his ultimatum on her… that could have thrown her off."

"Speaking of which… What about Ray?" Jackie asked, and the three friends turned toward Darby, awaiting her response.

Darby sighed. "I've already boxed up his things," she admitted. "I just wasn't ready to move them to the porch until now."

CHAPTER 6

THIS IS BULLSHIT, John thought staring at the stack of papers. He pushed back from his desk, wandered to the credenza, and poured himself a cup of coffee. The second of the morning, with more to follow. Coffee mixed with the bile this office generated was anything but good for his health.

John McAllister's hair was more salt than pepper these days, and it had nothing to do with having a ten-month old at home. He had never wanted the job as Secretary of the Department of Transportation. The pursuit was nothing but a means to an end. However, as the game had proceeded forward, he'd begun to believe he could make a change and the position would be deserving. Unfortunately, there had been no chance in hell for him to have been nominated for the position, especially after they'd learned his investigation included the President of the United States.

Yet, President Jim Drake had appointed him anyway. It was Drake's parting gift before he'd gone to prison. John learned of this appointment as Drake spoke into the camera, directly to John. The look and words still chilled him to this day.

They were up to something. John's boss had said to go with the flow and see what that 'something' might be. Keep your friends close, but your enemies closer. John suspected that was why they were keeping him close as well.

Sipping his coffee, he glanced at his watch. 'Manage by meetings' was definitely not something he was used to. He had worked as a top national transportation investigator at the NTSB, in a place where he had actually accomplished something. As frustrating as that job had been, at least they were able to identify problems and make recommendations. Whether the FAA took them, or not, was another story.

Unfortunately, the DOT was nothing more than a glass house where he could look out at the chaos, but wasn't allowed to put his fingerprints on any of it. If he stood inside his office and didn't touch the glass or get too close, everyone was his friend. If he pressed his nose against the glass looking into places where he was not welcomed, the glass became frosted, obscuring all vision. His blood ran cold at the reactions from the FAA.

The Department of Transportation's mission was to develop and coordinate policies and, most importantly, create an economical national transportation system taking into account necessity, the environment, and national defense. This position was an education in itself. The reality of this job was to oversee eleven agencies, and the FAA was simply just another grain of sand, where those in power thought he was clueless. Economics in his position were highlighted as the government's greatest concern—to hell with safety.

Rumors ran rampant that they were planning to replace the FAA administrator with someone from an airline. Who that was, or which airline, was the mystery. Mike Hackman had been in place since 2013, and his term would end in January of 2018, the same month and year that Safety Management Systems (SMS) would become a Federal Aviation Regulation. At least someone had taken action to improve safety.

Hackman was also the individual who'd determined airlines would not be required to give pilots mental health examinations as the standard, in the shadow of the Germanwings accident. His justification, as outlined in the Aviation Rule Making Committee report on mental health, made sense.

John pulled a hand through his hair. So, why the hell did they put Darby through that testing? Global was up to something, but he'd be damned if he knew what it was.

Global was an industry leader, but he had never seen so many aviation safety reports from a singular airline in his career. They also did not address the issues with a solid fix. Global only addressed those that were near catastrophic. In addition, those fixes never addressed the root cause of the problem, yet the local FAA always approved them.

Each year John peeled back a level of corruption within Global. The airline as a whole had never been named. While the entity was responsible, there's difficulty in blaming a company for one or two individuals' corruption—as long as senior management held people accountable. Global management appeared to be doing all they could. Until now. The actions they took against Darby were a mystery. He wondered at what point the board of directors would step in.

Returning to his chair, John continued perusing the morning notices. Too much shit slid through this office daily. There was virtually no way one person in the DOT position could be an expert on all the departments under their responsibility. It wasn't long until he realized how easy overlooking something could be. He found himself allowing processes in departments to fall to the individual in charge of that department, simply because he did not have the knowledge to assist or oversee. He hoped they were on the right path. There was far too much information for one person to grasp and to fully understand in this position. Success depended upon those in charge of individual departments. However, the FAA side of the house was a different story.

John's dream job was actually the position of the FAA administrator. However, they needed him to pursue the DOT position to help weed out the next level of terrorism. The NTSB had nothing to do with terrorism, and he'd been lying to those whom he'd loved with the illusion he still worked there. His paychecks came from that department, but he hadn't worked there for years.

There had been something brewing within the walls of the government, and they were close. Who would have imagined that a top official in the FAA, the CEO of Global Air Lines, *and* the President of the United States were involved?

The CEO and the FAA executive were both dead, and President Drake was in prison. Drake had known exactly what he was doing when he'd placed John into this position …a prison all his own. John suspected his actual boss knew more than he was willing to share, as well.

Was the new Global CEO on the same level? Was Darby's flag on SMS the reason they tried to silence her? Who the hell was running the FAA? The airlines? John wondered. There were many more questions that haunted him daily. He only hoped he could find the answers before it was too late.

Something was up. John felt it in his bones. Similar to the feeling of walking onto an accident site. Sight and scent would overwhelm his senses. Closing his eyes, he could envision the events … sometimes with prescient knowledge. Kathryn Jacobs had that instinct as well.

She had been his partner in another life. They now were both too busy to discuss much of anything. That needed to change.

Aviation safety had been John's life. While the DOT was an overload, this was the first time in history someone in this position actually knew what in the hell was going on within the aviation sector. While Hackman wasn't pleased that John had been breathing down his neck for the better part of a year, they had gained a mutual respect. At least he assumed so.

When Vice President Ronald Kohler took over as President, he had inherited John McCallister as the DOT secretary and Mike Hackman as the FAA administrator. He suspected their selections would change, but they never did. Hackman's term was over in three months. John was trapped in his position, wondering who would replace Hackman.

John scanned another document and then the next and the next. He stopped at an interesting article from Pacific Marine Institute—PMI. The shipping industry was a fascinating sector, with many problems similar to aviation regarding automation dependency. It appeared they were well ahead in training harbor pilots, more so than the aviation sector was at training airline pilots. That may have had everything to do with the high volume of pilots on the airline side. Volume was no excuse not to ensure the best training possible.

He jotted a note to drop by PMI when he was back in Seattle. He could see firsthand what they were up to and determine if he could integrate PMI's processes into the airline sector.

John lifted his cup as his phone rang.

"Mr. McAllister, Chairman Chambers is here," John's secretary announced.

John glanced at his watch and sighed. "We've got a meeting in a few minutes."

"I'll remind her."

Mary Chambers was the House Transportation and Infrastructure Committee Chairwoman, and a strong proponent of the privatization of the air traffic control system. She was also married to the Senate Majority Leader, Donald Jones. Chambers was encouraging a replica of the Canadian model. She had also been well-rewarded from the airline industry the year before, receiving close to $150,000 in personal campaign contributions. Not much money in the whole scheme of things, but enough to cause a conflict of interest that went unnoticed.

A rapid knock at the door and then it opened. "John," Chambers said stepping into the office. She closed the door. "Thank you for enabling me to drop by unannounced."

John contemplated if he had a choice in that matter. He stood, and moved around to the front of his desk, extending his hand. "What can I do for you?" he asked as they shook.

"A cup of coffee would be appreciated."

"My apologies. We've got five minutes before they're expecting us down the hall."

John had no intention of a lingering discussion over a cup of coffee. He also could not circumvent the chill that entered the room with Chambers. He couldn't pinpoint the reason. Perhaps it was nothing more than her having openly received funds from an industry where she was obligated to be neutral that irked him.

"This will only take a minute," Chambers said, walking over to John's coffee pot. She poured herself a cup.

John folded his arms and stared without comment.

The chairman dumped two scoops of sugar into her cup. "We plan to push ATC privatization through, and I would appreciate your support."

John waited until Chambers looked his way and then he said, "No way in hell."

Chambers chuckled. "We all love a good challenge in DC. But as the new kid on the block you have a lot to learn." She sipped her coffee and stared over the brim, eyes not moving from John's.

John lifted his arm and checked the time, and then returned his attention to Chambers. "You've got two minutes to educate me, and then we have a meeting to attend."

"This *is* going to happen. You can fight a losing battle and die a slow death in this city, or you can get on the right team and earn your place." She set her cup of coffee on the edge of his desk. "I'll see you at the meeting."

Mary Chambers walked out of John's office and closed the door. He returned to his desk and sat. His heart rate increased. The increase was due more to an internal fight to keep his mouth shut than anything else. If he ever changed his mind and decided it was appropriate to hit a woman, she might just be the one.

John glanced through the remaining papers, perhaps more to calm himself through a moment of distraction. Then he stopped short at the brief on the bottom of the pile. "What the hell?"

He could not believe what he was reading. Classified was stamped on the top of the page. *Fucking classified material*, he thought. This was nothing short of what Darby had said they were planning. He had never believed it could happen, but she'd been right. He gathered the sheets of paper, carefully stuffed them into his briefcase, and closed it firmly. If they wanted a fight, he was the person to give it to them.

CHAPTER 7

JOHN WALKED INTO the meeting and found a seat at the boardroom table. He was ready for the fight. This was classified information that, as Darby had said, would open the door to the next level of terrorism, and he had to end it before it began. Unfortunately, lying on the table was a press release from the President regarding a different issue. John lifted it, and read the document.

Ronald Kohler had been the Vice President until Drake had been sent away. Everyone knew Kohler had been nothing but a puppet, and Drake the puppet master. *Who the hell was pulling Kohler's strings now?* John wondered.

Managing the government like a business was a great idea for financial reasons. However, there had to be a balance. Politicians and legislative leaders needed to care about the people. Corporations as a whole did not. That was, in part, the reason that many or most executives had sociopath tendencies. They needed to make the financial decisions for their corporation which could cause harm to thousands. He understood that concept. However, allowing private enterprise to profit from safety organizations was open for corruption. *Not-for-profit, my ass,* John thought.

The White House

Office of the Press Secretary

For Immediate Release

October 25, 2017

Letter from the President to Members of Congress

Dear Mr. Speaker: (Dear Representative:) (Dear Senator:)

(Dear Mr. Chairman:)

I am pleased to transmit to you my Administration's principles for reforming our Nation's Air Traffic Control (ATC) System. Each year, our ATC system contributes $1.5 trillion to our economy—roughly 5 percent of our gross domestic product. To protect and improve this critical infrastructure asset, we must focus more attention on our ATC system and enact much needed reforms.

Despite using 1960s technology and operating in outdated facilities, United States air traffic controllers remain the best in the world. Every day, they safely manage the largest, most complex airspace system in the world. As air traffic has increased, however, the FAA has had to sacrifice system efficiency to maintain safe operations.

Our Nation's air traffic is only going to increase, and today's ATC system simply will not be able to handle the volume that is expected over the next two decades. Without immediate attention to comprehensive ATC reform, aviation congestion and delays—which already cost the United States economy more than $25 billion per year—will worsen and our economy will further suffer.

The Federal Government's $1 billion per year investment in the NextGen Program's improved ATC technology has proven insufficient. Unfortunately, political interference, budget uncertainty, and a bureaucratic government procurement system have continued to impede modernization efforts. The NextGen Program was originally estimated to cost $40 billion. By the Inspector General's most recent estimates, however, it may cost an additional $80 billion to complete. By the time it is fully operational, the technology may already be obsolete.

Efficient operation of our airspace requires significant investments in rapidly evolving technology. In this environment, bureaucratic efforts are unlikely to succeed. That is why all other industrialized countries, with the exceptions of the United States and France, have separated their ATC functions from government. By taking that critical step, those countries have accelerated modernization, maintained or improved safety, and lowered operating costs. We must take bold action now to preserve the competitive economic advantage in the world economy that our ATC system provides. The enclosed proposal describes a new, not-for-profit ATC entity that will leverage private capital to enable faster modernization and immediate safety and operational improvements for all users of the system, from passengers to shippers to operators.

I look forward to working with you to enact these important reforms into law.

Sincerely,

President Ronald Kohler

CHAPTER 8

GEORGE WYATT PRESENTED his ID to the doorman and was escorted to the elevator. Another doorman entered the elevator with him, and pressed the PH button. He rode to the top floor with Wyatt, and then extended a hand. "Have a good night."

George nodded, exited the elevator, and the door closed.

He glanced around the foyer and breathed deeply. It wouldn't be long until he, too, could live in style. George had been making two-million a year as the Director of Flight Operations at Global Air Lines, not bad for a pilot. However, the real money was in Washington. The real money was also not taxed as nobody knew it existed.

He walked to the door and pressed the doorbell. Within seconds the door was opened by a woman in uniform. "Welcome, sir. May I take your coat?"

George removed his coat and handed it to the woman just as Mary entered the room.

"George!" Mary Chambers exclaimed. "It's wonderful to see you. Thank you for joining us tonight."

"My pleasure," George said, walking with Mary as she tucked her arm in his.

"I'm sorry we've been busy your last couple visits," she said.

"They've been quick trips," George said. Then he added, "My father said to tell you hello."

"How's the old man doing?" Mary asked, stopping before they entered the living room.

"Still up to his old tricks. Just not as quickly."

"Wonderful," she said. Then they were back in motion. They stepped into the living room with an entrance framed by two ten-foot tall carved doors. "And how are your wife and children?" she asked.

"My youngest is about to give us our first grandchild."

She patted his arm, "Wonderful," and then she released it as they walked into the living room. "What are you drinking these days?"

"Scotch. Neat."

Mary looked at the servant, who immediately disappeared.

The living room was close to 400 square feet overlooking Washington DC, and filled with elegance. A gas fireplace was alive on the opposite side of the room. The furnishings were exquisite. The artwork alone was worth more than his home. *One day*, George thought.

"Donald, you remember George," Mary said.

"Of course," Senator Jones said, extending his hand as he approached. "Nice to see you again."

Within minutes the young servant reentered the room with three glasses. She served George first, then the others.

Donald raised his glass to George. "Balvenie single cask, 30 years."

George raised his glass with an air toast and sipped. "Very nice." It had been years since George had tasted a thousand dollar bottle. That, too, was about to change.

"Please, have a seat," Mary said. "Dinner should be ready in thirty minutes."

They all sat and Mary began talking about George's dad. Senator Jones did not appear pleased. She was sharing stories of the good ol' days when the doorbell rang. Both Mary and the Senator rose and excused themselves.

Within minutes they returned, followed by another guest. George stood as they entered the room. He placed his glass on the coffee table, and turned to say hello. He froze for a second, then worked to calm his nerves.

"Nice to meet you, Mr. President," he said, extending his hand.

"Please, call me Ronald," the President said shaking George's hand.

By the time greetings were complete, the servant was standing off to the side with a fourth drink on the tray. Mary took the drink and said to the woman, "That will be all. Thank you." Mary handed the glass to the President of the United States.

This time, when the woman left, she closed the large double doors with the President's Secret Service on the outside of the room. They all sat, and Kohler placed a briefcase on the coffee table. They spoke small talk about the weather and joked about global warming.

George could not stand Ronald Kohler. He never understood why they had made him the Vice President. Kohler was so bad, in fact, that everyone thought President Drake would be secure from removal of office for anything, because Kohler couldn't step up to do the job.

However, Kohler surprised everyone when Drake went to prison. Perhaps he even surprised himself, as he seemed to grow into the position. Absolutely nothing changed when Drake went to prison. Ronald Kohler was managing well. He was also the person who would secure George's future.

President Kohler leaned forward and opened his briefcase, removing three sheets of paper and handing them each a copy.

George glanced at the paper he'd just received. *Classified.* Then he read the subject. Everyone in the industry knew this was coming.

He glanced over the document. *Theatrics*, he thought. However, this answered many questions.

"We need support to push this through," President Kohler said. "Could we count on you as the FAA Administrator?"

"Of course."

Kohler stared at him with intensity. "I've got some questions I need answered."

"Anything."

"Global has two ongoing AIR 21 cases against them. Any validity?" Kohler asked.

"I don't think so," Wyatt said.

"*Don't think so* won't cut it," Senator Jones stated. Mary placed a hand on his leg and he fell silent.

George looked from the Senator to the President and said, "Let me rephrase. Absolutely no to the first case. The second case, our legal team says no..."

"But?" Kohler asked.

"I personally believe she has a case." George reached for his drink and sipped to buy time and measure his words.

George Wyatt was also an attorney and knew the law. But the law was an illusion when it came to justice. He returned his glass to the table, and leaned forward. With arms resting on his legs, he held the document in one hand and looked directly at the President.

"Darby Bradshaw gave us a report exposing concerns, which could impact your work here," Wyatt said, setting the document on the table. "My second in command, Rich Clark, thought she needed to be silenced."

"And you?" Mary asked.

"I think we could have used her."

"Why didn't you?" President Kohler asked.

"Corporate legal and labor relations got involved. This was their call. They wanted her gone."

"Will she give up?" President Kohler asked.

George paused a moment and then said, "No. I think she'll fight us."

"Where does her case stand?" President Kohler asked.

"The OSHA investigator has it now. He'll rule for the company. We've got a doctor who is giving her a career-ending diagnosis. We had one FAA inspector in Oklahoma City who supported her. He was conducting the investigation, but was forced to recuse himself because he knew her. However, he changed his tune after we placed him on the Global certificate. More money and the respect he deserved won him over."

"When will OSHA be ruling?" President Kohler asked.

"Three to six months."

"And the medical report?" Mary asked.

"The company has already been notified of her diagnosis. The doctor is waiting for the best time to tell Bradshaw. He said a notification over the holidays could push her over the edge and support his diagnosis."

"If she doesn't fall?" President Kohler asked.

"We could push her," Senator Jones added, with a grin.

"That's possible." George breathed deeply and said, "Darby loves flying. Giving her a diagnosis that would end her career… it would be plausible she could take things into her own hands."

"We don't need any attention," President Kohler said. "Drake is concerned with the publicity of all this."

George didn't show any response to that comment. However, now he knew Drake was controlling Kohler's moves from within prison. Everything was making sense. *Interesting.* He wondered why Kohler simply did not pardon the President to get him out of prison. Perhaps he didn't want attention brought on him, either. There was no other reason he could think of, as to why Drake would remain locked up.

"I am going to put someone else in the position of FAA Administrator in January."

George stared, holding down the emotion he felt. How the hell could they refuse him because of Bradshaw? *God damn that fucking Clark and his teenage reactions*, George thought. Clark had reminded him how effective the mental health allegation was to remove a pilot. But it had been his call. He could have ended it, but he didn't. He had no one to blame but himself.

"Sir, nobody has ever come back from a mental health challenge at Global. Bradshaw won't be any different," George finally said.

"I hope so." The President assessed George, and then asked, "Were you involved with the action against her?"

"Yes."

"Then you're just what Washington needs," President Kohler said with a grin. "We need people who are not afraid to get their hands dirty. The position is yours if you want it. However, we need time to allow the dust to settle on the AIR 21 cases. The appointment we'll put in place will be temporary. When the dust settles, you're in."

"Thank you, sir," George said, trying hard not to display his emotions.

"You've got some loose ends to tie up at Global," President Kohler said while standing. "Finish your work there, and we'll talk again."

"Ronald, won't you join us for dinner?" Mary asked.

"Not tonight. But thank you."

After President Kohler was gone Mary smiled. "That went well. Better than I'd imagined." She placed an arm in George's and looked at her husband. "Senator, shall we eat?"

CHAPTER 9

PRESIDENT DRAKE HAD met Bill Jacobs inside the Lompoc Correctional Institute two months earlier. He respected the man for taking action for a cause. Jacobs was someone who was not afraid of death. Not afraid of doing the hard stuff. What impressed Drake most was how Bill got pilots to crash their own aircraft.

Despite Drake having more influential power than anyone, he wasn't sure he could convince someone to commit mass murder without paying them. Suicide was tougher, because the dead couldn't take the money with them. Foreign nutcases were easy to persuade in the name of some effing god, but not the pampered pilots from the United States.

There was a reason Drake had pulled Jacobs into the Lompoc prison to join him. The very reason Drake was there in the first place. Together they could take the aviation industry to the next level. He not only wanted Jacobs' help, he needed it. Who would have thought Jacobs actually loved the industry and would do nothing to hurt it? That had made no sense. However, nobody told Drake no, especially a pilot.

Drake sent Bill a message when he had him shipped to San Quentin.

San Quentin was the oldest prison in California and known for its death row. The expression on Jacobs' face was priceless when they told him he was being moved. Drake had smiled and spread his hands. Then he'd winked at Bill.

Jacobs was not only moved to San Quentin, but then was placed on death row for a month. Jacobs would never again doubt Drake's power. Drake subsequently relocated himself to San Quentin, too, but he moved into a cell with a million-dollar view.

Now Drake stood with hands on his hips staring out the window at San Francisco Bay. Why the hell were they wasting twenty acres of priceless land for prisoners? Hell, he could buy this property and pay off half the state's debt. Build a prison in the desert. Sell that to the government. Then develop this property and quadruple his investment.

There were opportunities everywhere, he thought.

"Mr. President, you have a visitor," the guard said from beyond the bars. The guard opened the cell door and Drake exited.

The guards allowed him to walk past the other cells without cuffs, sending a message to the inmates. They exited the hallway. The door closed behind them. He was cuffed, and then the next door opened. They proceeded to a room where inmates met with their attorneys. But Drake knew his attorney would not be there. He knew who would be waiting for him.

The guard opened the door. Drake entered the room, and then turned toward his escort and lifted his arms. The guard removed his cuffs and then stepped out of the room, closing the door behind him.

"Good morning, Bill," Drake said turning toward him. "How do you like your new location?"

"Fuck you."

Drake smiled. He pulled out a chair, and sat across the table from Bill.

Bill's cuffed hands were resting on the top of the table. A two-foot chain connected to thick ankle cuffs and kept his legs bound.

"Want to get off the row?" Drake asked, folding his arms. He leaned back in his chair and crossed his legs.

Bill's glance flashed to Drake's deliberate act of leg crossing. Something he himself couldn't do within his constraints. He shifted in his seat, clearly frustrated by the reminder of his limitations. Bill lifted is hands and rubbed his face. When his hands dropped with a thud, he said, "I want out of this fucking place altogether."

"It's not so bad if you have a room with a view." Drake grinned. "Work with me."

"Can you get these off?" Bill asked with a slight lift of the chains.

"I had us both moved to a state prison. What the fuck do you think?" Drake said, his eyes never leaving Bill's. He allowed the realization of his power to settle in, and then called, "Jack!" The door opened and two guards entered. Drake nodded to one of the guards.

He walked around the table and unlocked Bill's wrist cuffs. Bill pushed his chair back shifting to pull his feet out from under the table. The guard unlocked and removed the ankle chains. The second guard stood with a hand on his gun. Then both guards left the room.

"What do you want?" Bill asked.

"I want you to tell me how to crash a few planes."

"Anyone who would do that for me is gone," Bill said. "The backsliding of the industry, pay loss, pensions gone… my friends became easy targets because they had nothing to live for."

Drake thought about that. The industry was on the upswing. Pilots knew pensions were history, therefore there were no expectations.

Contracts were providing top pay. "Commuter airlines have shitty pay scales," Drake said. "Could that be leveraged?"

"There's hope for better," Bill said. "Besides, the idiots who made the 1500 hour rule created a pilot shortage for the regionals. They'll go out of business because they can't get pilots. The majors will have to cover those routes with their own equipment. So, the pilots will simply go to the majors for better pay."

Drake allowed the 'idiot' comment to slide, and then asked, "What about excessive fatigue?"

"Exhausted pilots make errors," Bill said, stretching his arms overhead.

The FAA had increased the single crew duty time from eight hours to nine in an effort to reduce fatigue. The justification was that nine hours would be a 'do not exceed' limit under any circumstances, whereas the eight hours had flexibility. This made no sense, but the public bought into it. Global was already exceeding that time limit, and Wyatt had requested a duty-time extension from the FAA to make it permanent. When the union found out, they forced him to pull the request. Not the union exactly, but one rogue pilot who was subsequently removed from his union position. The change would happen sooner than later. *But was it enough?* Drake wasn't sure.

"What if the FAA gave an extension to the nine hours?" Drake asked. "Say… an additional forty-five minutes?"

"Nine forty-five single crew?" Bill said. "Yeah, you'll see some problems."

Drake thought about that for a moment. "What are your thoughts on automation and controlling aircraft from the ground?"

"It will never work." Bill leaned back and crossed his legs.

"The technology is there," Drake said. "They're just waiting to get a grip on security."

"Even so, it won't happen."

"Why not?" Drake asked, interested in Bill's perspective.

Bill uncrossed his legs, placed his arms on the table, and leaned forward. "Passengers won't get on an airplane flown without pilots."

"Give them cheap tickets and they will," Drake said.

Bill grinned. "Can't argue that."

Everyone knew that passengers would fly on any airline if they could get a cheap fare, even if the airline duct taped the engines to the wings.

"How do we create confidence in technology versus pilots?" Drake asked.

"You're already doing it."

Drake folded his arms and assessed Bill. He might be more valuable than he'd previously thought. "Not well enough," Drake said.

"Airplanes are safe." Bill leaned back and clasped his hands behind the back of his head. "Even when the pilots don't know what they're doing, the automation is creating a safer operation."

"Therefore, we've proven the automation is safe," Drake said.

"Yeah, but the passengers don't know how weak the pilots' flying skills are. You need to break some equipment and show the public what they can do. Or not do, as the case may be."

Drake nodded. He knew exactly what needed to be done. However, there was a problem that needed to be dealt with first.

"I understand your wife is friends with a Ms. Darby Bradshaw."

"Ex-wife. But, yes." Bill's eyes narrowed.

"Do you know Bradshaw's been removed from duty?" Drake asked.

Bill nodded, and his expression shifted slightly. "I've heard."

"Will she go away on her own?"

"No chance in hell."

Chapter 10

OPERATION 'GATHER DATA' for Kathryn's research was well underway. Darby had been more or less living at the airport twelve hours a day, handing out business cards to pilots with the survey website address printed on the bottom. She had been doing this for a month and a half. At night she'd reached out to pilots on LinkedIn. It had taken her three days to upload Kathryn's survey to Survey Monkey. From then on, she had been at full speed gathering data. A perfect distraction from life as she knew it.

She pulled her car into her garage and climbed out. After closing the garage door she entered her house, locking the door behind her. Darby had hoped to catch a glimpse of Ray at the airport, but no luck. However, it was fun talking with the pilots, and they all appeared very supportive.

Exhausted and hungry she opened the fridge and stared at the contents. Far too empty for comfort. She grabbed an apple and a package of cheese, and then removed a bottle of water. She set her feast on the kitchen table and plopped onto a chair.

She powered up her laptop and logged into Survey Monkey. That morning, before she headed out to the airport, she'd had 1450 surveys. All she needed was 1599. She bit into her apple and popped a piece of cheese into her mouth for the perfect combination. She waited for the numbers to populate.

"Holy cow!" Darby said. She had 1703 completed surveys. She pulled her cell phone out of her purse and pressed *favorites*. Then she selected Kathryn's number. Two rings and Kathryn answered.

"Hey, Darb, how's data collection going?" Kathryn asked, before Darby could say hello.

"We did it," Darby said. "1703 surveys."

"Are you kidding? Congratulations."

"Thanks. I can't believe it. It's time to celebrate," she said, glancing at her wine rack. She stood and selected a bottle of pinot. "I was thinking about texting Ray to tell him, but thought better of it."

"Have you heard from him?"

"I heard he already has a girlfriend," she said, pulling a bottle opener out of the drawer.

"Wow. That was quick. I'm sorry."

"That's okay." Darby stuck the corkscrew into the cork. "It was inevitable. I packed his stuff for the road and opted out of his proposal," she said, twisting the cork and pulling it from the bottle. She pulled a glass from the dishwasher.

"Doesn't make it any easier."

"No, it doesn't," she said, filling her glass.

Darby slipped back into the kitchen chair as she and Kathryn discussed the best way to proceed with the analysis. Darby had put an ad out on Craig's List to find someone to help her with the stats. This was far too important to make any errors. Kathryn had also told her she could publish her results. Darby had discussed this with her editor, who was looking forward to reading it. However, her editor had also been after her to finish the novel, which she had been dabbling at for over two years. She was so close to completion. She refreshed Survey Monkey.

"Holy shit," Darby said. "We've got 1849 surveys."

"Since we've been talking?"

"Yes. Looks like this has snowballed."

"What if you wait for, say, three weeks to run the data?" Kathryn said. "Get through the holidays and see if more come in."

"That's a great idea." Darby sipped her wine. She was too wiped out to jump into data analysis anyway. "At least I can sleep in tomorrow."

"You deserve a break," Kathryn said. "I'm just amazed you did this so quickly. To get this kind of result normally takes many people collecting data, and multiple years."

"Never underestimate the power of crazy," Darby said lifting her glass, thinking about Ray again. She wanted to share her excitement with him.

Then she froze. "Kat, I think I just heard something upstairs," she said quietly, setting her glass on the counter.

"Get out," Kathryn said.

"Just hang with me," Darby said, and she walked quietly to the back door. Locked. Then to the front door. Locked. "The house is secure downstairs."

"Want me to come over?"

"No. Just call 911 if I scream," Darby said, picking up her fire poker. Memories of Bill and a shower came to mind. Regardless, she would not be the paranoid person they had accused her of being. On the other hand, if they were really out to get her, she would finally get vengeance. She crept up the stairs.

She stepped to the top of the landing, heard something in her room, and stopped. "Someone's in my room," she whispered.

"Get out, Darby."

Instead of running, she slowly opened the door and a cat flew past. "Shit!" she yelled, falling back against the wall.

"Was that a scream?"

"Not really. It was the neighbor's cat," Darby said, placing her hand to her chest. She walked into her bedroom. "My window is open." She stood for a moment looking out, and then pulled it closed. She hadn't remembered opening it, but she'd been pretty tired lately. More like running on fumes.

Darby sat on her bed, and they talked about plans for the holiday. She promised she would be at Christmas dinner with Kat and the girls. Everyone would be there. Everyone except Ray. Darby sighed. *Sometimes life has an idea all its own when we're busy making plans for something else.*

CHAPTER 11

RICH CLARK SAT in his den sipping a single-malt scotch. The wine bottle sitting on his credenza that he'd received as a gift weeks earlier, had given him the idea. He could not help but smile. They wanted Bradshaw gone and he had wanted her to suffer. A win-win. If he got lucky, she wouldn't die, but rather become a vegetable. He doubted he would get that lucky. However, statistics proved only 5% of all suicides by pills were successful.

He leaned back, swiveled his chair toward the window, and stared out. The snow was falling. It would be a white Christmas. At least his wife would be happy. He took another sip of his drink, and glanced at his watch. The doorbell rang. He pushed up from his chair, walked into the entry way, opened the door and smiled.

"Merry Christmas," he said, stepping aside so George Wyatt could enter. "Join me for a drink?" he asked.

"A short one," Wyatt said, following Clark into his den. Wyatt closed the door behind them. "I only have a few minutes. Holiday party tonight."

"This will only take a minute," Clark said, opening the bottle of scotch and pouring a couple fingers into a glass. "Any word on the position?"

"It's official," Wyatt said, accepting the glass with a nod. "However, they're putting Deke Elmer in as a temporary, until the dust settles with the legal action."

"That dust will be settled soon," Clark said, sitting in his leather recliner. He extended his hand toward the couch for Wyatt.

"I hope so," Wyatt said, making himself at home.

Wyatt stared into the glass for a long moment. "She's not going to give up," he said. Then he sipped, looking over the brim of his glass at Clark.

"Won't matter," Clark said, leaning back. "Dr. Wood is sending his death sentence on Christmas Eve."

"That won't do a damn bit of good," Wyatt said. "She's been gathering data for some fucking research, and I don't think at this point she'll do anything but make our lives miserable."

"Maybe not," Clark said. "But the autopsy will tell a different story."

"Autopsy?" Wyatt's eyes narrowed. "How?"

Clark leaned forward and rested his arms on his legs. Lowering his voice he said, "Sleeping pills in her wine."

"How the hell do you get pills into her wine?"

Clark shifted his glance to the credenza. The bottle he'd doctored was now inside a gift box. "Liquify the drugs, remove the cork, pour them in, reseal."

"No pill bottle at the scene," Wyatt said. "It won't be believable."

"Taken care of," Clark said.

"How do you get the wine to her?"

"FedEx delivery. Overnight."

"How do you know she'll drink it?" Wyatt asked.

"She'll drink it." Clark grinned.

"Who's it from?"

Clark handed him a printed card with a typed message.

"She'll never believe this," Wyatt said after reading it. "He's…"

"She'll buy it," Clark snapped. "Because she'll want to believe it."

Clark had done a little research on Darby. Getting Ray drunk over a year ago had been informative. He had offered Ray the opportunity to become an airline pilot, and with that, he had willingly shared information. Clark had learned a great deal about Ms. Darby Bradshaw, none of which Ray had thought would be useful. Everything was useful.

"Not sure this is the right move with the AIR 21," Wyatt said.

"A perfect way to save the taxpayers' money." Clark grinned, and then tipped back his glass. He placed the empty glass on the table and then stood. "We will never have a better opportunity than the moment she learns her career is over."

"I'm not sure…"

"I don't think we have a choice," Clark interrupted.

CHAPTER 12

CHRISTMAS EVE WAS in full motion, but nobody would have known it by the inside of Darby's house. This was the first year Darby hadn't decorated a Christmas tree. She hadn't decorated the house, and her Christmas CDs were collecting dust in a cabinet someplace. The only music was her fingers tapping across the laptop keyboard.

Darby was still grounded. It had been a year. To be specific—12 months, 3 days, and 18 hours. To date, nobody had told her why. There'd been ups and downs throughout the year. She'd remained stoic for the first six months, then had become depressed. But she had snapped out of it thanks to Linda. Then the breakup with Ray. She couldn't fight those tears so she allowed them to flow. Only six weeks of turmoil and then her friends pulled her out of that funk, too.

Kathryn had allowed her to gather data for her research. Linda's prescribed therapy. The perfect distraction was a productive distraction. However, when she was done with data collection, waiting until the New Year to analyze it, the emptiness returned. Emptiness which was magnified by the holiday.

Darby allowed that feeling to last for one day only, and then she jumped back into her novel. She had not realized how close she was to finishing it. There was no time like the present.

Nobody would believe what they were doing could really happen, so she turned it into fiction. The names had been changed to protect the guilty. Actually, the names were changed so they couldn't fire her for a social media violation. Darby decided to finish it as a Christmas gift to her friends, and that wish came true. She'd hunkered down for the previous nine days and had done absolutely nothing else.

She sat back, thinking how to end the novel, and then the words simply flowed.

> *A shadow crossed his face.*
>
> *"I heard you wanted to see me," the man said.*
>
> *"You're blocking my sun," the President said, not opening his eyes.*
>
> *The man moved aside and warmth covered him again.*
>
> *"What can I do for you?"*
>
> *"Depends… on who the hell you are."*
>
> *"Captain Phil Malcom."*
>
> *The President of the United States opened his eyes, and a smile spread across his face.*

Darby typed *The End* and then leaned back in her chair. She glanced at the time on her laptop. She'd done it. Now, she just needed to get this sucker printed—three copies. Then she would gift wrap a first edition novel for Linda, Jackie and Kathryn.

Darby stood and stretched, and then loaded the printer with paper and pressed print. She reached for her cell phone, and walked to her bed. Falling flat on her back she typed DB into her phone and pressed dial.

Within no time, Deloris Brooks answered. "Merry Christmas, Darby."

"I'm done," Darby told her editor.

"With the research book?"

"No. The novel," Darby said. "I haven't even run the data on the other."

"I have to admit it. I didn't think you could do it."

"Never underestimate the power of crazy." Darby had used that line on Kathryn, and somehow it was growing on her as her tag line.

Deloris laughed. "Did you settle on a title?"

"Oh, yeah," Darby said. "I think the only appropriate thing to call it is *Flight For Sanity.*"

"*Flight For Sanity*...Yes, I like that," Deloris said. "How much truth is in this one?"

"Let's just say the only fiction is the murder and the sex. The sinister plot is all too real." She glanced at her bedside clock. She was running out of time to finish printing, binding, and wrapping. Not to mention getting ready for Christmas Eve dinner. Darby promised to send Deloris the final manuscript after the New Year, and another edit or two. The research book would be about six months out. She wished her a Merry Christmas and said goodbye.

Christmas was so much easier without decorating. Darby wandered into the bathroom and turned her tub faucet to hot. There would be no need to put away decorations. No pine needles on the floor. Who needed *Santa Baby* anyway? She dumped bubble bath into the tub.

Besides, she could celebrate at Kathryn's beautifully decorated home. Bubbles grew as they filled the tub, and Darby returned to her bedroom to add more paper to the printer. She removed pages, pressed the button to continue printing, and stacked the first set of pages on her desk. She returned to the tub filling with bubbles.

Global Air Lines pulling Darby from flight duty was nothing but a tactic that airlines used to remove pilots who became irritants. The only problem, Darby wasn't an irritant. All she had done was tell senior management the areas where they could improve safety. Maybe that constituted irritant status in their minds.

Plus she had spent years trying to improve safety within the airline industry, a fight she learned nobody else was willing to take on against Global. Everyone was afraid of speaking out, and for good reason.

Her union rep had warned her not to point out Global Air Lines' safety flaws. But she didn't listen, and they sure as hell went on attack. But for the life of her, she could not figure out their game plan or why the union didn't support her. Granted, being off work with pay wasn't so bad, it gave her time to write, but... Who the hell was she kidding? This was the worst torment she could experience, money or not.

Darby returned to her bedroom and opened the closet. She removed a green sequin dress, and then one made of black satin. Holding the green sequins in front of her, Darby tilted her head and assessed herself in the mirror. Then she held up the black satin. The green sequins won. She chose a pair of red four-inch heels from the closet, and tossed them and the dress onto the bed.

She checked on the tub, felt the water and increased the temperature. After three mandated visits to a psychiatrist in Skokie, Illinois, she still waited for the quack's findings. Dr. Wood was one of the strangest people she'd ever met. If they cast him in a horror film, starring himself as the psychopathic doctor, they would tell him to downplay his theatrics.

Over a year later, they still couldn't figure out her mental health. Darby wasn't sure if the psychiatrist was soaking the company, or if he was part of their master plan to drive her nuts. Either way the results were the same. She was out of the flight deck *and* she was being driven nuts. Assessing the water level, she returned to her printing project, removed the printed pages, and added more paper.

CHAPTER 13

DARBY RAN TO the bathroom, but the tub wasn't filled, yet. She sighed and sat on the edge of it. Time had clicked by more slowly each day. Her life had turned into a rollercoaster. She swirled her hand through bubbles. Lifting a handful she blew, watching them fly and then drift downward. She'd had a year to digest the company's behavior, and still couldn't believe they could get away with this.

The airline's attitude toward safety was appalling. The entire concept of pulling someone for a mental issue because they'd reported safety concerns pissed her off. Hell, it violated the essence of a safety culture. Proactive safety demanded that people come forward—see something, say something.

Darby slapped the bubbles a second time and this time they splattered onto the floor. Taking her anger out on innocent bubbles was nothing short of therapy. She stared at the pile of bubbles as the tiny spherules popped and dissolved before her eyes. Her *Flight For Sanity* book might just be enough to push Clark over the edge. She grinned. Data collection done. Novel done. Jumping into the analysis would keep her going through the New Year.

Linda had said Darby was experiencing the five stages of grief, much like losing a loved one. Having a friend who was a psychiatrist was a welcomed benefit. Linda was right. Darby had lost her love—she'd lost her ability to fly. Flying was what helped a pilot survive the everyday shit-storms of life by escaping into the sky. Bubbles began sliding over the edge and dropping to the floor.

Darby shut off the water. She dunked her hand into the tub, and removed it quickly. Hot. *Too hot.*

There was no way in hell Global Air Lines could do this to her—but they did. Realizing her fate made her madder than hell. Then she began bargaining with God, praying that if he let her come back, she would make sure this would never happen to anyone again.

Pulling her robe a little tighter, she left the bathwater to cool and headed downstairs to the kitchen. Opening the fridge, she removed a bottle of champagne and assessed the contents for a snack. This was an exciting day. She had finished writing her novel, she had 3,289 surveys completed on Survey Monkey, and there was real food in her immediate future. There was only one thing that could make Christmas Eve better. Maybe two.

After struggling with the foil wrap, Darby pulled the seal from the bottle and twisted the wire to remove the contraption holding down the cork. Within seconds there was a loud pop. Holding the champagne glass at a tilt, she filled it. Darby stared into the liquid as bubbles rose to the top. Her stomach grumbled, and she thought of Kathryn's prime rib.

Kathryn was battling a jungle within the walls of the Federal Aviation Administration. The good ol' FAA had many problems of its own—mostly the incestuous relationship with Global. Passengers didn't know they were playing Russian roulette every time they stepped onto a Global airplane.

Darby sipped her champagne and glanced out the window, wondering where the twins were. She glanced at her phone, but no messages. She stuck it into her pocket. Kathryn's girls, Jessica and

Jennifer, should have already been there. They had said they were bringing her a "big present" and Darby suspected it had something to do with decorating her home. Perhaps they would give it to her at their house tonight.

She loved being Aunt Darby, even though she wasn't their real aunt. It had been so much fun watching them over the years. It was hard to believe they had almost lost the twins in a car accident… an accident designed for her and Kathryn. A shiver shot through her body and she wrapped her arms around herself, careful not to spill her drink, and then pushed away that memory.

The last stage of grief would be acceptance. She would never accept what those corporate assholes were doing to her. Darby held the bottle of champagne and her glass, and headed up her staircase toward the tub. She was halfway up the stairs when a pounding on the front door told her the girls had finally arrived.

A smile spread across her face. She bounded down the stairs, tucking the bottle under her arm, she freed a hand and reached for the doorknob. "It's about time you got here," she said opening the door.

"I got here as soon as I could," Dan, the FedEx delivery driver, said with a twinkle in his eye, eyeing her robe, the bottle tucked under her arm, and her glass of champagne.

"I'm sorry. I thought you were my nieces." Darby stepped outside and set the bottle and glass on the railing. Then tightened the belt on her robe.

"If I were twenty years younger you would be in trouble, young lady," he said, handing her a large box. "Hopefully this is your Christmas bonus," he added, handing her an envelope. Darby took the envelope and thanked him, as he headed down the steps toward his truck.

"Merry Christmas, Dan!" Darby yelled.

Dan's envelopes were usually filled with a royalty check from her book sales. A box—that was new. A Christmas gift perhaps. She reached for her glass of champagne when her phone dinged. She removed it from her pocket and read her text message. The girls would be there in two minutes. She sat down on the porch steps to wait for the twins.

She sipped her champagne then set it aside, and began ripping the tape off the box. Inside was another box carefully wrapped in bubble wrap. She removed the plastic to find beautifully gift-wrapped package.

She ripped opened her gift. *Stags Leap Pinot.* "Wow." She read the card. *Merry Christmas. Enjoy in the tub. Lovely memories. Love, Ray.*

Was this a joke? Darby thought, fighting tears. She didn't know quite how to take his gift. She should be happy he was thinking of her. Why did she feel so weird? *It's just a card and wine.*

Darby set the gift down on the porch, and opened her envelope. But there was no check. Instead, she removed a letter. A letter from Dr. Wood. Her eyes grew wide as she read it.

She looked to the sky and asked, "Is this a fucking joke, too?"

CHAPTER 14

DARBY KNEW CRYING on the front porch in her robe might not be the best look on Christmas Eve. But somehow, she could not find the energy to stand and go inside. Then she was busted. The twins pulled into her driveway.

She returned their wave and dried her eyes with a sleeve of her robe.

Darby watched them climb out of the car. Jessica climbed out of the passenger side, ran around to the other side, and opened the back door. Jennifer leaned in with her, and they produced the largest most beautiful poinsettia Darby had ever seen. She began crying harder.

Jessica ran to Darby. "What happened?" she asked, sitting beside her.

"It's just so beautiful," Darby replied. "I've never seen anything so beautiful."

"Bullshit," Jennifer said, standing there holding the plant. She set it on the porch. "What's wrong?"

Jessica lifted the note laying on the box and read it. "Did you and Ray get back together?"

Darby shook her head no. "I'm not sure why he sent that. He's got another girlfriend."

"What's this?" Jennifer asked, taking the letter from Darby's clutch. She sat at Darby's other side and read the letter. Within moments she said, "Holy shit."

Jessica reached in front of Darby, pulled the letter from her sister, and read it as well. "No effing way," she said. "What are you going to do?"

Darby shrugged and sucked a deep breath. She wiped her face with the sleeve of her robe, and then said, "This is a career ender."

"I don't believe it," Jennifer said, standing. "Just because they say this, doesn't make it true."

Jessica wrapped an arm through Darby's and pulled her close. "That doctor is a rat bastard." She leaned her head against Darby's arm.

Darby laughed. "Where did you get that language?"

"Really?" Jennifer said, as she extended a hand to Darby. Darby knew exactly where they got that language, and smiled. She took Jen's hand and allowed her to pull her to her feet.

Jessica stood, too. "This sucks, but you'll fight it. Right?"

"I will," Darby said flatly.

"I love the outfit," Jennifer added. "Wearing that to dinner?"

"You think your Mom would care?" Darby said, swinging her belt. The truth was, Kathryn wouldn't care, and Darby didn't know if she was up to fixing herself up for the night. She actually wanted to stay home. She sighed. "I think I'll go jump in my bubble bath and clean up my act."

"As long as you don't jump off a cliff," Jessica said.

Darby gave her a slight smile. If a cliff were within range at this moment in time, she wasn't so sure she wouldn't jump.

"Here you go," Jennifer said, handing her the box with the bottle of wine. "I think a bath and glass or three of this is exactly what you need."

"I like the way you think," Darby said.

"My short-term advice," Jessica said, "Uber."

Darby hugged them good-bye, then stood on the porch holding the bottle of wine from Ray close. She waved with the best smile she could fake as the twins drove off.

She walked inside and set the box on the kitchen counter and then returned to the porch.

How the hell a doctor could come up with such a diagnosis was beyond her. Darby stuck the letter from Dr. Wood into the FedEx envelope and then tucked it into the poinsettia branches.

Wood was a little freakazoid and had asked her some really asinine questions—whether or not her mother had expressed her milk to feed her as a baby had absolutely nothing to do with her mental health. And when he said, *Oh, here is a good question for you West Coast people,* she knew she might be in trouble since she was one of *those* people.

But for him to give her such a diagnosis was beyond comprehension. She had actually thought they were simply going to punish her for bruising their egos. How the hell did they get a doctor to become part of this?

Darby tipped back her champagne glass to finish it off. Then she reached down and lifted her poinsettia and the bottle of champagne. Arms full, she walked into her house and kicked the door closed behind her.

CHAPTER 15

EVERYONE FLEW DIFFERENT directions with their busy schedules throughout the year. However, Christmas Eve was the one night Kathryn was guaranteed to have everyone whom she loved gathered around the table at once. She opened the oven and checked on the prime rib—Darby's favorite.

Kathryn had never stopped worrying about Darby since Global had begun their attack against her. Unfortunately, she wasn't able to do anything about that, other than keep her eyes and ears open inside the walls of the FAA. This entire mental health assessment was absurd. Darby's report was spot on, and the FAA had issued a violation against Global for violating FARS. But that didn't seem to matter to anyone. Closing the oven, Kathryn glanced at her watch. The twins should be back anytime. Everyone would be arriving soon.

Thank God Linda had suggested Darby run the data collection. Kathryn was so proud of how Darby had excelled at that. Then, nine days later, Darby had gone into lockdown and Kathryn and her friends hadn't seen nor heard from her. Darby had told them not to worry, as she was working on something. Kathryn worried. Ray having another girlfriend so quickly was also a bit much to grasp. Not flying for over a year and Ray's departure were both tough on Darby. But at the very least, they could give her a wonderful Christmas.

She was opening the refrigerator to gather the ingredients for her caesar salad dressing when pounding on front door was replaced by "Merry Christmas!" Seconds later, John, Chris, and Jackie with the baby in her arms were entering the kitchen.

Kathryn gave Jackie a hug and then took the baby. "Merry Christmas," she said, removing baby JJ's coat. It was hard for her to believe she was a year old already. "Chris, the girls will be back any minute. Grab a soda and you can hang in the game room if you want."

Chris smiled in clear relief of escaping kitchen duties. He grabbed a Pepsi and made an expeditious exit. John located a beer and headed into the living room, not to miss a moment of the game. Kathryn put JJ in the highchair that had once been the twins.

"Thanks for pulling this out of the attic for us," Jackie said, placing the tray into position and locking JJ into place. She dropped a handful of Cheerios onto the tray. "Where's Darby?"

"Not sure. I called, but she didn't answer."

"What can I do to help?" Jackie asked, pouring herself a glass of merlot.

"You could wash the lettuce," Kathryn said, removing a salad bowl and lettuce spinner from the cupboard.

By the time Jackie was spinning the lettuce dry, Linda walked in.

"Merry Christmas, ladies," Linda said, hugging Kathryn and then Jackie. "Where's Darby?" she asked, removing her coat.

"I'm sure she'll be here soon," Kathryn said. It was unusual for Darby to miss one minute of a party. They all worried about her a little more each day. "Where are Frankie and Niman?"

"Frankie's picking up something for the girls. She'll be here in about thirty minutes. Niman's in the living room with John. I'm sure they're solving the world's problems by now." Linda poured herself a glass of wine. "Hello, my little sweetie pie," she said, as she kissed the baby.

The kitchen door burst open, and Jessica and Jennifer bounced inside.

"Hi, girls," Jackie said. "Chris is in the game room, and Frankie's on her way."

"Thanks," Jessica said, as she opened the fridge and grabbed a Pepsi.

Jennifer gave Linda and Jackie a hug, and then headed straight for the baby. "Can I take her out to play?" she asked Jackie.

"Of course," Jackie said, and Jennifer lifted JJ out of the highchair.

"Did you girls stop by Darby's?" Kathryn asked.

"Oh, yeah," Jennifer said, bouncing the baby on her hip. "Good thing, too."

"I can't believe that asshole did that," Jessica said, pulling the tab on her soda. Everyone stared her way, as she lifted the Pepsi to her lips. "What?" she said returning their stare.

"What asshole did what?" Kathryn asked calmly. "Ray?" Keeping up with teenagers was a challenge.

"The doctor. He sent her a letter saying she was bipolar," Jennifer said. "FedEx no less."

"What the hell?" Kathryn said, grabbing her phone and pressing Darby's name. She finally understood what that saying, your heart jumped to your throat, meant.

"Sweetie, are you sure that's what the letter said?" Linda asked.

"Positive," Jessica answered for her sister. "I read it, too."

Linda flashed a look of alarm Kathryn's way. Darby's phone went directly to voicemail.

"How was she doing when you left her?" Linda asked.

"She was sad, but tried to fake happy," Jennifer said. "She had definitely been crying when we showed up."

"She said she needed time alone," Jessica added. "But she promised she wouldn't be late for dinner. But don't be surprised if she's in her robe."

"Ray sent her a bottle of wine with a love note," Jennifer added. "But I don't think that made her happy, either."

"Why don't you girls go give Chris some company?" Jackie said. Once they were gone she said, "I don't like this."

"Call Ray," Linda said. "If he sent her a gift, they might have talked."

Kathryn hesitated, and then dialed his number. When he answered she said, "Ray, this is Kat. Have you talked to Darby?"

"No," Ray said hesitantly. "Why?"

"Darby got her diagnosis today."

"On Christmas Eve?" he said. "That's quite a gift."

"Not exactly," Kathryn said. "They said she's bipolar."

"No fucking way." Ray said. "That's permanently disqualifying. That will kill her."

"I know," Kathryn said. "We're just trying to track her down, and wondered if she called you."

"I haven't heard from her," he said.

"Okay, thanks." Kathryn ended the call, assuring him they would be there for Darby.

"What'd he say?" Jackie asked.

"Darby can never fly again."

"Doctors have a Hippocratic oath to help, not harm the patient," Linda said. "Telling a pilot they would never fly again on Christmas Eve would be enough to push them over the edge. You also don't FedEx a message like that. You talk to the patient in person."

"Especially on Christmas," Jackie snapped.

"The company left her hanging for a year, and I'm afraid she's been internalizing much of what's been going on," Linda said. "Now this. Today? Christmas Eve?"

"She'd been pretty upbeat doing data collection. But once that was over... I don't know." Kathryn contemplated the best way to deal with this. She pulled the prime rib from the oven and turned the oven to off. "Let's get over there."

"Should we call someone?" Jackie asked. "Just in case."

"No." Kathryn waved a mitted hand.

"But what if…" Jackie hesitated.

"No what ifs," Kathryn said. "Tell the kids to watch the baby. Linda, will you drive?" Kathryn attempted to show a cool exterior which she didn't feel. She pulled the potholders off her hands, tossed them onto the counter, and headed for the living room.

"Merry Christmas, Niman," she said, and gave him a quick hug. "John, the ladies and I are going to Darby's for a bit. Chris and the twins are watching the baby."

"Everything okay?" John asked, raising an eyebrow.

"I'm sure it is." Kathryn hesitated, holding his stare. "But, would you mind keeping your phone on and where you can hear it?"

CHAPTER 16

THE WIND WAS blowing hard when Kathryn, Linda, and Jackie headed out the door. They ran to Linda's car. Jackie climbed into the backseat and Kathryn into the front. Jackie shivered. She was scared. Scared for her friend, and scared for what the world would be like without her.

Kathryn always remained so calm, but every part of Jackie's body feared the worst. Darby would rather be dead if she couldn't fly. That quack psychiatrist probably knew that after interviewing her, and it was the only reason he had waited so long to tell her.

Snowflakes began to fall as Linda backed down the driveway. *Darby loved the snow*, Jackie thought. Jackie knew that Kathryn wasn't willing to imagine Darby being so depressed that she could hurt herself, but Jackie wasn't as sure. She wanted to believe Kat, but her gut told her otherwise. She could not imagine walking into Darby's house and finding her just lying there.

"We probably should have told John and Niman what was going on," Jackie said, as she stared out the window.

"Nothing to tell," Kathryn said glancing back at Jackie. But Jackie wouldn't look her way. "She got bad news, news that we will fight. I'm certain she's just in shock. This is not the end of the world."

"But why is her phone off?" Jackie snapped, shifting her attention to Kathryn. Jackie knew that if Darby was unable to fly again that would be the end of her world.

"She wants time alone to think this through," Kathryn said. "Or she forgot to charge it."

"Maybe Jackie's right," Linda said, glancing sideways. She looked both ways, and drove through the intersection. "Let's not panic. Darby is one of the most resilient people I know."

Jackie wasn't so sure how anyone could be that resilient to go through the hell they'd put Darby through for a year. Jackie would have gone postal on those assholes at Global months earlier. She wiped a tear from her cheek and sucked a deep breath.

It felt like forever but it was actually only minutes before they were pulling into Darby's driveway. They climbed out of the car, then ran up the path and steps to the porch. Linda rang the doorbell. Nothing. She pressed the button multiple times, and Jackie knocked while Kathryn stuck her key into the lock. She turned it and the door opened an inch, but the security chain prevented the door from fully opening. Darby was inside.

"Darby!" Kathryn yelled through the door. "Open the door."

Linda continued to press the doorbell. They could hear it ring, but no Darby.

"We have to break in," Jackie said.

Kathryn reached her fingers inside the door crack to see if she could lift the chain, to no avail. "I'm going to see if this key works on the back door."

Jackie yelled through the partially opened door. "Darby! Open the door!" Panic was consuming her. She could not lose another person she loved.

Linda put her hands and face to the glass and looked through the window, "I don't see her."

Kathryn came running from around the side of the house. "The key doesn't work."

"We have to call someone," Jackie said. "We need help."

"I'm afraid Jackie's right," Linda said to Kathryn.

Jackie slammed her body into the door, but the chain wouldn't break free. "This can't be."

"Stand back," Kathryn said, as she bent down and grabbed a large rock. She smashed it into the glass pane on the door, and then crushed the edges of glass away. She reached her arm through the window and removed the chain.

They all ran into the house, calling for Darby. The house was deathly quiet. The only signs of life were the dancing flames in the gas fireplace.

"I'll check the hot tub," Linda said, heading that way.

"Already checked," Kathryn said, and Linda turned and followed Kathryn up the stairs, taking two at a time.

Jackie followed her friends to the stairs, but she couldn't bring herself to follow them upstairs. Instead, she sat by the fire and closed her eyes. She was in the middle of a silent prayer when the most blood-curdling scream she'd ever heard came from above.

CHAPTER 17

DARBY'S EYES WERE closed and her headset was in position with the volume cranked up and she began to sing with the music. "Like a small boat… On the ocean… Sending big waves into motion… Like how a single word can make a heart open… I might only have one match… but I can make an explosion!" Her hands were in balls under the water and she spread her fingers wide and exploded bubbles into the air.

"And all those things I didn't say… wrecking balls inside my brain… I will scream them loud tonight… Can you hear my voice this time? This is my fight song! Take back my life song…" Darby punched her hand into the air in beat with the music. "Prove I'm alright song… My power's turned on… Starting right now. I'll be strong… And I don't really care if nobody else believes… 'Cause I've still got a lot of fight left in me…"

Darby opened her eyes to people in her bathroom and she screamed. When she realized it was Kat and Linda, she said, "What the hell?"

Kathryn said something, dropped to her knees at the edge of the tub, and began to cry.

Darby pulled the headset from her ears and tossed it. She said, "What happened?" Her first thought was something had happened to the kids.

Kathryn looked up and she swiped the tears from her cheek and started to laugh. Linda knelt beside Kathryn, closed her eyes, and said, "Thank God."

"Okay, you two are really starting to freak me out," Darby said sitting up. But naked in the tub was no reason not to be hospitable. "Champagne?" she asked, reaching for the bottle.

Then Jackie poked her head into the bathroom, and she began crying.

"Is this one of those bathtub intervention things?" Darby asked, filling her glass. "Or was I seriously late for dinner?"

IT WASN'T LONG before Darby was dried off, wearing her fuzzy robe inside out, and sitting on the hearth in front of her fire holding a cup of cocoa with whipped cream on top.

"If you expect me to start this conversation, it's going to be a long wait," Darby said. "I don't know where to begin. What in the heck are you all doing here?"

"The girls told us about your letter," Kathryn said from the couch. "Then we couldn't get ahold of you."

"Something like this could push anyone over the edge," Linda added. "We were worried."

"I thought you'd hurt yourself," Jackie remarked flatly, moving from a chair to sit on the floor beside Darby. "You didn't hear us pounding on the door, or ringing the doorbell."

Darby glanced at the hole in her front door and smiled.

"Why aren't you upset about this?" Kathryn asked.

"The glass can be replaced," Darby said, knowing exactly what Kathryn meant. Then she added, "I am upset. It's only been a few hours, but I actually hate being bipolar. It's awesome!"

Linda grinned and shook her head. Then she began to laugh.

"At least they didn't steal your sense of humor," Kathryn said.

"Who gives someone this kind of news on Christmas Eve?" Jackie asked, laying her head on Darby's leg. "The truth is, I was scared you'd do something because I know how much you love flying."

"How can you be so calm?" Kathryn asked. "Are you drunk?"

"Not anymore," Darby said. "You guys are super buzz killers." She grinned, sipping her hot chocolate. She was thankful they had all cared enough to be there for her. "I was actually only into my third glass of champagne."

"I'm afraid you're back to stage one of denial," Linda said with a wink.

"This actually hit me pretty damn hard. I cried. But the truth of the matter is… there's nothing I can do right now about it. Thus, I decided to find my peace that passes all understanding, and enjoy the holidays."

"Huh?" Jackie said looking up. "Your piece of what?"

Darby chuckled. She realized she had to hit her bottom before she could figure out that she had to let this go, and accept. There were some things she could not control, and this was one of them. She would fight it, but not give into it emotionally.

"Kiddo, there are things we can control, and others we can't," Darby said, placing a hand on Jackie's shoulder. "I can't control what the company did, or what that doctor wrote. At this point the only thing I have control over is my attitude."

"The eye of the storm," Linda said. "No matter what chaos flies about, you maintain your calm."

Darby smiled and nodded. "Absolutely. So, I decided to shelve it for now. I'm not going to let these bastards ruin my holidays. Today at least, I can't do anything about this. Then, we'll just see. One day at a time, I suppose."

"Shelve it?" Jackie said.

"Yep. Literally. In the hall closet." Darby glanced toward the entryway closet.

Linda stood and went to the closet and retrieved the FedEx envelope. "Can I read it?" she asked turning towards the room.

"Of course," Darby said. "The point is… they took a year of flying from me. Dr. Wood defied my trust. I think the company is definitely working on stealing my sanity. But I'll be damned if I'll give them Christmas, too."

"This is so much bullshit," Linda said, looking up from the letter.

"Worst case… if it sticks, you can get half pay on disability for the rest of your career," Jackie said. "Right?"

"It's not about the money," Darby said. "If this sticks, I will never fly again, because I can't hold a medical certificate."

"But you haven't lost your medical, yet," Linda stated. "Have you?"

"Nope."

"Can you fight it?" Jackie asked.

"Hell yes," Darby said. "They can't get away with pulling this crap. That's why I was listening to Rachel Platten's *Fight Song*—motivation to kick ass and make an explosion or two."

"Listening?" Kathryn grinned. "I think you were singing *with* Platten. You were pretty damn good, too."

Darby knew better.

"I'm concerned about this on so many levels," Linda said, walking over and sitting on the hearth beside Darby. "Far beyond you being prevented from flying."

"Why?" Kathryn asked.

"From a medical perspective, Darby has no signs of being bipolar whatsoever. From a legal perspective… If a doctor is willing to put his reputation on the line by falsifying such a diagnosis, he must think he has significant power protecting him."

"If he thinks he has the FAA protecting him," Kathryn said, "he's got another thing coming."

"John won't let this fly, either," Jackie added. "You've got a lot of people who know and care about you, Darby. Global won't get away with this."

"Now what's this about a love letter and bottle of wine from Ray?" Kathryn asked.

CHAPTER 18

GEORGE WYATT WAS madder than hell. He never should have allowed Clark's interference. He glanced over at Clark and shook his head. This was not how the events were supposed to play out. Nobody should ever play their hand, expecting someone else to throw him the right card. Counting on the unexpected never worked. Apparently, Clark was not as smart as he thought he was.

"Gentlemen, Mr. Croft will see you now," Rose said.

"Thank you," Wyatt said. He and Clark stood.

Rose had been the secretary to three CEO's, and Wyatt wondered how much she knew. She had played her part well regardless. Wyatt opened the door and stepped through before Clark. His urge to slam the door in Clark's face was placated with professionalism.

"What the hell did you two do?" Walter Croft asked, looking between the two men as they entered. Wyatt closed the door behind them.

"You don't want to know," Clark answered.

"I'll determine what the hell I want to know." Walt ran a hand through his hair and paced for a minute, then sat heavily at his desk. "Brief me."

"We anticipated…" Clark began and then glanced at Wyatt, who returned the glance with a look that could kill. He then said, "I anticipated that we could end this. Set the stage that Bradshaw committed suicide on the day Wood's diagnosis was delivered."

"How'd that work for you?" Walt asked, already knowing the answer.

"Not well," Clark said. "But she could drink that wine at any time. We could have the same results. Call it delayed gratification."

"Do you agree?" Walt asked Wyatt.

Wyatt shook his head no. "Absolutely not."

"Explain," Walt ordered.

"Many scenarios could do us in. Most pointedly, if she shared the wine with Jacobs, or McAllister, there would be an investigation we could not undo. Trouble we don't need."

"The bottle is not traceable," Clark said.

"Everything is traceable," Walt snapped. He returned his attention to Wyatt. "Anything else?"

"If she were to drink it alone, say in a couple months, and they find the empty pill bottle, they will suspect foul play."

"How so?" Clark said.

"If she fights this and makes headway, nobody would believe she'd kill herself. If there's hope, there is no way she'd quit," Wyatt said. "There is no telling when she might drink it. The only plausible time would have been at the moment of a negative diagnosis."

"Then we'll make sure she loses all hope," Clark said.

"People who fight don't kill themselves," Wyatt said, exacerbated.

"I agree with George," Walt said. "Clean up this mess."

"Okay," Clark said, stuffing his hands into his pockets.

Walt assessed Clark and then asked, "On that note, can you remove all hope?"

Clark nodded. "Of course."

"Then do it," Walt said.

Wyatt shook his head and said, "If you fuck this up, you'll be drinking the wine."

"I'll help you pour it down his throat," Walt said. "But I want that bottle to disappear sooner than later."

"I will take care of this," Clark said. "Don't worry." With that, Clark and Wyatt exited Walt's office, and Wyatt closed the door behind them.

Walt returned to his chair. He wished he'd known that Clark had been planning to kill Bradshaw. Clark had failed simply because revenge was never a good reason to remove someone in business. Revenge destroyed clear thinking. Far too much emotion became involved. Now they had to beat her in court. He had the power. The money. The connections.

He was contemplating how Clark would clean up this mess, and decided to put Wyatt in charge, when Rose buzzed his office. "Sir, the President is on line one."

He had not been expecting this call so soon. Walter Croft sucked a deep breath, picked up the phone, and pressed line one. "Mr. President, good to hear from you."

CHAPTER 19

THERE IS NOTHING like a really good plan, Darby thought. Despite her stellar effort of an attitude of acceptance, she had been pissed since her Christmas Eve gift of insanity. The decision not to ruin everyone's holiday was a gift to her friends, so she kept her feelings to herself. Besides, she figured if she faked it long enough, that calm exterior would work itself into her soul. Guys faked it until they made it, why not her? That plan wasn't working so well. However, anger was better than depression, and the only way to break free from both was to do something proactive. That's when inspiration hit.

Early that morning Darby had emailed Dr. Wood and asked him if he could prescribe medication for her bipolarism. He was now officially a criminal, and the reason criminals got caught was because of stupidity. If he prescribed something for her, she could nail his scrawny little ass for malpractice.

Darby had just returned home, dropped her purse and gym bag onto the kitchen table, and opened the fridge. One of her many New Year's resolutions was a year of health, both physical and mental.

She had been trying to get her union to access her medical report to no avail. They had sent her a link to download it, but it hadn't worked. She removed a container of chicken wings and opened it, smelled them, added five to a plate, and stuck them into the microwave.

Waiting for the buzzer to beep, she thought about being pulled from pay status. She was now officially out on medical. At least she had 250 hours of sick leave to get her through a few months of pay. The buzzer beeped and she popped open the door.

Removing the plate, she set it on the table and grabbed a couple paper towels. Then she pulled a Diet Pepsi from the fridge. That's when she noticed the red light flashing on her landline.

She lifted a wing from the plate and sucked the juice from it. She licked her fingers and then pressed play. She stripped the wing bare, with her teeth, while she leaned against the counter listening to the message.

Hi. It's Dr. Fourberie from the ALPO aeromedical office calling. Hey, I just got a little bit more correspondence on your situation and some information from Dr. Wood. I saw with you requesting, sort of, his actual diagnosis from him and also a suggestion for a treatment plan that might get you back to flying… and he defers on the treatment plan because he's correct. As an evaluator, he's not in the role of your treating physician, so he would not, sort of, determine a treatment plan. You would go to your own specialist or provider to manage any condition like that.

The problem is, is that with—you know—the only way back to medical certification is to dispute the diagnosis of a bipolar spectrum disorder. That's disqualifying. And even if you were to say, okay, I'll do a mood stabilizer or some other thing and get into either pharmacological or non-pharmacological treatment or therapy, that's not going to be satisfactory to the FAA because all of the medications for it are disallowed. It's considered a condition that can be treated and managed, but is not essentially curable and is always disqualifying, even if it is fairly—you know—effectively treated for the time being. So unfortunately, sort of, getting treatment is not going—for a condition like that. I don't think we're going to have any luck with regaining medical certification.

The one option to regain medical certification would be to effectively and completely and convincingly dispute the presence of the diagnosis to begin with. That's the—based on our experience with the FAA—that's the one and only way that a bipolar spectrum disorder can have any sort of success with. So we are, of course, standing by to assist you with this however and whenever we can.

That is our next, sort of, step with this as far as medical certification goes, which is my primary function in assisting you here, is to try to get an independent evaluation that would very, very effectively counter Dr. Wood's conclusion of a bipolar spectrum disorder, and that's going to be tricky because Dr. Wood is sort of a big gun with the FAA. You'd have to convince the FAA that he's totally wrong and that you do not have any sort of bipolar spectrum disorder, and that would be a difficult situation. But I think I gave you Dr. Brody's name and number. She's certainly a good person for you to talk to and explain your situation to, and she would probably be the best next step. As I stated, she would read your report for free and tell you if this is hopeless.

But as I say, we are here standing by. I'm here for a little bit longer, at least, today and a little bit next week and Dr.

Max is also covering for me next week. So, if you have any questions or want to talk strategy on that, please feel free to give us a call. Thanks.

"What a fucking idiot," Darby said. *Who the hell leaves a rambling message like that on someone's phone?* Darby thought setting the bone on the plate, and licking her fingers. She wiped them on a paper towel, reached into her purse for her cell phone, and called Linda.

"Linda, I need your professional opinion," Darby said. "I just listened to a really weird message. Do you have a couple minutes?"

"Of course," Linda said.

Darby explained what she wanted Linda to listen to, and who it was from. "I'm going to hold my phone to his message so you can hear it."

With that, Darby pressed play. It felt like forever listening to the discombobulation again. The message was no better the second time than the first.

"What the hell?" Linda said, when the message ended. "There are so many things I could say about this. But, is this the same guy who told you *not to* disclose you were seeing a psychiatrist on your medical form?"

"None other. My ALPO medical representative at his best, but my captain representative concurred."

For a pilot not to disclose they were seeing a doctor on their medical application was subject to a temporary loss of license. The FAA viewed omissions equally as bad as a falsification. Something every pilot should know.

"Who the heck is Dr. Brody?" Linda asked.

"She's a doctor who's doing the same thing to pilots over at Air Western Airlines that Wood did to me. Take money to sink a pilot."

"These doctors should be put away," Linda said.

"More than that, Wood, Marsh, and Dr. F. should have their nuts chopped up in a grinder," Darby said. "Dr. Brody... half of me wants to go meet with her."

"No." Linda snapped. "I would not recommend that. But... is Dr. Wood really a big gun at the FAA?"

"Maybe in his own mind," Darby said, eyeing her wings. "And perhaps ALPO's, too."

"Want my advice?"

"Of course," Darby said. Linda had been a practicing psychiatrist for a few years, but she had more intelligence and real life experience than anyone with twenty years over her seniority. She was also a wonderful friend.

"Stay away from Dr. Fourberie. That man is not on your team."

"Ya think?" Darby said with a chuckle. "But he's my ALPO representative and he's here to help."

"Tread cautiously," Linda said. Then she asked, "Are you okay?"

"I will be, as soon as I get Wood's medical report."

"When you do, I'll help you with it any way I can," Linda said. "I'll see you on Saturday. But if you need anything before then, call. I mean it."

Darby assured Linda she would call and said goodbye. She listened to Fourberie's message again. He had to be part of their game. How couldn't he? She stood and opened a kitchen drawer to remove a note pad, and then located a pen. She began to write...

1. *Dr. Marsh— Global's Director of Health Services good friends with Fourberie. Why is Global's Dr. friends with ALPO's Dr.?*

2. *Marsh good friends with Wood. Both working for Global management.*

3. *Dr. Brody works with Wood—Air Western has 98 pilots on leave. Brody involved in how many?*

These doctors appeared to be in bed with each other. But how the hell could doctors accept payment to down mentally fit pilots? Why wasn't anyone stopping them? Why hadn't they been removed by their respective medical boards? Had anyone reported them before?

Whores, Darby thought. Apparently, they would take money for screwing anyone. She hated having those thoughts. It was so disrespectful comparing any hard working woman, regardless of her occupation, to unethical doctors. They were the lowest form of life.

She opened her Diet Pepsi and assessed the wings, which were now cold. She stuck another into her mouth. She had to figure out what the hell Fourberie was up to and why. But then she wondered if that was even necessary. Maybe her best bet was to forget he existed. Unfortunately, she needed that report, and he may be the only way to get it. Darby picked up her phone.

CHAPTER 20

DARBY SAT AT her kitchen table and sipped her Diet Pepsi while she waited on hold with the ALPO aeromedical office. She was sketching airplanes and clouds on the paper when someone finally answered.

"Thank you for waiting. How may I help you?"

"Is Dr. Fourberie available?" Darby asked.

"May I tell him who's calling?"

"Darby Bradshaw from Global Air Lines."

"Standby."

Darby had been a damn good sport at standing by, but those days were done. She was done going for a ride on a company sponsored ticket, where the union pushed her into the front of the line. That message he had left was a combination of unprofessionalism and ridiculousness. The more she thought about it, the angrier she became. The thought of ignoring him was short lived.

How the hell could Dr. Wood be the FAA's big gun?

The previous year had been the most frustrating of her life. If Global's fucking management hadn't done this to her, she would be flying and she and Ray would be together. He wouldn't be with some other pilot, who apparently had a kid. He certainly found a way to get an instant family. The worst part was he knew what was going on, and wasn't coming clean with her. But none of that really mattered. Those concerns were just misdirecting her anger.

Her AIR 21 attorney had been charging her a fortune, and was doing nothing. The union had fought against her every step of the way. The grievance was delayed because they couldn't get Abbott to show up, and Abbott was the company's star witness.

Ms. Abbott was the woman whom Rich Clark had claimed was an H.R. Safety Investigator, assigned to investigate Darby's report. As it turned out, she was the manager of the pass travel complaint department and equal opportunity manager. They had sent the lady who resolved employee pass travel complaints to investigate a safety report.

Darby had been set up from the beginning. Yet she had a hard time believing Ms. Abbott was involved. There had to be some misunderstanding. Abbott had to be a pawn. Darby had no idea what she'd allegedly said to Ms. Abbott a year ago, because they had never told her. Did Abbott tell them something that wasn't true? Or, did Abbott tell them what Darby had actually said, and Clark created something that was not? The only way to find out was to read that report.

Darby glanced at the time on the phone, and tapped her pen on the paper. Man, these guys didn't care about anyone's time. She thought about hanging up and calling back.

She stood and paced. Her union doctor was incompetent. Dr. Wood was a criminal. Her attorney was a nightmare. Darby didn't have control over much, but she could get herself a new attorney. She could also fire her ALPO medical examiner.

"Darby, we got some bad news," a voice broke into Darby's thoughts.

"Dr. Fourberie?"

"Yes. Dr. Wood told me that you are bipolar, which is very, very bad. Pilots just don't *ever* come back from that."

"Yep. I heard that. I just listened to your message. Three times. Not sure how you got the house number, but my cell phone is probably best."

"Oh, well… we'll have to update that."

"We'll do that," she said sitting. "More importantly, do you know why Dr. Wood diagnosed me as bipolar?"

"He said it was something about you having a three or four year manic episode twenty years ago while you were working two jobs, taking flying lessons, and attending college. Apparently, you were caring for some kids during the day, attended college at night, worked a part time job, while flying. Most recently, you wrote a safety report which also exhibited grandiosity."

"I was a nanny to pay for flight lessons, and I—"

"I'm not here to debate. I'm just telling you what he said," Dr. Fourberie snapped. "Dr. Wood is a powerful force, and this will be difficult to challenge."

"You said that in your message, too." Darby rolled her eyes, and sucked a breath. *Don't argue, just get the report*, she told herself.

"I guess you could get a second opinion."

"I'm going to use the Mayo Clinic."

"Uh, well… Mayo is good. But… the FAA doesn't really respect the Mayo like they do an aviation private practice psychiatrist."

"The Mayo gives medical clearances to astronauts." Darby's incredulous look would have spoken volumes had Dr. Fourberie been there to see it. What the hell was he thinking? "You cannot be serious."

"I've got a good friend here in Denver," he said. "Dr. Brody. I mentioned her in my message. Let me give you her number."

"Oh… I've heard of her." Darby sighed. *How the hell could he be sending her down the river like this?* Brody had a reputation of removing pilots from other airlines. She suspected Brody was nothing less than another unethical doctor for sale like Dr. Wood. "Do you know her reputation?"

"I do know she will read your report without charging you. She'll tell you if your case is hopeless or not. That way you don't have to waste your money or time for further evaluations."

He gave Darby her phone number and address, and she wrote it on her pad. As if she would use her. Ironically, Brody's office was located in the ALPO aeromedical office's backyard. Then something else occurred to her.

"I'm allowed a second opinion—an *unbiased* second opinion. So why should *anyone* be able to read Wood's report to evaluate me based on his rhetoric?"

"You have a bipolar diagnosis. This is now a forensic investigation. That means whomever you go to from here on out must have a copy of Dr. Wood's report for a valid evaluation."

"Are you frigging kidding me? A doctor can make up shit, and then all evaluations will be based upon his falsified records?"

"Dr. Wood is a big gun with the FAA," Dr. Fourberie said.

"Big gun or not," Darby said. "If this is a forensic investigation, then don't you think I should go to a forensic psychiatrist?"

"Not necessary."

She breathed deeply and counted to five to not say something she'd be sorry for. How the hell would she ever get a valid evaluation? She wouldn't. But she did need to see what the hell he wrote. This was crazy. Her union dollars were paying for this shit. Pilots deserved better.

"Do you have a copy of my report?" Darby finally asked. "I've been requesting this from your office and always get one excuse after another. Dr. Wood won't give it to me. Dr. Marsh won't give it to me. Your office is giving me the runaround."

"Yes, we have it all. Your neuropsychological tests are included. I think the audio is there, too."

"Can you send me the audio on a disk, along with a printed copy of the report?"

"We're going to have to charge you for printing, uh… just a sec… Yep, here it is. Uh… five hundred eighty-nine dollars."

"What the hell? Why so much?"

"The report is three hundred and sixty-six pages in length, but the entire packet is thirteen hundred and nineteen pages."

"As in one, three, one, niner?" she asked clarifying, her mouth hanging open.

"That's correct."

"Holy shit. Can you just email it to me?"

"Our server can't handle it."

"How'd *you* get it?"

"Email. I think."

"Am I missing something?" Darby closed her eyes and breathed deeply, shaking her head.

"Well they uploaded your report to the server a week ago. I think you can access it from there."

"I tried, but the link doesn't work."

"It must have expired. I'll make sure you get a new link."

Dear God, please give me the strength, Darby prayed.

"I have one final question," Darby said. "If Dr. Wood is a big gun, whose finger is on the trigger?"

CHAPTER 21

DARBY ENDED THE phone call and wrote the word *ACTION PLAN* on the pad of paper. She tapped her pencil for a moment and then added:

1) Call Dr. Johnson—Mayo?

2) Call Samantha—Air Western Airlines... Brody?

3) Get medical report.

4) Don't give up!!!

But her attention went back to Brody. What was with this woman?

It was Samantha who had mentioned her name, and that she had been working with Dr. Wood. Darby sprinted up the stairs to her bedroom to find her laptop. It was about time she searched Brody's background. Dr. Fourberie was pushing this woman hard. Darby needed to know why. She typed Brody's name into the search engine, and multiple listings popped up.

"Bingo! Dr. Angela Brody," Darby said. "What the hell?"

The FAA respected this woman more than the Mayo Clinic? No way in hell Dr. Angela Brody should be touching pilots unless it was to fix their bunions. Something was not right with any of this. A chill overcame her, knowing that ALPO was not simply incompetent, but they were in fact part of this.

Darby grabbed her list of items and wrote notes under Dr. Brody. Then she circled Dr. Johnson's name. He'd been her Aviation Medical

Examiner for the previous ten years, and the best AME a pilot could ask for. He'd known what was happening, and he'd had no problem giving her a medical after she had been pulled.

Contrary to Dr. Fourberie and her union rep telling her not to notify the FAA on her medical application, Dr. Johnson had agreed with her—disclose everything. Darby listed all the doctors she'd been seeing and wrote—labor dispute and AIR 21 filed. The FAA allowed her to keep her medical. The was the first indication that the FAA knew what the company was doing—no questions were asked, and she retained her medical certificate.

Dr. Johnson had been positive everything would be fine before she went to Dr. Wood. Darby hadn't been sure how to tell him of the diagnosis. So, she'd decided to do it like drinking a bad shot—quickly. She had called him four days after she'd heard. He'd said, "You need to go to the Mayo Clinic."

She knew it would be another six months to get in, but she trusted his opinion. She doodled clouds around his name while she sat on hold.

Within minutes he answered. "Happy New Year Darby."

"Thanks. You, too," Darby said. "Sorry I missed your call."

"Don't give it another thought. But I've got great news. You have an appointment at the Mayo."

"What? Really? Oh my God." She could not believe it. "When?"

"February 13."

"Are you kidding?" Darby said, raising her arms and doing an air scream. "I thought it would be months out."

"I made a few calls, and explained what was happening."

"Thank you. My medical is due in February. If I can get cleared before the end of the month, then I won't lose it."

"We'll make that happen."

Darby wrote the contact information to the Mayo Clinic, and the date, on the paper. They said their goodbyes and then Darby scrolled through her phone looking for Samantha's number.

Samantha was a captain at Air Western Airlines. Well, until they'd pulled her from duty three years earlier. She had never lost her medical, either, but that didn't stop them from keeping her from flying. From the best Darby could assess, she pissed off some pilot who had friends in management. A mutual friend had connected Darby and Samantha when she'd heard they shared a similar story.

Darby found her number and pressed call.

"Sam, this is Darby. Happy New Year."

"Happy New Year. How are you doing?" Samantha asked. "I've been meaning to call, but life has been busy."

"I've been bipolar since Christmas Eve," Darby joked. "But other than that, I'm doing great."

"Those bastards," she said. "I'm so sorry."

"That's okay. If I can't laugh, I'd cry." Perhaps only those going through such an ordeal could truly understood.

"What's next?" Samantha asked.

"Mayo Clinic. February 13th," Darby said, as she stood and stretched.

"Wow. That was quick. It took Janice seven months to get an appointment. But she got her job back after they cleared her. Hopefully you will, too."

"Have you talked to her since?"

"Nope. She's gone radio silent, and put the rest of us on the no talk list," Samantha said. "I think she's afraid they'll get her again."

"Can't really blame her, I suppose," Darby said, opening the fridge.

"We can't. We've got close to one hundred people out on forced medicals. Some have been required to take psychiatric evaluations.

Some eventually quit. Most get jobs elsewhere. This medical process gives them the opportunity to destroy pilots' lives without just cause. They certainly are killing mine."

"It's got to stop," Darby said, removing the last Diet Pepsi on the shelf. "I thought the AIR 21 was the way. But I'm beginning to wonder. My attorney is soaking me. He says I'll get all my attorney fees back, so I'm listening to him. However, I'm not sure how much longer I can do this. When sick leave runs out, I won't know how to fund it."

"Welcome to my world," Samantha said. "I'm going to have to sell my house."

"I'm really sorry to hear that. I might not be too far behind you," Darby said. "So, I have a question. Do you remember that doctor's name who was talking to Dr. Wood about you?"

"Yeah. Dr. Brody," Samantha replied. "Why?"

"I thought that was her," Darby said. "My ALPO doctor is trying to encourage me to go to her. Said she'll read my report for free, and let me know if it's hopeless. Says the FAA respects her more than the Mayo."

"That fucking bitch. Stay way the hell away from her," Samantha said.

Darby chuckled. "How do you really feel about her?"

"Why the hell is your union pushing Brody?" Samantha asked. "That's criminal."

"I don't know. But apparently whoever does my second evaluation is required to read Wood's report because this is now a forensic investigation." Darby returned to the table and set the Pepsi by her computer.

"Have you read it?"

"Not, yet," Darby said. "I'm having a difficult time getting it." She logged into to her email to check and see if Dr. F. had sent her the new link. Nothing. Frustrated, she popped open her Pepsi.

"Was that an adult beverage I just heard?" Samantha asked.

"It probably should be," Darby said with a grin, and then took a sip. "I'm really curious how he could craft this diagnosis. Bipolar is a medical diagnosis, kind of like cancer. Either you have it, or you don't."

"There's nothing legal about any of this," Samantha said. "Unfortunately they get away with it. I wish there was something we could do to stop it."

"Me, too. Any word on you getting back to flying at Air Western?" Darby asked.

"None in sight. Union limbo. But I got a job flying 757's with the new Eastern. The pay will be a fraction of what I made before. But at least it's something."

Samantha told Darby about the airline and the training she'd been experiencing. It felt good catching up with her. She still couldn't believe the airlines could keep pilots away by saying they were mentally unfit. Just because they said so. Yet, those exact same pilots could go fly elsewhere, as Samantha had.

You know," Samatha said. "I think you should call Dr. Strat. He's helped a few of our pilots, and has been working with Jack. He might give you some information that could help."

"Jack told me about Strat. But I was hoping I wouldn't need him," Darby said twiddling her pen. "And now I have the Mayo appointment."

"It couldn't hurt to talk to him," Samantha said.

She gave Darby Dr. Strat's number, and the two said good-bye. Darby texted Jack to see if she could use his name for the connection and he replied—*absolutely! It's about time*. She dialed Dr. Strat's number and he answered on the second ring.

"Dr. Strat, my name is Darby Bradshaw, and Captain Jack Brown said to call you. I'm a pilot for Global, and they pulled me for the inability to hold a first class medical. They sent me to a doctor who diagnosed me unfit to fly."

He sighed heavily. "I normally don't take calls like this," he said, "but for Jack I'll make an exception."

"I really appreciate it."

"Who's the doctor?"

"Wood," Darby said. "He has a 366-page report defending his diagnosis."

"Wood's known for that," Dr. Strat said. "He writes voluminous reports that nobody reads."

He rattled on about Dr. Wood and his experiences with him. None of it was good. Then he disclosed his normal fees, and the reason why he doesn't take calls from pilots. His time is money, and any pilot going through this could take an hour or more telling him their story, and he still may not have the full picture.

"What's your diagnosis?" he finally asked.

"Bipolar."

"Well I'll be damned," he said with a chuckle.

"What's so funny?" she asked.

"Normally they give a narcissistic personality disorder," he said. "It appears they don't just want you gone from the airline, they want you gone from the industry."

"It appears so," Darby said.

Why in the hell they wanted her out of the industry, she had no idea. All she did was point out the areas they would not meet the SMS mandate, and called out their substandard training. All she had done to get here was to give them an internal report. What the hell were they afraid of?

"I want you to contact someone," Dr. Strat said. "He's a friend of mine, and a forensic psychiatrist. Tell him I sent you."

CHAPTER 22

DARBY STARED AT the number Dr. Strat had given her, wondering what to do with it. She opened the fridge and grabbed an apple. Taking a bite she walked into the laundry room to throw a load into the dryer. She opened the lid. With one sniff, she skipped that idea. Setting the apple aside, she added detergent and pressed the start button for the second time on the same load that week.

Pulling her coat on, she walked into the backyard with her phone. Sitting on a patio chair she stared at her unused hot tub and ate the apple. She contemplated calling the forensic doctor, wondering if that would be a good move or not. It wouldn't hurt to call. *Would it?* But her AME had gone to such an effort to get her into the Mayo Clinic, Darby didn't want to cause problems there.

Darby lifted her phone and pressed Kathryn's number, but got her recording.

"Kat, it's me Darby. I have a question for you, call when you can."

She tossed her apple core across the patio at the garbage can lid, and actually hit it. Then she dialed Linda who answered on the first ring.

"Did you get your report?" Linda asked.

"Not yet," she said. "But my AME got me into the Mayo in February."

"That's wonderful. That's exactly where you need to be."

"It is. But here's the thing. There are a group of pilots at Air Western Airlines out on similar mental health accusations. A couple of them told me to call Dr. Strat. He's been helping them. I called, and Strat said my case was like none other, and recommended I see a psychiatrist friend of his. He also told me that I could use his name to get in."

"Would you go there instead of the Mayo?"

"I'm thinking, yes. But only if he can get me in sooner." Darby stood and walked around the patio, and opened the side gate.

"I know you want to get this done," Linda said. Darby headed toward her front yard as she listened to Linda explain the Mayo Clinic's strengths. "I don't know," Linda finally said. "The Mayo is highly respected and you would have a team, versus a singular doctor's opinion."

"I could not agree more," Darby said. "Did I tell you that my union doctor told me the FAA doesn't respect the Mayo Clinic?"

"Seriously?" Linda said. "Like I said... I would stay away from your union. Something stinks to high heaven over there."

"It certainly does," Darby said sitting on her front porch. "On the other hand, this new doctor is a forensic psychiatrist so he could testify in court. I'm not sure if the Mayo doctors could do that."

"I suppose that could be positive," Linda said. "What happens if he disagrees with Dr. Wood?"

"Then we go to a neutral doctor," Darby said, returning a wave to a neighbor walking her dog.

"Who selects the neutral doctor?"

"The two doctors. Wood and whomever I select," Darby said. "So, if I don't cancel my appointment with the Mayo, then we could use the Mayo for the neutral if I can get this other doctor to meet with me first."

"That sounds reasonable, but..." Linda hesitated. "Are you sure they would choose the Mayo Clinic as the neutral?"

"I don't know why they wouldn't," Darby said. "If two private practice doctors disagree, common sense says they would select a clinic with a panel of doctors."

"Nothing has made sense with any of this," Linda said.

"I'll give you that one," Darby said, brushing some dirt into the cracks on her porch, thinking about which way to turn. Normally she knew exactly what to do, but her thinking was being clouded by her singular goal—to get back to work sooner than later.

"It can't hurt to call," Linda finally said. Then she added, "Why is your case different from the others?"

"Huh? Oh… he said that airlines do this often, the fake diagnosis thing. But my bipolar diagnosis was a first for him." Darby stood and opened her front door. "He said it had something to do with them wanting me out of the industry."

"We need to talk to Kat," Linda said. "I have been thinking the exact same thing. None of this makes medical sense, and I simply don't know how far they will go."

"I'm not sure, either," Darby said.

She had wondered how far they would go for a year, then they'd shown her with the bipolar diagnosis. Now, she wasn't sure, and afraid to voice that concern because of the paranoia accusation. A doctor with Wood's credentials who would give her a medical diagnosis with such error, was bewildering. Bipolar symptoms began appearing in childhood or late teens. This was not something a person caught later in life. She needed to see that report.

There was even a time she had carried a gun as an FFDO. When she'd become a part of the Federal Flight Deck Officer program, she'd been evaluated by a psychiatrist in order to be armed. All she could say now was, Rich Clark was a very lucky man that she wasn't crazy, or his ass might be in trouble.

Chapter 23

KATHRYN WAS PULLING lasagna from the oven when Jackie and John walked into her kitchen. "Hey, guys," she said, as John set two bottles of wine onto the counter.

She hugged Jackie, and then removed her potholders and set them on the counter next to the wine. She lifted one of the bottles and read the label—*Vie*. "Thank you, John. This is nice, and quite appropriate under the circumstances."

John nodded, "Besides, you can never go wrong with a Las Madres Syrah."

"Can I help with something?" Jackie asked, opening the fridge.

"You can help yourself to a glass of wine," Kathryn said. "Not too often do you get to put your feet up these days."

"I forgot how hard babies were," Jackie said, closing the refrigerator. "I might be too old for this," she whispered.

"Never," Kathryn said, wrapping the bread in foil and placing it into the oven.

As John opened one of the bottles, he asked, "Have you talked to Darby since she got her report?"

"Oh, yeah. You might say she was a little pissed yesterday," Kathryn said with a laugh, closing the oven door. "I'm joking about the little part."

"I can imagine," John said, pouring the wine. "She's been through hell."

"I think her statement was, 'this is bullshit' and then she headed to the gym," Kathryn said.

"Exercise is good stress management," Linda said from the doorway. "Beats drinking your troubles away."

John sipped his wine and then added, "Depends on what you're drinking." He extended a hand to Niman. "Good to see you." He shook Niman's hand and then hugged Linda. He poured two more glasses of wine, and then opened the second bottle while Kathryn prepared the salad.

"Linda, would you mind taking the plates to the table?" Kathryn asked.

"What can I do to help?" Jackie asked again.

"You could fill the water glasses," Kathryn said, knowing Jackie would not be content to sit. The men wandered into the living room. Assigning tasks was one way to get them out of the kitchen.

Once they were gone Linda asked Kathryn, "How is Darby?"

"I'm not sure," she said. "She was doing great until she got the report, and then she kind of went on tilt. She was having a hard time just reading the Abbott section."

"This has been tough for her," Jackie said, pouring water into the glasses.

"I don't know if she even slept last night," Kathryn said. "I had some interesting text messages this morning, that arrived throughout the night."

"Venting," Jackie said, setting the pitcher on the counter.

"She flipped out when she read Ms. Abbott's report," Kathryn added. "I'm not sure what else she's learned, but I feel so bad for her."

Niman and John returned to the kitchen, holding two more bottles of wine, and the ladies fell silent.

"If I knew it was that easy to quiet women, I would become an alcoholic," John said, setting the bottles onto the counter. "Regardless, I thought we could use a couple more."

"Who's Abbott?" Niman asked, grabbing a handful of nuts.

"She was the purported HR safety investigator that Rich Clark asked to investigate Darby's report," Kathryn answered.

"She wasn't even an HR manager. She was the manager of the pass travel complaint department," Jackie added. "She knew nothing about safety or flight operations."

"They met in a hotel lobby, no less," Linda said. "I wouldn't trust anything that woman had to say. If she were a doctor, she would be disbarred simply for the evaluation location."

"She's also a fucking lying bitch!" Darby exclaimed standing in the doorway, holding a bottle of wine.

Everyone turned toward her, and she continued. "I wish someone would bring her right here, right now, with a big, bow on her head, so I could tell her what a cheap, lying, no-good, rotten, four-flushing, low-life, snake-licking, dirt-eating, inbred, overstuffed, ignorant, blood-sucking, dog-kissing, brainless, dickless, hopeless, heartless, fat-ass, bug-eyed, stiff-legged, spotty-lipped, worm-headed, sack of monkey shit she really is!"

A moment of silence filled the room, and then Jackie burst out laughing and Linda joined her. Kathryn asked, "How many times did you watch Chevy Chase Christmas Vacation this year?"

"Too many," Darby said with a wave of a hand. She set the bottle of wine onto the counter and then lifted a glass. "But why am I the only person with an empty glass?"

CHAPTER 24

DARBY SAT AMONGST her friends at the end of the table. Kathryn was at the other end. They exchanged a glance and a warm smile. Jackie and John were to her right, Linda and Niman on the left. It had been a long time since they'd had a grownup dinner without the kids.

Darby handed her plate to Jackie, who held it out for Kathryn, who scooped a large serving of lasagna onto it. Kathryn knew how to comfort Darby with her homemade lasagna.

"This smells so good," Darby said, setting her plate on her mat. "Thank you."

"Makes coming back to Seattle worthwhile," John said with a wink, as he leaned away from his wife.

Jackie slapped his arm. "Hey, mister," she said with a laugh, "you'd better be coming back for more than Kat's lasagna."

"Brave man," Niman said, and sipped his wine with a smirk.

"I was thinking the same thing," Linda said, adding caesar salad to her plate. She then handed the bowl to Darby.

"Thanks," Darby said, accepting the bowl.

Once all the plates were filled Kathryn asked, "Darby, do you want to make the toast?"

Darby nodded, and then lifted her glass and assessed the faces around the table before she spoke. "May the best of your past be the worst of your future. And most importantly, to friends."

Everyone lifted their glasses, and they all said, "To friends."

Darby felt lucky to have these people in her life. This fact was magnified by all the mistruths Abbott had written about their meeting. There were unethical people running around the world, but there were also really good people, too. These were good people.

Darby stuck her fork into her lasagna and lifted it, a string of cheese hung down and she used her finger to wrap it around the fork. Then she stuck the bite into her mouth, and realized they were all watching her. "What?" she said with her mouthful.

"We're dying to know what Abbott wrote," Jackie said.

"I have to say, you're surprisingly calm," Kathryn said. "Especially with the Griswold commentary and the midnight text messages."

"Well, it goes with being bipolar," Darby said. "One minute you're up." She raised her glass. "Then you're down." She lowered her glass. Then she said, "Actually this is not really something to joke about. It pisses me off that this company is using an extremely debilitating condition as a tool of retaliation."

"That's bothers me, too," Linda said. "There are close to six million Americans with this condition. You're right, it's extremely debilitating, especially if not treated."

"So, what exactly did Abbott say?" John asked, mirroring his wife's question.

"I'll give you the *Reader's Digest* version," Darby said, "but first..." she raised a finger and then took one more bite of lasagna and said, "Kat, this is exceptional."

"It is quite delicious," Niman added.

"Thank you," Kathryn said, touching a napkin to the edge of her mouth.

"Apparently," Darby began, "I was crying for the entire time during our three hour meeting."

"In the middle of the hotel lobby?" John asked, and Darby nodded.

"Can you get the video, or ask the clerks working there to stand up for you?" Jackie asked. "They could prove that didn't happen."

"That was over a year ago. Nobody remembers anything from back then, especially something that didn't happen. The video's gone," Darby said. "Had they told me then what she'd said, I would have done just that. Now it's too late."

"It's your word against hers," Niman said. "The very reason why they didn't tell you."

"I suspect as much, too," Darby agreed. "I am also paranoid because I told her pilots had warned me that I had a target on my back, and that they'd said if I came forward with the report, management would get me."

"Get you how?" Niman asked.

"Line checks, mess with me in training, stuff like that," Darby said.

"But they were out to get you," Jackie said. "Because they did."

"Yep," Darby said, stabbing another bite of lasagna. "But, remember, you're only paranoid if they really aren't out to get you."

"This is unbelievable," Niman said. "When Linda told me, I thought it was strange. But now it makes even less sense."

"Well, I have to give her some credit, because she did say that I did not literally say I was going to be physically harmed. Abbott said she'd inferred it."

"Did Dr. Wood ever ask you if you thought you'd be harmed?" Linda asked. When Darby shook her head no, she asked. "What about Dr. Marsh?"

Dr. Marsh was their director of health services and was supposed to have made the initial assessment. It had taken him six weeks until after she'd been pulled to meet with her, and at that time he had said it was a misunderstanding.

"Dr. Marsh asked," Darby said. "I told him the same thing about the line checks, training, oh, and that they could give me a Section 8. Which is exactly what they did."

"I'm confused," Kathryn said. "How did she infer you were going to be physically harmed? Simply because you told her you had a target on your back?"

"Well, because I told her I gave Linda a copy of the report."

"What?" Linda said, her fork stopping midway to her mouth.

Darby turned her attention to Linda. "Apparently, I gave you the report for safe keeping, for when I was murdered. Then you could give it to the media."

"That's simply ridiculous," John said.

"Why did you tell her you gave it only to me?" Linda asked. "You also gave it to Kat."

"Well, after the meeting we were standing at the elevator, and she had been so clueless about everything, I wanted to convey that I'd given the report to someone who wasn't aviation savvy. I explained that, if you understood, why wouldn't an HR safety investigator get it," Darby said. "No offense."

"None taken," Linda replied, and ate her bite of lasagna.

"The most interesting thing about her report was that she had 62 questions listed, that she claimed she asked, and I answered. They were all written with extremely articulate answers."

"What's unusual about that?" John asked, refilling wine glasses.

"She didn't have a list of questions with her when we spoke. She had my safety report." Darby stabbed her salad, and asked, "How could anyone remember that many questions, without reading them, let alone remember the detailed responses?" She stuck the bite into her mouth.

"Did she have a pad of paper at the meeting?" Linda asked.

"Nope. The only thing she had was a copy of my report."

"How long did you say your meeting lasted?" John asked.

"Three hours," Darby said. "Oh, but she also claimed I was erratic, jumped from topic to topic, couldn't stay focused, and did all the talking."

"Yet she was able to ask 62 questions, and then write articulate answers?" Linda asked.

"Apparently so," Darby said, glad that Linda understood the conflict.

"What did you talk about besides the target on your back?" John asked.

"I gave her examples of near crashes at Global. Training concerns. Fatigue. Policy violations. For example, she asked me about the instructor falsifying records. Then I explained about AQP and…"

"What's APQ?" Linda asked.

"Advanced Qualification Program," Darby said. "It's how we train pilots." She took a sip of her wine and then continued. "Anyway, Ms. Abbott asked how bad it would be if he just did it once."

"Who did what just once?" Jackie asked.

"I'm sorry," Darby said. "The instructor falsifying records. If he falsified them just once and got caught."

"Are you kidding?" John asked, glancing toward Kathryn with an incredulous look.

Kathryn nodded at John and then turned to Darby and said, "Tell John what you told her."

"I asked her how bad it would be if she got caught robbing a bank. If she just did it once." Darby sighed. "I had told her that documentation was the only way we have to monitor our performance under the new program. Bad data does nothing and that we could lose our AQP certification, which would be a huge financial hit to Global."

"Is there any way to prove she was lying in this report?" Jackie asked.

"Kind of," Darby said. "There are things she said that I can prove are false. Like, she said I was exhausted because I was busy babysitting kids and writing books while flying. But I haven't babysat kids for years."

"Besides, when you're with the twins," Kathryn said, "we have to wonder who is watching whom."

"Exactly," Darby agreed, and raised her glass in an air toast. The truth was, Kathryn was probably right. "Abbott made me sound like I was afraid, irrational, and an emotional wreck crying the entire time, and she was afraid I would harm myself and others."

"I'm sorry for being dense," Niman said. "But if you were, say, behaving that way in the middle of a lobby, wouldn't a reasonable person cut the meeting short and change the venue?"

"One would think," Darby said.

"What's the next step?" Niman asked.

"That's the good news," Darby said. "I am going to the Mayo Clinic in February. And I have a number for a forensic psychiatrist who I am calling on Monday. If I use him, then we could use my Mayo appointment for the neutral. I'll be back on property by March."

"Sounds like you have all medical bases covered," John said. "What about the legal issue?"

"That's another problem," Darby said. "My attorney claims to be a big wig. I've been paying him a lot of money. But he really doesn't seem to be moving forward. I can tell when he's busy, he agrees with the union attorneys. When he's not busy with something else, he's billing me for one thing or another."

"I've got a coworker who's related to an attorney," Niman said. "I think he's got an aviation background of some sort. He might know someone. I'll see what I can learn." Linda squeezed his hand.

"That would be great. Thank you," Darby said.

"What I'm confused about is how Dr. Wood used Ms. Abbott's report against you," Linda said. "Nothing you've said so far identifies a bipolar diagnosis."

"I'm not sure. I haven't got beyond her report," Darby said.

"What have you been doing all this time?" Kathryn asked.

"I wrote up a rebuttal on her report, challenging everything she wrote."

"You've got to finish that report before you see the next doctor," Linda said. "We need to know what he said, and how he created this diagnosis."

"I will." Darby played with her fork and pushed the salad around her plate. "It's just so hard reading the lies. It's also been so long since I talked to Abbott, and I was trying to give her the benefit of the doubt that she misunderstood, but…"

"Misunderstood crying for three hours?" John said.

"Exactly. The things that woman said were so diametrically opposed to what actually happened, it's beyond belief. She needs someone to slap her silly, or hang her by her toes."

"Did she call anyone to come and get you after the meeting?" Niman asked.

"No, she didn't," Darby said, knowing exactly what he was getting at.

"If she had actually thought you were a danger to yourself," Niman added, "that would have been required."

"Did the company connect you to their employee assistance program?" John asked.

Darby shook her head. "They did not."

"Did anybody ever follow up on your safety report?" Kathryn asked.

"No, they didn't," Darby said.

"Besides, she's the manager of the pass travel complaint department," Jackie added. "What was that all about?"

"Not anymore," Darby said. "Two months after her report, she was promoted to manager of HR in another base."

"How convenient," Linda said. "They were either rewarding her for the false report, or covering their asses for not sending an HR investigator to the meeting."

The group fell quiet as they ate their meals. But Darby suspected they were all deep in thought about the situation.

"When are you going to analyze your data?" John finally asked.

"Good question," Darby said. "The surveys keep coming in, so during the wait I'm not losing anything. However, I really need to get through the medical report. After that, I'll start crunching numbers."

"I think we should see what those surveys tell us," John said, glancing at Kathryn. Darby could read their exchange. Something was up.

Darby finished off her wine and headed to the kitchen. She returned with the bottle she'd brought from home. "Merry Christmas from Ray," she said holding up his bottle. "Does anyone want to try a glass?"

CHAPTER 25

DARBY'S OFFER TO open Ray's bottle of wine was vetoed by Kathryn for one reason only—Roulage and coffee. Kathryn had laughed at how quickly that bottle of wine ended up back on the counter. Roulage was Darby's favorite.

The friends enjoyed dessert in the living room, and the discussion shifted to politics in Washington D.C., and then to children. Something told Darby there wasn't a large difference between the two discussions.

Jackie was the first to say she needed to get home. Linda offered to take her, when John indicated he wanted to stay and chat with Kathryn for a few minutes. Jackie knew that John's position as the DOT secretary and Kathryn as the head of the Seattle FAA office meant they had work related issues they needed to discuss. There had been a time when it bothered Jackie to be kept out of the loop, but Kathryn was grateful that Jackie now understood.

Kathryn hugged Jackie good night. John said he'd be about thirty minutes behind her. Everyone hugged goodbye. They all thanked Kathryn for a wonderful dinner and then left. Everyone except for Darby. She sat on a barstool and looked between John and Kathryn.

"Want me to call you an Uber?" Kathryn asked, clearly indicating they wanted to be alone.

"Nope. I'm good. But thanks," Darby said, popping off the stool. She grabbed her coat and pulled it on. Then lifted her purse and threw it over her shoulder.

"Want to take Ray's bottle with you?" Kathryn asked.

"Nah. You can keep it here," she said, hugging Kathryn. "Thanks again for an incredible dinner." Then she hugged John. When she stepped back, she said, "I'm only leaving you two alone because I'm counting on you to solve the world's aviation problems."

Kathryn grinned. "We'll try."

Darby left the house and climbed into her car. Kathryn waved good-bye from the kitchen door and then closed it. She was thankful wine had been replaced with coffee.

John was holding the bottle of wine Darby had left behind, and when he looked up, he said, "Ray gave this to Darby? I thought they split up."

"He did, and they are," Kathryn said taking a stack of plates to the counter and setting them beside the sink. "I thought it was nice." She began scraping them into the garbage can.

"Nice is one thing. But this bottle is probably worth six to seven hundred dollars."

"What?" Kathryn stopped scraping and turned. "Are you sure?"

He nodded as he set it onto the counter, pulled up a bar stool, and sat. "So, what do you think is really happening with the situation with Darby and Global?"

"I'm not sure. She'll let me see the report after she reads it, but the question as to how a psychiatrist could concoct a report to support such a diagnosis is interesting. We've known Darby for years, and there's never been any sign. He had to have been paid to falsify that report."

"That's what I'm wondering, too." John slid the bowl of nuts closer and said, "We now have a temporary FAA administrator."

"I heard."

"Something's amiss. Rumor had it that they were putting a management pilot from one of the big three airlines into that position. Then they made a military guy a temporary. This makes no sense. Why a temporary?" He grabbed a handful of nuts and popped a couple into his mouth.

Kathryn just listened. She knew John well enough to know he was expressing his thoughts, not seeking answers. She set her dishtowel on the counter, then sat on a stool beside him. She, too, reached into the nut bowl and selected a pecan, and popped it into her mouth.

"They're pushing for ATC privatization," John said. "They are also authorizing freight operators to use drones. Simply a test bed for passengers."

"A lot of issues happening all at once," Kathryn said. "Do you think any of it has anything to do with Darby?"

"I do," he said. "It's only a gut feeling, but yes."

"Why?" Kathryn asked, standing. "For what purpose?" She walked to the sink and began rinsing the plates. Keeping busy helped her to think.

John gathered a handful of glasses and set them beside the sink. "That's the question—*why?* But look at the facts." He turned and leaned against the counter. Folding his arms, he continued. "We had been watching Global. The CEO and the woman who held your position were murdered. Both were working with President Drake."

"Who is now in prison," Kathryn added. "So, they are all out of the picture."

"Not exactly. Drake was moved to San Quentin," John said.

"To put him on death row?" she said with a smile.

"Bill was moved there in October."

"What?" she said turning, a plate slipping from her grasp. It hit the floor and glass shattered everywhere. "Why didn't you tell me?"

"I just found out," John said, walking to the closet. He retrieved a broom and dustpan and began sweeping. "Drake and Bill have been in communication."

"Shit," Kathryn said, half under her breath. She could not believe this was happening. "Could President Kohler pardon President Drake?"

John nodded, and said, "Yes he could, and Kohler could pardon Bill as well."

Kathryn walked to the kitchen table and pulled out a chair and sat. She finally understood what the term 'turning your blood cold' meant. Goosebumps appeared as a chill shot through her body. If Bill got out, her girls would be in danger. She looked at John, "But how does this have anything to do with Darby?"

"She brought that safety report forward," John said. "The pilot who pulled a gun on that captain was murdered. The old Global CEO was forced off the bridge. Your boss was murdered. He was ordered to stop your research. Research based on Darby's report, no less."

John filled the dustpan and dumped it into the garbage can.

Kathryn stared, not sure what to say.

John continued. "People are being removed permanently. Then Darby was pulled for a medical condition which will discredit her." He leaned the broom against the counter. "Then you are put into a position that has kept you so busy, you haven't had time to do your research."

"President Drake makes you the DOT secretary," Kathryn said. "Parting shot?"

"I suspect so," John said, taking a seat across the table from her. "There is far too much happening right now. It feels like a slight of hand. Distracting me with one thing, so I will miss what they are really up to. I just wish I knew what the hell I'm missing."

"Whatever it is, do you think President Drake is involved from prison?"

"I have no doubt."

"Then Bill is involved, too."

"Yes." He glanced at his watch, then stood and walked to the hallway and returned with his coat. "We have to keep this between us, for now."

Kathryn nodded, and asked, "What can I do?"

"Be smart, and go back to the beginning."

"How far back?"

"Back to Darby's initial report. The one she gave to Wyatt and Clark," John said. "There is something in that report that I believe is the reason they're trying to silence her."

"But it's now my research," Kathryn said. "Why don't they silence me?"

"I think they tried," he said.

Kathryn's hand went to her mouth. "Oh, my." How could she have forgotten her daughters' car accident? The accident designed for her and Darby. "Do you think...?"

"You and the girls are safe."

"Is Darby in danger?"

"Not if they think the diagnosis will stick," he said pulling on his coat. "But I do know management at Global has read her medical report. That concerns me."

"That diagnosis is not going to stick unless they bought off everyone at the FAA. And we know that didn't happen," Kathryn said.

"What if we allowed it to stick?" he asked.

"Oh, John," Kathryn said folding her arms, shocked at the mere suggestion. "I don't know if Darby would survive that."

"You're probably right," he said, reaching for the doorknob. "Sorry I mentioned it. But to be safe, if anyone asks if you know anything about her gathering data, lie. Say you aren't sure what she's doing, but you'll check into it. Do not become involved in this any more than you have. You know nothing."

"I don't like any of this," Kathryn said holding the door open for him.

"I don't either, but for now... keep your distance from that research. When it's complete, I'd like to see those results. And no mention of Bill to anyone."

CHAPTER 26

THE TWO MEN slipped through the side gate and into the backyard. They walked across the patio in the dark. No flashlights were allowed. The man in charge lifted a rock, hesitated, and then smashed it through the glass of the back door. He smiled, exposing his yellow stained teeth. "Told ya' there wasn't an alarm." Reaching through the hole he unlocked the door.

"What kind of wine we 'sposed to get?" the other man asked.

"Some fancy shit," he said as they walked into the laundry room, and worked their way into the kitchen. He opened the fridge to give them some much needed light.

"Shit, she's got five bottles on her counter," the man said. "Which one?"

"Who fucken' cares, dumb shit," he said, opening one of his duffel bags. "We're taking them all."

The man in charge began setting the bottles into the bag. Then they walked into the living room, with nothing but the streetlights leading their way, clanking bottles as they went.

"Jackpot," the assistant said. "Nuther' wine rack, and she's got some good shit."

"Take it all," the man said. "Put the hard stuff in this bag."

"Hope it don't break," he mumbled. "How many bags did ya' bring?"

"Three," he said, handing him the third bag.

"Grab them pillows, an' use 'em for padding."

Then he had a better idea, and returned to the kitchen. He began opening drawers to find dishtowels. He returned and removed the pillows, then wrapped the bottles in towels so they wouldn't break.

"Is this all we have to do?" the man following the lead asked. "Just take it?"

"Hell no," he said. "We have to get rid of the evidence."

He was grinning at his joke, when the other guy asked, "Can't we just drink it?"

"You're a dumb fuck, aren't you?" the man said. "That's how we're gunna' get rid of it."

"Think we should see what's upstairs?" the other guy asked, just as a car pulled into the driveway, shining lights across the window. They both ducked, and then the garage door began opening.

CHAPTER 27

DARBY LIFTED HER purse as she climbed out of her car. Tossing it over her shoulder she headed toward the door and pressed the garage door button to lower it. She stepped into her kitchen and closed the door. A draft whipped through the kitchen and she shivered. She turned on the lights and headed toward the laundry room and froze. The back door was open and the window had been broken. Glass covered the floor.

Her 'oh shit' moment was fueled by *don't touch anything* and *get the hell out of the house.* Whoever it was could still be in there. She retreated to the garage as quickly as possible, pressed the button, and ran around to the driver's side of her car. She climbed in and locked the doors. Her heart beat rapidly.

She pulled her purse onto her lap and dug out her keys. She then tossed her purse onto the passenger seat. Heart racing, she fumbled with the key and then stuck it into the ignition. Turning the key, she looked over her shoulder to back down the driveway. Two figures were running across her lawn and then they headed down the street. They were carrying bags.

"You bastards," Darby shouted. She dialed 911, set her phone on speaker and placed it on the passenger seat. She backed out the driveway, and followed them.

"911, what's your emergency?"

"Two guys broke into my house. Looks like they filled bags with my stuff," she yelled. "They're running down the street."

"Are you in danger?"

"Danger of running them over," she answered, pointing the car in their direction. She drove close, then shined her brights on them and she honked her horn multiple times. "I'm in my car following them."

"What's the address?"

Darby gave the woman her address, but attempted to explain she was in hot pursuit. Her hot pursuit wasn't that fast. She rode the brakes so she wouldn't hit them. The thought of stopping the car and jumping them crossed her mind. She definitely could outrun them. However, there was nothing in her house they could have taken worth her life, or theirs. Unless they took her computer. "Oh shit, my computer!" she gasped.

One of the guys looked back and flipped her off.

"Seriously," she almost laughed. "Oh, you're so dead."

"Excuse me?" the operator said. "Ma'am, you need to return to your home."

"They're heading between two houses at the end of my street. South side." Damn. Damn. She stopped her car and unlocked the doors, ready to run after them. Then she sighed and relocked the car. A quick slap on the steering wheel, and she circled back toward her house. She stayed on the phone with the 911 operator, and together they took the short drive home.

She pulled into her driveway, but stayed in her car with the doors locked.

"Please don't hang up," Darby said, turning off her car. "Will you wait until the police come?" She gave the woman her description, and that of her car, so when the police arrived, they wouldn't try to shoot her. She pulled her driver's license out of her wallet while she waited.

Within minutes the police were driving down the street with lights flashing. She jumped out of her car, and waved.

Two policemen climbed out of the car. Both with hands on their guns.

"I called 911. Here's my ID," she said, extending the license.

One of the cops took it and shined his light on it, and then shined the light at Darby. "Doesn't do you justice, ma'am."

Oh, God. If one more person called her ma'am, she would go crazy.

"Could anyone else be in the house?" the older of the officers asked.

"I'm not sure," she said, and then she began to shake even though she was still wearing her down jacket. "But I doubt it."

"Do you know what they took?"

Darby shook her head no, and then said. "Can we go take a look?" God, she hoped it wasn't her laptop. Years of her life were in that computer.

"Lead the way," the younger officer said, extending his hand toward the garage.

They walked through the garage and she opened the door into her house and stepped back. The officers entered first and she followed. Then she pointed to where they had broken in through the back door. Darby stayed in the kitchen, and then noticed all her kitchen drawers were opened.

When they returned, the older officer said, "I think that's how they got in."

Ya think? Darby thought. "It appears they were looking for something in my kitchen."

"Did they take anything?" the older guy asked. "Can you check without touching?"

Darby removed gloves from her coat pocket, waved them, and pulled them on. She looked inside each of the drawers that had been opened, and then said, "They stole my dishtowels." Then she glanced around the kitchen. "And my wine off that counter," she said pointing.

"How many bottles?"

"I don't remember. Three or four," she said. Then she headed directly for her living room. The officers followed. The wine rack was empty, too. She opened the cupboard and all the booze was gone. "They took all my alcohol."

Darby attempted to remember what she had. It didn't matter. There would be no tracking it regardless, and she wouldn't be making an insurance claim for alcohol and a window.

"We need to inspect the house, and make sure it's clear," the older officer said. "Is that okay?"

Darby nodded. "Will you see if my laptop is on my desk in my bedroom at the top of the stairs? I'm too afraid to look." They agreed, left her downstairs and headed up the stairs. Darby sat on the couch and pressed favorites on her phone and called Kathryn.

"I'm home. Cops are here. Someone broke in and took all my booze. They also stole my dish towels. Maybe to clean up their barf after they drank everything. I'm hoping they didn't take my laptop," Darby said.

"I'm on my way," Kathryn said.

"You don't need to come. I'm fine." She tried to talk Kathryn out of coming over to no avail.

The officers returned to the main level and the older guy said, "All clear upstairs. There's a laptop on your desk. I'll finish looking around down here. If that's okay?"

"Yes, of course." Darby placed a hand to her heart, thankful the one thing she couldn't afford to lose was still in place.

The young officer removed a pad from his pocket and asked her what had happened. Darby proceeded to tell him the details, and how she called 911 and followed the guys. They were carrying a total of three bags. Not hers. Black, appeared to be worn. No writing on them. She described what they looked like—homeless. But now that they only stole booze, they could have been homeless teenagers.

Burien, the neighboring city, had become the place for teens to live on the streets. She also told him that one guy flipped her off. She said she wasn't sure if they knew it was the homeowner who was following them, but she was tempted to run them over. The more she thought about it, she didn't think they were teenagers because the guy who flipped her off looked pretty weathered.

The officer turned the page and asked, "Ma'am, were you speaking to the 911 operator while driving?"

"Yep. That's how I called for help and followed them at the same time." Darby's patience was running thin, and she was tired. However, she avoided telling him what she was doing before the robbery because there had been alcohol involved, and she had been driving. However, she was thankful she hadn't called an Uber, or she would have been left without a means of escape.

He wrote while he asked, "Do you know that it's illegal to speak on a phone while operating a motor vehicle?"

"Are you kidding me?" She stared at him, not believing that was his focus. Just then there was a knock at the door and she jumped to her feet. The officer handed her the paper and she grabbed it, and stuffed it into her pocket on the way to the front door. She opened the door to Kathryn.

"Are you okay?" Kathryn asked, hugging her.

"I am," she said, just as the older officer walked into the room. Darby turned and said, "This is my friend Kathryn Jacobs."

"Nice to meet you," the older cop said, and turned to his partner. "Tom, let's check out the backyard." Tom nodded to Kathryn and then followed the old guy out of the room.

When they left, Kathryn and Darby went to the kitchen. "Want a cup of tea?" Kathryn asked. Darby sat at the table while Kathryn opened the cupboard and retrieve two cups without waiting for an answer. She placed a bag of Yogi Stress Relief tea in each cup.

"Good choice," Darby said, and then, "What's that?" looking at the floor.

Kathryn turned, and followed Darby's stare. A lighter was lying on the floor, by the fridge. "Not yours?" Kathryn asked.

"Nope." Darby stood and pulled out a Ziploc bag from her drawer. She walked over to the lighter and took a picture of it. Then slipping her glove back on, she picked up the lighter by the end you weren't supposed to touch when lighting it, and dropped it into the bag.

The officers walked into the room. "What's that?" the older officer asked.

Darby handed the bag to the older guy. "Not mine. I didn't touch it," she said, waving her gloved hand. "Check it for fingerprints and if they have a record, you've got our crooks."

The older officer thanked her, and then recommended she get an alarm system. He also advised her against following potential criminals. She should leave that to the police. This statement raised Kathryn's eyebrow. The younger officer reminded her to not drive and talk on the phone, to which she gave him a tight lipped smile and nodded.

After the officers left, Kathryn pulled the broom out and walked into the laundry room and began sweeping up glass. Darby went to the garage looking for wood to close up the hole in the window. She could not find any, but she did find cardboard and duct tape.

It wasn't long until the window was taped closed, and the floor was cleaned. Darby pulled her car into the garage and lowered the door.

The tea was thoroughly steeped by the time they sat down to drink it, and a bit cold. Kathryn set one of the cups into the microwave. When it beeped, she set it onto the kitchen table in front of Darby. Kathryn stuck the other cup into the microwave and asked, "You followed the guys who broke into your house?"

"I did. I should have run their little asses over. I thought they were probably homeless teenagers." She sipped her tea, then added, "The guy who flipped me off didn't look much like a kid. But it's hard to tell age when the person looks like shit."

"Why did you take a picture of that lighter?" Kathryn asked, sitting at the table with her cup in hand.

"I've seen one like it someplace, but can't remember," Darby said, and zoomed in on the photo. The pattern looked like crisscross of white on blue, and was anything but a random pattern. She showed Kathryn.

"Airplanes?" Kathryn said, stating the obvious.

"This isn't a normal homeless guy's lighter."

"Kind of weird," Kathryn said, staring at the picture.

"It is," Darby agreed. Then she sighed, remembering the ticket the cute officer had handed her. "There is absolutely no justice in life. That cop actually gave me a ticket for talking to 911 while I was driving!" She pulled the paper out of her pocket and handed it to Kathryn.

"I'm glad he didn't you give a DUI," Kathryn said, unfolding it. "*Which* officer gave this to you?"

"The cute one."

Kathryn read the paper and grinned. "Uhh…. he didn't actually give you a ticket, he gave you his phone number."

Darby took the paper and looked at it, and grinned. "Looks like I misread that one."

"Clearly," Kathryn said, holding back a smile. "A robbery will do that." Kathryn sipped her tea and then added, "There could be benefits to having a cop car in your driveway at night."

"The main benefit I can see is if his car is in my driveway at night, that means there's a cop in my bed," Darby said with a grin.

"Regardless, you'd better get that alarm system set up tomorrow morning."

"I will," Darby promised. "I've actually been planning to do that since Ray left. I just never got around to it."

"Will you come spend the night with me tonight?" Kathryn asked.

"Thanks, but I don't think we'll see any more action around here tonight."

"Unless that cop comes back to check on you," Kathryn said with a smirk.

Darby was about to say something profound, but instead she just grinned and sipped her tea.

CHAPTER 28

RICH CLARK COULD not believe he was taking Bradshaw's damn survey. Wyatt's idea. George Wyatt had directed him to tell all his managers to take it as well, in an attempt to skew the data in their favor. How the hell could they do that? He had no idea how to answer in order to skew it. Some of the management questions were evident, and he could make himself look good. But the others? Who the hell cared when he disengaged the autopilot? *What in the hell was she trying to prove?*

Clark knew damn well this survey was based upon the report Bradshaw had given him and Wyatt. But they had assured him her report would be silenced after they removed her. There was also an assurance that Jacob's research would never come to light. They were wrong on all accounts.

He finished the survey and then walked out of his office and across the hall to Wyatt's office. "Jane, can you tell George I'm ready?" Clark asked Wyatt's secretary.

"Of course," she said. Within seconds Jane said, "He'll see you now."

Damn right he'll see me, he thought. *He's the one who called me.* He smiled at Jane, entered the room, and closed the door.

"Thanks for coming over," Wyatt said. He had no time for problems, and he needed this one resolved sooner than later. "Did you get rid of the wine?"

"I took care of it," Clark said. "Last night."

"As we discussed?"

"I had a friend pay a couple bums to remove it."

"How do you know they took the correct bottle?"

"Assumed they would take everything," Clark said.

"That's a safe assumption," Wyatt agreed. "Won't they be eye-witnesses?"

Clark stared for a moment wondering if that question deserved an answer, then replied, "They won't be alive to identify anyone after they finish that bottle."

"What about your friend?" Wyatt asked.

"Not a concern."

Wyatt nodded. "And the other bottle?"

"No big deal. It's empty. No identification. If she ever finds it, it could have been Ray's."

Wyatt pushed back from his chair and walked around the desk. "I know you want her gone. But we've invested far too much time and money into this. This Section 8 is something that you started. You got us into this, you will get us out. Legally."

"Nobody has ever come back from a mental health assessment," Clark replied. "We'll make her go away."

"What was the poisoning shit about?" Wyatt asked.

"Permanently getting rid of a problem. Save the company some money. I don't know." Clark placed his hand on his hips, taking a mirroring stance to Wyatt. They had all told him she needed to be taken care of. What the hell did they think that meant? "You have to admit, receiving the diagnosis on Christmas Eve would have been the perfect time for her ending it."

"Yes. But that didn't happen. Now we're too deep to attempt that again." Wyatt walked to his credenza and poured himself a glass of water. "Want one?"

"No, thanks," Clark said. The only thing he wanted was Wyatt's position when he moved on to DC. Unfortunately, that was delayed because of Bradshaw.

Wyatt turned holding his glass, and took a sip. Then he said, "You took us down this mental health path. Make that stick. Then we'll be back in the driver's seat."

"What about Jacob's research?"

"Ms. Jacobs is not conducting the research, Darby is. If she becomes mentally unfit, there will be questions as to the legitimacy of her data. We've got media power to kill any results she may find."

"Good," Clark said with a nod. "We've got a doctor lined up for her as the neutral. The union is assisting. She's as good as gone."

CHAPTER 29

DARBY'S SLEEP WAS restless, as she half listened for intruders throughout the night. Finally the light of day hit. She could end the turmoil and get her butt out of bed. Sitting up, she yawned and stretched, then dropped her feet to the floor. God, she wished she could awaken to the smell of coffee. There was a time she didn't have to get out of bed for a coffee, but those times were gone.

She sat for a moment, then glanced at her clock. If she didn't get moving, Dr. Gelder would be at lunch before she could call him. Grabbing her robe off the end of her bed, she pulled it on, fuzzy side in, and headed downstairs. She walked straight for the kitchen, carrying her laptop, with her coffee machine the goal. *Best invention ever.*

Entering the kitchen, a thought occurred to her. She peeked into the laundry room. The duct-taped cardboard to the window confirmed that part of her night wasn't a dream.

Darby returned to the kitchen and set her laptop on the kitchen table. Then she stuck a pod into the coffee machine, placed a cup into position and pressed start. The machine did its business while she called the glass repair company who'd fixed her front door. By the time her coffee was ready, she had an appointment to have the glass fixed that afternoon.

She sipped her coffee and allowed her fingers to search a security company. As it turned out her cable company offered a security system, so she decided to take the easy way out and use them—for better or worse. They would be at her house on Wednesday, sometime between 12 and 4 pm. Her coffee mug was almost empty, and she had not yet called Gelder. This would definitely be a two or three cup day. She had never thought about how much coffee she drank until Dr. Wood had grilled her. As if coffee were a mental health issue.

Darby stuck another pod into the machine. She leaned against the counter and folded her arms, glaring at her computer. There was a time when she only used her computer for good, not evil. She was so thankful she had left it in her room last night, and not on the kitchen table. Now she did not want to leave it out of her sight.

Sighing, she knew she had to get into the remainder of her medical report. But what she had read so far was far too painful. To be honest, she was a bit nervous to read the rest of it. Well over 300 pages of what? She could only imagine based on what she'd already read.

Darby added cream to her coffee, and picked up her pad with notes. She headed into her living room and set her supplies on the table. Once snuggled onto the couch, she found Gelder's number and then typed it into her phone. He answered on the third ring.

"Gelder. How may I help you?"

"Dr. Gelder, my name is Darby Bradshaw. Dr. Strat recommended I call you."

Darby proceeded to tell Dr. Gelder what happened and how she'd been pulled from duty. She told him about the safety report she'd written, and about her book. She told him about the bipolar diagnosis on Christmas Eve after the year-long delay, and that she needed a second opinion. Dr. Gelder listened without comment until she finished.

"How long have you been flying?" he asked.

"Over 20 years."

"Have you ever had any failures in training?"

"No."

"What about sick leave?" he asked. "Do you miss a lot of work?"

"No," she said. "I maybe had three sick calls in the last twenty years."

"Did you attend college?"

"Yes. I have a master's degree."

"What was your GPA?"

"Three point seven, I think."

"Have you ever been to a psychiatrist before?" Dr. Gelder asked. "I mean before Dr. Wood."

"Once, but that was because I was applying to be an FFDO."

"A what?" he asked.

"Federal Flight Deck Officer," Darby said. "I was one of the pilots who carried a gun while flying. So, they had us evaluated before we were accepted into the program."

"Do you take any medications?" he asked.

"None, unless coffee is considered a medication."

"As far as I'm concerned, it should be," Dr. Gelder said, with a chuckle. "You're not bipolar."

"Thank you," Darby said with a huge grin. "So now what happens?"

"I've got to meet you in person. I would also like to read Wood's report."

Darby and Dr. Gelder scheduled her appointment for February 5th. Perfect timing to get her results back, and retain her appointment at the Mayo Clinic. Everything was falling into place. She would be back before anyone knew what hit them.

"I'll call ALPO's medical office and have them send you the link to the report. It's quite lengthy," Darby said. "The report, that is."

"I've heard that about Wood," Gelder said. "I've also worked with ALPO before. I'm looking forward to meeting you."

"I'm looking forward to meeting you, too," Darby said.

They said their goodbyes and Darby called the ALPO medical office.

"Hi, this is Darby Bradshaw, and I would like you to send my medical report to Dr. Gelder."

"Standby," the woman said. Darby sat on the couch and sipped her coffee. Within minutes the woman was back on the line, and said, "I'm sorry, we've already sent it to the Mayo Clinic."

"Well, I'm now going to Dr. Gelder."

"We are unable to send the report to more than one doctor."

"Why not?" Darby asked, setting her cup on the coffee table. When there was no reply she added, "I pay my dues. Your services are to help. Nowhere does it say one doctor only."

"But we already sent it to the Mayo."

"I changed my mind. It's a link, or an attachment. Please, just send it again," Darby said. "Besides, the neutral will need it and there won't be any wasted effort."

"I'm sorry," the woman said.

"If you will give me Dr. Gelder's email address, I will send it myself."

"I don't feel comfortable giving his email out," the woman said.

"I just spoke to him. He's expecting the report."

"If you'll give me his number, I will call and ask him."

ALPO had his number if they had worked together before. They had his email address. Darby was getting tired of this. Did they not realize how transparent they were? She sucked a deep breath and said, "I don't feel *comfortable* giving his number out."

She ended the call quickly so she wouldn't tell the woman how she really felt. What the hell was that all about? There was more than one way to get things done. Darby dialed Dr. Gelder's number again.

When he answered, she said, "I am so sorry to bother you, but ALPO is having difficulty sending you the report. As in, they don't want to. Do you mind if I send it directly to you?"

"Not at all," he said, and he provided her his email address.

Darby logged into her computer, typed in his email address, attached the report, and pressed send. Then she located and booked a hotel room for her visit. She logged into the Global website and purchased an airline ticket to Portland, Maine. She bought a positive space on Global, since she'd lost her pass privileges.

Now, it was time to eat that elephant. Darby opened up Dr. Wood's report and began to read beyond Abbott's allegations.

She hadn't been reading more than thirty minutes when she stopped.

Pacing the living room, she fumed. How the hell did this guy call himself a psychiatrist? She now fully realized the magnitude of what they were doing. He was nothing but a tool, and they had paid him for a false diagnosis. What a bunch of crap.

The problem was, if anyone were to read this report who had no knowledge of the facts or a solid understanding of aviation, and believed his words, he had painted an ugly picture so far. "God dammit," she said. "That asshole!"

There was only one thing she could do at a time like this, and coffee had nothing to do with it.

CHAPTER 30

DRAKE WAS ENJOYING his winter in California. The weather was far better than the East Coast freeze. He was also far enough away from D.C. to avoid conflict. None of his acquaintances were in Quentin, even if they deserved to be.

He stood at the wall and scanned the view his hotel would one day encompass. Then he glanced across the yard, enjoying the respect he received in prison. Everyone wanted something. Everything was for sale. If it wasn't for the lack of business suits, he might as well be in Washington D.C. He would not remain here forever, but for the time being it served a purpose. Bill Jacobs came into view and Drake raised a hand.

Bill was someone he could have used in another life, but his value going forward would be priceless. There were not many people whom Drake called friends. Perhaps there was something about being locked up together which connected people. He actually liked Bill Jacobs. Each hour they spent talking gave him a better understanding of how he was able to get his pilots to crash those planes, and the more he admired him.

"Good morning," Drake said, as Bill approached.

In another life they would have shaken hands. In this world there was no touching in public. Bill stuck his hands into his pocket and looked out. "Good morning."

"What do you think, hotel or condos?" Drake asked.

"Whatever makes the most money."

Drake grinned. "I like the way you think." He patted Bill on the back and said, "Priorities." Only Drake could get away with breaking the rules and touching an inmate in public, and he did just that to show the others who was in charge.

The two men wandered to their bench where they held most of their conversations, away from others. A place so quiet he could analyze his options without distraction. Drake's intention was to own the aviation industry and reduce the operational expense by removing pilots. It was his company which would provide the technology for security. That, too, was an ironic thought. It was unfortunate that his two partners were gone. He grinned. A misfortune he created.

Together they'd initiated the pilot shortage with the flight hour change. They killed pensions worldwide. They made the piloting job less attractive with longer workdays and less pay. Then without realizing how he was helping Drake, Bill Jacobs had stepped in and took his plan to the next level by showing the public how vulnerable they were in the pilots' hands. He did a marvelous job. That was the reason Drake had protected him. But it didn't end there.

Companies worldwide reduced training, effectively leaving pilots without knowledge. FAA mandates to utilize automation reduced piloting skills and the industry pressed on. Pilots were becoming mere button pushers and skill was being thoroughly destroyed. Why more planes weren't crashing was perplexing.

"I've got an interesting question," Drake said. "Pilots are stressed, tensions are high, they lack flying ability, and they are disgruntled. Why the heck aren't planes crashing now?"

Bill eyed him. "Because of people like yourself."

"How so?"

"Technology is improving daily. You and others are building reliable equipment. So reliable a monkey could fly it," Bill said.

"Then we don't need pilots," Drake said with a grin. "We could pay monkeys with bananas."

Operations without pilots were exactly where the industry was headed. He owned the patent on the singular component which would ensure security on an aircraft to be flown from a ground-based system. It wasn't foolproof yet, but nobody needed to know that small detail. By the time the world was ready to accept this concept, he'd be ready.

"You need pilots when the planes break," Bill said.

"But if they can't fly them…"

"They don't need to fly them," Bill said. "They just need to manage them. Even broken, these aircraft have redundant systems."

"Take the redundancy out, and then there's a problem?" Drake asked.

"Perhaps," Bill said watching an airplane depart from San Francisco International Airport and head west.

"Do you miss flying?" Drake asked, glancing at the aircraft.

"Every day," Bill said. "Hell, they could have grounded me and that would have been prison enough."

Drake nodded. He understood being locked away from your passion. He leaned back with his arms behind his head, and closed his eyes, enjoying the morning sun's warmth. "That's the reason I don't mind being in this place. My life continues as if I were in my office."

"With fewer interruptions," Bill said with a smirk. "You probably get more done here than anywhere."

"That I do." Drake dropped his arms to his legs, leaned forward, and looked sideways at Bill. "What would be the most challenging failure on an aircraft today?"

"Hmm. Good question," Bill said, leaning back and crossing one leg over another. "Probably an uncontrollable fire over an ocean with no place to land."

"That wouldn't be associated with pilot error, would it?"

"No," Bill said. Then Bill's mind began working.

Drake knew that look. He fell silent waiting for Bill to tell him what he needed to know.

Bill finally said, "A runaway stabilizer."

"Hmm," Drake murmured. "That's bad?"

"A runaway stab trim, just after takeoff," Bill said, "could ruin a perfectly good day."

"Huh," Drake said, curious as to the timing. "Why after takeoff?"

"The power will be in max takeoff thrust. If the stab runs forward, the nose goes down. With full power, stabilizer running forward, unless you knew what was happening, that would be a bitch. If they didn't cut the stab trim motors and pull the power back when the nose pitched down, and control the plane, I don't know if they could pull the nose up. The autothrust would be engaged at takeoff power."

"Do the airlines train for a stabilizer event?"

"Maybe on initial training," Bill said. "But for some, that could have been 20 years earlier. And not necessarily during takeoff."

"Is this something that pilots could handle?" Drake asked.

"Maybe the older guys," Bill said. "But the truth is, in training we know the failures are going to happen as part of the lesson plan, so we're ready. But it never happens in real life. I doubt anyone would be expecting it. If it hit during takeoff, with all the fucking bells and warnings they now have to alert the crew when something goes wrong, that could be a surprise. Especially if it were to happen on an aircraft that was already unstable."

"What would make a stabilizer spin uncontrollably?" Drake asked.

Bill explained the aircraft systems to him with great detail, as if he were reading from a manual. Drake enjoyed Bill's passion for detail and the memory that man had was incredible. His value was definitely multiplying. He questioned him about an unstable aircraft, and Bill explained the issues with B737 Max and how the MCAS system was designed to improve stability.

"The reality is," Bill said, "I don't think they're training for this anymore because of the redundancy of systems. One component breaks, there's always a backup."

"Redundancy is a good thing," Drake said.

CHAPTER 31

JACKIE HAD NEVER been more concerned about anyone in her life than she was about Darby locked in her house reading that medical report. It was as if Darby had fallen into quicksand. The more she read, the more she fought it, and as a result was sinking daily. Jackie just hoped there would be a way for Darby to get out. Each day Jackie called her, and each day Darby seemed to get worse. One week turned into two, and Darby had not finished reading the report.

Walking into Starbucks, Jackie glanced around the room, and spotted Linda. She headed her direction. When their eyes met Linda waved. "I got you a raspberry mocha and a croissant," Linda said. "Where's the baby?"

"Day camp." Jackie removed her coat, and draped it over the back of her chair and sat. She reached for her drink. Sipping chocolate through the whipped cream was a moment of decadence she had learned from Darby. "Thank you. This is exactly what I needed."

"Been a morning?" Linda asked.

"Every day is 'a morning' with a baby," Jackie said. "Day camp is a sanity saver."

"What kind of camp do they have for a one year old?"

"That's the thing… *anything* you want," Jackie said with a grin. "Apparently by calling daycare a camp, stay at home moms feel justified dropping their kids off for their own opportunities of growth. Meaning, mommy sanity."

"But it's a daycare?" Linda asked raising an eyebrow.

"Oh, yeah," Jackie said, breaking off a piece of her croissant. "God, back in the day we condemned the working moms for having daycare kids." She stuck a bite into her mouth. "But in today's world it's hard for Moms to get their hair and nails done or hit the gym with kids under tow."

"I never went to a gym back then," Linda said. "Had the best body ever running after Francine at the park and cleaning my house."

Jackie lifted her cup in a toast of confirmation. "Touché. But I'm too old to worry about justifying what I do." She sipped her mocha and then said, "I'm completely comfortable ditching my little wild thing. I also couldn't live without my housekeeper. Not sure how I survived in those early days."

Linda chuckled and said, "Today I think I'd do the same thing myself."

Jackie's thoughts shifted to Darby, and the reason she had asked Linda to meet her. Her face became somber at the thought of Darby's pain. "I'm really worried about Darby. As worried as the day she got that letter."

"That's what you were saying," Linda said. "What's been going on? I haven't been able to talk to her."

"I think that report is really getting to her," Jackie said leaning in and lowering her voice. "The things that come out of her mouth… let's just say Darby has taken swearing to a new level."

"Sounds like she's expressing her anger," Linda said. "Seriously, that could be a good thing."

"Yeah, but… it's what she says… or doesn't say… in the middle of those tirades." Jackie searched to find an example. She needed to explain what she meant, but that was hard because it was more of a feeling. "She keeps saying she can't believe it. She's shocked. I think she's getting really depressed."

"That's to be expected," Linda said. "When I call, she doesn't answer. But she always follows up with a text, saying she'll call me back later. She never does."

"Doesn't that worry you?"

"As long as she texts me, I know she's alive," Linda said. "For now, that might be all we get."

"I just keep calling until she answers," Jackie said. "I'm a pain in the ass, but then I get an earful."

"Has she said anything about the content of the report?"

"Bits and pieces," Jackie said. "Two days ago, it was something about finding a letter from over three years ago. Some check airman said she was a threat to the safety of the operation while flying the plane."

"Are you kidding me? Why hadn't she said anything?" Lind asked.

"That's the thing. She never heard about it." Jackie picked at her croissant. "The line check happened, but there was never an issue."

"Could it be an event that they would only put a letter in her file, and not tell her?"

Jackie shook her head no. "Kat said that if an event like that had ever happened, they would have been required to divert. They would have pulled her immediately. It just wouldn't be a non-event; it would be a huge event. A shutdown-the-flight event."

"So, it was a manufactured letter?"

"Sounds like it," Jackie said. "It was written by the instructor whom she had turned in, like over six years ago. They never did anything to him, but then he was promoted to a line check airman. He gave her crew a line check when the captain wasn't due for four months."

Linda sighed. "Each time I say this might be worse than I thought, it gets worse."

"How so?" A million thoughts ran through Jackie's mind, none of which were good.

"If there are multiple people involved, and they're falsifying records trying to have her removed, this puts their action against her on a different level. They're not just forming opinions to justify some result. They are actively falsifying records, which is fraud. This is more than a personal attack; they are resorting to criminal activity. What this means is, if Darby identifies this to be the case, she could fall into a sense of hopelessness."

"Yes," Jackie said, slapping the table. "That's exactly what I'm getting from her. A sense of hopelessness."

Linda glanced at her phone and then set it on the table. "Okay. She is heading to Dr. Gelder in less than a week. For now, she still has hope because he already told her she's not bipolar. Their meeting is a formality. As aggravating as the lies are, I think she'll be fine."

"But if Gelder talks to her when she is this stressed out, that can't be good."

"No, it can't," Linda said. "Her claims of the falsified report could make her appear paranoid."

"Even though she isn't paranoid, because it's true they are plotting against her," Jackie said. She could totally feel Darby's frustration and pain. "This makes me so mad. It's not fair."

"No, it's not," Linda said reaching out and placing a hand over Jackie's. "But with friends like you, she's going to be okay."

"Will you talk to her before she sees Dr. Gelder?" Jackie asked. "You always have the right things to say."

"Absolutely. I will make a point of it, even if I have to sit on her porch until she talks to me."

"I just hope that nothing happens before she gets there."

"Like what?" Linda asked.

"Like her going postal on someone," Jackie said, and sipped her drink.

CHAPTER 32

THE DARK NIGHT of the soul was the best way to explain Darby's experience going through the report. Where the hell this doctor got his information was beyond her. He quoted policies which did not exist. He accused her of violating social media policies when she hadn't. Basically, he pulled shit out of his ass and threw it at a wall to see if anything would stick.

"Reasonable degree of certainty my ass," Darby said, as she dialed Linda's number.

"I was going to send out a search party," Linda said.

"Oh, you won't believe this document," Darby said, flopping onto her couch. The snow had begun falling early that morning. She had shifted her attention between watching the flakes drift past her window and the flames dance in the fireplace. "I'm done, but now I'm not sure where to begin."

"The beginning is always best," Linda said.

"Okay… here we go. I'll read you his summary to this 366-page medical report," Darby said turning to page one. "He said, *Based upon interviews, a review of documents and information from other sources, I would conclude, applying the FAA medical standards, Captain Darby Bradshaw's diagnosis is bipolar disorder.*"

"Interviews?" Linda said. "Who?"

"He doesn't say." Darby turned the page, and said, "But he said that this diagnosis was with a *reasonable degree of certainty.*"

"How did he come up with bipolar?" Linda asked. "That has been driving me crazy."

"Welcome to my world," Darby said, turning to the end of the brief. "I think his insights at the end of this piece of crap might best explain what he did. Do you remember that interview I did with the doctor on the News Media radio show for mental health?"

"I do," Linda said. "Excellent interview."

"Thanks," Darby turned the page. "Okay… ummm… this is what he took from that interview."

> *At points during the process of this evaluation, Captain Bradshaw has provided comments which suggest a sense of the experience of mania. The first is that the person who is mentally will not recognize that a problem exists.*

"A person who is mentally?" Linda chuckled.

Darby grinned. "Yep. Not sure how he got through medical school. At one point he referred to undue influence spelled u-n-d-o. But he goes on to say, *From September 11, 2017 News Media video Bradshaw stated, I believe… if you're mentally unstable, you don't know.*"

"Because you stated that a mentally unstable person may not know they have a problem, he associated you with being unstable?"

"Yes, he did. But he actually agreed with my statement," Darby said. "You don't know you have a problem, if you have a problem."

"Not only is he corrupt, but he's an idiot, too."

"It gets better." Darby leaned back in her chair and found the page identifying her mania symptoms. "I've got seven points to the manic episode criteria. First is that I have an inflated sense of self-esteem or grandiosity."

"Does he know you're a pilot?" Linda said.

"Ha. Ha," Darby said. "Actually, it's because I referred to the CEO as Walt."

"But doesn't everyone at your airline call him by his first name?"

"Yes, they do," Darby said. "But he also said that I have grandiose delusions of thinking I have a special relationship with a famous person."

Linda laughed out loud. "He thinks the CEO is famous?"

"It appears so. He also said that a person with an overestimation of abilities, or a belief they could write a book, is grandiose."

"But you did write a book," Linda said.

"He also said that I had increased speed in talking," Darby said. "Oh... and my medical condition was further characterized by my jokes and puns."

"I'm not sure if I should be laughing or not," Linda said. "You talk fast, but not in a manic way. Most women do. Besides, how the hell did he determine an *increase* in the speed if talking fast is your normal?"

"He didn't," Darby said. "Oh wait, here's a good statement."

People in a manic state believe they are managing everything exceptionally well. In addition, what they are trying to achieve is usually virtuous. The difficulty is that more and more life problems are developing and because they do not see them, negative events will ultimately occur.

"What you are doing with the safety report is virtuous," Linda snapped. "What problems is he talking about?"

"Maybe my breakup with Ray?" Darby said, trying to think of what other problems were ongoing in her life. "But that happened way after I saw him."

"Personally, I think more women are crazy staying with someone they should not be with."

"Maybe he's blaming me for Clark doing this," Darby said. "You know… this could be my fault because I shouldn't have been so grandiose as to email the CEO and refer to him by his first name, but also the audacity of me to think that I could impart safety information to airline management."

"I'm speechless," Linda said.

"Here's a good statement," Darby said. "Ready for this?"

"Ready as ever."

"He said from 2010 to 2017, that I presented myself as an authority and… or an expert in safety, training, marketing, psychological and psychiatric assessment, and, I quote, *being the CEO of Global*."

"You want to be the CEO of Global?"

"Hell no," Darby said. "Besides, I'm not qualified because he didn't give me a sociopathic diagnosis."

"That's really funny," Linda said. "But this is pissing me off. This guy needs to be put away."

"If I have anything to do with it, he will be. I wrote a rebuttal as I went through the report. It took me a lot of time, but it was worth it. I'm sending it to the FAA and the Illinois medical board."

"Good for you. Global won't get away with this."

"I hope you're right," Darby said. "But there's more."

"I can hardly wait."

"While I don't have a history of hallucinations that he knows of, I do have paranoid delusions and I also exhibit formal thought disorder."

"I've got to read this report," Linda said.

"You will," Darby said, tucking her legs up onto the couch. "He also said that I don't need sleep, I have too many goals, and that I'm preoccupied with unjustified doubts about loyalty and trustworthiness. I'm afraid to confide in my friends because they will use it against me, and I read hidden, demeaning or threatening meanings into benign remarks or events."

"What a fucking lunatic," Linda said.

Darby laughed. It was a rare event when Linda spewed a swear word. "Was that a statement with a high degree of medical certainty or just your opinion?"

"Medical certainty," Linda said. "When you meet with Dr. Gelder, make sure you take your rebuttal."

"Yes, and I'll email it to him before I go, too," Darby said. "But what if he changes his mind based on this piece of crap report? What if he doesn't allow me to clarify? What if they support each other as part of a doctor's club?"

"I wouldn't worry about any of that. It's evident this is anything but a medical report," Linda said. "Dr. Gelder will see through it."

Darby hoped Linda was right. Besides, who in the hell was manic for having goals? Tony Robbins beware. She promised to bring Linda a copy of the report first thing in the morning, and they said their goodbyes.

Darby wandered into the kitchen, opened the fridge. She seriously needed to do some shopping. Pizza delivery was sounding better by the minute. She pulled a Diet Pepsi from the rack and popped the top as she sat at her kitchen table and opened up her laptop to send Gelder her rebuttal. She logged into her Gmail account, but Dr. Gelder had beaten her to the email. She opened his email and read the two words—*call me.*

CHAPTER 33

DJ HAD NO idea what he was delivering or why, and that's the way he liked it. He simply did what his father requested. Not asking questions was the easiest. As was not arguing with the old man. It had been a long flight, but he'd slept for six hours, eaten a couple meals, enjoyed three drinks, and watched two movies. He blended well with the riff raff of society. He could not remember the last time he'd watched a movie, a decadence to which he was not accustomed.

They had just pulled into the gate and the passengers began the deplaning process. This had been a humbling experience. He normally had people to carry his bags. Every time he'd come to Shanghai, he had also taken their private jet, but he was told his suitcases would be handled better via commercial this time. That *was* a first. But whatever they said, he did.

Thirteen hours on the airplane had gone by quickly, and the Global Air flight attendants had taken very good care of him. He was surprised. Perhaps they didn't recognize him. Perhaps they simply sucked up to all business class passengers. His purpose was not to ask why.

He stood and stretched. Then he removed his briefcase from the overhead compartment. He checked under his seat. After he was sure he had not left anything behind, he walked down the aisle and stepped off the airplane. Walking down the jetway, DJ followed the other passengers toward customs. He scanned faces as he walked. As he approached the baggage claim area a young man in a suit approached him.

"Mr. DJ?"

DJ smiled. "Yes. And you are?"

"Your assistant," the man said. "Please, come with me. I will escort you."

DJ knew exactly who the man was, as he'd been shown a picture. The escort's directions were to pick up his bags and accompany him through security. Then he would meet the client.

They walked into an unoccupied room off to the side of baggage claim. His bags were waiting. He gathered them both, and then followed his escort to an unmanned inspection booth. They stood at the red line, four feet from the window. Waiting.

Within minutes a short, stocky man opened the booth. He waved them forward. He accepted DJ's passport and looked at his documents, and then at him. He returned his passport without electronically scanning it and said, "Welcome."

DJ walked through the customs terminal with bags in hand, and followed his escort. Once outside, a black limousine which had been parked five yards back crept forward. The escort placed the bags inside the car, and motioned for him to enter.

There was another man in the car. Not a word was spoken until the limo pulled into traffic. "Do you have a key?" the man asked.

DJ pulled a key out of his jacket pocket and handed it to him. "Here you go."

He stuck the key into a lock, and turned. The clasp opened. Then he opened the case. He removed a cardboard box from inside, and opened the lid. His eyes narrowed and a slow smile crept across his face.

"Exactly what we need," the man said nodding. He looked up. "How many available?"

"How many do you need?"

"200."

"We can do that," DJ assured him.

"How much?"

"For you… half price of what you would pay elsewhere," DJ said.

The man's eyes narrowed. "What do you want?" he asked.

"These two cases will be sent to Boeing, and worked into the system on the Max aircraft. We'll ship you two hundred parts from one of our Asian factories first of the week," DJ said. "You can pay that station cash for the order."

"Conditions?" the man asked, warily.

"No tracking. No paperwork. And these are a gift," DJ said patting one of the cases, "but they must go into production immediately. Whatever price you receive on these, it's yours."

"Very generous," the man acknowledged.

The limousine pulled up to the curb and stopped. A door was opened and DJ stepped out of the limo. He turned, looking back towards the man in the car, and nodded. The man inside returned the nod and then the door was closed. The limousine drove off.

DJ turned and headed towards the building carrying only his briefcase. Once inside, a woman said, "Your departure is scheduled whenever you're ready, Mr. Drake."

"Thank you," he said, appreciating the respect. His father had always been Mr. Drake, while he'd been dubbed Drake Junior, shortened to DJ. Despite the fact his father had become President

Drake, DJ stuck. Perhaps his father being in prison was good for both of them. He headed out the glass doors toward the ramp where one of his corporate jets awaited. Drake Industries was painted on the tail.

The carpet was rolled out as he approached, and he boarded the plane. Once inside the aircraft he smiled. His favorite flight attendant was working today. They would be the only two passengers on the flight returning to Honolulu. His vacation was about to begin.

Chapter 34

DARBY TOSSED AND turned all night wondering why Gelder had sent her that cryptic message. Whatever he wanted to talk to her about, was something he wasn't willing to put in writing. *This could not be good,* she'd thought. Unfortunately, by the time she'd read his message, it was six p.m. on the East Coast and he hadn't answered his phone.

She opened her eyes and looked left, bringing the clock into focus. While it was only six a.m. in Seattle, he should be in full business mode on the East Coast. There were only three things she had to do before she called him, and two were in the bathroom. She dropped her feet to the floor.

Sitting on the toilet she brushed her teeth, wondering what Gelder could possibly want, but not be willing to email. The last time she'd received a "call me" email was from Captain Rich Clark, who was in the process of setting her up for the fall of a lifetime.

In a futile attempt to stop the Section 8 action before Clark went too far, she had attempted to meet with the CEO, Walter Croft. First, Darby had tried to schedule a meeting. Then she'd invited him to her presentation. Finally, Darby had placed a silent bid of $4000 for a cancer charity auction to have lunch with him. She won him for $1650. But when she reached out to Mr. Croft for scheduling the lunch, it was Clark who'd responded and told her she had to wait.

Walter Croft was an amazing leader, and there was no way he could possibly know the truth of what Clark was doing, or he wouldn't have allowed this to continue. Clark had to be lying to him. When she had congratulated Walt for becoming CEO after Patrick died, he had written her and told her he looked forward to writing a few safety chapters together, and he'd signed—Best, Walt. Then he'd asked to see her safety report. She'd sent it with a personal note saying she was fighting for her career after she'd been pulled.

When he didn't respond, she reached out to see if he'd received it. That email was also responded to by Clark, stating that Walt received her email and Clark would be her point of contact. She brushed her teeth even harder. Clark had started all this with a 'call me' email.

Sadly, the personal note that accompanied her safety report to the CEO was in Darby's medical report. Darby wasn't sure if Walter Croft ever received her note or the report. However, someone had given it to the doctor.

Rich Clark was definitely keeping her from speaking with Walter Croft. He had to be selling him a bill of goods. Clark was definitely an asshole and he should be very lucky that she wasn't crazy. Darby flushed the toilet, then spit in the sink and washed her hands.

Step three, before she made her call, would be a cup of coffee.

Coffee in hand, sitting at her desk, Darby dialed Dr. Gelder's number.

"Gelder, how may I help you?"

"Dr. Gelder, this is Darby Bradshaw. I saw your email."

"Yes, Darby. Thanks for your call," Dr. Gelder said. With note of hesitation in his voice he added, "I'm sorry, but I cannot take your case."

"Why not?"

"A conflict of interest just came to light."

Darby's heart sank, as a whirlwind of thoughts filled her brain. "Can you tell me what it is?"

"Not now, but perhaps in six months," he said. "But I am going to tell you why there is no indication of bipolar diagnosis in this report."

"You read it?" Darby asked, pulling a pad of paper close, and grabbing a pen from the top drawer of her desk.

"I did," he said. "I want you to know that a key to mania is a distinct, abnormal period of time when a behavior stands out from normal behavior. There is no indication that your behavior is any different from your normal life or anything from your history. Your high energy, goal-setting behavior and accomplishments indicate a baseline stemming from adolescence. Would that be a fair statement?"

"Yes," Darby answered. "Anyone who wants to become a pilot has to be extremely goal directed, and many pilots worked two or three jobs just to pay for flight lessons."

"It's a tough career to break into," Gelder said. "This report does not identify any period of time during your life which is different from all the other times. There is absolutely no indication of mania."

"What about his statement that I have psychosis?" Darby asked.

"There is no evidence of psychosis either. Psychosis identifies a severe mental disorder where your thoughts and emotions are so impaired that you've lost contact with your external reality," Gelder said. "This statement borderlines on absurdity. Just because Dr. Wood said you had psychosis, doesn't make it true. He provided no support."

"Thank God," Darby said scribbling his words on the pad.

"His concerns about your grandiosity," Gelder continued, "are quite interesting. You are highly experienced, and have written a best-selling book. I also viewed your social media interactions, and have found no indication that you have an unrealistic sense of superiority."

"It looks like he took confidence and success, and turned that into a disorder," Darby said.

"That it does. He also attempted to create a pretense of your superiority by interjecting words and statements into his report that created an illusion of grandiosity, which were not actual statements. Uhhh... here's an example," Gelder said. "He stated you were ready to be CEO. However, it was he who asked you if you could run an airline, and you answered yes. Nowhere did you say you were ready. I also have no doubt you could run an airline."

Darby was liking Dr. Gelder more with each statement. "He also said that I had expert knowledge, but I never said that, either," Darby said.

"He assumed all of that because of your book. However, I would guess that you do have expert knowledge in many areas."

"Knowledge doesn't come easily," Darby said. "I just have a passion for safety and do a lot of research. But I wouldn't call myself an expert."

"I can see that. I was impressed with your AME's statement when he said, Ms. Bradshaw is a rational, empathetic and extremely intelligent person. She is capable of multitasking and functions consistently at a high energy level, and universally with the best interest of other human beings in mind."

"He's a good guy," Darby said.

"Perhaps so, but what is most impacting about that statement is that, while it's present in the supporting documents, Dr. Wood ignored his opinion and never placed it into the report. It also appears he never spoke to your AME. He simply included it as a side note, and left it unaddressed."

"He didn't call or talk to anyone but Global management," Darby said. "He said he conducted interviews, but he doesn't say with whom."

"I noticed that," Gelder acknowledged. "His assessment of delusions with formal thought disorder and claims of rapid speech are also non-supported. The short amount of time that you and I have spoken, and your dialogue within the transcripts, have not indicated any signs of Dr. Wood's claims of disorganization, derailment, poverty of speech, tangentiality, illogicality, perseveration, neologism, or thought blocking."

"That's a mouthful," Darby said with a chuckle.

She had looked up poverty of speech, and tangentiality, on the internet. Poverty of speech was the lack of additional, unprompted content, whereas tangentiality was the tendency to speak about topics unrelated to the main topic of the discussion. She learned that most people move to other topics on occasion, but not an issue unless extreme. Both conditions were associated with schizophrenia.

"What's Neologism?" Darby asked. "I looked that up, but forgot."

"That would be a new word coined by a person affected by schizophrenia," Gelder said.

"Oh, yeah. Like if I were to call Dr. Wood a psychobastard?" Darby said.

Dr. Gelder laughed. "Well, that wouldn't count because the coined word is only able to be identified by the coiner. I understand that meaning precisely. It might fit in this case, as well."

Darby laughed, and said, "At least I'm not schizophrenic."

"No. You're not paranoid either," Gelder said. "While Dr. Wood alleged paranoia, your research of SMS concerns is clearly a proactive risk mitigation strategy."

"You know safety management systems?"

"I'm a proponent of SMS in the medical field. I disagree with Dr. Wood that proactive risk mitigation is fear based. Your concerns represent the foresight of what could happen, and are necessary to create processes to reduce the chance of occurrence."

Darby wanted to cry. This was the man who could help her, but his hands were tied for some unknown reason. She only wished he could take this case.

"Dr. Wood also expressed concerns, based upon Ms. Abbott's report, that you were paranoid and feared physical harm by unidentified sources. However, in a word search of his twelve hours of interviews, I have ascertained he never spoke of or questioned you regarding any harm that may come to you."

"No, he didn't," Darby said. "I had just told Ms. Abbott I had a target on my back because my union rep and other pilots had warned me management was planning this."

"What was most interesting and could have been the biggest indicator of a problem was this letter from an instructor stating, 'First Officer Bradshaw was unstable, emotional, displayed odd behavior and was a threat to the safety of the operation.' You should have been pulled immediately," he said. "Did anyone ever speak to you about this event?"

"No. Never," Darby said. "I first learned of that letter in the report."

"I suspected as much. I could not find any source documents identifying it. I also found it odd Dr. Wood never addressed the letter during his evaluation with you. He simply slipped it into the report," Gelder said. "Much of this report was regarding social media, uniforms, your book, trip buys, and a variety of policy issues.

"I reviewed Global's policies, and it appears he did not understand them in most cases, and in other areas he was provided inaccurate information. I'm curious who educated him on these policies."

"During one of our sessions he had a transcript of recurrent training, and we argued whether or not manual flight should be considered an emergency," Darby said. "I asked him who provided the documents. He said that he would tell me in our final meeting. Then he refused to tell me. He said I did not take 'no' well."

"I'm not sure who does," Dr. Gelder said with a chuckle. "He also attempted to distort your good will regarding speaking at schools, and donating your time by altering the facts. Honestly, none of this has anything to do with mental health."

"Dr. Gelder," Darby said, "I am really sad that you cannot help me with this."

"I am, too," he said with sincerity.

"I feel bad for all the time you've spent on this, and you're not getting paid," Darby said.

"Don't worry about that," Dr. Gelder said. "Can you get your money back for your plane ticket? If not, I would like to reimburse you for it."

"I'm certain I can exchange the ticket with a minimal change fee," Darby said. "Either way, I would never ask you for money. I appreciate you taking your time like this."

"It's been my pleasure. I'm simply sorry I can't help more."

Ending the call, Darby stared at her empty cup. Thank God she had not canceled her appointment with the Mayo Clinic.

CHAPTER 35

DARBY COULD DO anything for twelve days, especially if it meant the result would be the reinstatement of her sanity. Her Mayo Clinic visit would arrive before she knew it, and that gave her an element of hope. Hope that didn't protect her from the other shoe being thrown at her.

Linda had been livid when she'd heard Dr. Gelder had backed out at the last minute. Jackie was sure Global was involved. Darby agreed with them both. However, Kathryn said his backing out might have been a gift in disguise. The Mayo Clinic would have more strength than a private practice doctor, despite Gelder being a forensic psychiatrist.

Darby received the greatest gift from him—assurance an authentic psychiatrist could see through Wood's report. With that knowledge, she felt renewed confidence.

In the meantime, she had decided to focus on the research and analyze the data. She had logged into her Survey Monkey account that morning and was shocked to see 7,469 surveys. "Time to do this," she said. Closing the survey, she downloaded data and began coding it.

This would definitely keep her busy for the duration. It also took her mind off losing Dr. Gelder. She signed into her Gmail account to reach out to her statistics guru. That's when she saw the email from her attorney. An email with and invoice, no less.

She wasn't sure why there would be an invoice since all she did was send him a message that she was diagnosed as bipolar. He'd been off the radar for a couple months before that.

"What the f?" she said, eyes widening as she read the document. Then she dialed his number. Within minutes he was on the phone.

"Darby, how are you today?"

"Other than Gelder cancelling my appointment, what's with the $3500 bill for bipolar research?"

"We had to determine if you could fly with that diagnosis."

"No you didn't. You could have asked me," Darby said. "A ten year old could have googled it and learned that in less than three minutes."

He laughed as if she were joking and then said, "There's nothing to worry about. Under the AIR 21 law you'll get *all* your attorney fees reimbursed."

"So, this is your license to run up the bill and nail Global?" she asked. A license to steal was not at all a bad concept, but $3500 meant nothing to Global. It meant everything to her on half pay with a mortgage.

"Filing lawsuits is not for the weak," he said.

"Or the poor," Darby added. Apparently only the wealthy had rights. She told him about the Gelder situation as quickly as possible. At $400 an hour this situation could cost her dearly, in more ways than one.

After she ended that call, Darby called Kathryn to tell her about the data, but instead told her about the recent bill. Which got her pissed all over again. She wasn't sure how she would survive this financially or mentally.

"I know it's only 3500 bucks, but this is ridiculous. Everyone knows a pilot can't fly being bipolar. What the hell does that have to do with the lawsuit anyway? He simply infuriates me."

"Rightfully so," Kathryn said.

"First Gelder cancels. Then my attorney runs my bill up. What next?"

"I'm afraid to say."

"Me, too," Darby said as she headed downstairs. "I'm thinking there is only one thing to do at this moment, and that's give up on the idea of any more work today. I'm going to pour myself a glass of wine and climb into the hot tub."

"That's a great idea," Kathryn said. "But you need to get a new attorney before this one bankrupts you."

"I'm working on that," Darby said, with a sigh. That had been her broken mantra for too long, but sadly she wasn't doing anything about it. The reason she hadn't made the extra effort was that the idea of starting all over from scratch was daunting. She walked into her kitchen, and yelled, "Oh God!"

"What happened?"

"I forgot to replace my wine," Darby said. "What is this, the friggen triple crown? First Gelder. Then I get screwed by my attorney. Now I'm out of wine."

Kathryn laughed. "Hang tight. Resources are on the way."

"Really?" Darby said. "Bring your bathing suit."

Darby said good-bye and pulled a glass from the cupboard and filled it with water. She leaned against the counter and took a long drink. She needed to get a grip. If she didn't de-stress soon, the stress alone would kill her. Then her mind drifted to her data. She could not believe the number of responses. Pilots really did care. Now all she needed to see is what was happening worldwide.

Kathryn had written the research questions based upon Darby's observations of Global's shitty training program and lack of safety culture. She knew what the results would be if she had only surveyed Global pilots. But she was very curious as to what the rest of the world was doing. Was Global alone in their dysfunction? She had no idea, but it wouldn't be long until she found out.

Darby ran upstairs and changed into her bathing suit. She was pulling on her terrycloth robe when she heard Kathryn's car pull up. She ran down the stairs and opened the door. But it was the cute cop standing on her porch. This time he was out of his uniform.

"Ms. Bradshaw," he said. "I hope you don't mind me stopping by like this." He smiled as he assessed her outfit. "I've got some information."

"Not at all," Darby said, closing her robe and tying her belt. "Want to come in?"

"Thanks," he said. "I just wanted to let you know we found the thieves."

"Drunk, I suspect," she said as they walked into the kitchen.

"That they were. Slept it off in the tank," he said. "Turns out somebody paid them a couple hundred bucks to come into your house and take your wine. They were told there was no alarm. Don't know who it was. Drank some, sold some."

"What the hell?" Darby said, turning toward him. "High school prank?"

"No," he said. "Did you piss anyone off lately?"

Darby began to laugh. She wasn't sure why that struck her as funny, but it did. "You might say that." She offered him a Diet Pepsi. "It's a really long story. I could tell you over a glass of wine sometime."

"I'd like that," he said. "I was beginning to think it was something I said when you didn't call. More importantly, did you get an alarm?"

"I did, and let's just say that things have been a little crazy around here. I lost your number. Actually, I think I washed it. Twice."

"That's what they all say." He grinned and then snapped opened the Pepsi tab.

"They all?" Darby raised an eyebrow.

"Figuratively," he said, and then sipped his soda, watching her over the top of the can.

"You look good out of your uniform."

This time he grinned. "I was hoping to hear that."

He was cute and funny, too.

"Knock, knock," Kathryn said from the doorway. She walked into the kitchen and looked between the two of them.

Darby startled. "You remember officer... uh..."

"Tom. Officer Tom Olson," he said extending a hand to Kathryn. "We met the other night."

"He dropped by to tell me they found the crooks who stole my wine," Darby said.

"I've got to get on my way," he said, writing his number on a sheet of paper. "I hope we can finish our conversation."

Darby accepted the paper and smiled. She walked him to the door, thanked him, and assured him she would not lose his number this time.

In no time she and Kathryn were soaking in the hot tub with a glass of wine in hand.

"Thanks for rescuing me," Darby said, raising her glass. "I can't believe I forgot to buy more wine."

"I needed the break as much as you," Kathryn said. "It's been a shitty day all the way around."

Kathryn shared the challenges of her day with Darby, and all the hell that she'd gone through. Darby didn't envy what Kathryn faced daily in the bureaucracy of the FAA. Between the two of them, they were quite a pair. Darby told her she had finally shutdown the data collection, and how far she'd gotten coding it. Then she told her about the thieves being paid to rip her off.

"To steal wine?" Kathryn said.

"He asked me if anyone was pissed at me," Darby said with a grin.

"There might be a couple people I can think of."

"But why would anyone pay homeless guys to steal my wine?" Darby asked. "That's just simply freaky." She twisted the stem of her glass and added, "Maybe they were trying to scare me."

"Freaky is one way to describe it," Kathryn said, raising her glass to her lips, eyes not leaving Darby's.

"Remember when the cat scared the shit out of me?" Darby asked.

Kathryn nodded.

"I'm certain I did not leave my window open."

"Any ideas?"

"None. And why my wine?" Darby said. "Most of it was cheap crap, except the bottle Ray sent."

"What was that all about, anyway?" Kathryn asked. "John said it was expensive, so I googled it. That was at least a $700 bottle."

"I googled, too," Darby said. "I found one for $895. Ray's cheap. He wouldn't spend more than 20 bucks on a bottle."

Kathryn chuckled. "John said that, too."

Darby tipped back her glass and emptied it, then reached for the bottle and refilled her glass, then topped off Kathryn's. "There's definitely something going on here."

"Do you think the research has something to do with this?"

"I thought about that," Darby said, "but you'd think they would have grabbed my laptop if that was the motive. Not my wine. So, I'm not so sure."

"Then *why*?" Kathryn asked.

"I've been thinking about that," Darby said. "Not to sound paranoid, but think about the timing. The same day I get my letter saying my career is over, a bottle of wine magically arrives from Ray. Which I doubt he sent."

"Did you ask him?"

"Texted. He hasn't responded."

"How is that paranoid?" Kathryn said.

Darby ran a finger around the rim of her glass and then looked up at Kathryn. "Those two items coming the same day. What do you think should have happened?"

"You'd be upset. Drink the wine," Kathryn said. "Probably the entire bottle."

"Exactly. But I didn't."

Darby sipped her wine, allowing the details to spin around in Kathryn's mind for a moment. These details were something she hadn't spent many brain cells on, but they were there waiting for something to glue them together. The fact the thieves were paid to steal her wine, may have just been that glue.

"If you ask me," Darby said. "I think whoever sent me that wine wanted it back when I didn't drink it."

Kathryn's eyes widened with acknowledgment. "It couldn't be," she finally said. "Could it?"

"It could," Darby said. "Where's the wine?"

"My pantry. I was going to save it for your return to work celebration."

"Would you give it to John and see if he'll test it?" Darby asked.

"Now you're making me paranoid," Kathryn said. "I'm sure he'd be happy to."

"If we're wrong, have him save it," Darby said, grinning. "I'd really like to taste an expensive bottle of wine."

CHAPTER 36

KATHRYN HAD BOOKED the boardroom on the tenth floor, and John had delayed his commute east. D.C. could wait a day for his presence. She needed to share the results of Darby's research with him. The research based on Darby's safety report. Kathryn wrote the survey questions, but this was due to Darby's efforts and the reason they had this data.

She firmly believed Global's actions against Darby had everything to do with her report—the question had always been why. Now she suspected the answer lay in front of her.

Placing all the documents into her briefcase, she threw the strap over her shoulder. Glancing at her phone to double check the time, she walked out of her office. Kathryn asked her secretary to hold all her calls, and headed toward the elevator. Inside, she pressed the button for the tenth floor. She tapped her foot while she waited for the elevator to make the climb.

The doors opened and she headed down the hall. Stepping into the conference room she flipped the light switch to on. The coffee was waiting, and a bowl of fruit sat in the center of the table. Kathryn was nervous, but not because of a meeting with John. She was concerned with what Darby had discovered and its significance.

Could someone at Global have attempted to poison her because of this? The thought gave her the chills.

Kathryn was pouring herself a cup of coffee when John knocked on the open door. "Good morning," he said as he entered.

"Thanks for indulging me," Kathryn said, glancing over her shoulder. "Black?"

"Please." He walked into the room and stood in front of the table. He stared at the papers she had laid out. "Darby did this?"

"She did," Kathryn said, filling his cup. She set his coffee on the table. "I wish she were here to go through this, but she's back in Rochester. Her Mayo assessment starts tomorrow."

John pulled out a chair and sat, then reached for his cup of coffee. "Where do we begin?"

"The office of the inspector general wanted to know why pilots were not manually flying," Kathryn said. "Well, I think the FAA and airline management are to blame."

"How so?"

"Safety culture turned out to have the greatest impact on pilot training, and pilot training is the underlying factor as to how pilots learn to operate their aircraft," Kathryn said. "Results identified that, in isolation, pilot training had a small but positive impact on pilots' willingness to manually fly. However, when safety culture was added as a mediator between training and manual flight, the impact was negative."

"I'm not sure that I follow."

"Pilot training has a negative impact on pilot performance. The more pilots train, the less they are willing to fly."

"How's that possible?"

"I'm getting there," Kathryn said. "Pilot understanding is a direct result of learning. And these results identify that the level of understanding also significantly impacts the pilot's decision to manually fly."

"Sounds more like an airline issue than the FAA."

"Yes, but the FAA is approving these programs. They're also supposed to oversee training." Kathryn was more frustrated than ever, because this problem was under her rule. She wasn't sure what to do with this, less than perform a major overhaul of the FAA which budgets simply wouldn't allow.

"How are these programs specifically impacting learning?" John asked.

Kathryn flipped through a couple pages. "Okay here… 43% of the pilots queried utilize rote memorization practices, 62% received less than a thirty-minute debrief, and 39% said there was no repetition for events." Kathryn sighed. "It also looks like 80% of the pilots utilized supplemental material that was not provided by the company, and 50% of them claimed this self-gathered material was necessary."

"This is what Darby pointed out to Global," John stated. "These were her concerns in the report she gave to them."

"Yes, they were," Kathryn said nodding. "These FAA-approved training programs are inadequate, airlines are non-compliant, and our recommendations are not being followed by operators."

Turning another page Kathryn showed John the data that identified 39% of the pilots received only electronic or written assessments. Therefore, the level of understanding is not adequately being assessed."

"But the FAA approved the electronic assessment," John said.

"Yes they did." Kathryn hesitated. "And this might be the reason lack of understanding is bypassing detection."

John nodded in agreement and said, "Please continue."

"Results also identified that 50% of the pilots did not have the correct crew complement during training," Kathryn said.

"Meaning that two first officers or two captains were being trained together."

"But AQP requires that the crew complement to be a captain paired with a first officer," John said.

"Yes, it does." Kathryn pinched the bridge of her nose and then looked at John. "What this means is, these pilots are getting half the training they're legally required to receive under such a scenario."

John pushed back from the table and stood. He placed his hands on his hips. "So, training sucks. FAA's not monitoring it. What else?"

"The flight line instructors are not requiring pilots to disengage the automation."

"Despite the safety alert requesting manual flight?" John asked incredulously.

"Appears so. They profess one thing, and do another. It appears unwritten policies are guiding their behavior." Kathryn removed another document from the stack and read. "Results identified that 69% of the participants reported their organization had unwritten policies regarding automation usage.

"Meaning, that our airlines have created policies to comply with FAA requests, but their unwritten policies direct the pilots to keep the automation engaged," Kathryn added.

"But why?" John asked. "This makes no sense."

"I didn't think so either," Kathryn said. "Until I came to the safety culture results."

"Maybe I need to sit for this," John said. Not waiting for a reply, he returned to his chair. He crossed one leg over the other, leaned back, and then folded his arms. "Let's hear it."

"To put it bluntly, safety culture sucks," Kathryn said. "And safety culture has the greatest influence over the ultimate impact on a pilot's decision to manually fly the aircraft."

Kathryn stood and poured herself another cup of coffee. Hers had turned cold. She returned to the table and then read the results that included 34% of the pilots would not critique the training program. They identified that 41% of the pilots believed that management involved in training did not have expertise. Learning culture was also an issue, where 54% of the pilots believed their comments would not be taken into consideration. The sad news was that 54% of the pilots also believed it was best to keep quiet.

"Another very telling stat was that 46% of the pilots believed their employer would not exceed regulatory compliance," Kathryn said. "SMS is worthless without a positive safety culture."

"Shit," John said, reaching for an apple. He took a bite and chewed, locking eyes with Kathryn's. Then he said, "This is why they pulled Darby."

"I believe so," Kathryn said. "Darby gave them the report that identified their safety culture was atrocious. She identified areas where they did not meet SMS compliance. She also pointed out areas deficient in training."

"We have a bigger problem than Global," John said. "These results implicate the FAA. If airline oversight is lacking..."

"Can Deke Elmer do anything?" Kathryn asked.

"A better question is, *would* he," John said. "But the truth is he's only the temporary administrator. There's nothing he can do now. Nothing anyone can do at the moment."

"Any update on who will replace him?"

"Rumors still confirm an airline guy," John said. "But they are keeping that tight to the chest."

"What do we do with this?" Kathryn asked waving a hand over the papers. "I told Darby she could publish it."

"Let me think on that," John said. "But we have another problem." He stood, and walked to the door. He opened it, stuck his head out into the hall, looked both ways, and then closed the door.

"What's going on?" Kathryn asked.

John walked toward Kathryn and lowered his voice. "The results for that bottle of wine came back," John said. "Someone tried to kill Darby."

CHAPTER 37

F*OR BETTER OR worse,* Darby thought sitting in the lobby of the Mayo Clinic. She sighed, and crossed her legs at her ankles. Then she uncrossed them. Then sat upright. This was her moment of truth. They'd told her she would be here for three days, so perhaps she'd have many moments of truth, But truth be told, she was scared. If that old saying *the truth would set you free* was accurate, she had nothing to worry about. Like hell. She had everything to worry about.

Just before she'd left Seattle, Jennifer had sent her a song to help with the nerves—*Just Be Held.* Darby stuck her headphones into her ears and pressed play for about the tenth time in the previous twenty-four hours. The words gave her strength. *Hold it all together. Everybody needs you strong. But life hits you out of nowhere and barely leaves you holding on, and when you're tired of fighting chained by your control, there's freedom in surrender, lay it down and let it go. So when you're on your knees and answers seem so far away, you're not alone, stop holding on and just be held. Your world's not falling apart, it's falling into place...* She closed her eyes and allowed the music to soothe her soul.

Darby had done absolutely everything she could do, now she had to have faith it would work out for the best. Because at this point, all she could do was to be herself. If that wasn't good enough for the medical profession, then so be it.

She hoped her life was falling into place. When the song ended, she switched her music to *The Fight Song*. She would be all right song. That had also been another mantra since the day she'd received Wood's letter. Grinning, she realized the irony of her two survival songs—one to fight, and the other to accept.

Glancing around the lobby, she saw more than a dozen people who had actual medical reasons to be at the Mayo Clinic. She wondered if they, too, would be all right. She glanced at the time on her phone, then removed her headset and stuck it into her purse. Darby turned her phone to silent. Depositing the phone into her purse, she reached for a magazine.

Life certainly wasn't fair. It was hard enough to understand when tragedy struck out of nowhere, but when a human intentionally drew blood from another, like Rich Clark, that was unconscionable. The results of Kathryn's research proved Darby had been spot on as to the impact on flight operations and operational performance when a negative safety culture was involved. She had tried to share this with her leadership, and this was where it got her. She glanced around the room again, and returned the magazine to the table.

"Darby Bradshaw?" a man announced, as he entered the lobby. He was tall, greying at the temples, and wore a nice suit.

Darby stood and smiled. Walking over to him she said, "I'm Darby."

He extended a hand. "Nice to meet you. I'm Doctor Sorenson."

Darby shook his hand and said, "It's nice to meet you, too."

"Your ears must have been burning yesterday," he said with a warm smile. "You're quite an accomplished young lady."

"Thank you," Darby said, with a questioning look. "But didn't you read Dr. Wood's report?"

"We all did," he said, his smile never fading. "But we also know the difference between a medical diagnosis and political corporate action." He extended a hand toward the door. "We are not here to get your job back. Our only goal is to assess you, and determine if you are fit for duty."

"That works for me," Darby said. They passed through the doorway and down another hallway. He then introduced her to the office staff as if she were a guest, not a patient. The women who had helped her over the phone to gather documents, sign waivers, and provide her the necessary details to find a place to stay in Rochester, were as nice in person as they had been on the phone.

He then introduced her to Dr. Andrews, the lead psychiatrist. He was as nice as everyone else. He said they would be spending some time together on the third day of her visit, and wished her well.

Once they stepped inside Dr. Sorenson's office, he closed the door and extended a hand for her to take a seat. He sat behind his desk and opened a manila folder. Placing his glasses into position, he perused the contents. "When did this all start?" he finally asked.

"A year ago December," Darby said.

"It took Dr. Wood a year for a diagnosis?" Dr. Sorenson asked, removing his glasses. That declaration appeared to be more of a statement than a question.

"The company pulled me a little over four months before I met with him," Darby said. "However, it took him another seven and a half months to come up with a bipolar diagnosis."

"What was he doing all of that time?"

"I have absolutely no idea," Darby said with a shrug. "We only met three times. But his grand finale was when he sent me my diagnosis via FedEx for a Christmas Eve delivery."

"He didn't," Dr. Sorenson said in astonishment, and his expression shifted to one of concern.

"He did," Darby said. "Probably one of those corporate decisions."

"I suspect you're right." He returned his glasses to the bridge of his nose, looked at a few more pages, and then said, "I've got you scheduled to meet with Dr. Triton this afternoon, but I'm not sure if he plans to administer the neuropsychological testing again. If so, we'll make sure you have ample time to do them."

"When I took the tests the first time, they had me do them all in one day."

"Really? But there were far too..." he stopped midsentence, and sighed. "Do me a favor and tell Dr. Triton they gave you this entire battery of tests in a single day."

She agreed to tell him, and then he asked her how she started flying. It had been a long time since she'd thought about those early days of flying, let alone talked about them. She had fun reliving the memories. Dr. Sorenson was an aviation medical examiner and he loved aviation as much as she did. She found him grinning as she shared her experiences. The time flew by and then her first meeting was over.

"We've got you scheduled for some blood tests in a couple of hours," he said, glancing at the clock. "Nothing to worry about. Just standard practice so we don't miss anything that could be medically wrong. But I would like you to go get a bite of lunch first."

He stood and walked around the desk.

Darby stood, and threw her purse over her shoulder. "Thank you for making this easy."

"We're going to try." Dr. Sorenson placed a hand on her back and reached for the doorknob. "Your appointment with Dr. Triton is scheduled for one p.m.," he said, opening his door. "Have a good lunch and then drop into the lab, say, around 12:15. You'll have ample time to get to Dr. Triton's office after that."

Darby left the office, and relaxed. Doctor's orders were to eat, and she would not disappoint him. He was a good man. If the other doctors were anything like Dr. Sorenson, then she had nothing to worry about. She was about to say, *what could possibly go wrong,* but then decided maybe she should leave well enough alone.

CHAPTER 38

IF TODAY WAS Darby's last day on earth and this was her final meal, it could not have been better. A five-minute power walk to Newt's, and she'd had the most incredible hamburger anyone could have asked for. She returned early, which gave her time to run to her room and brush her teeth. Nothing like fresh breath when being analyzed.

Dr. Sorenson was spot on about the timing of the blood tests and they got her in and out without issue. She had wondered if the burger would turn her blood to sludge, but it flowed quickly. After donating a couple vials, she found her way to Dr. Triton's office. Now she sat in a chair and waited for her appointment.

She reached for a magazine and glanced at the pictures as she flipped through the pages. Within minutes, a man stepped into the lobby, walked toward her, and asked, "Ms. Bradshaw?"

"Yes. I'm Darby," she replied, setting the magazine onto the table and standing.

"I'm Dr. Triton," he said, warmly shaking her hand. "Very nice to meet you."

Darby followed him into his office, and once they were settled into their seats, he asked her how her trip had been so far. They chatted like old friends for about fifteen minutes and then he said they should get to business.

"We are not going to repeat the neuropsychological testing," he said.

"That's a shame," Darby said. "I actually practiced for them this time. I've improved my pegboard score by 6 seconds with my left hand, and 8 seconds with my right."

"How'd you do that?" he asked, leaning back in his chair with a grin.

"I found a board online," she said. "Then I practiced."

He laughed, "Well, at least you prepared."

"There's actually a doctor who teaches pilots how to pass this test," Darby said. "I found out *after* I was tested that Global's doctor uses him."

"They didn't send you to prepare before this test?"

"No. I asked for time to do so on my own, and he told me that it was impossible to be trained."

"Do you think that's true?"

"Of course not." After having taken the tests, Darby knew she could train anyone to pass them. "It's somewhat like shooting an approach down to minimums, after you do it a few times you get better."

"I suppose it is," he said with a chuckle. "Why do you think the Global doctor told you that it was impossible to train?"

Darby shrugged and then said, "My guess is they were hoping I would do poorly and have a reason to get rid of me."

"Well, they didn't get their wish," he said with a smile. "You did exceptionally well in most areas, and those where you didn't were just fine. We'd learn nothing new by testing you again."

"Well, thank you," Darby said. "But practice or not, I probably could have done better if they hadn't been crammed into one day."

Dr. Triton shook his head ever so slightly, and tapped his pencil on the desk. "Well," he said when the tapping stopped. "I'm going to administer the MMPI once again. My assistant will take you to a room and get you started."

The MMPI was the Minnesota Multiphasic Personality Inventory to test for personalities, and apparently could identify mental health issues as well. Darby had taken that evaluation numerous times throughout her career as part of pilot hiring and the FFDO program. The reality was they could give a crazy person who was intelligent the MMPI, and they probably would do fine. The intelligent part of the brain could hide dysfunction. It was fairly obvious with some of the questions as to why they were being asked.

Before she left with his assistant, Darby said, "Can I ask you something?"

"Of course, anything."

"If I did so well on the cognitive test, why did Dr. Wood write in his disqualifying letter that he took into account my testing as part of his diagnosis for my being bipolar?"

"That is a very good question," Dr. Triton said. "And one we discussed yesterday amongst the team."

Darby nodded. She was glad to know there were others who could see through the inconsistencies of Wood. She followed the assistant out of the room to take the MMPI.

AN HOUR AND a half later, she was done and back in his office.

"That was fast," he said.

"Well, those questions are not really something I needed to think about in order to answer," she said. "Test me on the electrical system of an A330, and that's something I might have to put some thought into."

Darby had also taken the same personality assessment test eight months earlier with Wood. The questions hadn't changed. Nor did her answers. She still liked flowers and taking bubble baths, and did not hate her mother.

"Did you have a chance to see your results the first time around?" Dr. Triton asked.

"Not exactly," Darby said. "I read what the psychiatrist from the brain injury facility said, about my K score being high. And the claim that they couldn't assess me accurately because I was trying to make myself look better than I am."

"I read that, too," he said. "I reviewed those results as well. See this," he said, pointing to a chart on a document. "This is what she was talking about. You did have a high K score. You still do. Your results are exactly the same."

"What's a K score?"

"It's simply an index that identifies how you think of yourself. A low score would mean you're self-critical, and a high score is making yourself better than you are," he said. "Research has identified that the K Scale can be related to educational and socioeconomic levels, with higher scores associated with being better educated and having a higher socioeconomic status.

"But this score is perfectly normal for you. Doctors, pilots, and anyone going for a new job are typically high. You want all three confident and positive that they'll achieve success."

He further explained how taking one set of questions out, her K score was higher than it should be, but that was because she was a woman.

Darby found this discussion fascinating. She wished she had a recording of his explanation to share with Linda. There would be no way she would remember his explanation. But the bottom line was, he believed she didn't make up her answers, and she was normal.

"Dr. Sorenson said I should ask you how you began flying," he said.

Darby chuckled. She wasn't sure why he'd asked that, but she shared her early flying days with him, as well. She told them about the moment she realized they were going to pay her to fly. Dr. Triton leaned back and smiled as she talked.

"Thank you," he said. "Dr. Sorenson was correct. You light up when you talk about flying."

"I love it," Darby said. "It's what I've always wanted to do. Anyone who can have a career that's their passion is the luckiest person in the world."

"There's something I've been wondering," he said, now scrutinizing her. "How are you able to sit here with such composure, after having gone through all this? What you have been through is enough to make anyone crazy. What have you been doing?"

"I've been writing a book, working on research, and exercising." She hesitated and played with the strap on her purse for a moment, gathering her thoughts. Then she looked up and said, "I guess, what really got me through this was a belief."

"Go on," he said gently.

Darby looked at him directly. "I had to come to grips that Global management might very well get away with this. And if they did, my career would be over. But I had to convince myself that while my career would be over, my life would not. It would just be different."

Dr. Triton stared for a moment and then said, "Don't give up this fight. You are stronger than you realize."

CHAPTER 39

I F CUPID HAD a heart, he would stab her in the butt and get it over with. Hopefully in front of one of the cute doctors whom she'd passed by the day before. The Mayo Clinic was full of them. She rolled to her side, and glanced at the bedside clock. Flopping to her back, she closed her eyes and pulled the covers over her head. *Valentine's Day was totally overrated,* she thought. Then she allowed herself to think about Ray.

An hour later Darby was standing in front of the line at Starbucks.

"Happy Valentine's Day," the young lady said with a hair flip, just a bit too enthusiastically for Darby before she'd had her first coffee of the day. The exuberance, however, wasn't unusual. Darby had spent the day prior at the Mayo Clinic and at night had wandered around Rochester. She had experienced nothing but really nice people. They were in the clinic. Around the clinic. Nice people were everywhere. Maybe Rochester simply raised kind people. Regardless, it was contagious and she liked it.

"May I have a Grande Raspberry Mocha?" Darby asked. "With whipped cream."

"You got it," the young lady said, "Anything else? How about a hot pastry?"

"I'd take a hot date," Darby said with a grin.

The gal leaned in and said, "Would you like to have that here, or to go?"

"How quickly could you wrap it up?" Darby asked. "I've only got forty minutes. Then I've got a date with a doctor."

"Is he cute?"

"I've never met him."

"Oh. I'm sorry," the girl said, placing a hand to her chest. Her smiling face changed to one of compassion.

"No, I'm not sick," Darby said with a wave of her hand. "I'm just a little bipolar. I'll be better by noon." She winked, and then glanced behind her. "If I gave you a twenty, would that be enough to buy everyone a coffee in line?"

"More than enough," she said.

Darby stuck a five dollar tip in the jar and said, "Tell them cupid wanted to wish them Happy Valentine's Day." Darby handed her the twenty, then went to the end of the counter to gather her drink.

IN NO TIME she was sitting on a couch waiting for Dr. Melnyk, the bipolar specialist. From the appearance of the building, he specialized in children. The reception area was yellow and felt warm in contrast to the temperature outside. Darby sipped her coffee as she waited. When she'd emptied her cup, she stood and wandered across the room and dropped it into the trashcan. Then she walked to the window and stuffed her hands deep into her pockets, and stared out the window.

The snow lined the streets, but roads had been plowed and sidewalks cleared. The early morning sun was shining brightly. She tilted her head back and closed her eyes, feeling the warmth on her face. She was so close to the end of all this, that she didn't want to become overconfident. However, what if she were bipolar? Would someone who was bipolar be able to self-diagnose? She could only assume they could. Yet if she were bipolar and never had a performance issue and no sick leave abuse, then why not allow pilots to fly bipolar?

"Ms. Bradshaw," the receptionist said. Darby turned. "The doctor will see you now."

Darby followed her through a door and down a short hallway. Then she escorted Darby into a room, and made a hasty exit.

"Nice to meet you, Ms. Bradshaw," a man with an accent said, as he stood and walked around his desk. He extended his hand. "Welcome."

"Thank you," Darby said, shaking his hand. "You can call me Darby."

"Darby it is. Please, have a seat." He extended a hand towards a chair, and then returned to his seat behind his desk. They exchanged niceties about her visit so far, and accommodations. Then he leaned back in his chair and asked, "Can you tell me what brings you here?"

She explained the events and the contractual process as he listened intently, nodding occasionally. He assessed her while she spoke, as they all had. He, too, had read Dr. Wood's report.

"That's about it," Darby said. "The synopsis."

"Why did you meet with the manager of the pass travel complaint department?" he asked.

"They said she was an HR safety investigator."

"And you believed them?"

Darby smiled. "Sadly, I did."

He tapped his pen a few times on the desk. "You do speak rapidly," he said. "Do you have anyone who's known you for more than, say, ten years I can speak to?"

"My best friend, Kathryn Jacobs. She's known me for eighteen or nineteen years. I met her when she was working for the NTSB. Now she's with the FAA."

He glanced at his watch. "Do you think it's too early to call?"

"No. I'm sure it's fine."

Darby gave him Kathryn's number and he pressed speaker phone, then he dialed.

"Jacobs' residence," Jessica said. Darby smiled when she heard Jessica's voice. This was the normal she needed to get her through this chaos.

"Is Kathryn Jacobs in?"

"Mom, it's for you," Jessica yelled. Then she said, "May I ask who's calling?"

"My name is Dr. Melnyk, I'm sitting here on speaker phone with Darby Bradshaw."

"Darby's listening?"

"Yes," Dr. Melnyk said, glancing at Darby.

"Hey Darby. It's me, Jess," she said. "When are you going to be home? We've got a game on Saturday and Jen and I were hoping you could come."

"Yes, of course, I'll be there," Darby promised. "Unless they make me an in-patient." She winked at the doctor and he smiled.

"Funny," Jessica said. "Mom's here, so I gotta' go. See ya'."

Darby and Dr. Melnyk shared a smile, and Kathryn said, "Hello?"

Dr. Melnyk made introductions and then he asked Kathryn how long she had known Darby. Eighteen years it was. Then he asked, "Would you say she talks slow or fast?"

"Definitely fast," Kathryn said, with a chuckle.

"Has she always spoken in the same speech pattern?" he asked.

"As long as I've known her," Kathryn said. "She's never changed."

The doctor and Kathryn chatted for a few more minutes about Darby. Darby said a quick, "Hey, Kat" and then they all said good-bye.

Dr. Melnyk then asked Darby questions similar to the ones Gelder had asked about work, school, performance, and sick leave. Her answers were the same. Good grades. No training failures. But then he asked her why she was single.

"I guess… I've been married to my job." Then she told him about Ray and how he had proposed, but had given her an ultimatum to quit her job. She told Dr. Melnyk about the breakup and how she felt about all that. Then she told him about Keith and how he had been killed.

"Do you miss him?"

"Who? Keith or Ray?"

"Either," he said. "Actually both."

"Yes," she said. "Both. But it's different. Keith's gone forever, and I'll never see him again so that's a different kind of loss. He was cheated out of life, and that makes me angry when I think about it. It wasn't fair. But it's occurred to me that life isn't fair. So you just have to live it the best you can."

Dr. Melnyk nodded, encouraging her to continue and Darby complied. "I hear Ray's happy with his new girlfriend, so that's good… I guess. I feel like he's cheating on me, so that's kind of weird." She smiled and said, "You know, there's no guarantee in life with anything. Sometimes all we can do is wake up and remember to put one foot in front of the other when times are tough. Oh, and make sure to smile along the way, too. Happiness is a choice."

"Have you been doing that?"

"I have," she said. "One foot at a time. Don't get me wrong, there have been some very difficult times with all this. But I have a lot to smile about, outside the job. I've also been busy writing." Then she told him about the research and her findings. He appeared genuinely interested, so she explained more in depth what she'd learned and the ramifications.

"Do you think they will do anything?" he asked about her results.

"All we can do is hope," she said. "But the FAA has known for twenty years and has done nothing."

"Couldn't Ms. Jacobs help, being with the FAA?"

"She's trying. But when these training issues began, she was with the NTSB. Now she's in a position where she could probably do something," Darby said. "But they are keeping her too busy. Her job and life were threatened a year ago."

Darby explained the details of what had happened with the girls and the car accident. Then she told him how Kathryn's boss had been murdered, as well as the CEO at Global.

"Yes, I remember that situation," he said nodding, with recollection etched in his eyes. "I read about that in papers. The President was involved. I thought I recognized Ms. Jacob's name. That's a lot to process."

"I hope you don't think I'm paranoid," Darby said. "There are just some facts, or I should say issues, in our industry which really need to be addressed. I suspect I'm here because of something I brought forward in my report. I'm just not exactly sure what."

He sighed, "Well, if you were in my country, you would have known they were going to do this to you."

Darby grinned. Apparently, she had been the only one with her head in the sand. She had never imagined that in today's world a Soviet Union style of retaliation was possible. But now she knew that anything was possible with money and power.

"Is there a clinical diagnosis for being naïve?" Darby asked with a slow smile.

"We might have to write a paper on that," he said.

"Please don't name it after me," she said. "We don't want to give Dr. Wood any ammunition."

He grinned broadly and pushed his chair back, and she thought he was going to stand. But instead he leaned forward and placed his arms on his legs and stared at his hands for a moment. Then he looked up and asked, "So how are you doing with all this? You have been put through a gauntlet. Most wouldn't have survived."

She shrugged. "Under the circumstance, I think I'm doing okay."

He nodded. "Yes. I think you're doing just fine."

CHAPTER 40

THERE WAS SOMETHING weird about walking into the Mayo Clinic dragging your suitcase behind you. In-patient came to mind. Darby wasn't sure why she found this funny. Perhaps if she were in her uniform, others might see the humor, too. Back in the day, a captain at her previous airline had a minor domestic charge and was sent to jail, but allowed out on work release. Therefore, when scheduling called the jail, he was released to fly his trips. When he was done, they threw him back into the slammer. Rumor had it, he was the resident hero in the jail.

Pressing the up button at the elevator, she smiled and then stepped inside. That would make a funny scene in the next airplane movie—releasing pilots from the mental ward to fly their trips. These days, some thought you had to be crazy to want a career as a pilot, anyway. Yet, when the flying bug caught someone, it turned into a virus that could not be cured.

Stepping off the elevator she headed toward the waiting room where her journey had begun two days earlier. Behind these walls sat a medical flight department with some of the most experienced aviation professionals she'd met in her career. There had been a time when Northwest Airlines had sent every pilot to the Mayo Clinic in Rochester, for evaluation prior to hiring them.

Darby was impressed. What impressed her most was everyone's humanness and compassion. If a person had an illness, there should be no other way to treat them.

Dr. Andrews was one of the best, if not the best. She had been lucky to get into the Mayo on such short notice, but to get into the office of Dr. Andrews, that was nothing short of a miracle. Dr. Johnson had heard him speak on mental health at an FAA seminar, and had told Darby this was where she needed to be. Then he made it happen. He was right.

Parking her suitcase beside her chair in the lobby, she was about to sit when she heard her name called.

Turning, she saw Dr. Andrews walking her way. He extended his hand. "How has your visit been?" he asked.

"It couldn't have been better," Darby said. "Everyone has been incredible."

"Good to hear," he said. "We've got a few more things to cover. But this won't take much time at all."

Darby followed him through the main doors and down the hallway. "What time is your flight back to Seattle?" he asked, as they approached his office.

"Six p.m. out of Minneapolis. I've booked a car to pick me up at three. But the driver said he would wait if we took longer."

"Three should be just fine," he said, entering his office. "Please, place your bags right there." He extended his hand toward the corner of the room.

Darby deposited her luggage and took a seat before him. "Thanks again for getting me in on such short notice. It feels like I've been grounded forever."

He smiled with an expression of compassion. "I'm sorry you've been put through this. Today's tests won't take long."

"Thank you," Darby said. "That means a great deal."

She had not been expecting more testing. However, this experience showed her that sometimes life threw in surprises when you were least expecting them. Nothing was ever as expected.

Today's tests were nothing she couldn't handle, as were the others she had taken. Simple cognitive tests. Counting backwards from 100 by 7 would have been more difficult had Linda not told her that it was all about adding 3. She had pointed out that 100 to 93 was easy, but then add 3 to the second digit, which would make 86. Then add another three—79. Next time subtract a 7 and so on.

They chatted a bit after all his questions were complete and then Dr. Andrews said, "From everything I've discussed with your evaluating doctors, and from what I've seen, you are not bipolar. You don't have a mental health diagnosis of any kind."

Darby could not be more relieved to hear those words. "Thank you." The pressure she didn't realize she had been holding in, finally released. She tried to hold it together, not sure if she should laugh or cry. The result was a huge smile and a calmness she hadn't felt in a long time.

"We do have one more step," he said. "We like to have a panel of doctors who have *not* met you, discuss these results. Personalities while meeting an individual can sometimes impact a doctor's opinion. Positive or negative. That's just human nature." He opened a folder and scribbled something on a piece of paper. "All physicians you met with will also be present, except for Dr. Triton. He's got an out of town appointment. However, he will provide us with a written report."

"When will that meeting be complete?" Darby asked. "My medical is due at the end of the month, and I've got my physical scheduled for Monday the nineteenth."

"We'll meet tomorrow and I will get a preliminary report to your AME by Friday," he said. "I must tell you, I had to laugh when Dr. Wood identified your comment regarding Hackman as a mental health concern."

Darby furrowed her brow as she tried to remember that passage in his report. "Do you mean when I commented about Hackman saying the psychological tests would not be of value to pilots?"

"Exactly," he said. "Dr. Wood's concern was that you'd quoted *one* individual, as if it were fact, because one person said so."

"But he was the FAA administrator. If I couldn't believe him, who should I believe?"

Dr. Andrews chuckled and said, "My point exactly. Have you read that ARC?"

When Darby told him she hadn't, he dug through a side drawer and removed a document, and handed it to her. The cover said—*Pilot Fitness Aviation Rule Making Committee*. Dr. Andrews directed her to open it to page A-2, where she found Dr. Wood's name.

"Wood was on the committee," Dr. Andrews said, "and yet, he had no idea the man who made the rules was the same man you'd quoted. Let alone the FAA administrator."

Darby looked at the top of the page and her eyes grew wide. "Joe Wolfe, Global's labor relations attorney was on the committee, too," she stated flatly. "But it doesn't say Global. It says he was representing Airlines for Americas."

Dr. Andrews leaned back in his chair and steepled his fingers. "The airlines like to have representation. They don't always want it known whose eyes are watching."

That was a polite way of saying Global did not want to be acknowledged. *But why not?* She wondered. Dr. Andrews was on the committee, as well. She turned to the beginning of the document and flipped the pages, scanning the document as she did. Andrews sat quietly as she read and flipped pages.

Then she came to the bottom of page ten. "No way," she said, and looked up.

"What did you find?" he asked.

"Can I read you something?" she asked. When he nodded, she began to read.

> The working group examined how an event is handled in which air carrier management receives a report concerning the emotional or mental health of a pilot. In those cases, an investigation is initiated to determine the credibility of the report. After this evaluation, if management determines additional research into the report is necessary, the pilot will be removed from flying status and a mandatory fitness for duty exam may be required.

Darby looked up from the page, and said, "But in my case, nobody *ever* did an investigation of the credibility of Ms. Abbott's report. They just sent me VFR non-stop to the shrink. Sorry, no offense."

"None taken," he said with a grin. "I noticed the omission of an investigation in Dr. Wood's report, as well."

"But Dr. Wood and Wolfe were both on the committee," she said. "They would have known this was supposed to have been the process."

All Darby could think was those dirty little rat bastards. How dare they do this to her. They had knowledge that this document existed, and that an investigation to the authenticity was part of process dealing with the mental health issue. Yet, they didn't follow that process. They knew exactly what they were doing.

"Director Hackman saved the airlines a lot of money by not mandating all pilots to take the neuropsychological testing," Dr. Andrews said. "It was his decision."

"I think he saved them more than that," Darby said. "After taking those tests, I'm not sure if most pilots would have passed." She hesitated, and then said, "I don't mean I'm better than most pilots because I passed. It's just I've been doing a lot of reading, writing, and playing Luminosity on the computer. Stuff like that. I'm not sure I could have done as well if I hadn't been active outside the flight deck. Four years ago, I don't know if I would have performed as well."

Dr. Andrews was nodding his head, "I think you may be correct. But now, we'll never know."

"Where's Hackman now?" Darby asked. "I mean what's he doing since he's retired as the FAA administrator?"

"I haven't heard a thing," Dr. Andrews said. "I'm sure he'll pop up somewhere, but right now he's simply disappeared."

"He gave the airlines quite a gift before he left," Darby said. "Do you mind if I keep this copy?" she asked, raising the report.

"Not at all," Dr. Andrews said. "What's your company's process now?"

"Dr. Sorenson and Dr. Wood will need to agree on a neutral doctor for the third opinion," she said. "The tiebreaker."

"I doubt that will be necessary," Dr. Andrews said. "After the panel rules, we'll send our report to Dr. Marsh. With our thoroughness, that should suffice and you should be returned to duty without another evaluation."

CHAPTER 41

SHE HAD ARRIVED late and slept long. Now, wide awake, Darby could not wait to tell Dr. Marsh she was coming back to work. That little creep had said it was a misunderstanding when this had all started, and yet he'd allowed it to continue. He'd also lied to her about the inability to train for testing. He was most definitely a double agent, but now there was nothing he could do. She was cleared and he had to accept that.

She sat up in bed, and pulled her laptop onto her lap. She was already on her second cup of coffee, but still in her pajamas and tucked under the covers. She allowed a yawn to escape and began to type.

Dr. Marsh, I have some great news, that I'm sure you will be pleased to see. It appears you were absolutely correct when you said this was a misunderstanding. I've attached a letter from the Mayo Clinic confirming your initial assumption. This letter was recently sent to my AME. I will be renewing my FAA first class physical on Monday. The complete report from all ten examiners will be headed your direction in a couple of weeks.

I explained Global's process of requiring a neutral examiner to Dr. Andrews (Mayo: PhD., MD., HIMS psychiatrist, official AME), and he said based upon the credentials and thoroughness of this expansive Mayo evaluation team, that he does not believe Global will require a third opinion.

The reason I'm writing to you, is to ask if that is a valid assumption... or do you still require a third evaluation? If you do require a third evaluation, would you please let me know this week so I can let Mayo know, in order to expeditiously coordinate with Dr. Wood to get that completed in a timely fashion?

As you know this process has been ongoing for over a year now. I'm hoping, based upon the attached report from this expansive team, you will concur there is no medical reason to keep me from flying, and we can expeditiously get me back to the flight line.

Please let me know about that third opinion, and we will coordinate as necessary. If required, I would like to start that coordination this week. Also, I've copied the team's credentials on this email, but they are included in the report.

Thank you. Looking forward to seeing you again, and I hope you have a nice weekend. Darby.

She hoped Dr. Andrews was correct and Marsh would accept the panel's decision. Why the hell would they want a third doctor anyway, when she was evaluated by ten? They shouldn't. But then none of this made sense. Now all she needed was her current medical certificate and she was good to go. This was going to be a great new year. She could hardly wait to get back to flying. And that day was just around the corner.

"Woohoo!" Darby yelled, raising her arms. "I'm going back to flying and there is nothing they can do to stop me!"

Chapter 42

TRUE TO HIS word, Friday morning Dr. Andrews had emailed the preliminary report to her AME, Dr. Johnson, stating Darby was cleared. It was the same report he had sent to her, where the ten professionals assigned to Darby's case had unanimously ruled in her favor—she was fine.

Monday had taken forever to get here. But it was here now, and today was an excellent day. Had they tested her excitement meter, she would have been off the chart. She had just finished her medical examination and stood at the counter to pay. She handed over her credit card to Dr. Johnson's assistant, and awaited her medical certificate. Not able to wipe the grin off her face, she didn't even try.

The office assistant gave Darby a receipt, and she waited. Never again would she take her medical certificate for granted. Not that she had ever taken her health for granted. But coming so close to losing her medical when nothing was wrong with her was unconscionable.

Doctor Johnson approached the counter, but his demeanor had changed from joyous to somber.

"Are you okay?" Darby asked.

"Can we step into my office?" he asked.

"Is something wrong?" He didn't reply, and she followed him into his office. He closed the door and then stepped behind his desk.

"I'm going to defer your medical," he said.

"What?" Darby said, dumbfounded. "But..."

"Just until this is all over and you're back to work," he said.

"But you know I'm fine. You recommended me to go to the Mayo Clinic because of their expertise. I did, and they agreed there was no issue. How can..."

"I wasn't sure what to do, so I had reached out to a friend in the FAA. This is his reply." He handed Darby a sheet of paper, a copy of an email. She read it silently.

From: Brian.silverdale@faa.gov

Sent: Monday, February 19, 2018 8:35 AM

To: GLJ@HealthcareLLC.com

Subject: RE: Question regarding return to work after normal psych eval.

Hey Grant,

I have spent most of the morning mulling over this case. Dr. Wood's consult is not in her record as yet (but I assume it will get there). Wood for the most part is highly respected in Washington. This case is a time bomb with Mayo versus Wood. It is best decided in Washington. I would just defer her case. Don't get yourself into the corner by advocating any more than you have for the airman. This is not your fault, the baddies are the Airline who went down this route with the airman. I will have the records you send scanned into her record.

Brian

"A political time bomb?" Darby asked, as she looked up from the letter. "You know the truth. This isn't right."

"This is just a delay. Not permanent."

"But, if I lose my medical, I may never get it back," Darby said. "Global owns the FAA in Oklahoma City."

Darby stared at Dr. Johnson. The pain etched in his face was evident, but it was she who wanted to cry. After all the effort to get this far, and someone at the FAA warned her AME not to give her a medical certificate. It didn't matter that she was fine, it was all about politics. This was nothing but appalling.

"A political time bomb is no reason to ground a pilot who doesn't have a problem," Darby said. "How can this even be possible?"

"I'm not denying it," he said, "just deferring it."

"What's the difference?" she asked, heading toward the door. "The results are the same."

"I'm sorry. I just wanted his advice."

"But I'm not just some airman," she said. "And I don't have a damn thing wrong with me and you, of all people, know that. Yet the FAA is telling you not to advocate for me?"

Darby opened her mouth to say something more, but she couldn't. She could not find the words that could possibly explain how impacting this decision was to her life. Who the hell did FAA inspector Brian Silverdale think he was anyway? His duty was to do the right thing, not the political thing.

Dr. Johnson had no reply, and there was nothing more she could say. She walked out of the office with a receipt for the payment of a medical certificate she did not have, and for a medical evaluation which she had passed. Now she had no idea what to do.

CHAPTER 43

DARBY SAT AT Kathryn's kitchen table eating apple pie and sipping whiskey, while Kathryn loaded the dinner dishes into the dishwasher. The girls were already in their bedroom doing their homework.

"Are you sure I can't help you?" Darby asked again. "It's the least I could do after barging in on dinner."

"You're fine. Enjoy your dessert," Kathryn said, as she placed the last of the silverware into the basket and closed the dishwasher door. "I simply can't believe Dr. Johnson gave you your examination, cleared you, but didn't give you your medical."

"You and me both," Darby said.

Kathryn turned the water full on and added dish soap. She set a couple of pans and a bowl into the sink as the water flowed and bubbles grew. "What was that FAA inspector's name?"

"Brian Silverdale," Darby said, sticking the last bite of pie into her mouth.

"That name sounds very familiar," Kathryn said, as she began washing the pans. "I know of him, but I can't remember why."

Darby opened the dishwasher and put her plate and fork inside, then grabbed a dishtowel. "He referred to Global as the baddies," she said standing to Kathryn's side. "Who says baddies? "

"Apparently, the FAA," Kathryn said, rinsing a pan and handing it to Darby.

Darby began drying, wondering how anyone could ever get a fair shake, if doing the right thing would back someone into a corner. Politics and power were strong forces.

"I guess I can't blame Dr. Johnson," Darby finally said, putting the pan into the cupboard. "It's just if the good guys are afraid to do the right thing, then how can anyone win?"

"They can't," Kathryn said, handing her another pan.

Kathryn and Darby finished washing and drying the last of the pots, each lost in their own thoughts. Once they were done, Darby handed the towel to Kathryn, who folded it and hung it over the sink. Darby retrieved her glass of whiskey from the table.

Kathryn turned toward Darby and said, "Medical or not, you have your clearance. Hell, they weren't allowing you to fly with a medical certificate regardless, so it doesn't really matter. Right?"

"I guess," Darby replied, sipping. "But retaining my medical certificate would mean something huge."

"Yes, it would." Kathryn sighed, and then she placed her hands on her hips. "Want to join me while I find out why I remember Silverdale?"

"FAA database?" Darby asked, and then she tipped back her whiskey.

"Google first," Kathryn replied with a grin.

Darby followed Kathryn into her office, and Kathryn powered up her computer. Kathryn typed in Brian Silverdale and multiple news reports popped up. "Oh shit," she said. "Now I remember where I heard of him."

Kathryn opened the first article and stood, giving Darby her chair to read it. When she was done reading, Darby looked up. "He was involved in a mental health case at Global?"

"He was," Kathryn said. "I had been working for the NTSB at the time. Bill and I were dating. Bill had been livid over the case. So much so, he scared me."

"Should have listened to that warning," Darby said, with a smirk.

"True, but then I wouldn't have the girls," Kathryn said, making an excellent point. "The doctor involved in that case had been working with Silverdale. He had a list of accusations against him a mile high."

"Why was Bill livid?" Darby asked, opening another article on Silverdale. "He was working for Coastal at the time."

"He'd done the same thing to a Coastal pilot. But after this, he was ordered to never work with Global again."

Darby continued with fingers dancing across the keyboard. "But that should be a good thing," she said, scanning a list of potential articles.

"One would think," Kathryn said. "Type in Michael Banks FAA."

Darby did as Kathryn asked. She opened the first article and froze. "Are you kidding me? He's the head of the FAA aeromedical department, and he pulled this shit at Global?"

"Many years ago, yes." Kathryn slid another chair close and sat beside Darby. "Silverdale worked with him back then. It was before his FAA gig. It would make sense that Dr. Johnson would query Silverdale due to his position. Especially if they were friends. But I pray to God he's not playing games with Banks and Global again."

Darby's fingers typed rapidly. Multiple articles popped with Global and Banks. Her blood ran cold as a list of atrocities alleged against Michael Banks populated the screen. How the hell could Banks be the head of the FAA aeromedical department? Then she came to the Global pilot's case Kathryn spoke of.

"Listen to this," Darby said, and she began to read.

Former Global pilot Norm Wallace was also grounded by Dr. Banks for alleged health and psychiatric problems in 1998.

Wallace, a Naval Academy graduate (class of '61) who won two Distinguished Flying Crosses in Vietnam, and despite his outstanding military career and 34,000 hours of flight time, was targeted by Global for dismissal after he and other employees began exposing pension fraud which led to the airline being forced to pay $640 million in federal penalties...

"Good ol' Global boys," Kathryn said.

"No kidding," Darby agreed. "It says that an FAA employee in Oklahoma City told this pilot that Dr. Banks had gone to Oklahoma City two or three times at the company's expense in an effort to get the FAA to pull his medical certificate. He also says other pilots personally told him Dr. Banks extorted them, asking how much it was worth to keep information that could ground them out of their files."

"Does it say what happened to the pilot?" Kathryn asked.

"Umm... oh, it says the NTSB ordered him to be reinstated at Global, but he never worked again," Darby said. "He told the reporter Banks is one of the most dishonest men he'd ever met, who has ruined far too many lives, all for power and money."

"Now he's in charge of every FAA medical examiner in the country," Kathryn said.

"This is crazy bat shit scary," Darby said, swiveling her chair toward Kathryn. "What the hell am I supposed to do now?"

"Get a neutral who cannot be bought," Kathryn said.

"That's the problem, it's not my choice. The Mayo and Wood have to decide."

"Then let's hope the Mayo has more weight than Dr. Wood on that choice."

"Dr. Andrews thinks Global won't need a neutral. Not after ten doctors ruled in my favor. I wrote to Dr. Marsh and asked him."

"Let's hope for sensibility," Kathryn said.

"I was counting on peer pressure," Darby said with a chuckle. "But sensibility works." After a moment, Darby asked, "What do you think my chances are of not needing a neutral?"

"Not a chance in hell," Kathryn said, her words mirroring Darby's thoughts.

CHAPTER 44

DARBY FOUND IT hard to believe her entire career was about to be placed in the hands of one person. With all that had happened, she also did not believe neutrality existed. She returned home to a dark house and turned off her alarm. She'd thought about setting it off to see if the cute cop, Tom, would come to her rescue, but not even hot sex could fix this.

She made herself a cup of tea, wondering what her next move would be. Kathryn was right, all she needed was to get cleared by the neutral. If the Mayo determined she didn't have a diagnosis, then most certainly another doctor would, too. But what if the FAA was in on this? She held the string, and bobbed her tea bag in the cup.

What if they bought off the neutral? She wondered, as she dropped the teabag into the garbage can. What if Dr. Banks was asked by Global to have Silverdale send that message? Corruption ran deep... but how the hell did Rich Clark get the FAA to help him?

Darby ripped open a package of stevia and dumped it into her cup, and then headed to her bedroom. With the cup in one hand, she grabbed her laptop with the other and climbed onto her bed. Setting her tea on the nightstand and laptop on a pillow on her lap, she powered up. Darby sipped her tea while she waited for her computer to come alive.

The more she thought about it, Dr. Marsh had to agree with Dr. Andrews. Dr. Andrews had been involved with cases like this, and would know the process. However, he also knew Wood's report was based upon a political action, not a medical diagnosis. Yet, he still thought they would agree. Maybe he was right. Once they knew the scam was over, they, too, would end it. She could only hope.

Darby logged into her Gmail account, and there was a response from Dr. Marsh. "Here's to good news," she said, raising her cup. Then she took another sip, then set her cup aside and pressed open.

MedicalInception@BellSouth.net February 19, 2018

Dear Ms. Bradshaw,

Thank you for your information and the summary report from the Mayo Clinic physicians. I will need to confirm that I have all information regarding the evaluations you had in response to Dr. Wood's findings and report. I have attached medical release authorizations for the Mayo Clinic physicians listed on the report as well as for Dr. Fourberie at ALPO Aeromedical and Dr. Angela Brody, who you mentioned Dr. Fourberie was going to have review your case.

As to your question about next steps, we will need to seek a third opinion given the differing opinions and as is stipulated in Section 8 of the Pilot Contractual Agreement (PCA). Before we can proceed with this third evaluation, we will need to get all the completed medical releases from you and then get the full medical documentation we need.

Regarding your mention that I "said this was a misunderstanding" and that the materials you sent me "confirm my assumption," I must correct you. I never told you that I believed a misunderstanding occurred and I have not made any assumptions in your case and in particular, no assumptions that you are medically fit. My recommendation to have you evaluated by Dr. Wood was to get his expert and professional assessment on whether you have an underlying mental health condition. It was his determination that you have a psychiatric diagnosis which makes you unable to meet the FAA airman medical standards. Based on this information, I made my recommendation to remove you from active flight status.

Finally, I have received your disability form to complete. I am not in the position to serve or be identified as your treating healthcare provider. However, in past cases, I have completed these disability forms, using the diagnosis provided by the Company Medical Examiner (Dr. Wood), to cover for a period of ninety (90) days. During these three months, you can find a healthcare provider that can verify your disability moving forward.

Please let me know if you wish for me to complete the disability form to cover you for the 90-day period. Again, thank you for your information. I realize you are eager to move on to the next steps in the process, and ask that you complete and return the attached releases to my office as quickly as possible.

Yours - Tom

"Yours Tom?" Darby said. "Fucking Dr. Marsh. Now we're on a first name basis?" She pushed her computer aside and stood. "Goddamn it!" she said, storming into her bathroom.

She turned the water to hot, and then plugged the tub. She grabbed her bag of Epsom salt and dumped it into the water, then sat on the tub edge and drummed her red nails on the tile. "Now what?"

"Oh shit!" she said, and ran back into her bedroom to read the letter again.

That little bastard had given her a release for Dr. Brody to review her documents—the same doctor who Fourberie had tried to talk her into going to instead of the Mayo. Darby had never mentioned to Dr. Marsh anything about Dr. Brody. It was Dr. Fourberie who had tried to get Brody to review her case.

Besides, Dr. F. wanted Darby to see Brody as the pilot medical examiner, instead of the Mayo Clinic. Now Marsh wanted her to go to Brody for the neutral. *What the hell happened to the contract requirements?*

Darby returned to the bathroom and turned her water off. Stripping naked she realized one thing—don't ever allow your excitement meter to peg first thing in the morning, because there was only one place for it go by the end of the day.

CHAPTER 45

DARBY AWOKE NAKED and alone with a slight headache to the sound of her phone ringing in the distance downstairs. She rolled to her side and opened one eye to glance at her clock. She closed her eyes and pulled a pillow over her head. Eight a.m. was not an unusually early hour to receive calls, but she wasn't quite sure why her phone was downstairs. She was also not sure if she were ready to get up.

Her mind drifted back to her tea in the tub the night before. Then she grinned.

The memory of going downstairs for an after-tub cocktail found its way through the gray matter. She'd had a scotch on the rocks, as she'd told Kathryn about Dr. Marsh's email. They had discussed Global's problems late into the night. She hoped she hadn't emailed Dr. Marsh drunk. She grinned, thinking that could be one of the most interesting emails she ever wrote. But it was actually Dr. Wood who would be the most fun to drunk email. She would love to tell him exactly what she thought of his scrawny little ass. Maybe after this was all over, she would do just that.

Rolling onto her back she threw the covers from her body. There would be no more sleep. She needed to create her plan of attack for today. She wasn't quite sure what that was, but coffee would clear the cobwebs.

She had her evening of upset, but she would not allow Marsh's denial to kick her off balance. All that did was just push things out. It did not stop her from returning. This delay was only a nuisance, not a catastrophe. She sighed, dropping her feet to the floor, and then she reached for her robe. It was Michael Banks who concerned her.

Once downstairs with a cup of coffee in hand Darby began wandering her house looking for her phone. What the heck? She moved her search to the living room. And then it rang again.

She ran to the kitchen and zeroed in on the noise. With a chuckle she reached into the cookie jar to retrieve it.

"Hey Kat," Darby said, leaning against the counter.

"Just checking to see if you behaved yourself last night."

"I think so," Darby said. "What time did we end our call?"

"It was a two-scotch call," she said. "Shortly after midnight."

"Did you give me any good advice?" Darby asked, reaching into the cookie jar for a cookie. "My brain is a bit fuzzy as of yet."

"Yes. Don't email Marsh."

Darby laughed. "I didn't. My trek back upstairs was directly to bed." She bit into her cookie and said, "Best advice ever."

Kathryn was at work so their call was short. Darby loved Kat—the best friend ever. Kathryn was always there when Darby's pieces were on the floor, and she always picked her back up and put her back together. That's what friends did for each other.

Darby looked at her phone and realized the first call hadn't been from Kathryn. The missed call had been from her AME's office. She sighed and pressed play, then listened to the message.

CHAPTER 46

WALTER CROFT FLIPPED the cap off the bottle. He dumped three antacid tablets into his hand, and popped them into his mouth. He supposed that making thirteen million dollars a year as the CEO was worth the price of an ulcer. Tums, however, were turning out to be a priceless commodity these days. Walt glanced at his watch just as his secretary tapped on his door and opened it.

"Your four-thirty appointment is here," she said.

"Thank you, Doris. Please send him in," he said, still chewing the tablets.

He swallowed them, then reached for a glass of water and took a quick drink. Walt pushed back from his chair and stood. He walked around the desk just as the door opened again. Doris held it open for his guest. She stepped back and closed the door quietly behind her.

The two shook hands and performed the perfunctory formalities of business associates, with the illusion of a friendship. Walt had known this man for over thirty years, yet they did not really know each other. They had built a mutual respect based on trust. So far, neither of them had screwed the other over. They had each been successful throughout their lives in their own right, but always down a different path. Until now.

The scotch was poured—the good stuff he served only to impress. His associate accepted his drink and settled onto one of the two couches. Walt reached over his desk and buzzed his secretary, then said, "Doris, we might be here for a while. Please take the rest of the day off. You can lock the door as you go."

He then took a seat on the other couch, across from his associate. The partition of the coffee table between them was proverbial neutral space. With Doris out of the office, they would not be bothered.

They chatted about absolutely nothing for the better part of ten minutes when Walt glanced at his watch. "What can I do for you?" he finally asked.

His guest uncrossed his legs, and set his drink on the coffee table. He leaned forward with his arms resting on his legs and stared at Walt for a moment. He clasped his hands and shifted his gaze toward them. Then he looked up and said, "We want you to cancel all Boeing orders."

"What?" Walt said with more emphasis and shock than he wished he'd expressed. "That's not what we discussed."

"No, it's not."

"But we don't have any Max aircraft on order," Walt said. "Why cancel all Boeing orders?"

How would he explain this to the board? He couldn't. He had been promised the rewards of a wealthy man, but the airline had already done that for him. If he displeased the board and was removed, then what would he have? Nothing.

"We can't take any chances," his associate said flatly. "I don't trust Drake."

"Shit," Walt said half under his breath, then tipped back his drink, emptying his glass. He should have known Drake would cause him grief. He stood with his glass and walked across the room to pour himself another drink. He held the bottle to his guest, in offering, who shook his head no. He set the bottle onto the credenza.

"Do you trust his kid?" Walt asked.

"No. He'll do anything the old man tells him to do."

Walt ran the current Boeing orders through his mind, trying to figure out how to get out of the penalties. "Do you have someone inside Boeing?"

"We do," he said. "Yes, we can remove the cancellation penalties."

Walt nodded. They both knew that cancelling aircraft orders for no reason would be costly. And something which could also bring unwanted attention.

"Is this the only way?" Walt asked. They were going into contract negotiations and pilots were expecting fifteen B777 aircraft and a dozen 737's. He didn't need one more thing to instigate an uprising amongst the pilots.

"Call it cheap insurance."

"Hmm," Walt scoffed, running the options through his mind. But that, too, was a waste of time. Apparently, the choice was taken out of his hands. But then most business decision weren't his. Who the hell was he kidding? No business decisions were his. He returned to the couch and sat heavily. He stared at the man who'd just thrown a wrench into the gears of his life.

Walt was nothing but a puppet and a poster child for the airline. A well-paid puppet. He sighed, knowing this was not the first time he'd felt that way and it would not be the last. This was going to happen whether he wanted it to, or not. But how the hell would he mitigate damages? He sipped his scotch, while his mind worked to solve the problem. His guest remained quiet.

"If we guarantee Airbus an exclusive, we could negotiate a better price," Walt finally said. "This could be a business decision that might pan out better in the long run."

"It could." His guest reached for his drink, leaned back and crossed one leg over the other. He extended an arm over the back of the couch and sipped his scotch. "What's the worst that could happen?" he asked. "Drake sticks to his demented plan, and Global is safe either way."

"No harm, no foul," Walt said. His associate was right, an accident was something he could not afford under his watch. "I'll make the call tonight."

"Status on Wyatt?" the man asked as he uncrossed his legs, and stood.

"He's ready to make the shift," Walt replied, also standing. "They've got a temporary in place until this AIR 21 bullshit blows over."

"Many people want to know when that will happen."

"I'm assured sooner than later," Walt said. "We've got a great deal riding on the future administrator."

The man nodded in agreement. He stared intently at Walt and then said, "I have another recommendation. You may need another drink. This one's from the board of directors."

CHAPTER 47

HER PHONE RANG as Darby headed down the stairs. She stopped and looked at the name, but was hesitant to answer. Dr. Johnson had left her a message, advising her of his plan to ask the western division regional flight surgeon to issue her certificate. She'd waited patiently for his call to learn of the outcome. But now she didn't want negative news. Perhaps this time she simply wouldn't get her hopes up. She closed her eyes, and answered.

"Hello?" she said hesitantly.

"Darby, Dr. Johnson," he said. "I have great news."

"He said yes?" she asked, opening her eyes and placing a hand to her chest, as she sat on the stairs.

"He did," Dr. Johnson said. "I gave him the rundown on your history, and what's transpired. I told him of Dr. Wood's diagnosis, and then sent him the preliminary report from the Mayo Clinic. He'd experienced this type of activity in the military and it didn't surprise him. He had no problem issuing you your medical certificate."

"I can't believe it," Darby said. "I'd cry if it wasn't considered a medical abnormality."

"Well, in this case happy tears are in order. I won't tell." He chuckled. "Check your email. You'll need to sign your medical and return a copy to both of us."

"I will," she said. "Thank you!"

Darby said good-bye. She stood and then ran up the stairs to her room, directly to her laptop. She logged in, and there it was. Darby printed her medical certificate and she signed it. She scanned it back into her computer, and then sent a copy to both doctors. She wrote a heartfelt note of gratitude.

Dr. Christopher Williams, the western division regional flight surgeon, was more than willing to give her a medical certificate based upon the facts. Dr. Johnson had conducted the physical, and the Mayo Clinic specialists had cleared her from being bipolar. There was no reason she shouldn't have a medical certificate and he issued it. Now, if she could only put it to use. "Thank God for honest people," Darby said.

There was one more person to whom she needed to send her medical, and that was Dr. Marsh. This time her message was short—*Dear Dr. Marsh, please accept the current issuance of my First Class medical to add to my files. Have a nice day. Darby.* She attached the scanned copy of her medical certificate.

Darby then sent a group text to Kathryn, Linda and Jackie—*I have a first class medical!* The return messages were, *Congratulations, you did it*, and emojis of hearts and flowers splashed across her phone. Now she needed to get the neutral examination and she was golden.

CHAPTER 48

JOE WOLFE HAD been Global's labor relations attorney since 2012, and the corporate fit worked well for everyone. They gave him freedom to deal with things as he saw necessary, and they always stood by him whichever way the wind blew. However, he never displeased them.

His hand raised to his mouth, and he bit a snag on a pinky nail and pulled it with his teeth. The nub began to bleed. *Shit*, he thought and sucked the drops of blood. He sat outside Clark's office, leg bouncing, waiting for his weekly meeting to disclose the status on Bradshaw.

He was not looking forward to this meeting. He hated giving Rich Clark bad news.

Leaning back he crossed one leg over the other, and his foot jiggled. He glanced at his watch, and rubbed a nail on his left hand with his thumb. He was just bringing his finger to his mouth when Clark's secretary looked his way.

"Captain Clark will see you now."

Wolfe stood and walked into Clark's office, wiping his right hand on his pants.

"Sit, please," Clark said, remaining in his seat behind the desk. "What's her status?"

Clark was in a mood, and this would not be welcome news. He would give him the easiest to swallow first, and then the time bomb. "Turns out the Mayo Clinic cleared her."

"We expected they would," Clark said. "Any news on the neutral?"

"We're sending her to Dr. Brody," Wolfe said. "She'll put her away for us."

Clark leaned back in his chair and said, "Bradshaw's not dumb. You guys burned the Brody card by trying to get Fourberie to talk her into going there instead of Mayo. How in the hell do you plan to make that happen?"

"Well, that's the thing. She doesn't get to decide on the neutral," he said, tucking in his fingers. He made his hand into a ball so Clark wouldn't see his nubs. "Mayo and Dr. Wood will decide."

"And if Mayo won't go along with it?" Clark asked.

"We've got two more in our pocket," Wolfe said. "Mayo will have to choose from one of them."

"Good," Clark said. "Anything else?"

"Well. Uh… yes. She got her medical certificate yesterday."

"What?" Clark said. "How the hell did *that* happen?"

"The western division regional examiner gave it to her."

"Goddamn it!" Clark snapped. "We have people in place for a reason. This really pisses me off." He pushed his chair back and stood. He walked over to his coffee pot, poured himself a cup, and returned the pot with force.

Wolfe stared without comment. As if Clark had to tell him he was pissed. He wanted to say, *really?* But thought better of it. So, he simply stared, trying to control his foot from tapping.

Clark turned, leaving the coffee cup in place and said, "How the hell can anyone give her a first class medical? Especially if our doctor gave her a bipolar diagnosis. That's permanently disqualifying."

Wolfe shrugged. He wanted to state the obvious—because Darby Bradshaw didn't have a problem. Something of which they both knew to be true. He folded his arms, tucking his hands, and responded, "I'm not sure."

"I want you to get ahold of Michael Banks immediately. Tell him you're challenging a medical certificate for a pilot who has been diagnosed as bipolar." Clark returned to his chair. "Stress the Germanwings issue and public safety. Besides, he owes us."

"Notifying the FAA is a clear violation of the contract," Wolfe said. "Something she'll grieve and win if she challenges." Wolfe never cared about violating the contract, but when it was as blatant as this, he attempted to avoid it. There was nothing he disliked more than failure.

"Who the hell cares?" Clark said. "Once that genie is out of the bottle there's no putting it back in. Even if she wins a grievance, what the hell does she win?"

"Good point. I'll tell Marsh to do it," Wolfe said. "That way when it comes down, we don't know anything about it."

"Make it happen yesterday," Clark demanded with a growl.

Chapter 49

THE SHIT HAS hit the fan, Darby thought as she read the letter from Dr. Sorenson. She texted a group message to Linda, Kathryn, and Jackie—*ladies… Letter from Mayo… I need to read to someone. Anyone have time right now?* The reply was from Linda—*I've got this. Call you in 10 minutes.*

Her solitude of writing her book was interrupted. Darby stretched, realizing she'd been writing for three hours. This was definitely good practice for when she got on her triple seven and flew the long haul flights. She headed toward the kitchen in search of food.

The battle lines are being drawn. She wondered who would win this one. The Mayo Clinic had sent three recommendations to Dr. Wood for the neutral examiner on February 28th. Dr. Sorenson had emailed her on March 8th, advising her that Wood had yet to respond and there was nothing else they could do. Darby had contacted ALPO, and they had given her more of the same—nothing. She had been in limbo.

There was absolutely nothing she could do, so she'd begun writing her book, *Normalization of Deviance*, based upon her research.

The time passed quickly when she wrote. The more she dug into the research, the more she realized the industry was not giving the passengers what they deserved—a guarantee of safe travel. However, her return-to-work plot was thickening.

There was nothing she could do about any of this. She was frustrated that she wasn't flying. At least her paychecks were still arriving, for another two months, anyway. She was using her unused sick leave, then she would default to vacation, and then go nonstop to disability. She wasn't quite sure how they would pay her on disability if she didn't have one. But that would be another chapter to this story she could deal with at that time.

Darby snuggled back into her chair with a cup of yogurt, and was just finishing it when the phone rang.

"Linda, thank you so much for calling."

"Of course," she said. "Did they agree upon a neutral examiner?"

"No. Just the opposite. Remember Dr. Brody?"

"That lady doctor whom your union wanted? Of course." Linda said.

"Yep, *and* the same doctor who Marsh sent me a release," Darby said. "Turns out, she's one of Wood's selections. Surprise. Surprise."

"Who would have guessed," Linda said.

"Can I read you the letter?" Darby asked.

"Please. I've got an hour until my next appointment."

Darby started at the beginning.

Darby, I talked to Dr. Wood yesterday and he recommended
three different names -- somewhat as expected -- they are: Dr.
Angela Brody, Dr. Alan Gendel, and George Thymes.

She licked her spoon, set it on the table aside the yogurt container and continued.

Dr. Brody provides individualized consultation, evaluation,
and management of cognitive, behavioral, and emotional

disorders due to neurologic conditions such as Alzheimer's disease, frontotemporal dementia, Lewy body dementia, mild cognitive impairment, traumatic brain injury and other acquired brain injuries, toxic exposures, brain tumors, central nervous system infections, movement disorders, Parkinson's disease, Huntington's disease, vascular dementia, stroke, cerebrovascular disease, hypoxic-ischemic injury, Multiple Sclerosis and other white matter disorders, Epilepsy and Non-epileptic Seizures, Pre/ Post-neurosurgical psychiatric management, deep brain stimulation, vagal nerve stimulation, normal pressure hydrocephalus shunting, surgery for seizures or tumor.

"Holy shit," Linda said. "She's a woman of many specialties."

"Oh… it gets better," Darby said. "He also says that she does medico-legal evaluations and consultations, fitness for duty evaluations, and independent psychiatric/medical evaluations."

"There's her cash cow," Linda said. "But, none of her specialties mentioned bipolar disorder."

"No they don't, and she's come a long way from being a pediatrist," Darby said. Brody had begun her career as a pediatrist. Years later she earned her psychiatric certification and worked in a VA hospital down the road from the ALPO office. She was a hack of all trades.

"He says Gendel's office is closed. He probably wanted to get out, when the getting was good."

"What about Thymes?"

"Sorenson says that Thymes has served as a medical doctor and psychiatrist for over 30 years. He received a Bachelor's degree in Psychology from Swarthmore College, earned a medical degree from Northwestern University Medical School in Chicago, and did his psychiatric residency at the Yale University Medical School."

"Didn't Dr. Wood go to Northwestern?" Linda asked.

"Yes he did," Darby said.

"Any specialties?" Linda asked.

"Yeah," Darby said and continued to read.

Dr. Thyme's post residency training included intensive studies in the treatment of alcoholism and substance abuse, which led to clinical experience in the treatment of adult, adolescent, and geriatric individuals with psychiatric and substance abuse problems, including alcohol and drug related issues, depression, and issues resulting from physical, psychological, and stress related traumas, including divorce. Since 1986, he has been helping families, attorneys and courts deal with the psychological consequences of divorce. Dr. Thymes has travelled throughout Texas as a forensic expert in family court cases, as well as conducting group presentations and divorce workshops, and treating patients involved in family disruptions.

"He would be a reasonable choice if you were an alcoholic going through a divorce," Linda said.

"No kidding," Darby said.

"Did Dr. Sorenson say what he's going to do?" Linda asked.

"He did," she said, finding the place in the letter where she'd stopped reading. "Here we go... He said, *As you know we offered three profession providers from medical and educational facilities specializing in bipolar disorder, which Dr. Wood refuses to accept. We had a lengthy phone discussion with him.*"

"I wish we could have heard that call," Linda said.

"Me too. But he did provide an email that Dr. Wood had sent him after the call."

"What did it say?" Linda asked.

Darby read his message.

As described per our call, my sense of the goal is to find a psy-
chiatrist who has both: An extensive background in evaluating
commercial airline pilots and thus would know the FAA
procedures and use the FAA medical standards to determine
fitness for duty. A forensic background to be able to integrate
and consider the multiple sources of data in this case. Looking
at the HIMS Psychiatrists from the recently published FAA list.

"HIMS?" Linda asked.

"It stands for Human Intervention Motivation Study. Basically, the program they stick alcoholics into," Darby said. "But none of the doctors he wants me to see have anything to do with aviation."

"This is getting more nonsensical."

"I could not agree more," Darby said. "Okay, so after the Wood's email, Dr. Sorenson continues."

We disagree with Dr. Wood in that he himself stated in his
report that you did not have a HIMS problem. I am sorry
you have been placed in this situation. However, we are at a
standoff. I will reach out to Dr. Wood and attempt a solution.
Perhaps your union could provide you support and intervene
on your behalf. I wish we had better news. Please do not give
up. With this said, we do not agree with Dr. Wood's selections,
and cannot in our professional opinion agree with any of them.

"Wow," Linda said. "Now what?"

"I'm going to call the union again," Darby said. "I don't know what else to do."

"What happens if they don't get the third doctor?" Linda asked.

"I suppose the standoff will keep me off property," Darby said. "And I'll be off disability in two years."

"Two years? I thought you would be on disability for the remainder of your career," Linda said.

"I thought so, too, but Global placed mental health into the drug and alcohol bucket. Therefore, it's only two years."

"Oh my God. They didn't," Linda said. "If Global associates someone with a mental health issue as an alcoholic or drug addict and cancels their disability after two years, nobody will ever come forward if they have a mental issue."

"That's exactly correct," Darby said. "This contract contradicts aviation safety on every level. They cry about the Germanwings pilot and spend thousands in recourses to determine what to do. Yet, they have created a process that forces anyone with a mental health issue into a hole. We need to change the contract."

"I'll help you fight that every step of the way," Linda said.

"I'm going to need the help," Darby said, shutting down her computer. "If pilots know they could be kicked to the street after two years, they will gamble that they can handle problems on their own. They won't get help."

"An accident waiting to happen," Linda said.

That it was, but nobody seemed to care. Especially not Global.

Chapter 50

THIS SITUATION WAS getting out of hand. However, it was turning into the most fun Joe Wolfe had experienced at Global to date. This process shifted from a legal strategy to a game, and there was one thing Wolfe was good at—games. Nobody ever beat him.

He sat at the head of the conference table with Dr. Marsh to his right. Captain Joel Iverson, the Seattle base Chief Pilot, sat to his left. Brian Talbot, from Brian Talbot & Associates law firm in Oklahoma City, sat to the left of Joel. They waited until 3 p.m. to call the final member to finish their meeting.

"Is everyone ready to go?" Wolfe asked, rubbing a thumb against his fingers. When they all confirmed they were, he dialed Dr. Wood's number.

"Hello," Dr. Wood said.

"Ken, it's Joe. I'm here with attorney Brian Talbot, and Joel, Bradshaw's chief pilot. Thank you for taking your time to discuss the situation with us."

"Of course," Wood said. "I'm frustrated. I've provided rationale to the Mayo doctors, and they are arguing with me. I'm not sure what else to do."

"Dr. Wood, this is attorney Talbot speaking. Do you have any documentation that can support your choice of doctors?"

"Well, uh… nothing other than they are qualified, and will believe my diagnosis."

Wolfe grimaced, glancing at the men in the room as he shook his head. Wood openly admitting that results would be forthcoming to reflect his opinion was not something he wanted as public knowledge. Not even in a closed room discussion.

"Fine. You've got qualified people who will make an honest assessment," Wolfe said. "I think what Mr. Talbot meant was, do you have any statistical data on the doctors?"

"Dr. Wood, it's Talbot again," he said, twiddling his pen between his fingers. "I'm a little concerned with the Dr. Brody selection. Her name has been brought up a few too many times. I'm also concerned with Thymes. He's a divorce substance abuse specialist. That would be easy for Mayo to fight in this case."

"Oh… but Dr. Thymes helped us win a FedEx case," Dr. Wood said. "We won."

"Good," Talbot said. "That's what we need."

"Gendel closed his practice," Wolfe said.

"I didn't know," Wood said flatly.

"That's fine," Talbot said. "My concern is back to Brody. Do you have any documentation that she's had any aviation experience?"

"She uhh… a few years ago she taught an FAA continuing education seminar. She explained a health issue of some sort to a group of pilots."

"Good," said Talbot.

"Darby's taught a half dozen FAA continuing education aviation seminars," Iverson said. All eyes looked his way. "I'm just saying. Two of those have been while she's been out for mental health."

"Seriously?" Talbot asked, directly to Wolfe.

Wolfe shrugged, and then a pinky finger slipped into his mouth to pull a nail nub off.

Talbot sighed heavily. "Maybe when Bradshaw gets pinched for money by losing half her pay on disability, she'll ask the boys at Mayo to acquiesce."

"She's got GPSI," Iverson said.

"What?" Talbot said, scowling at Iverson.

"Global pilot supplemental insurance. This is private insurance she's paid into which will protect her for one year," Wolfe said. "The union organizes it. It will essentially pay her the other half of her pay if she loses her medical due to a disability."

"Make it go away," Talbot said. "If she says she doesn't have a disability, then tell them not to pay it."

"The problem is," Wolfe said, "If she doesn't have a disability, then why can't she fly?"

"Dr. Marsh," Talbot said, turning Marsh's way. "You're on the board of HW Alliance Insurance, aren't you?"

"Yes, sir, I am."

"Make sure she qualifies for disability," Talbot ordered.

"I will," Marsh said. "I can also walk down the hall and make sure GPSI won't pay her."

"Good," Talbot said.

"How do we justify one and not the other?" Wolfe asked.

"The other is not managed or controlled by Global," Talbot replied. "You don't have to justify a damn thing. How much is two years at half pay?"

"That's about six thousand a month on her new equipment," Wolfe said.

"New equipment?" Talbot asked.

"She bid the triple seven in Portland," Iverson said. "That's officially her new base and new pay scale."

"How big is that base?" Talbot asked.

"Maybe sixty pilots is all," Iverson answered.

"Close it. Move her to Los Angeles," Talbot said. "California will take the other half of her paycheck for disability insurance. Close the base and you remove a quarter of her disability paycheck."

"It's not that easy," Iverson said. "Besides, we close a base and she can bid back to Seattle."

"Not now," Wolfe said. "She's officially off property and can't bid a new plane."

"Her attorney is sucking over four hundred bucks an hour from her," Talbot said. "With a quarter pay, she'll not only give into Dr. Wood's suggestions, but she might even drop her lawsuit as well."

"Won't she get the other quarter back from filing paperwork with California for a disability?" Joel asked.

"Yes, she would," Talbot said, "but… she would first have to admit she has a disability. If she admits to a bipolar disability, we have her. If she denies her diagnosis, California will not pay her."

"But closing a base…" Iverson said.

Wolfe stared at Iverson a moment, knowing exactly what he was thinking. However, he liked the thought, and the results the closure would produce. He turned toward Talbot and said, "Displacing an entire base is expensive endeavor."

"I was under the impression no expense was spared on this one," Talbot said. "Might be money well spent."

"Tom, what was the FAA's response on overturning her medical certificate?" Wolfe asked.

"I actually haven't contacted them yet," Dr. Marsh said. "It's been a busy few weeks, and I asked my staff to, but I think they forgot. I'll make sure they prepare a letter first thing tomorrow."

Wolfe held his breath, and stared at Dr. Marsh for a moment. He wanted to smack the man. "This is not a paper trail we want," he snapped, more firmly than he'd intended. "Make a call directly to FAA Inspector Banks, tomorrow."

Marsh nodded, and said, "Consider it done."

Marsh had been fired from his last position at FedEx. Now Wolfe understood why—he was a lazy sonofabitch. He'd been asked to take care of this damn issue nearly a month ago. He had told Clark it had been taken care of, simply because he'd thought it had. He'd fire Dr. Marsh right now if he wasn't such a valuable tool. On the other hand, he was a likeable guy when he was taking his medication. Just inefficient as hell.

"Dr. Wood," Talbot said, breaking the tension. "Prepare a medical release for Ms. Bradshaw that enables you to speak to anyone at the FAA regarding her case."

Wood agreed, and the men said goodbye to him. Wolfe thanked him for his time and ended the call. Darby was about to be squeezed tight, and there was not a damn thing she could do about it. Wolfe actually looked forward to seeing what she might try next.

Chapter 51

IF SHE WASN'T crazy before, she most certainly should be now. It had been a week since Darby had emailed her union representation asking for help, with no response. She'd called three times to no avail. The doctors were in a standoff and she didn't know what to do. Her answer to this dilemma was to hit the gym, work on her book, and let time fly. So far, she'd been successful at all. But time was in slow flight. Perhaps that saying was true—*fun flies when you are serving time.*

Darby had just returned from the gym, and she logged into her computer. Her inbox was unusually full and the names populating the screen indicated something was up. A storm was in full motion.

Dr. Williams, the regional flight surgeon, had emailed her.

Dear Ms. Bradshaw, the FAA is requesting additional information regarding your first class medical certificate. Please sign a release to enable your doctor to send a complete file with Dr. Wood's medical report. This is not denying your medical certificate, simply evaluating additional material.

"What the hell?" Darby said.

Dr. Williams would never ask for more material after he'd given her the medical certificate. Would he? That information would have come before he'd issued it. This couldn't be right. Darby called Kathryn, but got her voice mail. Maybe John would know what to do. She glanced at the time on her phone, it would be lunchtime on the East Coast.

She stood and paced as the phone rang. Then he answered.

"McAllister, how may I help you?"

"John, it's Darby."

"Everything all right?"

"Not really," she said. "I'm sorry to bother you, but Kat didn't answer, and I just got a message from the regional examiner saying he wants more information. I think Global is trying to take my medical certificate."

"The issuing doctor requesting more information at this stage doesn't sound right," John said. "Especially since you just received it. Nothing works that quickly in any government office."

"I don't think the examiner would ask, either. Don't these requests normally come from Oak City?" She sighed. "I really should have called them instead of you, I'm sorry."

"They do come from Oak City. That might be your best bet, at this time," John said. "But, it's never a bother. You can always call me. If we need to, I'll dig deeper."

"Thanks," Darby said. "I'll let you know what I learn."

She ended the call and googled the FAA Oklahoma medical certification branch. She found the phone number and dialed. She'd be damned if they would get away with this.

"FAA medical certification, how may I help you?"

"My name is Darby Bradshaw and I have a strange question," she said. Darby then proceeded to tell him what had happened with

Global, then Mayo, and how the regional examiner had issued her certificate. "But now he's asking for more information," she said. "So, the question is, did anyone in your department place this request?"

"Let me take a look," he said. "What's your social security number?"

Darby gave him the number and then she waited. She knew that once a medical was issued, and if the FAA wanted more information, that request would come from this office after a review of the medical application form. The request would then be sent directly to the airman, not to the issuing doctor.

"Ms. Bradshaw, thanks for your patience."

"Of course," Darby said. "Any luck?"

"Yes, I found your file. It hasn't been opened yet."

She sighed heavily. "Thank you."

"Those little bastards," Darby said, after she'd disconnected.

She went to the fridge and grabbed a Diet Pepsi and bag of carrot sticks. She returned to her computer and opened the next email. This one was from Dr. Wood—*Dear Ms. Bradshaw, please find the attached release enabling me to speak to anyone at the FAA regarding your case.*

"Like hell I will," Darby said. Anyone? She typed him a simple message—*Dear Dr. Wood, your services are not needed. I will provide a release to Dr. Marsh to send your report. Thank you.*

Darby typed up a release for Dr. Marsh. She then typed in Marsh's email address, and copied Dr. Williams—*Dear Dr. Marsh, please find the attached release for you to send Dr. Wood's report and the Mayo Clinic files in full to Dr. Williams for his review.*

Then there was a letter from Global crew resources. "Geez," she said. "There must be a full moon." She opened that email and read.

> *Dear Ms. Bradshaw, please be advised the Portland B777*
> *base has been closed. Due to your current status you have*
> *no bidding rights. The B777 flying from Portland is being*

moved to Los Angeles, and this will be your new base, should
you return to duty.

"*Should* I return to duty?" Darby said, rolling her eyes and sticking a carrot into her mouth. "Of course I'm returning." But closing the Portland base, that was just weird, especially without any notice. She began deleting all the crap which had filled her box until she saw an email from her editor, and another from her attorney. She sighed.

God, she hoped there was good news. She needed something positive to go her way. Darby opened her editor's email first.

Darby, I love what I've seen of the book so far. Scary stuff.
I wonder what the FAA will do when they read it. Fix things?
Could they be part of the problem? Absolutely fascinating.
Keep up the good work! Loved the novel, as well. Deloris.

Darby smiled, and then opened her attorney's email. Then she said, "What the fuck?" She leaned back in her chair and closed her eyes, fighting the urge to cry.

CHAPTER 52

DARBY COULD NOT believe her attorney could be so criminal. How in the hell could he think this was right? This was beyond anything which could possibly be just, in any sense of the word. There was no way she could survive if this continued. It wasn't fair. How had she been so suckered? She paced her kitchen holding her phone, waiting to be connected.

"This is Donner," her attorney said, after he finally answered.

"Bob, this is Darby."

"Good to hear from you. What can I help you with?"

"I just opened my monthly bill," Darby said. "What the hell? On top of my thirty-five hundred dollars to determine I couldn't fly being bipolar, this…"

"Calm down. Research doesn't come free."

"Calm down?" Darby snapped. "You didn't need to spend a penny looking up the consequences of a pilot being bipolar, but you charged me $3500 for that research. Now this?"

"I told you not to worry about these bills…"

"How can I not worry?" Darby said. "Over four grand to determine if I had a fraud case? I never asked you to investigate fraud."

"We discussed the aspect of a fraud case against the doctor."

"Discussed, yeah. But I *never* asked you to do research," Darby said. She had never signed a contract for anything beyond the AIR

21 and it was he who wrote the stipulation in her current contract, in which any additional lawsuits must be established with another contract.

"Besides, I googled fraud and made a couple phone calls to fraud attorneys. For *free*." She emphasized the free part of that equation, and then continued. "Wood isn't technically my doctor because he was employed by and worked for Global. I have no recourse."

"Our research concurs that's a correct statement."

"But I'm out an additional 4800 dollars?" Darby snapped, sitting heavily. "And we haven't even moved the case forward. I am no closer to getting back to work than I was a year ago."

"Litigation takes time."

"But this isn't litigation, and it isn't helping," Darby said, drumming her nails on the table working to relax. "And yesterday the company told the FAA the diagnosis. Which was in violation of the contract." She regretted telling him that news the moment the words left her lips. He would undoubtedly figure a way to bill her for legal advice.

"You can't fly, anyway," he said. "But you could file another grievance. Speaking of which, we must move your grievance to the board for a hearing. If you don't exhaust all your options under the railway labor act, it will cost you your AIR 21 case. I also need to be there. I need to protect the process. We can't afford to have something spoken that could harm us."

"How much will this cost me?"

"Probably another fifty to sixty thousand dollars, just to prepare."

"Holy shit," Darby said. Tears filled her eyes. That would be on top of the AIR 21. Once she hit court this could be upward toward a half million dollars. How the hell was she going to pay for this?

"I will only need another twenty-five thousand dollar retainer, and that could get us started."

Darby wiped the tears from her cheek, and then sucked a deep breath. "I don't know if I can afford both the grievance and the lawsuit."

"Well you don't have much choice."

Darby ended the call with an assurance that she would get back to him with a decision as to whether or not he would represent her on the grievance. She could not believe he'd told her she did not have much choice.

Then again, that's what she'd been told throughout her situation—she had no choice. But she always had choices. She'd had the choice to not give them her safety concerns, and she'd chosen to anyway—despite the warnings and threats. After she'd been pulled from the flight line, her union attorney had told her not to go to the neuropsychological testing and to take an unpaid leave of absence. She chose to fight. There were always choices, and today would lead to more.

Darby grabbed her keys, set the alarm, and headed out the door.

CHAPTER 53

THIRTY-FIVE MINUTES LATER, Darby pulled into a spot in an underground parking garage in Tacoma. She took the escalator up to the ground floor lobby and found the elevator that would take her to the offices. She pressed the PH button, and rode the elevator to the top floor. Darby stepped off the elevator and into the center of an expansive space, with the most beautiful views she'd seen since living in Seattle—outside an airplane.

Yachts floated in the marina below, with the waterway spanning westward to Puget Sound, and Mt. Rainier stood as a sentinel to the right. She accepted a bottle of water and walked to the north windows and looked down at the marina below. The sun glistened off the water and Darby smiled.

In her search for another attorney, one of her friends had connected her to a law firm with offices in both Seattle and Tacoma. Her friend had spent the better part of a year fighting a case of another kind, and had been sharing Darby's story with his legal team along the way. One of the attorney's had become intrigued with Darby's case, and had requested a meeting.

"Ms. Bradshaw, Melanie will you see now."

Darby stood and followed her into a conference room with a window that perfectly framed Mt. Rainer, as if the mountain were a painting. She accepted her seat, and they conducted the formalities of introductions.

Melanie, as she preferred to be called, was one of hundreds of attorneys in this law firm. She had no understanding of aviation law, no knowledge of arbitrations, and lacked knowledge of an AIR 21, but she knew employment law.

"Thank you for meeting me today," Melanie said.

"I appreciate your time, more than you know," Darby replied.

"This is quite an interesting situation," Melanie said. "From the timeline you provided us and everything we've read, we'd like to take your case."

"Thank you," Darby said, somewhat in shock. "Would this be in addition to the AIR 21?"

"No. The suit against Global would be a discrimination suit based on gender. Global would have to prove you were not placed into a psychiatric evaluation because you're a woman, and quite frankly I don't know how they could do that based upon the continued harassment you've received, and the low percentage of female pilots at Global."

"But the harassment has all been because I reported an instructor and reached out to the CEO, reporting safety concerns."

"Unless they can prove they pulled the same shenanigans on the men, we have a strong case," she said.

"The truth is, I have no doubt they did this in part because I'm a woman. They're the most sexist airline I've ever experienced. I've got a friend who received a letter from them years ago, where they told her she didn't qualify to be a pilot at Global because they didn't hire women. She was hired at Coastal and came over to Global with the merger. She ended up quitting because of the culture."

"That's exactly the kind of information we can use," she said, writing on her legal pad. "Anything else?"

"Oh, yeah. I have another friend who had an impeccable career. She was a 747 captain and stood up to a captain during an emergency, preventing what could have been a huge catastrophe."

"What happened?" Melanie asked, with concern lining her eyes.

"An engine fire on the outboard engine. It took both bottles to put it out," Darby said. "The other captain overreacted and wanted to dump fuel, despite a burning fire. She stood up to him, and you don't do that at Global."

"Do these events happen often?" Melanie asked.

"Engine fires? No," Darby asked, and then answered, "but making someone mad if you bruise their ego? Yes."

"Where is she now?"

"She's out on medical in part because of harassment that followed in the simulator. The stress impacted both her performance and her health. She also has text messages from a management pilot, check airman no less, listing all the graphic things he wanted to do to her. The guy who was supposed to help her placed a contingency on his help. She first had to, and I quote, put it in her mouth."

"That's disgusting," Melanie said. "She has those text messages?"

Darby nodded. "Yes, she does. The company saw them and did nothing about it."

"Can we get her in here?"

"No. Rich Clark, the guy who did this to me, warned her that if she took legal action against them, they would pull her disability. She couldn't afford to pay her mortgage, even if a law firm took the case on contingency."

"This is horrible," Melanie said, shaking her head.

"I couldn't agree more. The airline had less than 1% female pilots when we merged. They have no female chief pilots, and the only women in leadership are HR."

"We could use all that for support, as well," Melanie said, writing on her pad.

"It's more than me being a woman," Darby said. "It's because I am a woman who reported safety concerns. That was the salt in their wound. They simply couldn't fire me for anything because I didn't have any performance issues and didn't do anything wrong."

"This creates an even stronger case. If you allow us to run with it, we won't charge you. This will be 100% contingency." Melanie leaned forward and said, "You'll win punitive damages. That means three times your earnings, until your normal retirement."

"But I won't get to fly."

"We can demand your job back, as well," she said. "But with that kind of money you could start over anywhere."

"That is a lot of money," Darby said. "But this fight has never been about the money." Her fight was simply to defend her career, and to support the contention that no airline had the right to retaliate because an employee brought safety issues forward. Her real fight was for safety, but when retaliation occurs, all efforts go into survival.

"We will need you to drop your grievance, and drop your AIR 21."

The implications of that were many. There was a moment of silence while Melanie waited for a response. Darby thought about the money. About the ease of winning the case. About not having to pay another penny in attorney bills, when her current attorney was draining her. She thought about paying her mortgage. She sipped her water and glanced at Mount Rainier, and then shifted her attention back to Melanie.

"I want them to pay for what they did," Darby said. "But their disregard for safety is wrong. If employees are fired, or forced into abusive psychiatric evaluations because they report safety, then nobody is safe when they step on an airplane. We can't allow them to do this."

"I appreciate your passion and concern for safety. I wish everyone cared that much," Melanie said. "Let me see if we can run this case parallel to that AIR 21."

"That would be the best option," Darby said. "This business is hard enough for a woman. I don't want to turn this into a girly thing."

"I appreciate that, as well," Melanie said. "I'll get back to you as soon as we see how we can do this."

They shook hands and said their good-byes. Darby took the elevator to the lower lobby, and sat on the couch to dial her attorney. This time there was no delay in his taking her call.

"Did you make a decision about the grievance?" he asked.

"No. I met with an employment attorney who wants to file a gender discrimination lawsuit."

"What? Instead of the AIR 21?"

"Well, yes, but no," Darby said. "She also wants me to drop the grievance."

"You can't drop the grievance, or you'll lose everything."

"But there is no gender clause in the Global contract. We don't have to run that through the Railway Labor Act because it's not part of the pilot contract. That's a federal law."

"You're wrong. All labor disputes must be heard in the grievance process," he said, his voice growing louder.

"I told her I didn't want to drop the AIR 21 case. She's checking to see if they can run it parallel," Darby said.

"You're wasting your time. It can't happen," he said.

"It's not going to hurt for them to check into it," Darby said, "because *they* are not charging me a penny for their research."

After a moment he said, "I've asked my clerks to reassess those bills to see if we can lower them a bit."

Darby shook her head in dismay, knowing he feared losing the bigger fish.

"We can win this, but you have to trust me," he said. "I've been doing this for thirty years, and have won many cases. I'm also adding a new attorney to the staff from Air Western."

"Great," Darby said, rolling her eyes. He should ask his new attorney why he didn't help the AW pilots get their jobs back for the same mental health accusations. "Can we talk later?" she asked.

"Of course. I'll be in the office tomorrow."

CHAPTER 54

SNUGGLED INTO A booth, 13 Coins never felt as comforting as it did this evening. Darby sat beside Jackie, with Linda and Kathryn on the other side of the table. She was experiencing déjà vu. They were well into their first bottle of wine, with a double bucket of clams and garlic bread on the table between them. She could make this a weekly habit.

"I'm completely confused," Jackie said. "You were cleared by the FAA, you have your medical, but they won't let you come back to work, and now the same guy who gave you your medical certificate wants more information?"

"Yep," she said. "And… my attorney charged another forty-eight hundred dollars for research which has nothing to do with my case."

"You need to get rid of him," Kathryn said.

"That may be sooner than later," Darby said, playing with the stem of her glass. "I met with another law firm today, and they want the case on full contingency." Darby proceeded to tell them of her discussion, and her concerns, as well as Bob's arguments against doing both.

"If they can't do both, then what will you do?" Kathryn asked.

Darby dipped a clam into the butter and said, "I think I'll do the AIR 21."

"But that attorney is raping you," Jackie said. "Can you afford it?"

"We'll definitely have a discussion on the billing issues," Darby replied. "But next week I go on disability with half pay. I think I can swing it. Oh, did I tell you they closed the Portland base and bumped me to Los Angeles?"

"When?" Kathryn asked.

"I got the notice a couple days ago."

"You would take half pay, and go broke with attorney fees to fight for safety?" Linda asked, ignoring the base closure discussion. "When you could get punitive damages, never pay another legal fee, and never have to work again?"

"Yep, I guess I would," Darby said, dunking a piece of bread into the melted butter, and stuffing it into her mouth.

"Maybe you *are* crazy," Linda said, lifting her glass with a grin. "Crazy with integrity."

"Is that a professional opinion with a high degree of certainty?" Darby asked, clinking her glass to Linda's with a smirk.

This was so much bigger than her. After analyzing the results of her research, she'd learned there was a problem in the industry. A huge problem. Airlines worldwide lacked safety culture, and pilots were not being trained. This was an accident waiting to happen. If pilots couldn't come forward to report freely, then they lost that first line of defense.

"Where are you with the selection of the next doctor?" Kathryn asked.

"Global's quack and the Mayo doctors still are arguing over the neutral. Rich Clark said it's my fault they have not agreed and that I'll be terminated if I don't make Mayo select one of Wood's choices. The FAA's regional doctor asked for Wood's report, and I'm hoping that seeing it won't change his mind. Mayo didn't, so why would he?"

"But he gave you the medical certificate," Kathryn said. "Why would he ask for more information?"

"I suspect his boss, Michael Banks, told him to do it," Darby said, staring directly at Kathryn. "This came from the top. My file had not even been reviewed at the time of the request."

"You're not afraid of Banks?" Kathryn asked, with a puzzled look.

Darby shook her head slowly and grinned. "No. I thought about it a lot because of what we read. But, in his current position, I don't think he'd want to open that can of worms."

Kathryn nodded in understanding. "I believe you're right."

"That report won't make a difference to another doctor," Linda said. "I have never seen such an effort to justify a corporate action. There was nothing about your mental health anywhere within that report. Wood should be barred."

"He's under investigation," Darby said. "The worst part is, he's still working while they investigate. Turns out, there are two more Global pilots that I've found whose careers he's destroyed, as well as a United guy, but I don't know how many more."

"Can't the union tell you?" Jackie asked.

"They could, but they won't. I've begged them to give my phone number to anyone who's experienced anything like this," Darby said. "They refused."

Kathryn lifted the wine and topped off everyone's glasses, emptying the bottle. "Did John tell you about the wine when you spoke the other day?"

Jackie and Kathryn exchanged a look, and Jackie nodded to Kathryn to continue.

"He got the wine back?" Darby asked, glancing between the women.

"He did. The bottle *Ray* supposedly gifted you at Christmas," Kathryn said, raising her glass and twirling the red liquid. "Let's just say someone was trying to remove you permanently."

"Seriously?" Darby said.

"It would have killed you if you'd drunk it," Kathryn said.

"It was poisoned?" Darby set her wine glass down. "Why didn't John tell me?"

"I convinced him not to," Kathryn said. "He told me the day you were headed to the Mayo."

"I concurred," Linda added. "You were going through so much with the medical evaluations. You didn't need one more thing to worry about. And honestly, you would have come across as paranoid telling the doctors someone was trying to kill you."

"But they were," Darby said.

"Yes, they were. But the truth is, in mental health cases it doesn't matter if it's true or not," Linda said. "They see what they want to see. Nobody believes this stuff happens in real life."

"Besides," Jackie added. "John was absolutely certain this was a one-time event, based on the timing."

"They were trying to get the wine back," Kathryn added. "Just like we thought."

"What was in it?" Darby asked.

"It wasn't actually poison. It was a sedative… a hypnotic type of sleeping aid," Kathryn said. "Benzodiazepine, a prescription with… let's just say some side effects. The amount in there would have been lethal with the wine combination."

"Wow." Darby lifted her glass and tipped it back, emptying it. "Anyone up for another bottle?"

Kathryn smiled. "I think that is in order."

They ordered their meals and another bottle of pinot. They shifted the discussion and talked about the kids while the waiter was in earshot. Darby, however, was still trying to figure out how they were going to pull off a suicide. She would never kill herself. Besides, she's never taken prescription sleeping pills. Dr. Wood knew that as well from his evaluation. How could they have pulled that off?

"They would've needed a pill bottle," Darby said, interrupting Jackie.

"Huh?" Jackie said, turning toward her.

"If they'd tried to drug me, there would have to be an empty pill bottle in my house, or they wouldn't have been able to pull off the fake suicide."

"Maybe they didn't think that far," Jackie said. "Criminals get caught because they're stupid."

"They probably had the wine thieves take it," Kathryn added.

The waiter returned with the pinot and new glasses, and poured half a glass for each of the ladies.

"Okay, I'm in more trouble than I thought," Darby said.

All eyes turned her way.

"They put me in a hole and now are piling on the bricks."

"Can a person breathe with bricks on them, more so than dirt?" Jackie asked with a nudge.

Darby sipped her wine and thought about that. "I think with dirt you suffocate and die. With bricks it's a slow, painful death because you can't support the weight."

"Focus ladies," Linda said with a chuckle, "or I'm cutting you off."

Darby gave her a thumbs up and focused on the facts. What she knew was easy. What they were doing and why was more of the challenge. Which path she should take to survive was another story.

"Rich Clark has gone to an all-time low," Darby said. "But I don't want a gender-based lawsuit, even if they are sexist assholes and I could become a multi-millionaire.

"I think she is crazy," Jackie said to Linda and Kathryn, nudging Darby.

"Maybe I am," Darby said with a chuckle. "The problem is... how do I afford court? More than that, I don't trust my attorney. I think he's a smart guy, but there are signs smacking me in the face."

"More than unreasonable bills?" Kathryn asked.

"Oh, yeah. I don't know if he's telling me the truth about whether or not I have to do the grievance. Not that he's lying, but his effing ego is such that he acts like he knows everything. I wish there was someone who had the knowledge that I could hire to answer my questions."

"Oh, is that all you want?" Linda said with a smirk. She pulled a folded piece of paper out of her purse, and handed it to Darby. "I have a name for you."

"Really?" Darby said.

"If you were going with the new law firm then you wouldn't have needed it," Linda said. "But, Niman had asked an associate at work whose son is a pilot and a lawyer, and teaches at an aviation university. He highly recommended this guy."

"Jack of all trades," Darby said with a grin. "That pilot sounds kind of bipolar." She unfolded the piece of paper and read the name— Robert Allen.

CHAPTER 55

MORNING COULDN'T ARRIVE fast enough for Darby. She had tossed and turned throughout the night. With the first sign of daylight she had given up on sleep, climbed out of bed, and taken a shower. Now she was curled up in her living room chair with a cup of coffee within reach, a legal pad in her lap, and the piece of paper Linda had given her the night before. Darby unfolded the paper. She stared at the number for a moment, then dialed. He answered on the second ring.

Darby introduced herself to Attorney Robert Allen, and explained how she'd received his number. She told him she'd given a safety report to management and they'd forced her into a psychiatric evaluation. She shared with him about filing the AIR 21, details of her company required psychiatric evaluation with Wood, and her evaluation at the Mayo Clinic. She explained the contractual process and the requirement for the neutral doctor, and how that doctor would be selected. She told him about the company violating the contract, and now the FAA was requesting more information in order to retain her medical. Then she told him about the meeting with the other law firm. She told him of her current attorney's adamancy that if she didn't do the grievance, she would lose her rights in court.

"I feel like I'm treading water," Darby said. "I don't have a job. I have an attorney billing me for fraud research, and I have another law firm who wants this on contingency but they want me to drop the safety case and do a gender discrimination suit. Now they're looking to see if we can do both gender and the AIR 21. But my current attorney says I can't. He also says I have to go through the grievance process first, and he needs to represent me, but at a huge price tag.

"The reason I want to hire you is simply to answer some questions, and help me to decide which way to turn and what to do. I guess I really need to know my legal rights."

"How much do you know about the AIR 21 statute?" Robert asked.

"I know it's the Whistleblower Law," Darby said. "That a company can't harm an employee who reports safety."

"Would you indulge me by allowing me to explain the AIR statute?"

"Of course," Darby said, her pen ready to copy.

"As I'm sure you know, it's illegal to discriminate on the basis of race, gender, and age. But, it's also illegal to discriminate against employees for reporting non-compliance with federal aviation safety standards. An AIR 21 action is a discrimination suit. However, it's different from other discrimination statutes, in that an AIR 21 was designed not just to protect the whistleblower, but to protect the public. With a gender discrimination suit you must establish a preponderance of evidence that the only reason they took action against you was due to gender.

"However, in a safety discrimination case you simply have to establish that reporting protected activity, in *part*, contributed to the employer's decision to take the adverse action against you."

"Would a forced psychiatric evaluation be considered an adverse action?" Darby asked.

"Absolutely," Robert said. "I recently lost a case where the judge ruled that submitting someone to a psychiatric evaluation was an adverse action."

"But you still lost the case?" Darby asked, trying to understand.

"Yes. There's more to this law than simply receiving an adverse action. If you're interested, I will send you the case."

"I would love to read it," Darby said, and then she gave him her email address.

"There are four elements in an AIR 21 case and you must prove all four," he said. "First you must engage in protected activity. Meaning you reported to your employer or the FAA what you reasonably believed to be a violation of a federal regulation, or an FAA approved program, and such. You don't have to be correct; you simply have to report in good faith."

"I reported violations of SMS and safety culture, fatigue violations, and an instructor falsifying training records."

"Good," he said. "That would qualify. Then you must show that your management representatives had knowledge of your reports."

"They did," Darby said. "I actually gave two senior leaders at Global an entire safety report."

"In writing?" he asked.

"Yes," Darby said. "Forty-five pages."

"Perfect," he said. "The next thing you must establish is whether you suffered an adverse action, and a forced psychiatric evaluation would clearly qualify. The fourth element is causation. The initial burden of proof is yours. However, unlike other discrimination cases, you simply must prove that reporting the violation had something to do with the adverse action. It doesn't have to be the employer's sole motivating consideration. Moreover, the case law allows a judge to infer causation from circumstantial evidence. Sometimes, simple temporal proximity is enough to establish that element. When you establish that there is a causal nexus between your protected activity and the adverse action you suffered, then the burden of proof shifts."

"In my case, they pulled me less than two months from the time I gave the report," Darby said.

"Excellent. An inference of causation has been based on a temporal connection more distant than two months," he said. "So, when the burden of proof shifts, then it becomes the company's responsibility to prove with clear and convincing evidence that they would have imposed the same adverse action regardless of the protected activity."

"This is fascinating. Is it true that at the end of this I'll get all my attorney fees paid?" Darby asked, hopeful she would redeem the funds she'd lost.

"No," he said. "The statute only allows for reasonable attorney fees."

"So, investigating whether I could sue for fraud wouldn't qualify?"

"No. The fees must be applicable to defending the case," he said. "The judge will determine the reasonableness."

"Am I required to also process a grievance with the union?"

"No, you're not. But if you do, you must be careful, as the company could claim collateral estoppel. Meaning any factual issue resolved by the arbitrator may be binding on you in the AIR 21 context. However, you have every right to go down both paths, in part, because there are different remedies in an arbitration versus the AIR 21, so these cases could run parallel."

"What are the differences?" Darby asked. "I mean, between the grievance and the AIR 21?"

"The grievance process doesn't provide provisions for discovery, attorney fees, or compensatory damages, as the AIR 21 does," Robert said. "The grievance can only award back pay. However, both can reinstate you to your job."

"What about running a gender discrimination case parallel with the AIR 21?" she asked.

"You could. In the gender-based case you must have evidence that they did this to you because you were a woman. The AIR 21 case is based on retaliation based on protected activity related to federal compliance issues," he said. "Now granted, some judge could throw it out. However, it would be no surprise that the company retaliated against you for two separate reasons—that it was that 'dumb bitch' who was reporting federal compliance issues."

Darby laughed at his language. She liked this guy. "Actually, I think that's exactly what happened."

"Are you planning on doing both?" he asked.

"I don't think so," she said. "Simply because women are less than 6% of the working pilot population. Global now has less than 3%. While I know they treat women like shit here, and are old school, I want this to stand on the merits of safety. We owe that to the traveling public. Safety should take full priority here."

"I agree," he said. "You're also fortunate that you filed in time. This is the shortest statute of limitations I'm aware of—ninety days is all you had from the date of the adverse action."

"I got lucky on that," Darby said, glancing at her watch. She had already gone over her allotted time. "I cannot thank you enough for this information. But I only paid you for an hour. I owe you another thirty minutes."

"Don't worry about it," Robert said. "Let me send you that brief. The judge's ruling in that case will explain a great deal. And please, don't hesitate to call if you have any other questions."

They said their goodbyes, and Darby immediately texted Bob— *Can you please email me all your AIR 21 cases you've tried? Thanks! Darby.*

Darby could not believe she hadn't thought about reading cases before. That was a fabulous idea. She also couldn't believe she'd been dealing with this for fifteen months and didn't know any of this. She wondered why Bob had told her she would get all her attorney fees reimbursed if the law didn't allow for it.

Her phone rang. *Speak of the devil.* "Hey, Bob."

"I just got your text."

"Can you email me your AIR 21 cases?"

"I haven't done an AIR 21 before," he said.

"What?" Darby said dumbfounded. She didn't know what to say. She'd trusted him. She'd paid him. He'd deceived her for the better part of a year. "How could you not tell me you haven't done an AIR 21 before?"

"I've been in front of an ALJ many times. It's exactly the same process."

"Maybe so, but this law is unique," Darby said. "Did you know that under the AIR 21 you cannot get *all* attorney fees back, only *reasonable* attorney fees?"

"Calm down," Bob said, not answering her question.

"Don't tell me to calm down," Darby snapped.

"I understand this is a frustrating process. But you have to trust me."

"No. I don't have to trust you," Darby said. She'd trusted far too many people and now she was going to trust herself. He had been the person extending a helping hand after she'd been beaten and left for dead, but he'd robbed her while she was down. She trusted Robert Allen.

Darby said goodbye, and immediately redialed Robert's number.

CHAPTER 56

THIS TIME ROBERT answered the phone on the first ring. "Do you have another question?"

"Would you represent me?" Darby asked. "Among other things, I just learned my attorney has never had an AIR 21 case before. I assumed he had by the way he represented himself. He said that it didn't matter because it's in front of the ALJ and he's been there hundreds of times."

"He's correct that you will present your case in front of an administrative law judge. But there are many nuances with this law unlike others," he said. "And yes, I will take your case."

"We don't get a jury?"

"No, an ALJ rules."

"That hardly seems right," she said. "What if they're bought off by the company?"

Darby had always imagined this being in front of a jury of real people, her peers, who would not be able to be bought. She wasn't so sure about judges. One person deciding on this didn't seem right.

Somewhat like the neutral doctor who would be the ruling party on her mental health, despite all the evidence on her side.

"These are federal judges. I wouldn't worry about them being bought. Regardless, most of my cases are settled well before we get to court. I believe Global will more than likely settle."

Darby sighed. If they settled, she'd be back to work even if they didn't agree on a neutral examiner. She liked the sound of that.

"Where do the OSHA and FAA investigations stand?" he asked.

"I'm assuming the FAA is finished because they gave Global a violation for duty time regulations," Darby said. "But OSHA, I'm not sure. I gave the investigator some pilots' contact information, all of whom said they would testify as long as they could remain anonymous. I also gave him my non-pilot friends' information, who know what's been happening. So far the investigator has not called any of them."

"Can you send me a copy of the FAA violation?"

"Of course."

"I'll also need a copy of the original AIR 21 filing, any communications you've had with OSHA, all your medical reports, and then we'll get me up to speed," he said. "You know this story better than anyone, so I'm going to depend upon you to fill in the blanks."

"Anything I can do to help," Darby said.

"You said you still have a medical certificate?" he asked.

"Yes. I've never lost it."

"If you have a medical certificate, why aren't you working?"

"Our contract says we need a neutral examiner. A tie breaker. But the Mayo Clinic doctors are in battle with Dr. Wood. Wood wants to send me down the river to a doctor who will rule in his favor, but the Mayo doctors are not agreeing with him," Darby said. "But now the FAA is evaluating his report, and they could be the tie breaker."

"Who's investigating?"

"The regional medical examiner," Darby said. "The same doctor who issued it."

"They're not going to pull your medical," he said.

"How can you be so sure?"

"The regional doctor is reevaluating his own decision. Something makes me feel he won't find fault with himself."

Darby chuckled. "You're right, he wouldn't." She smiled. Smart and logical, too. Excellent qualities in an attorney and something her last attorney was missing.

"And the grievance?" he asked.

"Scheduled for July 11th. But I'm not sure if ALPO is really helping me."

"That's only a month and a half away," he said. "Okay... tell your reps that I will be representing you at that grievance. Let's see how the company and ALPO respond to that. Then we'll decide what to do. As far as they're concerned, we'll let them think we're pressing forward."

"Sounds good to me," Darby said, writing notes as fast as she could.

"I'm going to read the initial filing, and then I'll make it official with the courts that I'm representing you," he said. "How long did you say this has been ongoing?"

"A year ago, December."

"Fifteen months." He sighed. "Normally I take an immediate loss because of OSHA's delays, and then I file an appeal. OSHA has a history of taking up to two years to conduct their investigations. By taking that loss, I can get the case to court in three months. But, in your case, we could go either way."

"If we lost and appealed, would it hurt our case in court?" Darby asked.

"Absolutely not," he replied. "However, you are simply one doctor away from getting back to work on your own, and it's going to take some time to get me caught up. If you're up for it, we could wait and see how OSHA rules. We'll have a couple months of depositions if this goes to court. Chances are OSHA will rule against you regardless, but you never know."

"This is so blatant," Darby said. "I'd like to think OSHA would do the right thing."

"Let's hope so, but don't count on it. In the meantime, let's spend our energy to make that neutral examination happen and get you flying again."

"I like the way you think," Darby said.

"One more thing," he said. "Your union hates me."

Darby grinned. "All the more reason to have you on my team." That was a story she could hardly wait to hear.

Robert said he would send her a contract and she could sign and return it to him, with a retainer, at her convenience. In the meantime, he would begin reading anything she would send his way. She would send him everything.

Darby went to the kitchen, filled a bowl with Lucky Charms and added milk. She sat at the kitchen table and took a bite of her cereal. And then another. Finally, someone was going to help her. She could not thank Niman enough for finding Robert Allen. She took another bite of cereal, and then opened her laptop and began uploading documents.

With a huge smile on her face she glanced out the window where a police car was driving slowly past her house. The officer raised his hand and waved. She blew him a kiss, and waved in return.

Stuffing one more bite of charms into her mouth, she lifted her phone and texted Bob—You're fired.

CHAPTER 57

THE DAY THEY removed pilots from controlling aircraft was the day they invited the next level of terrorism into the sky. Mary Chambers printed that invitation today by giving permission for the freight operators to use ground-based operations instead of pilots. Pilots were on their way out.

Chambers had no clue what she was doing, but John McCallister did. He knew where the industry was headed if this went through. He gripped the memo tightly and headed out of his office.

Mary Chambers was the house transportation and infrastructure committee chairwoman. John stormed down the hall, walked past Mary's secretary, despite objections, and into Mary's office. He froze when he saw her guest, and then he closed the door using the action to cool his emotions. He stepped forward and stood before them. It made sense Deke Elmer, the temporary FAA administrator was with her. John had no doubt they were discussing NextGen and the elimination of pilots.

The Next Generation Air Transport System was underway in which satellite-based systems would replace ground-based systems for air traffic management. Pilots would taxi with moving maps, execute satellite-based landing procedures, and assume responsibility for aircraft separation versus air traffic control managing that separation.

Unfortunately history has shown that anytime new technology was introduced, a period of instability associated with a learning curve developed, creating an environment ripe for catastrophe. Increased complexity and additional responsibilities would reduce situational awareness and create an environment susceptible to human error. Human error was nothing but an excuse to replace pilots with technology.

"What the hell do you think you're doing?" John asked Mary, with his voice as calm as he could force it. Frustration grew below.

"I should ask you that same thing," Mary said with a grin, "barging into my office unannounced." She glanced at Deke and back to John.

"If you push this through, you will destroy aviation safety."

"Don't be so melodramatic, John," Mary said with a flick of her hand. "Automation has been replacing pilots for years. If we can gain confidence with the public, by showing them freighters can operate without pilots, then we can cut back on operational expenses worldwide and give the savings to the public."

"This has nothing to do with savings to the passengers," John snapped. The money would go directly into CEO and administrative official's pockets at the sacrifice of safety. "This is irresponsible."

"I'm with John. This is more than irresponsible, this is negligent," Deke said. "Even if you could guarantee that airborne systems were secure from hacking, you still cannot secure the ground-based facilities."

"You don't have a voice in this," Mary said as her attention snapped to Deke, her eyes narrowing.

"He's the damn FAA administrator," John said. "He does have a say."

"Temporary," Mary said. "He's the *temporary* administrator."

Everything suddenly made sense. This was the reason they had not assigned a permanent replacement. They needed to be assured that their appointed official would push this through. If Deke ever had a chance of a permanent position prior to this, that chance was history with his current stance. His respect for the man increased tenfold.

"Temporary or not, you will never convince an administrator this is a positive move," Deke said. "Hell, those freighters fly over our cities."

"When you open this door to freighters, passengers will be next," John said. "God forbid the day this becomes a reality."

Mary scoffed as she looked between John and Deke. "What part of this are you two missing?" she asked. "That is exactly how we intend to utilize the data."

John threw the memo on the table in front of her. "You think automation is the answer to safety? You're as crazy as this idea."

"Safety has never had anything to do with this. We're talking about profitability and ensuring we have enough aircraft to service the traveling public's needs. This will be the solution to the pilot shortage."

"You don't give a damn about the public's needs," Deke said. "Pay the pilots what they're worth and you wouldn't have a pilot shortage."

"You can't control commercial aircraft from the ground," John said. "Nobody would fly without pilots."

"We can and we will," Mary said. She stood and reached for the memo. "You think you can delay this? Perhaps. But you will never prevent it. Automation is improving as we speak. Manufacturers are building equipment that doesn't need pilots. Have either of you looked at the statistics of pilot error?"

John was intimately familiar with the data. He had also read Darby's analysis of safety culture and training. The truth was, pilot error was the fault of airlines' poor training and lack of safety culture, and a critical issue with lack of FAA oversight and compliance.

Operating commercial aircraft as drones was not the answer. Errors would extend to those ground-based operators. Equally concerning, and exactly as Deke had expressed and Darby stated many times over, there would be no securing the ground-based facility.

It would only be a matter of time before those facilities were broken into. The security needed would be greater than the White House. Yet, when employing minimum wage, non-educated operators, no amount of security to keep someone out would account for what could happen from within.

CHAPTER **58**

I T MIGHT AS well have been April Fool's Day, but there was nothing funny about the news she'd just received. Darby wanted to believe someone was playing jokes on her, and that neither of these events had happened. She sighed heavily, not sure which to address first. Her disability paycheck was only a quarter of what she should have received, and she was denied Global pilot supplemental insurance.

She had paid into the supplemental aid, and that should have covered the other half of her paycheck for the next year. To make matters worse her disability pay from the company was only half of what she expected. "Shit," she said, and reached for her phone.

Pacing, she waited on hold with corporate payroll. She wondered if a judge could award an allowance for a new floor after her stress-induced pacing had worn a path. She'd been transferred at least four times.

"This is Barbara. How may I help you?"

"This is Darby Bradshaw," she said, somewhat startled by the live person. "I just converted from sick leave to disability and my paycheck is a fraction of what it should be." Along with her measly paycheck, Darby had also received a letter in the welcoming packet that included a medical form for the State of California.

"Yes, I'm aware of your case," the woman said. "The problem is, you're based in Los Angeles, and therefore we pay half your disability, and then the State of California pays the other half."

"But I've never flown out of California. I'm not even checked out on the equipment. I actually was forced there because the Portland base was closed."

"A simple solution. Fill out the paperwork and they will pay the other half of your disability," she said.

"Did you hear what I said?" Darby asked. "I am only there on paper."

"I did hear you, Ms. Bradshaw, but none of that matters," Barbara said.

"But I don't have a disability," Darby said. "A psychiatrist at the Mayo Clinic and I filled out the paperwork and he wrote no diagnosis. We lined through the word disability, and wrote medical hold status. The State of California is not going to pay a person for not having a disability, especially one who has never worked in their state."

"There is really nothing we can do," Barbara said. "Just fill out the California forms if you want the remainder of your pay."

"But I am *not* going to falsify records and tell them I have a medical issue when I don't have one. That would be fraud," Darby said.

"Then call them," Barbara said. "If we receive a letter from them stating they are not paying you, then we will pay the entire amount."

"Does this make *any* sense to you?" Darby asked, with eyes closed slowly shaking her head.

"Ms. Bradshaw, if you want your pay, you have two choices. Fill out the form or call them and get us a letter. I cannot do anything more to help you."

Darby was beyond frustrated by the time they ended the call, but she began a search for a phone number to speak to a person in the California disability system to explain her status and get that letter.

An hour later, after multiple calls and never actually speaking to a real person, Darby gave up. Instead, she found an email address for the governor of California. She decided to write him a letter.

Dear Governor, I am a Global pilot, and the company forced me out on a medical issue because I gave them a safety report. I am on a medical hold status awaiting the contractual obligation to return, and I qualify for disability under our contract, but I do not have a disability. My company said California will pay half of what is owed, but your paperwork is forcing me to state I have a disability. I will not falsify documents. The company will accept a letter saying my disability is denied. The problem is, I cannot find a real person to speak with. Would you please provide me a telephone number to a live person, or provide someone my number to call me? Or simply request someone to write a letter and deny my disability?

Darby added her phone number and snail mail address and pressed send. Then she called the people at the Global Pilot Supplemental Insurance office.

That call went through immediately and Darby provided her employee number and password. Then she was forwarded to her representative. She introduced herself, and explained what is happening.

"Can you please tell me why I was denied my supplemental insurance?"

"Because you don't have a disability."

"I know I don't have one, but I'm not allowed to fly because the company says I do," Darby said. "The company is paying my disability, why was this denied?"

"I'm not sure how I can make this any clearer," she said. "I told you because you don't have a disability."

"I know that," Darby said again. "Then why aren't I flying?"

"You have to ask the company."

"No, I don't. I know it's because *they* say I have a disability," Darby said. "What did they tell you?"

"Well, I'm not exactly sure," the woman said. "But if you want to fill out the paperwork acknowledging you have a disability then we could get this going and a payment to you ASAP."

There was no way in hell Darby would admit to having a disability when she did not have one. She had filled out this paperwork exactly like she did for the company disability. This did not make sense. Furthermore, if she acknowledged a disability, then they could use that to keep her from flying.

"I'm not falsifying records," Darby said. "But I paid into this as a supplemental insurance in the event I couldn't fly. I can't fly because of a medical hold status."

"The company is keeping you from flight status due to a medical reason," the woman said. "But you're not acknowledging that here. Therefore, we can't pay you."

"Yes, you could," Darby snapped. "I am being prevented from flying and the FAA is evaluating my medical certificate. I filled out the paperwork exactly the same. How can the company pay me, but not you?"

"I don't speak for the company," she said. "I know this is frustrating for you, but I am sure you will get it sorted out. However, there is nothing we can do to help you."

"I know pilots who had a medical, were perfectly fine, and they were paid their GPSI."

"But those pilots began with an issue, and then due to FAA delay we had to wait for their medical to be reissued."

"What's the difference? I started out being bipolar, found out that I was not, and now I'm waiting for *my* medical issuance to go through."

"You didn't start with a real medical issue."

Was she fucking kidding? She ended the call before she said something she would regret. When this went to court, she'd have to get this woman on the stand and testify in support of a fake diagnosis. She looked at her paycheck. It would not cover half her mortgage and she had attorney bills to pay.

CHAPTER 59

THERE WAS NO way Darby could survive on a quarter of her paycheck. She'd all but wiped out her bank account sending the retainer to her new attorney after her first one had drained it. If they went to court, she wasn't sure what she would do for funds. The thought of selling her house broke her heart. Besides, that would only be a delay of the inevitable. She didn't have enough equity to make a long-term difference.

Then inspiration struck. Darby pressed speed dial on her phone and it rang directly to Deloris Brooks' private line.

"How are you doing, sweetheart?" her publisher asked, genuinely concerned.

"Oh, I've had better days," Darby said. "Good news is I have a new attorney who is awesome. I learned more from him in one phone call than I learned in the previous year. I think we're going to beat this in court. However, with any luck… we won't have to go to court."

"Are you flying, yet?"

"No, we're waiting for Global's doctor and the Mayo Clinic to agree on a neutral doctor to break the tie."

"Is there any way they could buy off the next doctor to give you another bad diagnosis?" Deloris asked.

"I never thought they could do this in the first place," Darby said. "But they did. Nothing surprises me anymore. So... yeah, maybe."

"I'll be praying for you, darling," she said.

"Do you have any word on *Flight For Sanity*?" Darby asked.

"You know, I think it's incredible," Deloris said. "I just haven't heard where it stands."

"I hate to ask, but I need your help. Do you think I could get an advance on it, or on the safety book, or both?" Darby asked. "They're playing with my paycheck and it's less than peanuts."

"I am so sorry, honey," Deloris said, followed by a heavy sigh. "When you sent me the *Normalization of Deviance* chapters, I knew we had a best seller in the making. *Flight For Sanity* was incredible, and would roll off the shelves. I suspected you could use the advancement back then, so I took it upon myself and submitted the request. They said no."

Tears filled Darby's eyes, in part at Deloris' effort without having been asked. "I appreciate you asking."

"Can I give you a personal loan?" Deloris asked.

"You are too kind," Darby said, running a finger under her eye. "I'll figure this out. If I end up on the street, I'll call."

"Now there's a book—from pilot to homeless."

"Well, most pilots feel homeless," Darby said with a chuckle.

"Hang in there, sweetheart."

Darby wondered where that saying—*hang in there*—came from. She also wondered how long a person actually had to hang in there, before they wanted to kick the chair out. She said goodbye to Deloris who promised to help push her sanity novel to market as quickly as possible, and Darby promised to contact her as soon as she finished the *Normalization of Deviance* book.

She had more motivation than ever to get it finished.

CHAPTER 60

S OMETIMES SURPRISES CAME in small packages, but this
one came in an envelope from the governor of California.
Darby carried her mail into her house and tossed all the bills onto
the kitchen table. The love letter from the governor she carried
upstairs. Finally, she had made progress and hopefully this would
stop the bleeding.

She piled pillows against the headboard, kicked off her shoes, and
sat on her bed with legs extended. The envelope was legal size, but
thick. She kissed it and breathed deep. Hoping to find some answers
inside, she opened the letter.

"What the hell?" Darby said, and then began to laugh. That
statement had rapidly become new mantra of her life. The contents
of the envelope were nothing but the exact same application, which
she'd had in her possession to apply for disability. Closing her eyes,
she tipped back her head on the pillow and dropped the letter to the
floor. *What part of her message did he not understand?*

Darby sat up and dropped her feet to the floor, then walked to
her desk. She pulled out the chair and sat. She opened her laptop.

While it came to life, she thought about what she would write. Then she said, "Why not everything?"

She decided to explain about the safety report, the obtrusive psychiatric evaluation, about the Mayo Clinic, and her being covered for disability despite not having one. She would give him each and every detail of what had transpired, and produce the disability application she had filed stating she did not have a problem. She might even give him a copy of the safety report and her AIR 21 filing, as well. Not might, she *would* give him the report.

Her fingers began tapping the keyboard, and two and a half hours later she'd written twelve pages, single spaced. She stood and headed downstairs for something cold to drink, carrying her phone. One last ditch effort, and then she would send the package.

She filled a glass with water, and then dialed Global's payroll department. A nice man connected her to someone who could help with the situation. Then Darby requested a manager. Once the manager was on the line, she explained to the woman everything she had been advised by the other representatives at the beginning of the week. The explanation was unnecessary, as the woman was well aware of Darby's predicament.

"As previously advised, we can only pay you a quarter pay until you get us a letter from California advising us that they are not paying you," the woman said. "I'm not sure how we could be any clearer."

"That's the problem, I can't get ahold of anyone to write that letter," Darby said. "Besides, I'm not living in California, and I am not trained on the plane. I am there on paper only. I don't even believe Global has paid into the state for my disability insurance, either."

"There's absolutely nothing we can do," she said. "I'm sorry."

"Okay, here's the deal," Darby said. "I have just spent a couple hours writing to the governor of California explaining what happened.

Every little detail. I am most certain that the Governor is not opening his own mail, but some clerk. I also think *The National Enquirer* would probably pay that clerk more than a year's salary for a copy of this letter and all the associated documents.

"I will not fill out a form saying I am bipolar and falsify records. Nobody answers their phone in the California disability system," Darby said. "The reality is, it's going to be your choice if you want me to send this letter, with the safety report included. If you want to risk airing Global's dirty laundry to the world, then that will be *your* choice. I simply don't know what else I can do. I also will send a copy of the AIR 21 filing against Global, with a copy of the FAA's notice of violation for exceeding FAR duty time requirements."

"Well… uh, can I call you back?" she asked.

"Sure," Darby said. "I can give you a few minutes."

"It might take me three days because everyone's gone home for the weekend, but I'd like to look into this."

"Okay, then. I'll give you until Tuesday before I send it," Darby said, feeling rather gracious. "Then I will FedEx overnight."

Darby glanced at her watch deciding if she should hit the gym or soak in the hot tub. Then she remembered her laundry. She was starting the dryer when her phone rang. She ran to the kitchen and answered it.

"Ms. Bradshaw?" a woman said.

"Yes?"

"This is Ms. Smith from Global. We just spoke a few minutes ago. I found the right person to talk to, and they said that we can go ahead and give you the full 50% of your paycheck without needing that letter from California. We'll deposit the difference immediately."

CHAPTER 61

FOCUS AND DETERMINATION, combined with confidence her attorney was working diligently to catch up on her case, enabled Darby to finish her book—*Normalization of Deviance*. After one final read, she would submit it and be back in the money when they sold it. With any luck, she would also receive a thumbs up on her novel, too. Unfortunately, there was still no agreement on the neutral doctor. She had contacted her union in hope they would help, but that hadn't gone anywhere. Her side disability insurance from GPSI was a dead end, and the union wouldn't help.

Darby loaded paper and pressed print. She would take a paper copy of her book to the gym and start her editing process. While the manuscript was printing, she logged into her Gmail account. These days she checked her email sometimes six or seven times a day hoping for good news. She said a silent prayer when she saw a letter from Dr. Sorenson at the Mayo Clinic.

All she needed to do was get that neutral. Unfortunately, her editor's words haunted her... 'What if they bought him off?' She opened Sorenson's letter and began to read.

May 4, 2018

Darby, I received a message from ALPO legal regarding your case—I've forwarded this to our legal team and talked with Dr. Andrews. I also communicated with Dr. Williams at FAA as requested.

To clarify—we are not obligated to either ALPO or Global contractually or per any written/verbal agreement to assist in an arbitration process—we provided a multi-professional in-depth independent medical review confirming no psychiatric diagnosis—confirming our opinion that you are fit for duty.

We know that the issue is in review at the Federal Air Surgeon's office per discussions at the recent AsMA meeting in Denver. They were informed that our team had reviewed the 800+ page report from Dr. Wood as part of our evaluation. Given this level of involvement Global and ALPO are in a bind—the formal processes that the FAA uses can be affected by politics—but the NTSB, the appeals body, has little tolerance for personal bias (see Bob Hoover's case) and a much more legalistic approach— meaning that if the FAA does not follow strict guidelines in its assessment it will show up in the NTSB review—the downside being the time and resources devoted to keeping the case alive.

It is clear there are some cultural/corporate concerns involved in this process—and the commercial aviation world is often intolerant of dissent—we can't guarantee that you will be successful addressing non-medical conflicts between you and Global, but we are confident in our findings and are happy to discuss those (given your permission) as needed or to provide further evaluations if necessary.

Relative to using FAA physicians—it is within the FAA's jurisdiction to review medical concerns re: pilot fit to fly

decision making—but they are required to follow the CFRs
(the law) in this process—we have already provided three
very reasonable options for a third review—and have yet to
see any suggestions with similar neutrality and/or expertise,
so we will hold pending our legal team's recommendations.

VR Dr. Sorenson

Darby googled AsMA—Aerospace Medical Association. "My case was at a medical conference," she said in dismay. So much for the contractual obligations of not giving it to the FAA until final resolution, or anyone else. She knew someone from Global had called the FAA, and the reason they'd requested more information. Now it was at a conference. So much for HIPPA laws. Privacy be damned.

Darby had no idea what the Mayo Clinic's legal team would say about all this, but hopefully they would be upset for being challenged, and fight Dr. Wood in their clinic's defense. At least Dr. Williams knew what had transpired. She also knew the doctors at the Mayo Clinic were honest; now she just needed the support of their legal department.

Darby replied.

Dear Dr. Sorenson, I cannot believe that my case found
its way to the Aerospace Medical Association conference. I
appreciate your efforts for speaking to Dr. Williams, and you
are free to discuss my case with anyone you deem appropriate.
I understand why Dr. Wood is not agreeing with your rec-
ommendations, and it falls back on that cultural/corporate
issue you spoke of, which was the heart of my safety report. It's
nice to know the NTSB appeals body has little tolerance for
this behavior. One step at a time. Will be looking forward to
your attorney's response.

Now Darby needed to tell Ms. Brooks her book was done, and get a check.

CHAPTER 62

INVESTING A FEW more days into reading her book to conduct a final edit before she sent it off to her publisher was worth its value in gold. Now it was as good as she could get it. The editors would take it from here. Relief that funds would replenish her bank account soon was a welcome feeling. She had forgotten how hard life was without money. She had been broke learning to fly, but flying had made everything worth it. She realized she should have flown Ray's plane when she'd had the chance.

Darby loaded paper into her printer and changed the ink cartridge, then selected print. Picking up her phone to dial Deloris, it rang before she could press call. Robert Allen flashed across the screen and she answered.

"Darby," Robert said, "I received an email in response to my representing you at the grievance."

"Nice," Darby said. "The union didn't contact me about it."

"The response wasn't from the union, but from Brian Talbot," Robert said. "Brian Talbot and Associates in New York. This guy is a piece of work. Arrogant little shit, and Global retained him."

Darby chuckled at Robert's commentary. "Global hired an outside law firm because you're representing me?"

"Apparently so," he said. "I just forwarded you the letter."

"Looks like ALPO hates you, and the company fears you," Darby said, as she removed pages from the printer to prevent the others from flying across the floor.

"Talbot also cancelled our scheduled dates because of his unavailability. He's playing right into our hands. He also offered three additional dates, as well as an option of four arbitrators."

"But we're supposed to have a strike off," Darby said. "Who did they select?"

Robert read the names of the four arbitrators and the dates Talbot had offered. "I can tell you we don't want Mike, or Jackson."

"The arbitrator schedule was just released," Darby said. "Hang on a sec, and I'll grab it." She sat at her computer, and within seconds found the file. "Here it is. Can you read the names again?"

"Of course," he said, and read them.

"We don't want any of them," Darby said. "The list of their availability was just released a week ago for the next six months. None of these arbitrators had dates available for when he offered. Meaning, he had to have called them in order to make accommodations."

"What is your airline's arbitrator selection process?" Robert asked.

"We have a list of eleven, and we strike off one at a time," Darby said, removing pages from the printer. "Each year it cycles as to who goes first."

"If you're okay with it, I'll draft a letter stating that we do not want any of these arbitrators, and will be standing by to schedule the standard strike off process."

"That would be great," Darby said. "Do you think we should still do the grievance?"

"We'll see," Robert said. "However, we won't go blindly."

"Would it be worthwhile to research cases to determine how the other arbitrators on the list rule?" Darby asked. "To find out who is more favorable towards the pilots?"

"It wouldn't matter," Robert said. "May I share a story with you?"

"Of course." Darby enjoyed their exchanges. He was a wealth of knowledge, and his stories were always of value, especially those worth a good laugh.

"Many years ago, I had a series of three grievances with the same arbitrator," he said. "As it turned out, the first two cases were not as strong as the third. But we won them both. So, now the third arrives and the arbitrator meets me in the hall before the hearing, and apologizes for the loss."

"Before he heard the case?" Darby said. "How's that possible?"

"He put an arm over my shoulder and said, 'You can't win them all. You've already won two, the third is for the company.'"

"Without ever hearing it?" Darby asked, dumbfounded.

"Arbitrators need to keep both sides happy," Robert said. "If they always rule for one side, then the other side could kick them off the list."

"So much for justice," Darby said. "They should just do the right thing."

"That they should. It also makes my job all the more challenging."

They ended the call and Darby sent a text to Deloris—*Book is finished! Printed. Will be shipping FedEx with an email copy leading the way.*

Within minutes the phone rang and Darby answered.

"Darby, we need to talk," Deloris said.

"Of course." But Deloris' tone hit her like she'd swallowed a pile of rocks.

"They've cancelled your contract."

"What?" Darby said, dropping to the edge of her bed. "Who cancelled it?"

"I'm not sure," Deloris said. "I received a memo from corporate that until further advisement we won't be publishing any more of your books."

"What about the rights to my other books?" Darby asked.

"We own them."

"Can I go elsewhere with *Flight For Sanity* and the deviance book?" Darby asked.

"You can," Deloris said. Lowering her voice she added, "Sweetie, I think your company got into the pockets of the biggest publishing houses. I'm not sure if it was the threat of a lawsuit, favors called in, or a promise of advertising dollars, but this is something I've never seen in all the years I've worked here. I'd heard about this type of behavior, but just hadn't seen it. Until now."

"It isn't right," Darby said, fighting tears. Global had taken their actions against her to an all-time low.

"It's not," Deloris said. "Please let me help you."

"No, I'll be fine," Darby said falling back onto the bed. "But thank you."

She said goodbye and then pulled a pillow over her head. She wasn't sure if she would be fine. But those bastards were not going to get away with this. Why the hell were they going to such lengths? She could either roll over to let them nail her, or she could fight.

Pilots never gave up flying regardless of the catastrophic failures or what was thrown at them. They always flew the plane, all the way to the ground.

Darby pulled the pillow from her face and sat up. She could refinance her house instead of selling it, and get a renter. She could self-publish her books. She didn't need a publisher. Hell, she could get a job at Starbucks for insurance. If it was a battle Global wanted, she would put on her gloves and fight.

"To hell with all of them!" she said, throwing her pillow against the wall.

CHAPTER 63

THERE WAS A time when Darby had lived paycheck to paycheck and had eaten Top Ramen to survive. She did it before, and she could do it again. This time she had credit to help her over the hump, and she used her card wisely. Jetstar Publishing was the name of her new company, and for a $135 fee she had obtained a business license. Then after a few hundred more, she'd aligned her company with a distribution source. Darby had just become her own publisher. There was one thing about publishing her own books. Global had no control over her. *Normalization of Deviance* would be the first non-fiction on her list of books, and *Flight For Sanity* the first novel.

She wandered into the kitchen, and began making a sandwich when her phone rang. She had been waiting for Robert's call regarding the arbitrators. If she could say one thing about Robert, he was responsive. She answered his call.

"Are you sitting down?" Robert asked.

"No. I'm actually making a sandwich," she said, holding a knife. "Shall I remove all sharp objects before we talk?"

"Perhaps that might be a good idea."

Darby set the knife down and asked, "What is it?" Her heart sank with his words.

"The OSHA ruling came in. They ruled against you."

"What? But how?" She turned and leaned against the counter.

"This is common," Robert said. "As I told you, I normally take the loss just to push the issue to trial. This won't impact anything. We'll appeal and press forward. The good news is they didn't wait another year for negative results. Especially since your company is fighting the neutral doctor. Court will be an avenue to get you back to work if we can't get that neutral doctor on board."

"But I thought because the FAA found a violation, that this would be a slam dunk."

"No. The AIR 21 is a joint filing with the FAA and OSHA. An FAA violation, or not, is irrelevant as long as you presented your concerns in good faith. If they hadn't found any, that would not have gone against you. However, that violation will help your case in the long run. You were right. You reported a serious violation of federal standards, and Global received a notice of violation for those actions."

"I never wanted it to go to the FAA," Darby said. "I only intended to make this an internal report." She walked across her kitchen, and pulled a chair out from her table, and sat.

"I understand that. Don't feel bad for Global," Robert said. "They did this to themselves. But… an odd event occurred. The investigator's supervisor left me a message yesterday, and said the ruling was coming in. I returned his call this morning, and no answer. Then we got his ruling."

"That's not normal?"

"No," he said. "I can't figure that one out. I attempted to call, but he is non-responsive. This is not an end all. Granted it would have been better to get a win, but that rarely happens. Especially against an airline Global's size."

"So, size does matter?" Darby said, trying to lighten the devastation she felt.

"It does," he said with a chuckle. "The only time I've seen OSHA support a pilot or mechanic on the first go is if they worked for a small operator. When the employee works for one of the big four, OSHA tends to rule in the company's favor."

"Cowards," Darby said.

"Now the fun starts," Robert said. "I already ordered Dr. Wood to retain and protect all his documents, and make duplicates as we would be requesting them in discovery. The form was quite intimidating. I'm sure he squirmed. However, now, the first order of business is to write the appeal. We'll immediately request discovery from the company and Wood.

"You'll eventually have to produce all your emails, notes, and documents with anyone you spoke to regarding your reporting, history, etcetera. They'll be requesting discovery from us and that would be standard. So, if you get started at your convenience, we'll have it ready to go."

"When will you need it?"

"Ahh… probably not for another couple of months. We file first, then we decide who to depose after we review the discovery. Write me a list of all the people you would like as witnesses."

"How much does it cost to do a deposition?" Darby asked.

"You can anticipate about ten thousand dollars a deposition," he said. "That doesn't include if we opt to video them. But it's a good ballpark."

They said their goodbyes. Darby returned to the counter and dumped her sandwich into the garbage can. She'd suddenly lost her appetite. She texted Linda, Kathryn and Jackie—*OSHA ruled against me in the AIR 21*. They had all been so supportive, and she felt as if she had let them down, too. This was something that would surprise them all.

Kathryn was the first to reply—*Dinner my house 5 pm! Who can make it?*

Linda—*What a crooked system! I'm there. I'll bring the wine!*

Jackie—*I'm leaving the baby at home, and bringing tequila. This sucks. Hang in there, Darby!*

Linda—*No. I'll bring tequila. Jackie you bring the limes.*

Darby responded—*Thank you.* She climbed the stairs to her bedroom, pulled back her covers, and climbed into bed. She pulled the covers over her head, hoping when she emerged she would realize this was nothing but a dream, not the nightmare she was living.

CHAPTER 64

DARBY TRANSITIONED FROM being pissed at life to gratitude the minute she walked into Kathryn's house. She had chastised herself for throwing a perfectly good sandwich away because the rumblings of an empty stomach combined with drinking tequila were never a good mixture. However, once she opened the door, moo shu pork and deep fried noodles met her senses, and she smiled.

"I hope you don't mind take-out," Kathryn said, hugging Darby. "I grabbed this on the way home."

"Are you kidding? My favorite," she said, opening a package of fried pork and selecting a piece. She stuffed it into her mouth. She looked at Kathryn and said with a mouthful, "Thank you."

"You're going to get through this," Kathryn said. "No thanks necessary."

Within minutes Jackie and Linda were knocking at the kitchen door, and letting themselves in, both carrying bags.

"Only the good stuff for a time like this," Linda said, handing Darby a bottle of Patron. She set a bottle of wine she'd brought onto the counter, as well.

"Did you write a prescription for that?" Kathryn asked, taking Linda's coat.

"No, but we might need one for what comes after the poison," Linda said. "How are you doing, Darby?"

"Great now," Darby answered, with chopsticks inside the carton of fried noodles. "But maybe we can shift the talk from poison."

Linda placed her hand over her mouth. "Oh my God, I'm sorry."

Darby laughed and hugged her with one arm, holding her chopsticks at bay. "It's quite all right."

Jackie dumped the bag of limes on the counter and said, "I'm starving. But first we have to do at least one shot." Jackie opened a drawer and retrieved a knife.

Darby smiled remembering the last time she and Jackie drank tequila. Then the smile left her eyes. Days later Greg had died. It just shows how fragile life is. Darby set the noodle container on the counter and removed four shot glasses from Kathryn's cupboard. Jackie was busy cutting a lime.

Kathryn grabbed the salt, and Linda poured the shots. Jackie handed out the lime slices. They all licked their hands, sprinkled salt, and then lifted their glasses.

"Who wants to make the toast?" Kathryn asked.

"I will," Darby said, raising her glass. "To good friends. Helping me lick the salt off my wounds."

"To good friends," the others said. They licked the salt, drank their shots, and then each bit a lime.

"This is really good," Jackie said, shaking her head with a contorted look on her face.

"So good, it bites you," Darby said, setting the empty shot glass on the counter. She lifted a stack of plates and placed them onto the kitchen table.

Jackie and Linda moved the Chinese food to the table, and Kathryn poured the wine. She told them that someone had to be responsible, and that more tequila was only available after they ate dinner. That would not be a problem as far as Darby was concerned.

They all filled their plates as Darby shared with them what her attorney had told her about the AIR 21 process, and the option for an appeal.

"So this is not over," Jackie said. "I'm so glad."

"Ah, but there is more," Darby said. "Remember I told you how I couldn't get an advance on my books?"

"They changed their mind?" Linda said. "Thank God."

"Nope. My publisher told me they're cancelling my contract," Darby said stabbing a spring roll. "They even own my previously published books."

"They didn't," Kathryn said, her fork clanking to her plate.

Darby nodded. "They did."

"Global?" Kathryn asked.

Darby nodded again.

"Oh, Darby," Jackie said, "all that work. I'm so sorry."

"It's okay. I'm publishing them anyway," Darby said. "I formed a publishing company today—Jetstar Publishing."

"Can you do that?" Jackie asked.

"I can, and I did," Darby said. "They can try to knock me down, but they won't get away with it. I'm like one of those blow up clowns that gets hit and tips, but doesn't fall over because of sand in my butt. I bounce right back up."

"You're anything but a clown," Linda said. "But I had one of those when I was kid, too. They were fun."

"What happened with your paycheck?" Kathryn asked with concern. "Did that ever get resolved?"

"Kind of, sort of. I got an additional quarter of my paycheck on disability." Darby stuffed a bite of noodles into her mouth. "Can you pass the moo shu pork?"

"I am so sorry," Kathryn said, handing her the carton. "I've been so busy at work, I haven't been here for you."

"Are you kidding?" Darby said, adding to her plate. "You have been here for me. You all have. I know you all are here whenever I need you. It's just... I honestly don't know what to do next. I never imagined this could be so out of control, and they just keep playing whack-a-mole with me."

"I'm so sorry," Linda said, patting a napkin to the edge of her lips. She reached for the bottle of wine and added more to her glass and then Darby's.

"Every time my head pops up, they whack me down. The fact they did this in the first place is stupid," Darby said. "I get it. Rich Clark got his panties in a bunch, and his little ego was bruised. So, he spanks me and sends me through the process. But how the hell could they get a doctor to fake a diagnosis?"

"Then they violated your contract," Jackie said. "Giving your information to the FAA was just wrong."

"Exactly. Oh... did I tell you my case was at some aerospace medical conference?"

"What the hell?" Kathryn said. Darby chuckled, as her life-expression was rapidly becoming contagious.

"One of the Mayo doctors told me about it." Darby sipped her wine and then said, "I think they closed the base and sent me to Los Angeles on purpose, so they wouldn't have to pay all my disability. Either that or get me to falsify records with the State of California."

"Do you think they would really go to those lengths?" Kathryn asked, scooping rice onto her plate. "It could be just a coincidence."

"It could be," Darby said. "But I didn't get my Global supplemental insurance either, even though I paid into it."

"That's wrong," Linda said. "Anything you can do to help on that?"

Darby shook her head no, and then sipped her wine. The alcohol was taking hold and she was relaxing. She pushed her food around her plate for a moment and said, "The fact someone tried to drug me is kind of freaky. We all know who it was."

"Who?" Jackie asked, and all eyes turned her way, trying to figure out if she was joking.

"Rich Clark," Darby said, realizing Jackie was serious. "I have no doubt he figured I'd kill myself being so distraught."

"He doesn't know what you're made of, does he?" Linda asked.

Darby shrugged. She was beginning to doubt if she knew what she was made of. "I don't know exactly how to survive this. You know, it's going to cost me about ten grand for each deposition. This could get really expensive by the time it's done."

"Wow," Jackie said.

"I can help you," Linda said.

"Me, too," Kathryn added. Jackie pointed at herself and nodded that she would, as well.

"Thanks, you guys. But you know... I have my house, and I can refinance. I don't really want to sell it. But if I had to, I would."

"You're not selling your house," Kathryn said. "You can refinance it for a chunk of money, then live with me and rent it."

Darby mouthed, "Thank you."

"I just can't believe the OSHA investigator ruled against you," Jackie said.

"I can't either. Did he ever call any of you?" When they each shook their head no, Darby said, "That's what I suspected. I don't think he really was doing an investigation. I thought he was a nerdy little guy who was overwhelmed, but I think that was an act. He knew exactly what he was doing. Nothing. He always intended on ruling for Global."

"Why can't you have your lunch with the CEO?" Linda asked. "He could fix this."

Darby shrugged. She had bought lunch with the CEO in a cancer charity auction, a couple weeks after this had all begun, in hopes he would stop the Section 8. Rich Clark kept denying it. Now, a year and a half later she still did have the lunch that she had bought and paid for.

"Clark said I couldn't meet with him until the AIR 21 was resolved and I'm back to work."

"Technically, the AIR 21 is done if you don't appeal," Linda said. "If he were to meet with you, you could avoid court and he could end this without further expense. I wonder if he knows the Mayo Clinic is in your court. If he knew that he could pull the plug."

"I like the way you think," Darby said. "This is not going to look good for Global if we go to court. I have a medical certificate. The Mayo Clinic cleared me, and they are still keeping me from work. Then we have this safety report that will destroy the public's confidence in Global Air Lines."

"I wonder how much they paid that doctor to make his fake diagnosis," Jackie said. "He should be in jail."

"I'm working on the jail part, too," Darby said. "I have far too many dragons to slay. It's getting exhausting." She stood, and retrieved another bottle of wine. "I just really need to get back to work so I can finance all this fun."

"Any word on that?" Kathryn asked.

"The Mayo Clinic has sent a request to their legal department to see if they can continue on my behalf. Technically they don't have to spend another moment on this. I paid them for an evaluation, and they gave me one." Darby removed the foil from the lid as she continued. "They found three doctors who would be excellent evaluators, but they didn't have to. I didn't pay them to spend that time, they were doing it on their own because they cared. They definitely don't have to debate Dr. Wood, and he's being a prick," she said as she screwed the opener into the cork.

"Is this all worth it?" Jackie asked.

"I keep asking myself that…" she began, when Kathryn's phone rang at the same time Darby's phone dinged with a text. Jackie's buzzed, and then so did Linda's. "Oh God," Darby said reading her text, and ran to Kathryn's living room.

CHAPTER 65

GLUED TO THE television for the better part of two hours, the chinese food was gone. They had finished two bottles of wine and were now sipping tequila, as the horrific details continued to unfold on Breaking News.

Darby had been in this exact spot with her friends watching another accident unfold on television not so long ago. But that had been so much closer to home, in so many ways. That one had been at SeaTac with a man they had all loved. This accident was on the other side of the world.

Tiger Air, operating a Boeing 737 Max, had crashed thirteen minutes after takeoff, killing all 189 passengers and crew. The reporter said, "This is the first major accident involving the new Boeing 737 MAX series aircraft, introduced in 2017, and the deadliest involving a 737 ever."

Remains of the aircraft floated in the ocean beyond the cameras, as rescue boats made a futile attempt to find survivors. Darby knew that none would ever be found.

Kathryn had been on the phone with John for over ninety minutes. He, in turn, had been feeding her details of the accident which were not yet released to the public. Finally, she and John said their goodbyes and Kathryn promised to take good care of

Jackie. John promised if he heard any additional information he would call. Kathryn lowered the volume on the television and set the remote on the coffee table.

"It appears there was a failure with the pitot static system that triggered a component that induced a runaway stabilizer," Kathryn said. "It's too early to tell the extent of the mechanical problem, but the pilots couldn't handle it." She hesitated, and then said directly to Darby, "Or... they didn't know what to do."

"Lack of training," Darby said, shifting her eyes back to the television, knowing their research had all but predicted this would happen. Airlines worldwide were short-circuiting training because they did not want to spend the money. Pilots were not being given the tools they needed to do their jobs. But it was always more than one thing, and Darby's research identified a problem far deeper than training. It struck the core of aviation safety.

"It's more than that," Kathryn said, and all eyes turned from the television toward her. "Apparently, they'd had a similar problem the day prior on this airplane. But a pilot in the jump seat told them to cut the stabilizer switches, and after doing so, the pilots were able to control the plane without issue."

"Then why wasn't the plane fixed?" Jackie asked.

"They not only didn't fix it," Kathryn said, "it turns out there were about thirty pages in the logbook that have gone missing. A history of problems, that will remain hidden. It also appears that the broken part in question came from an unknown source. Nobody knows the origin. The paperwork is simply a mess."

"A knock-off part?" Linda asked, and Kathryn nodded.

Darby reached for the bottle on the coffee table and added more tequila to her empty glass. "It's all about lack of safety culture. It's about shitty training, and non-reporting, and documenting, and maintenance, and doing the friggin' right thing." She fought emotion. "It's the whole point of SMS and nobody gives a shit."

"It's everything you identified in your research," Kathryn said, taking Darby's glass and sipping her drink. "It's everything you wrote about in your safety report."

"Safety culture," Darby said. "*Everything* has to do with safety culture. The FAA oversight. Manufacturing the parts. How the pilots are trained. This is why we're supposed to have SMS… so this shit doesn't happen." Darby extended her hand toward the television.

The room became quiet. They were all remembering and reliving the accidents that tore their worlds apart. Sadness filled the room, but Darby was pissed. She did not want to be sad. She did not want to cry. She wanted to get mad and fight this bullshit.

"This is ridiculous because those people didn't have to die." Darby stood and wobbled, steadying herself with the back of the couch. The alcohol combined with the year-and-a-half of hell she'd gone through, and the fight she was in to get her job back and simply to survive, was driving that anger. She wanted to kick ass, or kick someone's ass.

"If Global thinks they are going to blackball my book so they can hide problems like this, or silence me by paying some quack to say I'm crazy, I'll show 'em crazy." She sat back on the couch, and sunk in.

Kathryn reached over and squeezed Darby's hand. "I'm with you on this one." Darby returned the squeeze, and Linda and Jackie nodded in agreement.

The room was beginning to spin, but Darby lifted her glass and stared into the gold liquid. She then looked over to Jackie and said, "The answer is yes."

"To what?" Jackie asked.

"Yes. It is all worth it, even if they fucking bury me."

CHAPTER 66

THANK GOD FOR *Uber*, Darby thought. Kathryn had offered for her to spend the night but Darby wanted to wake up in her own bed. She really didn't know why, but home felt like the right place to be after a drunk night surrounded by death. She gave the driver her phone to tip himself and to give himself stars. He returned it and then she stumbled toward her front door.

Tripping on steps, she fell sideways and landed in the garden. "Shit," she said. She stood and brushed off her butt, then closed one eye and made her way directly toward the house. It took a few tries to get the key into the hole with her world spinning, but she finally succeeded and opened the door.

Stumbling into the house, she dropped her purse and keys onto the floor, and made her way to the living room. She sat on the bottom stair and looked up. The room spun. If she could only make it, she would find her bed. Closing her eyes for a moment, she decided crawling might be the better option. She opened her eyes. On hands and knees, one step at a time, she began working her way towards the top of the staircase.

She wondered what the hell that beeping was, but her only goal was to get to the top. Just as she made the landing, her stomach rolled and her hand covered her mouth. She scrambled to her feet and lunged toward her bathroom, hitting the doorframe along the way just as her alarm went off.

Darby bent over the toilet bowl and heaved the reminders of the night, her alarm screaming in the distance. Unfortunately, her phone was in her purse and she had left it downstairs someplace.

This wasn't the first time Darby had set off her alarm, but it was the first time she didn't answer the call. Hopefully they would call Kathryn, and she would explain Darby's drunkenness and the high probability that it was she breaking into her own house.

In what felt like forever, the alarm finally silenced and Darby looked up. Flashing lights from outside her window identified she had company.

"Knock, knock," a voice said, and Darby waved her hand without looking, as she knelt before the bowl. "You okay?" he asked.

She wasn't sure how to answer that. She really wasn't okay, but she was better than she had been before she had a wine and tequila combo. She gave a thumbs up.

"I talked to your friend, Kathryn Jacobs. She said you might not be feeling too well. Is there anything I can do for you?"

"Turn off my alarm?" she said.

"Already taken care of."

Darby turned his direction, trying to bring the man into focus. "Do I know you?"

"You do," he said. "Your purse was on the floor with your door open." He set it onto the bathroom counter. "I think the noise kept the bad guys from stealing it."

"You're that cute cop," Darby said, turning her attention back to the toilet.

He stuck a washcloth under the water and then knelt by Darby and then wiped the side of her face and under her chin. He tucked a strand of hair behind her ear. She closed her eyes, the warmth felt great. He not only was a cute cop, but he was a nice cop, too.

Darby made a grand attempt to stand, but her world spun. "I'm going to rest here for a few minutes," she said, lying on the bathmat. Then she said, "I found it," and closed her eyes.

CHAPTER 67

S HE WASN'T SURE what had awakened her, but Darby opened her eyes and assessed her surroundings. She was in her own bed. Room spinning, she looked around and then closed her eyes. She opened them as quickly as she had closed them, and stared a moment at her jeans. Nicely folded in the chair. Not something she would have done by her own volition. A dead giveaway she had nothing to do with putting herself to bed. There wasn't enough alcohol that could encourage her to fold her jeans into a little package. She lifted the covers and took a peek. She was still wearing her tee-shirt with bra and panties on.

She rolled to her side to check the time, but it was the two Tylenol lying on her nightstand next to a bottle of water that caught her eye. The pills were crying to be eaten, so she popped them into her mouth and downed the entire bottle of water. She flopped back onto her bed and closed her eyes, waiting for the pills to take hold, and she drifted into dreams of the accident.

A noise from downstairs popped her eyes open again. She listened intently. But it was the scent of bacon which brought the smile. *Kathryn.*

Two hours had passed since she'd first glanced at the time. Darby lay there for a moment remembering the night. The crash. The drinking. The Uber. Her alarm. There had been a cop at her house. The cute one. She smiled and then dread filled her heart.

"Oh God," Darby said, pulling the pillow over her face as the pieces of the previous night fell into place. "I am so embarrassed," she mumbled into the pillow. She had two options—pretend she was still sleeping, or go downstairs, eat bacon, and tell Kat about Tom coming to her rescue.

Sucking a deep breath, she threw back the covers and headed to the bathroom to brush her teeth. Once her teeth were shiny clean, and all necessities taken care of, she pulled on her fluffy robe and headed downstairs.

"Kat, you'll never guess what…"

"Good morning," he said, placing bacon on a paper towel covered plate. Then he extended his hand to Darby, "Tom. Alias cute cop."

"I know your name," Darby said with a grin, and took his hand. "But… I was drunk."

"Yes, you were," he said, pulling out a chair for her and helping her into the seat. "How do you like your coffee?"

"Hot cream and a couple stevia," she said. "Have you been here all night?"

"Nope. Tucked you into bed, and left," Tom said, setting the plate of bacon onto the table. "I'm officially off duty now."

"How did you get in?" she asked.

"The first time, I came through an open front door with the alarm blaring," he said placing a cup of cream into the microwave.

"And this morning?" she asked, picking up a piece of bacon.

"If I tell you that, I'd have to kill you," he said, setting her coffee and cream in front of her. "Did I tell you I carry a gun?"

"Nope. I just thought you were happy to see me."

"I am happy to see you're alive," Tom said, opening the oven door with a grin. He pulled on potholders and removed a pan of muffins.

"You baked?" Darby said. *Was this guy for real?* She sipped her coffee, while he dumped the muffins into a bowl.

"Blueberry. Best thing for a hangover." He placed the bowl onto the table, and removed the potholders. He made himself a cup of coffee, and sat across from her.

"Great way to make an impression," Darby said, reaching for a muffin. She peeled back the paper and took a bite. "These are really good."

"I try," he said, reaching for a muffin. "So, what'd you find last night?"

Darby's brow furrowed, trying to figure out what in the heck he was talking about. "Religion while praying to the bowl?" she said.

"When you were making out with the bathroom floor you said, *I found it.*"

"Oh shit!" Darby said. "I think I found the bottle."

"Bottle?" he said.

Darby stared at him for a moment. He had been her savior in her time of need last night. He was an officer of the law, and he made perfect bacon and exceptional muffins. She sighed and then said, "You're pretty good at everything else so far, how good of a listener are you?"

"One of my best talents," he said. Then he grinned. "Make that the second best."

Two hours later Darby and Tom were still sitting at the kitchen table, each on their fourth cup of coffee. They had finished half the muffins and all the bacon. Darby had told him everything, from her report to her being pulled to the bipolar diagnosis, and the break-in to steal the wine. She told him about Rich Clark. Tom had offered to put Clark in jail next time he came to Seattle. Then she told him about the crash.

"So, you're crazy?" Tom said. "I knew there was something I liked about you."

"That's all you got out of that?" she said, and tossed a muffin wrapper at him. "I think that bottle up there was a prescription for the same drug they put in my wine. The question now is, do you want to do your police shit, or should I have John deal with it?"

"This is John's baby. He's keeping this quiet for a reason, and that's good enough for me," he said. "As far as my department knows, I don't know anything about this."

"Okay. I'll call him," Darby said. Tom had integrity over ego, something that was rare.

"I would, however, like to offer my services," Tom said. "You could use a bodyguard."

"Oh yeah?" she said tucking a strand of hair behind her ear. "You want to guard my body?"

He grinned. "It would be my pleasure."

Chapter 68

BILL WALKED INTO the room, and the television was still airing the Tiger Air accident. He had watched it for an hour, earlier in the morning, and nothing new was being broadcast. Being an outsider looking in gave him a different perspective than when he had a part in the crash. Not nearly as gratifying. But interesting all the same.

He glanced around the room and spotted Drake leaning against the back wall with his arms folded. He headed that way. The smirk across Drake's face and the glint in his eyes indicated that he took great pleasure in this event, more so than Bill's fascination.

"You were right," Drake said as Bill approached.

"About what?" Bill asked, as he, too, took position against the wall. He assessed the room. Never a moment went by when he was not on guard, even with Drake's alliance and protection.

"Runaway stabilizer," Drake said. "Looks like it was more than they could handle."

"This was a bit more than a runaway stab," Bill said. "The MCAS system triggered because of a failed system."

"Parts. You can never depend on them to work when you need them to," Drake said with his smirk, shifting to a Cheshire cat grin.

"You did this?" Bill asked, with a nod to the television. A response he would have expected was—what's an MCAS?

Drake shrugged. "Looks like incompetent pilots to me. We may need to replace them with automation."

"This was due to faulty equipment." Bill folded his arms, and said, "Looks like an automation problem to me."

"Perhaps, but if pilots can't handle their equipment, then why do we need them?"

"This was an isolated case," Bill said.

"Don't count on it," Drake said returning his attention to the television.

CHAPTER 69

NORMALIZATION OF DEVIANCE, A Threat to Aviation Safety. Darby leaned back in her chair and assessed the cover of her book. *Normalization of Deviance* was a term explaining why an organization's culture and associated behavior violated FAA requirements and encouraged pilots to violate their own policies. It also explained how management knew pilots had insufficient knowledge, lacked understanding of their aircraft, and were losing manual flight skills, yet were doing nothing to solve the problem. This was nothing but gambling on passengers' lives.

Maybe this was why managers at Global thought it was okay to assist Rich Clark in nailing her because she'd given him an internal safety report. It was hard to imagine anyone retaliating against someone offering suggestions for safety.

As it turns out, experts say employers who retaliate against others don't recognize their behavior as deviant because the behavior has become a normal occurrence within the organization. Thus, the term *Normalization of Deviance*. That rationale was a bunch of bullshit. These guys knew they were doing something wrong, and they simply didn't care. Perhaps abhorrent behavior was the new norm.

Initially, experts had attributed the deviant behavior to pilots who were not following standard operating procedures, or SOPs as they called them. This behavior subsequently became the norm for the pilots. She actually remembered when it was okay to break the rules and push the envelope. No harm no foul. Plane pushing was the norm. It was actually expected. If you didn't make it work, you were on their shit list.

Now was a new time and a new world, and SOPs were the key to safety. Unfortunately, the results of her research identified the deviant behavior as having shifted to within the organizational structure with management, more so than within the flight deck… a clear marker identifying a poor safety culture.

Darby began scrolling through her photos to see which would be the most appropriate for the cover. She had not realized how fun this process was until she had to do it herself. There were also professional editors she could employ. Figuring out how to pay for them was another story, but she would make it work.

The ding on her phone pulled her attention. She could not help but smile, thinking of Tom. That's when she read the message—*Can you talk?* Her smile faded as she stared at the name. Reluctantly she typed—*Yes.* But her finger hesitated over the button to send. She sighed and then finally pressed the button.

Within a couple minutes the phone rang.

"Hey," she said. "What's up?"

"Sorry I haven't called you sooner," Ray said. "I've been hiding since I allegedly tried to kill you."

"You talked to John."

"I did. He asked me to not talk to anyone about this, so I haven't," he said. "That's why I hadn't called you back."

"Not even Jane?" Darby asked. When he didn't respond, she asked, "How's that going?"

"Pretty good," Ray said. "But I don't really want to talk about her."

"That's fair." Darby pushed back from her desk and walked downstairs. She really didn't want to talk about Ray's new girlfriend either. But he certainly traveled quickly from wanting to marry her to a serious relationship with someone else a few months later. Not only that, she had a two-year-old, as well. An instant family. She couldn't help that it bugged her just a little bit.

"Do you think Clark sent the wine?" Ray asked.

"I have no doubt," Darby said. "But we can't prove it."

"John indicated there was an ongoing investigation, so if I were you, I wouldn't give up hope finding out who did it."

"I'm not. They're just screwing with me big time. They actually got my publisher to dump me," Darby said, opening her fridge. She removed a bottle of water and twisted off the top.

"Rat bastards," Ray said. "Did you ever have your lunch with Croft?"

"Nope. Clark won't let me," Darby said, and then sipped her water. "Linda recommended I ignore Clark and write to Walt directly. I might just do that."

"I wouldn't if I were you," Ray said. "You're already on Clark's shit list."

"What's he going to do... try and kill me?" Darby said rolling her eyes. "He tried that, and it didn't work." *Besides*, Darby thought, *I have a bodyguard.*

"Good point," Ray said. "But I wouldn't kick that hornet's nest."

Yeah. Yeah, Darby thought as she stepped onto her front porch. She sat on the step and leaned against a post. The sun felt warm on her face. She thought about Ray's words. His warnings. They were more of the same since the last time they had spoken. He had to know more than he was letting on.

"You still there?" Ray asked.

"Yep. Just thinking about the hornets," Darby said.

"You know what I mean. Rich Clark's an asshole."

"I'm not going to argue with you on that."

"Okay. Well…" Ray began.

"Why are you calling me?" Darby finally asked when he grew quiet.

"I just wanted to tell you I'm sorry this happened. Everyone is talking about it on the line, and rumors are flying. You got screwed by our union, but I didn't really know how bad. I'm in the best job I've ever had, and it's really all because of you."

"I'm glad you're liking it," Darby said, just as a police car drove by. She raised her bottle toward the car with a wave, and Tom responded with a spurt of his siren, then continued on.

"I don't think you should go to that third evaluation," Ray said.

"Why not? It's my ticket to return to work."

"That neutral doctor is going to sink you."

"How do you know?"

"It's pretty obvious," Ray said. "You can't trust any of them."

"There aren't too many people I can trust."

"Not fair," he said.

The police car drove down the street from the other direction and stopped in front of her house on the opposite side of the street. Darby stood and then walked to the edge of the street, smiling at Tom. "You're right about that. But sometimes life sucks," she said.

"I care about you, Darby," Ray said. "I just wanted to tell you that if you get that third evaluation, you'll be done."

"I've got my AIR 21 case," Darby said. "I've got a new attorney. I'll get my job back with that."

"Maybe. It won't happen for another three or four years. Then if you win, they'll appeal. That could take years. You'll be over sixty-five before you get your job back. It will be too late. That's if you can afford to go to court without working."

"Aren't you the confidence builder," she said. "All the more reason I need to work through the process."

"If they find you unfit by two doctors, you're done. One more year at half-pay and that's dried up. If that third evaluation comes in negative, you might end up losing your AIR 21 case, too," Ray said. "At least if you don't get another negative evaluation, and you win your AIR 21 case, you'll end up getting reimbursed."

"I'd never fly again if I don't proceed," Darby said flatly. "Besides, I'm not going to get a negative evaluation."

"For God sakes, Dr. Wood gave you a bipolar diagnosis," Ray said. "Don't think that the neutral will be any different."

Darby walked across street and stood within a couple feet of the police car. Tom was smiling. His elbow hanging out the window as he waited patiently for her to end the call. It was amazing how supportive and understanding this stranger sitting in front of her was, but the man who'd wanted to marry her was clueless.

"I've got to go," Darby said. "But thanks for the warning."

She stuck her phone into her pocket and tried to keep her cool exterior as she approached the car to talk to Tom. But Ray's words had unraveled her confidence and ignited the fear buried deep inside.

What if Ray was right? What if that examination was the beginning of her end? At least she didn't have to worry about it now, because, so far, the Mayo was not agreeing on any of the doctors Wood had selected. Besides, if the Mayo was involved, how could they possibly buy a bad-guy neutral doctor? Ray had to be wrong on this one.

CHAPTER 70

O N HOLD WITH the Mayo Clinic, Darby paced her kitchen waiting for Dr. Sorenson to come on the line. This entire process had been taking over her life. Now she knew why there were so few pilots who came forward to report safety. They simply wouldn't survive the process. And she hadn't even begun the court process, yet. She hoped Robert was right and Global would settle.

At the very beginning, her union attorney had advised her to take a non-paid leave of absence because he'd known what was in store. Losing a flying job at Global might have been less painful than fighting for a career when the odds were stacked against her. Darby pulled out a chair and sat at her kitchen table.

Despite Ray's concern that she shouldn't go to the neutral doctor, Darby understood the legality of the process. As long as the Mayo was willing to work with Dr. Wood, she wasn't violating the contract and they could take all the time they needed.

She was afraid, however, if the Mayo wasn't willing to continue to work with Wood that they would make her start the process all over again. Since the union wasn't helping, they could allow Clark's threat of termination to take hold, and there would be nothing she could do.

"Darby? This is doctor Sorenson."

"How did your talk with your legal department go?" Darby asked, jumping to the chase without the niceties.

"I'm sorry. They don't want me to engage in this any longer," he said. "Legal advised me to stand down. The problem is that your company reached out to the FAA, who challenged us at the conference. Legal believes it's in the hands of the FAA now, as they are the controlling agency. We don't have authority over their decisions."

"So, technically the FAA makes the decision?" Darby asked.

"Yes. Legal confirms that Global abdicated their rights to the contract by reaching out to the FAA. In doing so, they have given this decision directly to the FAA, therefore making the agency the neutral doctor."

"That sounds logical," Darby said. "I'm just surprised they didn't accept your clinic's panel of experts."

"Honestly, we thought they would accept our decision," he said. "But now this has been taken out of our hands. The FAA will decide."

"I understand," Darby said. She didn't know what else to say. She also didn't know what to do. She understood his perspective and it was completely rational, logical, and made nothing but sense. But they were dealing with Global.

"We were employed to give you a diagnosis and we did. We spent many hours trying to work with Dr. Wood to no avail. We simply cannot expend any more resources toward this."

"I understand," Darby said. She sighed. "I guess my next step is to wait until the FAA clears me and we'll see what we can do with that. I really do appreciate all you have done on my behalf."

"No thanks are necessary. We were just doing our job," he said. "Don't give up on this. You're a strong young lady, and this setback is not permanent. I believe justice will prevail. It may take a little time. But as I stated in my previous email, the NTSB does not look highly on politics."

Unfortunately in politics, anyone and anything could be bought.

Chapter 71

GLOBAL'S LABOR RELATIONS attorney Joe Wolfe walked out of his meeting with corporate attorney Martha Jones and attorney Brian Talbot. Jones and Talbot stayed behind, and he headed directly to Rich Clark's office. Despite the options they'd discussed during that meeting, he had an idea of his own that might just work.

Dr. Wood had forwarded him the Mayo Clinic's response stating they were no longer involved in the Bradshaw case. Wolfe hadn't been quite sure what they could do with that. This had never happened before, and there were no provisions in the contract. He decided a discussion with Jones and Talbot was necessary. He didn't really need their help. But if this fell apart, he would be damned if they would point a finger at him. Diffusing liability was never a bad strategy. Together they formulated options. Now he had to present them to Rich Clark.

Wolfe decided to take the stairs instead of waiting for the elevator. He opened the door and began a slow climb, nibbling on a frayed nail as he did. He formulated his thoughts along the way.

He reached the third floor, and entered the lobby. Catching his breath, he stood up straighter to fake the confidence he didn't feel, and walked towards Clark's office. Rich Clark was an asshole. Most of Wolfe's job was cleaning up Clark's mistakes. At least they paid him well, but Clark could show him some respect. He never knew what mood to expect when entering his office.

"May I speak to Rich?" Wolfe asked Clark's secretary.

"Is he expecting you?"

"I believe so."

It irritated him to be asked that question, but then again, she was only showing Clark the respect she thought he deserved. Maybe she treated him with respect because her job depended upon it. On the other hand, Clark could be screwing her, too. He sighed. If Clark would keep his dick in his pants, his job would be so much easier.

She picked up her phone, spoke a few words into the receiver and placed the phone on the cradle. "He'll see you now."

Wolfe walked into the office and closed the door.

"Joe, thanks for coming," Clark said, leaning back in his chair. "What's the status?"

"Mayo is backing out."

"What?" he said, with a mixture of shock and surprise, sitting forward. "Why?"

"The Mayo doctors were approached by the FAA at some medical conference, and now they believe this is out of their hands, and they won't participate in the selection process."

"What does the legal team think?" he asked, ignoring the fact that Wolfe was on that team making the decisions.

"We believe this could cause problems if not handled correctly," Wolfe said. "There is nothing in the contract identifying how to move forward under these circumstances. The questions are—do we force her through an entire new process advising her that the Mayo Clinic evaluation is no longer good? Do we allow Wood to pick the neutral doctor? Or should we let her sit in limbo, never to return?"

"Four. Fire her ass for not following the contract," Clark said.

"Not legally admissible," he said. "This is not in her control."

"You're the fucking contract expert," Clark snapped. "What do you think we should do?"

"That I am," he said, pulling up a chair and taking a seat. "But it was you who wanted the FAA to hear about this. This situation is Global induced, and now we have to mitigate the damages."

"Does Bradshaw know who contacted the FAA?"

"I'm sure she has a good idea."

"I'm equally sure it was Dr. Wood," Clark said never breaking eye contact. "We have no control over him. Right?"

"We can play it that way if you want. On another note, Talbot has been writing letters on behalf of Dr. Wood. Unfortunately, I think he's aggravated Dr. Sorenson."

Clark leaned back once again, and crossed his legs. Then he asked, "How do we get rid of her?"

"Legally, we get her that third evaluation and make sure the doctor agrees with Dr. Wood."

"If Mayo is out, how do we conduct the selection process?"

"We send Darby a letter and explain to her that since her doctor is no longer available, she can continue with the process and she can select one of Dr. Wood's options. If she chooses not to exercise that option, then she gives up her rights under the Section 8 process."

"Will the union support us?" Clark asked.

"They will. But we have a bit of a problem," Wolfe said, standing. "She's employed Robert Allen as her attorney in the AIR 21 case, and he's representing her in the grievance process, as well."

"God damn fucking shit!" Clark yelled. "What the hell?"

"My thoughts exactly." Wolfe sighed. "You wanted a sparring match with Darby, now you have one. She has employed one of the sharpest legal minds as her wingman, and none of this will be easy going forward. He won't allow *any* violation of the contract."

"Send a letter and give her the option to select the neutral from Wood's list, or go back and get another fucking evaluation."

"Consider it done," Wolfe said. He stuck his hands into his pockets and said, "But... I've read Sorenson's correspondence with Dr. Wood. It appears he's taken a personal interest. More so than just doing his job. It looks like he actually cares about Bradshaw. He's been writing fairly persuasive letters trying to get Wood to listen to reason on her behalf. He's also not backing out willingly. He's backing out because his legal team ordered him to do so."

"You're telling me this why?" Clark asked.

"I think our response to Sorenson, if written properly, might get him back on board."

"How so?" Clark asked.

"Tell him Bradshaw is losing her career because of him," Wolfe said. "Make him feel responsible."

"Would that give him the push to go with Dr. Wood's selection?" Clark asked.

"Guilt is powerful. It very well could," Wolfe said. He headed toward the door and hesitated. "We don't actually need Wood's current selections. As long as we can get Sorenson to pick any private practice doctor versus the institutions he's been proffering, then we can control the outcome."

Chapter 72

RICH CLARK IS evil and Wyatt has no balls. Darby grinned, not sure if she should scan that note into the files, but then again why not? The grins were far and few between these days. Gathering information was a pain in the ass. Most of her emails were communications with the company, so they already had them. She had no idea why she had to give them documents they already possessed. Unless it was a trap if she forgot to give them something.

There were more written notes than emails, and scanning them one at a time was a tedious process. She was putting all her emails into one file and then scanning other notes into the same file. Then she could provide it all to Robert who would send it to the bad guy attorneys when the time was right.

Darby had set up a make-shift office in the middle of her living room so she was closer to the kitchen, and she could watch movies while she scanned and searched documents. She had finally caught up on *House of Cards*. Whoever wrote that script must have gone to the same school of business ethics as Global management. Or perhaps there was simply deviant behavior everywhere, even in the government. Which meant, getting a fair shake at trial might not be in her future. Global was a powerful beast.

Dr. Marsh had asked her to choose one of Dr. Wood's selections and she'd refused. She told them she would go to one of the Mayo's selections. He refused. They were no closer than they were when this started. Marsh told her she would have to get another medical evaluation. She said she would hire a doctor to work with Wood in selecting a neutral doctor, but there was no reason she had to take another evaluation. They were at a standoff.

Robert hadn't filed the appeal yet, but Darby was getting everything in order, ready for when he did. She did not want to cause any delay. This process was a time suck, and a drain, but at least it kept her busy while she waited to return to flying.

She liked her new attorney. He kept her informed, allowed her to express her opinion, and encouraged discussions. He educated her on the process, and allowed her to be part of it. What she didn't know, he taught her. They were turning into a team, and she trusted him implicitly. He also was a quick study on SMS, and the legality of safety culture.

Her books were both in the hands of an editor. Ray had texted her that Wyatt had retired. Tom... well, that was an interesting story. She was keeping him at bay, simply because she could not afford another heartbreak.

Darby was sitting in the middle of her floor with papers everywhere when her cell phone rang. She could hear it, but it was nowhere in sight. She lifted a stack, but no phone. Then she stood, closed her eyes, and listened for the ring. She darted for the couch and lifted a pillow. She answered.

"Darby, this is Dr. Sorenson."

"Hey," Darby said. "What a nice surprise."

"I found you a neutral doctor."

"What? How?" Darby said. "I thought you weren't allowed to be involved."

"I'm not allowed to spend any more time on this. But I was thinking about your predicament, and was sitting at my desk between appointments and perused a list of doctors in the military. I recognized a name that fit all of Wood's requirements. Dr. Stuart Hanover. I had a minute, so I gave him a call. He's still in the military, but he's conducting private practice evaluations on the side, one or two days a month. He said he'd be willing to take your case."

"Really?" Darby said, simply dumbfounded. "What about Dr. Wood?"

"That's the thing. Wood agreed. He was one hundred percent onboard with the choice."

"That's concerning," Darby said, a chill taking over her body.

"If I didn't know Hanover, I'd think that, too," Sorenson said. "But he's a good guy."

"I don't know what to say. But thank you."

"Thank me by getting your job back," Dr. Sorenson said. "I tentatively booked you for June 25th."

Darby thanked him again, and he promised to send her the contact information. They ended the call, and she dropped onto the couch. She had an appointment in less than a week.

This felt like she was being invited into a lion's den for dinner. Was she the dinner or the guest? This is what she wanted, but why the heck did Wood agree with Sorenson's selection? Maybe Ray was right, and they were setting her up. Maybe Dr. Sorenson didn't have current information on Hanover. Hell, maybe Hanover and Wood were long lost lovers. Something didn't feel right.

Darby dialed her attorney. "Robert, they selected a neutral doctor."

"That's great news," he said.

Darby explained what had happened, and how Sorenson had taken it upon himself to find a doctor. She also told him what Ray had said about them setting her up.

"I'm sure it's just nerves, but I don't know about this," she said.

"You'll be fine," Robert said. "Once you are back on property, they won't have anything to win going forward. Now, they are fighting to keep you out. If you get back, they'll be more apt to settle the case."

"That makes sense," Darby said. "But why the hell did Wood agree?"

"I'm not sure. Perhaps he realized this is going to become a public nightmare for him, as well," Robert said. "But I would trust Dr. Sorenson's opinion regarding this doctor. Besides, you have to follow the contractual requirements. Even though they used this section as retaliation, you still have to do your part in the process. We'll settle the rest in court."

Chapter 73

JOE WOLFE'S LEG bounced under the table as he waited for Dr. Wood to answer the phone. Dr. Marsh sat to his right, finishing his second cup of coffee. Attorney Talbot sat across the table from them, biting into a pastry. Martha Jones, the corporate attorney, sat at the end of the table scribbling something on a notepad. The morning meeting had lasted a little over an hour, and now it was time to bring Wood into the fold.

"Hello," Dr. Wood said, when he finally answered.

"Ken, thanks for joining us," Wolfe said. "This is Joe Wolfe speaking. We won't keep you long. This meeting is simply to further discuss the email I sent you regarding the neutral examiner."

"Dr. Wood, this is Brian Talbot. Thanks for joining us," he said.

"It's my pleasure," Dr. Wood said.

"We just want to ensure you understand that the decision to select the neutral examiner is yours," Talbot said.

"As I previously advised," Wolfe added, "if you don't feel comfortable with Hanover then we don't have to use him."

"I know Stuart rather well," Dr. Wood said. "We have… uh… a history. He won't contradict my decision, or admonish my report in any manner."

"Can you be certain?" Wolfe asked.

"Absolutely," Dr. Wood said. "But I am a bit concerned with the FAA medical appeals board's involvement."

"We think they'll pull her medical," Wolfe said.

"If the appeals board rules in her favor, then what?" Dr. Wood asked.

"Don't worry about that. We'll cross that bridge if it comes to that," Dr. Marsh said. "But I doubt they will go against you."

"Legally it won't matter," Wolfe said. "The FAA doesn't have control over our contract."

"Dr. Wood, we would like you to contact Hanover to ensure we won't have a problem with his alliance," Talbot said.

"Consider it done," Dr. Wood said and ended the call.

Chapter 74

NOBODY CHALLENGED HIS decisions. Those conceited bastards at the Mayo Clinic ruled against him. If ALPO would have gotten their act together and sent Bradshaw to Brody, then he wouldn't be in this position. This situation infuriated him on another level. Dr. Wood squeezed the paper in his fist as he unlocked his door.

He stormed into his office and slammed the door. Wood had been paid to do a job, and that's exactly what he would do. He created reports that nobody challenged. He could prove a gnat had a mental health issue if he wanted to. Now he had to deal with an entirely new challenge.

A woman had to have something off balance to think she could be a pilot. In Bradshaw's case, to tout herself as a safety expert, she was nothing short of psychotic, which made his job easier. Global wanted her gone, and they'd paid him a hell of a lot money to make it happen. He would do just that. He threw the paper onto his desk and reached for his phone.

Dr. Wood was a big gun at the FAA, and they had undermined him. Dr. Hanover would turn the tables in his favor. Hanover owed him, and besides, they had a bond from another life. He'd delayed long enough.

Wood dialed the number, and then sat at his desk.

"Stuart, it's Ken Wood."

"Kenneth, good to hear from you," Dr. Hanover said. "It's been too long."

"It has," Wood said, drifting back to early years in their career. "I'm sorry we fell out of touch."

"Hopefully that will change once I'm out of the military," Hanover said.

"I'm sure it will. I'd like to talk to you about that pilot we're sending your way," Wood said. "Bradshaw. She's been a problem at Global for years. She has memory issues, violates social media, exhibits grandiosity, and experiences delusions with faulty thinking such as believing the CEO is her peer."

"I read that in your report."

"Did you read the entire report?" Wood asked, smoothing out the letter on his desk.

"I did," Hanover said. "I also read the Mayo report."

"And?" Wood asked, as he lifted a pencil and circled Michael Banks' name on the letter.

"What's happening here?" Dr. Hanover asked. "I don't see a medical diagnosis."

"This woman is a problem at Global," Wood said. "She may not exhibit your typical bipolar tendencies. However, she's got a history of doing more than a normal person, so that diagnosis was the best fit. That diagnosis also keeps her from the industry overall. That was the strategy we decided upon.

"She can't hold a relationship. She exhibits paranoid tendencies, believing management is out to get her. She writes to the CEO and violates their social media policy."

"Are they?" Hanover asked. "Out to get her?"

"They want her gone. This is far more serious than can be identified on paper. She appears to be causing long term problems within the company. Problems that could harm the future of the airline." Wood tapped his pencil on the letter. "This could impact more than the airline, including the selection of the FAA administrator."

"Long-term harm because she gave them an internal safety report?" Hanover said. "I'm not following."

"If an airline can't control their pilots, those pilots begin running rogue. Not following policies and procedures. They don't do what they're supposed to in the airplane. This becomes a safety issue to all concerned."

"How often are you faced with situations like this?" Hanover asked. "Diagnosing a pilot without medical support."

"A few times a year. Sometimes more," Wood said. "The opportunities are lucrative, but the outcome is always in the interest of public safety. Airline management, the board of directors, and even the FAA understand there are times we have to do what is necessary. Not necessarily what is popular. We are the safeguards of the industry."

"I had no idea," Hanover said.

"You can play it safe and establish a client list, with a nice little practice," Wood said. "Or you can run a solid operation and make a year's salary with one client. The time spent is the time it takes to write the report. Airline evaluations are the most lucrative and efficient means of profiting in this field. More so than anything else. You'll make a lot of money. Depending on the problem, the price increases."

"Pilots are losing their careers who are mentally fine," Hanover said. "I'm trying to get my head wrapped around this."

"I'm sure you faced this in the military."

"Yes, I did. But that simply removed them from the military," Hanover said. "They had an opportunity to leave the service and earn a living in the civilian world. In some cases, it was a better option for them."

"There's nothing different here," Wood said. "These pilots can earn a living in a different field."

"I see your point," Hanover said. "But I thought once I retired from the military that part of my life was over."

"These processes came from the military," Wood said. "They were extremely effective there, and they have been very effective for the airlines."

"We were warned we'd have to make the hard decisions," Hanover said. "I had no idea the extent…"

"Assessing mental health is a duty to the public," Wood said. "This is a duty we can't take lightly."

"I suppose the 911 attacks and the Germanwings crash are poignant examples of terror by aircraft," Hanover said. "We do hold a responsibility to the public."

"That's exactly what I'm talking about," Wood said. He smiled broadly. He had him. "We must trust management to identify those risks, and they reward us well for doing our job. If the airline wants a pilot gone, then we make it happen. No questions asked."

"The FAA knows about this?" Hanover asked. "They're okay with it?"

"They do. We make their job easier." He glanced at the letter on his desk.

"Have you ever faced legal action?" Hanover asked.

"Nobody has successfully challenged this." Wood drew a line threw Banks' name, and said, "It works."

CHAPTER 75

DARBY SIGNED THE return receipt, and thanked the postman for the letter. She carried it inside her house with trepidation. A certified letter from the FAA was nothing short of nerve-wracking. A certified letter determining her diagnosis could be life altering. She tossed it onto the table, and then pulled out a chair and sat. She stared at the envelope.

It really wouldn't matter if she was turned down, because Global wouldn't allow her to fly regardless. She drummed her nails on the table, trying to convince herself that it would be okay. But it really *did* matter how they ruled. If it were in her favor, then she could return to work. There would be no way to keep her from flying. If they cleared her, she was good to go. If they didn't, she would be sucked further into the hole of quicksand.

Her phone rang and she jumped. She smiled at the name, and stuck a headphone into her ear. "Hey, what's up?"

"The stars, the moon, and, well…" Tom replied. "But that's not why I'm calling. I think we should move our relationship to the next level."

Darby laughed. "What level might that be?"

"That level where I suck up my fear and ask you out on a grownup date, and you say yes."

"You want to guard my body *and* date me, too?" she said. "Would that be a conflict of interest?"

"Consider it a twofer," he said. "I've already seen you blow your beets."

"Chinese food," Darby said, correcting him.

"Fair enough," he said. "You might be bipolar. Some think you're crazy. You've got executives trying to kill you. But, none of that matters."

"You certainly know how to sweep a girl off her feet," Darby said, grinning.

"I try. What are you doing right now?"

"Sitting at my kitchen table, staring at an unopened certified letter from the FAA," she said, reaching for it. "I'm trying to get the courage to open it."

"Do you know what's in it?"

"One of two things. They either agree with Dr. Wood or with the Mayo Clinic."

"Bipolar or not. Hmm. That's big."

"It is," she said. "Kind of funny how a letter will define a person, more so than the person holding it."

"Then open it."

"You make it sound easy," she said, tapping the letter on the table. "Kind of like asking someone out on date, you just suck up the fear and do it. Right?"

"Exactly."

She ripped the top of the envelope open and removed the letter. Before she read it, she said, "By the way, yes. I would love to go on a date with you."

CHAPTER 76

DARBY UNFOLDED THE letter and read it to Tom.

Dear Ms. Bradshaw, I have reviewed the documentation you sent to our office, your agency medical file, and your application for a first-class airman medical certification. I have determined that the available evidence does not support a current or past diagnosis of any mental health condition that would be disqualifying under Part 67 in Title 14, Code of Federal Regulations. I affirm that you are eligible for the first-class airman medical certificate issued to you at the time of your current application.

I do not find any aeromedical basis for continued examination of your current mental health status. This does not, however, preclude further re-examination in the future. You are cautioned to abide by 14 CFR 61.53, which prohibits action as pilot in command or as a required pilot flight crewmember while unable to meet medical certification requirements due to a disqualifying medical condition or use of disqualifying medications or treatments.

You have my best wishes for the future.
Best wishes,
Michael Banks
Federal Air Surgeon

"Oh my God!" Darby shouted.

"This is fantastic," Tom said. "They can't stop you from flying now."

He was right. The FAA had ruled in her favor and she would not have to go to the neutral. This was finally over. "I'm going to send an email to Dr. Marsh. Can I call you back in ten or fifteen minutes?"

"Of course."

Darby said good-bye to Tom, scanned the letter, and sent it to her computer. She logged into Gmail, to download the scanned letter. There was an email from the regional flight surgeon, Dr. Christopher Williams. He, too, was congratulating her. He had written that she could keep her first class medical. He listed all the FAA officials who were involved, and how happy he was for her. She responded with a quick thank you note, and then selected forward on his email, and typed in Dr. Marsh's email address and copied her attorney.

> *Dear Dr. Marsh,*
>
> *I am not sure if the FAA informed you of the results of the investigation that you requested, but we have them. Please find this forward from the Airmen Certification Program Analyst, FAA, Northwest Mountain Region with the attached letter stating that I can keep my first class medical certificate, issued February 22, 2018. Please note that during this entire process that I have never lost my medical.*
>
> *Dr. Michael Banks also sent me a letter stating that I do not have, "Any diagnosis current or past of any mental health condition that would be disqualifying." He further stated, "I do not find any aeromedical basis for continued examination of your current mental health status." In addition, he gave me his best wishes for the future.*
>
> *I am certain that since you requested the FAA's involvement, that you most certainly will accept their decision as the neutral doctor.*

I will be looking forward to the next steps to get me flying again.

Darby called Tom, and read him Dr. Williams's email, and then the letter she had written to Dr. Marsh.

"I like it," he said. "Did you send it?"

Darby pressed send. "I just did."

"Did Dr. Marsh actually request the FAA to investigate?"

"I'm not sure," Darby said. "I'm guessing so."

"Regardless, you're officially going back to flying," he said.

"I can't believe it," Darby said, with a sigh. Another glance back to her computer screen and her eyes widened. "Wow. Dr. Marsh already responded."

"What did he say?"

Darby opened his email and read Marsh's response to Tom.

Dear Ms. Bradshaw, Thank you for forwarding the letters from Dr. Banks and Dr. Williams. The Medical Review and Evaluation process pursuant to Section 8 of the Global-ALPO PWA is ongoing, and no determination regarding your return to flying will be made until that process is completed.

"No way," Tom said. "He violates the effing rules, and now he wants to play by the contract?"

"So much for a doctor's code of ethics," Darby said.

"On a better note, where do you want to have dinner to celebrate our date and your FAA clearance?" he asked. "This will be a double celebration."

"How about Anthony's Home Port?" she said. "They've got king crab on the menu, and I suddenly have a craving for something I can hit with a mallet before I eat it."

CHAPTER 77

A LUXURY HOTEL, a nice meal, and a comfortable bed at Global's expense had made the trip to D.C. slightly less painful. He sat in the back of the cab and glanced at his watch. Their meeting was scheduled for eleven a.m. and should take no longer than thirty minutes. His return flight departed at five p.m. At least he could get home the same day.

Despite Wood's assurance, Wolfe had said they were not taking anything for granted after the FAA fiasco. Then he'd ordered Marsh to do the dirty work. He wasn't quite sure why Wolfe wouldn't fly to D.C. and take care of the preliminaries himself. Wolfe and Chief Pilot Iverson had met with Wood in Chicago for an entire day, and they hadn't invited him to that meeting. Not that he'd wanted to go. But he wasn't sure why they'd made him do this. He was willing to do anything they needed, but sending him out of town caused logistical problems with his schedule.

Marsh was not only the Global doctor in charge of returning pilots to duty, but he was also an AME. As an Aviation Medical Examiner, he had over two thousand pilots he cleared twice a year to maintain their medicals. In addition, he sat on the board of HG Insurance. Marsh was a busy man, and did not have time for this bullshit.

He stared out the window, then glanced at his watch. He actually had nothing to complain about because, at the end of the day, Global had made him a very wealthy man.

Minutes later, the cab pulled up in front of an old home which had been converted to an office. He paid the driver and asked him to wait. Then he climbed out of the car with his overnight bag in hand.

Once at the door, he turned the handle and entered. A bell rang upstairs, followed by a voice saying, "I'll be right down." Seconds later, a middle-aged man wearing a sweater walked down the stairs.

"Dr. Marsh," Dr. Hanover said as he approached. When he reached the bottom of the stairs, Hanover extended a hand and said, "It's nice to meet you."

Dr. Marsh shook Hanover's hand. "Thank you for making time for me."

"Please, join me in my office," he said, and headed toward the stairs. "It will be more private upstairs."

Hanover's office was on the second floor. The room was nondescript. His bookshelves were filled, and a number of certificates hung on the wall. Hanover obviously dedicated his life to his work. That would be a plus for their future working agreements.

"Please have a seat," Hanover said, extending a hand towards a leather couch. Hanover sat on the matching love seat across from him. "To what do I owe this pleasure of an in-person visit?"

"As we spoke about on the phone," Marsh began, "I have a contractual obligation as Global's Director of Health Services to explain the requirements for an FAA evaluation."

"That's what you said," Hanover said. "Is there something more?"

"Joe Wolfe, our labor relations attorney thought an in-person meeting was necessary to explain the delicacy of this situation."

"Go ahead," Hanover said, crossing his arms. His eyes had not wavered from Dr. Marsh's.

"Ms. Bradshaw is a risk to Global Air Lines," Dr. Marsh said. He allowed those words to settle before he continued. "Dr. Wood has conducted an extensive and thorough evaluation. He has also created a report supporting a bipolar diagnosis. This is an FAA disqualifying diagnosis, and Bradshaw will be unable to fly at Global, or anywhere else."

"The Mayo Clinic had a different opinion," Hanover said. "How do we justify that?"

"We don't need to. This is often the case in these types of evaluations." Dr. Marsh said. He leaned forward, arms resting on his legs, and clasped his hands as if in prayer. He stared at them a moment, and then shifted his eyes up to Hanover's. "The pilots will always select a doctor who will clear them. That's why the pilot working agreement has a process for the tie-breaker. That will be you."

"Who pays for this evaluation?"

"She'll pay you for the visit. However, per the contract, if a pilot were to be found fit, the pilot would be fully reimbursed. If the pilot is to be found unfit to operate an aircraft, then it will be a shared expense." Marsh leaned back and crossed his legs. "With Bradshaw, this *will be* a shared expense."

Hanover stared without comment. Marsh's eyes never wavered from Hanover's as he waited for a response.

Hanover finally asked, "What kind of report do you want?"

"While I'm leaving this to your professional judgment as to what activities are required to produce a sound medical determination, to answer your question directly I would say it is anticipated that you will interview, examine and evaluate Bradshaw, as well as review and analyze all relevant medical reports and related materials.

"That includes discussing the case directly with Wood and the Mayo Clinic, interviewing any sources inside or outside of Global whom you feel would assist in completing your evaluation, and reviewing analyzing information regarding First Officer Bradshaw's behavior since the reports were submitted. I believe this is all consistent with what Dr. Wood discussed during your selection process."

"I simply wanted to know how detailed of a report you would like," Hanover said.

"Oh. I understand. Whatever you feel necessary to build your case," Dr. Marsh said with a wave of his hand. "That's at your discretion."

Hanover nodded. "I've read both reports and I'm meeting with Ms. Bradshaw in two days."

"Good. We're willing to fly *anyone* out here, as you see fit to help with your evaluation."

"I think I'll be fine," Hanover said as he stood. "That won't be necessary."

The bell rang from below announcing the next patient had arrived. Dr. Marsh stood, and he followed Dr. Hanover down the stairs. Hanover told his next patient he would be with him in a moment, as Marsh headed directly toward the door avoiding eye contact with Hanover's patient. Hanover held the door open.

Marsh stepped out the door and stopped. He turned toward Dr. Hanover and said, lowering his voice, "Please know, there will be no expense spared with this. Global Air Lines is fully vested in this process."

CHAPTER 78

DARBY'S SUITCASE WAS tucked safely in the backseat of her car beside her computer bag. She climbed out of her car, clicked the lock, and ran up the path to Kathryn's house. She headed for the side door, as they would all be in the kitchen.

"Something smells great," Darby said as she entered. Kathryn, Linda, and Jackie were all sitting at the table, with JJ in the highchair. Jessica, Jennifer, and Chris were cooking breakfast.

"Aunt Darby," Jessica said, pulling back a chair. "Sit. We're making you breakfast."

"Because we love you," Jennifer said, hugging her.

"You're going to make me cry," Darby said as she sat at the table.

"Just how you like it," Chris said, setting a coffee in front of Darby. "Thanks for teaching me to drive, by the way."

"No kidding," Jennifer said. "Some of the guys at school saw him driving with *you*, and he's now the coolest guy in our school."

"Don't kid yourself," Jessica said, placing a platter of pancakes on the table. "He's got coolest kid status because he hangs out with us." She winked at Darby, and then pulled a pancake off the top of the stack and gave it to JJ.

Chris set a platter of bacon on the table, and Jennifer set down a bowl of scrambled eggs. Champagne glasses were filled with orange juice. Jessica sat to Darby's left and Jennifer to the right, while Chris sat beside his little sister.

Darby reached out and took each of the twins' hands and squeezed. She looked around the table and tears filled her eyes. "Thank you all so much."

"Tomorrow's a huge day," Linda said. "We can't send you to the East coast without a homemade meal and a bit of moral support."

"It's going to be fine," Kathryn said, scooping eggs onto her plate. "You have the FAA medical appeals certification in your pocket. Even though Dr. Marsh won't take it, the FAA did. That means something."

"I'm sure it will impact Dr. Hanover, too," Linda said.

"John's really looking forward to having dinner with you in D.C.," Jackie said. "He said whenever you're done, just text him."

"I will," Darby said, taking the bowl of eggs from Kathryn.

"Are you afraid?" Chris asked.

"I am," Darby said. "My biggest concern is that Wood agreed to accept Hanover as the neutral. We all know they're trying to get rid of me. So there has to be a reason he agreed with this selection."

"Jen and I think they finally realized they can't get rid of you that easy," Jessica said, dipping a rolled-up pancake into syrup. "So, they're giving in."

"Think about it," Jennifer said. "The FAA ruled in your favor. They're done. They can't win."

"But then why are they making her see this doctor?" Chris asked. All eyes turned his way and Jessica threw a strawberry at him. "What? They should just let her back," he said.

Darby grinned. "He's got a point."

"Mom, if they make this stick, can Darby work for you at the FAA?" Jennifer asked.

"I'm going to be fine," Darby said, before Kathryn could answer

Jennifer's question. Everyone, but the children, knew that if Darby's bipolar diagnosis stuck, she would never be allowed to work with the FAA. "Besides, if I don't get back, then I'm thinking I'll work at Starbucks for insurance and become a fulltime author."

"You could write a movie and buy your own plane," Jessica said.

"Excellent plan." Darby raised her glass of orange juice.

They finished their breakfast and Darby helped the kids to do the dishes. When they finished, Darby glanced at her watch. As much as she wanted this day to last forever, she said, "I think I'd better get going."

"Are you sure you won't leave your car here and let me drive you?" Kathryn asked.

"Thanks," Darby said. "But I get back in really late, and it will be nice to have my car."

Everyone hugged Darby goodbye, and told her they loved her. Jennifer began crying. Then Jessica started to cry, and Darby's eyes watered. "It's going to be okay," she said wrapping the girls into her arms.

"Girls, come on now," Kathryn said. "Darby's going to be all right."

"This is going to be a mini vacation," Darby said. "Everything will be fine." However, the reality was, she really didn't believe everything was going to be okay. She didn't have faith she would get a fair shake. Chris was right. If they were going to do the right thing, they would accept the FAA's ruling. Unfortunately, she had absolutely no control over the outcome. This entire situation had taken on a life of its own.

CHAPTER 79

DARBY SAT IN a coach seat and accepted her second Bloody Mary on her way to DC. The flight attendants were taking exceptionally good care of her. She suspected Jackie had something to do with this. Despite Jackie giving up her flight attendant job, she'd kept in touch with many of them. They all knew where Darby was headed, and were helping her to make the journey better.

Staring out the window she sipped her drink, thinking about all she'd been through. She contemplated Jackie's question about if it was worth it. Then she wondered how one doctor's opinion could determine her entire career, even if it was in opposition of the ten doctors at the Mayo Clinic and the FAA medical appeals board. If she didn't have her job, she wasn't sure how she could afford an attorney.

A single tear slid down her cheek, and she swiped it away. The best bet would be to take Kathryn up on her offer to move in. She just wasn't sure how that would work in the long run.

"Are you okay?" the man sitting in the aisle seat asked.

Darby looked in his direction. The seat between them was empty. He was in his late sixties, nicely dressed, with compassion in his eyes.

"I hope so," she replied. "If not, I'm sure I will be."

"Do you want to talk about it?" he asked. "What's said on an airplane, stays on an airplane."

Darby laughed. "You're not a pilot, are you?"

"No. Attorney," he said.

She grinned. "Hmmm. Then I should employ you for the flight, and we'd have attorney client privilege."

"That we would," he said. "But I have to disclose, I'm a divorce attorney."

"Perfect," she said. "Please accept these peanuts as payment for your services for the remainder of the flight." Darby set her unopened package of nuts on his tray.

"Are you married?" he asked, opening his payment.

"Nope."

"Works for me." He removed a pen from his pocket and wrote on a napkin—*Payment in full for listening and advice services for the passenger in 13A.* He signed his name and slid it to Darby.

Darby chuckled. "Why aren't you in first class where you belong?"

"Full flight, and I'm not that persuasive."

"Not a good trait for an attorney," she said raising her glass.

"No, it's not," he said grinning, as he raised his plastic cup of wine and toasted Darby.

Darby gave him the abbreviated version of what had happened and why she was headed to D.C. He listened intently, asked a few clarifying questions and shook his head as she spoke. His eyes were expressive and caring. His anger of what had transpired was obvious.

"There you have it," she sighed. "Tomorrow's kind of a big day."

"If I didn't know there were pilots, like yourself, willing to fight so hard for aviation safety, I don't think I'd ever fly this airline again," he said.

"I'm not really sure if it's worth the fight," she finally admitted. "I've never said that out loud before now. These guys really are stacking the cards against me. They've all but destroyed the life I knew, and it's not getting any better."

"It is worth it," he said. "Look around you. These people are depending upon you. I depend on you."

"But how much pain does a person have to go through in order to do the right thing?"

"As much as it takes," he said. He shifted in his seat and turned his body towards her. "What's happening tomorrow is not your end game. It doesn't matter if that doctor clears you or he doesn't. You have accepted the challenge of taking on something very important. Your AIR 21 ruling will impact change. Identifying doctors who take money for false medical diagnoses is important. Having the courage to shut them down takes strength. Your research is essential." He reached over and placed a hand on her arm. "You are not alone in this. Keep the faith that either way, whatever happens tomorrow, this is part of your destiny."

"I wish I knew my destiny," Darby said. "It would make this so much easier."

"You don't need easy," he said, removing his hand, his smile kind. "The challenges you have faced, and will continue to face, are preparing you for something big. I don't want to sound melodramatic, but there is evil at work here. Obviously, you accepted the challenge to fight it. Not many people would do that."

"I don't know about that," Darby said, remembering the note about Wyatt having no balls and Rich Clark being evil. She stared into her glass, thinking about how malicious Clark really was. She wondered if he would ever be held accountable.

"I know," he said, pulling her from her thoughts.

Darby looked his way. She sucked a deep breath and said, "Fighting evil would be so much easier if I had a sword to slay all the dragons."

"You have that sword," he said. "Just keep the faith, and use it."

CHAPTER 80

DARBY HAD FORGOTTEN how beautiful D.C. was, and was thankful she had taken the opportunity for a morning run. She stretched one leg and then the other, reaching her arms over her head. She leaned left, and then right. Then she sat on the steps of the Lincoln Memorial. Opening her bottle of water, she stared at the Washington Monument. *Breathtaking*. Maybe she would stay another day and take in all the museums. She took a long drink of her water and thought, why not? She really had nothing to be home for.

Wishing she could stay here all day, she glanced at her watch. She'd better get her butt back to the hotel for a quick shower, so she wouldn't be late. She stood, ran down the stairs, and headed north. One thing she learned during this mental health process was that timeliness and how a person was dressed were indicative of a person's mental health. It didn't matter if the taxi got stuck in traffic, or if a person could not afford nice clothes, it only mattered if they were on time and looked put together.

In no time, Darby arrived at her hotel, out of breath. She jumped into the shower and shortly thereafter, emerged from her hotel dressed for success. Well at least what she hoped would be a success. The taxi was waiting for her as promised. She gave the driver the address, and then leaned back to wait out the twenty-five minute drive. She and the driver became fast friends chatting the entire way. Darby wasn't quite sure where to go, but the driver knew the place. He'd actually taken someone there three days earlier.

"Do you want me to wait for you?" he asked.

"That's nice of you to offer, but I have a four-hour appointment," she said. "Could you come back?"

"It would be my honor, Ms. Darby."

She paid him, giving him a generous tip. Something a little extra for being so kind. She really appreciated the distraction this morning. Darby climbed out of the car, and then stood for a moment assessing the beautiful home. If she had her own office, this is exactly what she would do with it. The yard was landscaped with wildflowers, and a stone path led to the front door.

Darby was surprised how nervous she felt walking up the path. With Dr. Wood's first visit, she had not felt any nerves until she'd stepped into his building, at which moment a feeling of dread had encompassed her body. The hallways had reminded her of the movie, *The Shining*. When she'd met Wood, he'd come across as an evil professor. His office was cold. He was creepy. She had shivered during the entire meeting—six hours without a break, and an event she would never forget.

This time, she was filled with dread knowing what they were capable of. She breathed deeply and stepped onto the porch. She opened the door and stepped inside. A little bell rang upstairs informing Dr. Hanover she had arrived. Muted voices came from above. There was a bicycle leaning against a couch. She sat on the opposite couch to avoid knocking it over. She picked up a magazine, looked at the pictures, and then returned it to the table.

A few minutes later someone came down the stairs, and headed directly for the bike. Darby said, "Nice bike."

"Thanks," he said, "and that's the reason I don't leave it outside."

She stood and opened the door for him.

"Thanks," he said, again.

"Of course." Darby closed the door after he was out. She turned and then jumped. "Sorry, you surprised me," she said, "I didn't hear you come down." The doctor had been standing a few feet behind her when she turned.

"The apologies are mine," he said. "Please, join me." He headed toward the stairs and she followed him. "Did you have any problem getting here?"

"None at all," she said with a smile.

His office was elegant, yet homey. The bookshelves were filled with leather bound volumes, and a number of certificates hung on the wall. There were no photos of family. "Do you have children?" Darby asked.

He smiled and assessed her a moment before saying, "No."

"Where do you want me to sit?" she asked.

"The couch is dedicated to patients."

He sat at his desk, and sighed deeply.

She smiled a smile she gave to those whom she felt empathy for. What in the world had he gotten himself into, at the brink of his civilian career? Everyone had choices to make and this would be his. What amazed Darby was the feeling of calm with him, completely unlike when she was with Dr. Wood.

Dr. Hanover was a very nice man. Her fear melted away the moment she met him. She wasn't sure if he had calmed her, or the fact that she had just given in because she had no control over the outcome. She thought about what the attorney had said on the plane.

"I've been reading the many files on you," he said at last. "I am a bit confused as to why your AME did not give you your medical certificate."

"Someone at the FAA recommended he not support me in order to avoid getting himself backed into a corner. So, my AME reached out to our FAA regional flight surgeon who said he would do it."

"The regional flight surgeon gave you a medical without meeting you?" he asked. "Even with a bipolar diagnosis?"

"My AME gave me my physical, and told him I was fit for duty. He further explained what was transpiring with the company. He also gave him the Mayo Clinic's report to read. Then he said he would have no problem with the issuance."

"What's his name?" Dr. Hanover asked, flipping through papers.

"Dr. Christopher Williams," Darby said.

"Oh… really?" He looked up from his search and said, "I know him. He was a General in the Air Force. Good man."

"Yes, he is." Darby smiled and said, "And that explains so much."

"About what?" he asked, setting the folder aside.

"When someone at Global called Michael Banks, the head of the FAA, and told him I'd received my first class medical, Banks contacted Dr. Williams and challenged him." Darby moved her purse off her lap, and onto the couch. "Having been a General, I suspect his decisions haven't been challenged too often in his career."

"I suppose you're right," he said. Then he asked, "Michael Banks challenged the issuance?"

"He did. But that's been cleared up. I received a notice five days ago of their decision." Hanover genuinely appeared surprised, so this was her opportunity to play her hold card. "I brought you a copy of the letter they sent." She opened her purse, retrieved the folded letter, and handed it to him. "Apparently, the entire medical appeals board unanimously ruled in my favor, saying that I don't have a problem and can keep my medical."

"Does the company have this letter?" he asked as he read it.

"They do," she said. "I sent a copy to Dr. Marsh the day I received it. He told me it didn't matter, because we had to continue with the contractual process."

"Do you see a problem with that?" he asked, and then added, "May I keep this?"

Darby nodded, and said, "As a matter of fact I do have a problem with that." She tucked a strand of hair behind her ear.

"Because you don't agree with the contract?" he asked. "Or is it because you think the contract isn't fair?"

"Neither," she said. "The point is… a contract is a contract, and we are required to follow it under the law. Despite the reason they did this to me, once I was placed into the Section 8, they were required to follow the process."

"But now you're saying you don't think they should follow it?" Dr. Hanover said, as he wrote something on a pad of paper.

"That's not what I'm saying. The contract states they were not allowed to notify the FAA until we completely finished the process and it was negative," Darby said. "In that the company violated the contract and notified the FAA, the notification indicated *they* chose not to follow our contract. They abdicated their contractual rights by notifying the FAA, and therefore acknowledged their willingness to enable the FAA to rule on the issue. In that the FAA ruled in my favor, that should have held. However, now the company won't accept the FAA's ruling."

"Do you have a law degree?" Dr. Hanover asked.

Darby wasn't sure if he was mocking her or not. "No sir. I have taken one aviation law class, but the law is fairly black and white.

As a matter of fact, that was the reason the Mayo Clinic backed out of the process. Their legal department determined this was now in the FAA's hands."

Dr. Hanover simply nodded. Then he asked her about her life, training, beliefs, the company, and why she thought Global did this. They spoke for hours. She had been right, he was a nice man, and the discussion was in no way combative like that with Dr. Wood. Unfortunately, she had no indication of how he was going to rule. He held his hand close.

Their time was over. She gave him her credit card and paid for the visit. Unfortunately, there was no discussion on her being cleared or not.

Darby walked out of the office and into the fresh air. The driver was waiting. She headed for the taxi.

"How did it go, Ms. Darby?" he asked, as she climbed in.

"Honestly? I don't know," she said. She told him she would be returning to the hotel. Then she texted John to tell him she was on her way back. Folding her arms, she looked out the window. The driver began talking, but Darby didn't hear a word he said.

CHAPTER 81

TRAFFIC WAS LIGHT and within no time Darby had returned to the Watergate Hotel. She entered and exited the elevator, heading straight for her room. She did not want to talk to anyone. She wanted to ignore the reality of what her future held. Holding the electronic key to the door, it unlocked.

Once inside, she tossed her purse onto the bed, walked into the bathroom, and turned on the shower. She returned to her bedroom and opened her suitcase.

She had brought a simple black cocktail dress and a pair of red heels. On the drive back, she made a resolve that she would not allow the doctors or Global to ruin her life, despite the fact they were doing a damn good job of trying. She laid her dress and shoes on the bed.

John had texted he was still forty minutes out. She stripped out of her clothes, piled her hair high on her head, and climbed into the shower. The warmth felt incredible.

Darby dressed quickly, touched up her makeup, and fluffed her hair. She grabbed her purse and headed out the door and down the hall. They were planning to eat at the Kingbird restaurant downstairs. She still had twenty minutes until his arrival.

Her only decision was where to wait—The Whiskey Bar or Top of the Gate. She opted for Top of the Gate, a rooftop bar at the

Watergate Hotel. Appropriately named for the city, she was looking forward to capturing the view, if only for a moment.

Darby stepped outside and onto the terrace. The view of the Potomac River and the city beyond took her breath away. She worked her way through the crowd to the edge, and stood at the railing. She wondered how many people jumped off the bridge in the distance.

"Miss," a man said, interrupting her thoughts.

Darby turned.

"We're about to leave. Would you like our table?"

"That would be nice," Darby said. "Thank you."

In no time she was sitting at the table sipping a Glenmorangie, straight up. She had texted John and told him where she could be found. Then she sipped her scotch and gazed into the distance, wondering what would become of her future. She thought about the man on the flight, and everything he'd said. He'd told her she already held the sword to slay her dragons. If only that were true. She had faith things worked out like they were supposed to, but where this would go… she had no idea. Perhaps all she could do was believe. Take one day at a time.

"Hello, beautiful woman. Are you waiting for someone, or is this my lucky day?"

Darby turned toward the voice and then she started laughing. "That is by far the worst pick up line I have ever heard in my life," Darby said. "Jackie has nothing to worry about with you." Darby stood and hugged John.

"Well, you do look beautiful," he said, glancing at his watch. "Our reservation isn't for another thirty minutes. May I join you?" he asked, nodding toward her drink. "This has been another day in purgatory."

"For you and me both," Darby said with a chuckle, holding up her glass. "Nothing like an eighteen-year-old scotch to make your day better."

John ordered two more scotches, and when they arrived Darby finished her first drink, and the waiter took her empty glass. Once the waiter was out of ear shot, she began to tell John about her visit with Dr. Hanover.

"I really liked him and I felt like we clicked. But…"

"But what?" John asked.

Darby sighed and stared into her drink, and when she looked up, she said, "He didn't tell me that he was going to clear me."

"Is that significant?" John asked.

"It is. Mayo told me how they were ruling before I left. I don't think they send a patient out of the office who has a mental issue with a death sentence," Darby said. "When they told that Germanwings pilot he was unfit to fly, he knew his job was over and he took that one last flight."

"I suppose they could put themselves in danger if they were alone in the office with a crazy person, as well," John said.

"Or worse yet, they might not get paid." Darby emptied her glass. "I think we should head downstairs, because I'm starving."

John threw back his drink, placed the empty glass onto the table, and stood. "After you," he said, extending a hand. "We have a lot more to talk about."

Chapter 82

JOHN AND DARBY arrived at their restaurant minutes later. They were immediately seated. Darby opened her menu and glanced through the many entrees until she found one that jumped off the page. "Lobster spaghetti sounds delicious."

The waitress arrived and John ordered the filet medium rare, Darby's lobster, a couple caesar salads and bottle of pinot. Within no time the wine was at the table and two glasses were poured.

"So, what happened with the Tiger Air crash?" Darby asked.

"A malfunctioning pitot static system, but we can't track its origination," he said. "It came from an unknown source."

"A knock-off part," Darby said. Nothing short of what Ray kept quiet about when he was in maintenance. She was surprised he hadn't been fired, but then again nothing with Global surprised her anymore.

"What's bugging me is that the pilots didn't respond to the malfunction appropriately. The problem impacted the MCAS system which reacted as a runaway stabilizer. They didn't know how to fly their plane." John sipped his wine and then added, "Of course, they weren't trained specifically for that failure, because Boeing hadn't disclosed that they needed additional training for an MCAS failure."

MCAS was an acronym for the Maneuvering Characteristic Augmentation System, a flight control system which was designed for the 737 MAX to improve pitch stability. The system was designed to push the nose over to avoid stalling due to the aircraft's instability. This was accomplished by automatic trim. The pilots' protection would be to disconnect the stabilizer.

"Why didn't the FAA mandate training?" Darby asked.

"They were trying to keep the same type rating on the 737 for the folks at Southeast Airlines," John said. "Pushing the plane to such a large capacity created the instability that mandated the MCAS. Nobody wanted the expense that an additional type-rating would create for the larger aircraft."

This wasn't the first time the FAA enabled a major aircraft change and allowed Southeast Airlines to avoid training. The shift between round dial systems to a highly automated glass aircraft with push buttons should have been a new type rating. But they had a workaround, which was supported by the FAA.

"Remember when the FAA allowed them to keep the same type rating by retaining the lever latch switches?" Darby asked. "It's all about money."

"This time it bit them," John said. "But shouldn't the pilots have known how to manage a runaway stabilizer?"

"I would think so," Darby said. "But it's hard to tell what the pilots knew based on how bad training is worldwide."

John held his wine glass and twisted the stem between his fingers. "The problem now is the underlying attack about to commence on Boeing. However, there were many factors that went into that crash. If they only point the finger at Boeing, nothing will get solved."

"That crash was about safety culture, SMS, and training," Darby said. "Everything identified by my research."

"I'm afraid you're right," he said, lowering his voice. "There's more at work here than an accident."

"Like what?" Darby asked. It had been a long time since she'd seen this amount of concern on John's face. It was more than the stress of the job. Something had him on edge.

"You were right. There's a movement afoot to remove pilots from the flight deck. More than just talk. They're looking at the freighters first," he said. "It's going to happen, it's just a matter of when. This accident was a starting point."

"You think this crash is connected to removing pilots?" Darby asked.

"I do. I also think your initial report should have encouraged Global to do things differently. Instead, they took the alternate path."

"Kill the messenger," Darby said. "But I have nothing to do with Tiger Air."

"No. But your findings in the research were significant," John said. "Instead of listening to you, or firing you, they did something worse. They gave you a diagnosis to remove you from the industry. I think this accident has something to do with automation and pilot removal, and inadequate training. You're a threat to them."

Darby had always suspected there was a greater reason than Rich Clark's ego being bruised. But something still didn't make sense.

"Okay, so they don't like my report, and they definitely will not like the results that support it. But how does a malfunctioning part help remove pilots?" Darby asked. "It just proves automation fails and we need pilots for when it does."

"It does," John said, "but..."

"But what?" she asked.

"The pilots could not fly that plane with the malfunction. The assertion is that if this failure had occurred and there *had been* ground-based control, that plane would never have crashed."

"That's bullshit. Only if the kid flying the plane on the ground had more information than those pilots. Who says he could have even identified the fault on the plane or known how to control it any better?" Darby asked.

"I agree. But the decision makers won't see it that way. They want a panacea for the public, and that will be their angle. Pilots cause accidents when planes break."

"But what about the airline knowing they had a problem and allowing the plane to fly?" Darby asked. "They should be accountable for something. Someone should have grounded that plane, or at the very least trained the pilots."

"Nobody will ground it. Boeing wants to sell planes. The FAA doesn't want to be accountable for the losses all those carriers who fly the Max would incur. Airlines won't ground their own aircraft." John sipped his wine. "But I do think this accident was intentional."

"It feels like Bill all over again," Darby said. When John's eyes locked on her's without comment, she asked, "What? What's going on with Bill?"

"President Drake and Bill are at the same prison," he said. "His son was in China shortly before the accident. He arrived with luggage and hours later left on his private jet without any."

"Are you kidding me?" A chill went through Darby's body and she shivered something fierce.

The waiter arrived with their salads. The table was quiet while he served them. Darby's stomach grumbled. She wasn't sure if it was from hunger or the sickening feeling that came over her with the thought of Bill's involvement.

After the waiter left, John said, "Bill is tied to Global. Global doesn't fly the Max. Drake Industries makes airplane parts. Bill and Drake are pals in prison. His son's visiting China. We also had intel there would be issues with the 737 Max from an unidentified whistleblower, but had no idea what, where, or how. Yet nobody heeded the warning due to the lack of details, and then the crash. We're told there is going to be another."

"But can't they ground it now?" Darby asked. "Especially since the first warning was proven to be true."

"They won't. Not until another accident occurs. This would financially undo all the airlines who operate the Max." He sighed and stabbed his fork into his salad. "Boeing and the airlines would have to ground their own aircraft."

"Yes, but like you said, no airline or manufacturer is going to do that. They would be fighting to not ground it," Darby said. "This is the FAA's responsibility."

"That's the problem. The FAA is holding back."

"So, they're going to kill another plane load of people?" Darby asked angrily. "Can't we get Kat to do something?"

They ate their salads in silence for a few minutes, each contemplating the reality of this situation. John filled both their glasses. He lifted his glass and stared at it for a moment, then looked at Darby.

"They are looking at a new FAA administrator," John said. "Someone from the airlines. Deke Elmer is temporary. He's got his head on straight so they won't keep him long. They need a pawn."

"From what airline?" Darby asked.

"We don't know," John said. "There are many issues on the forefront. Joint venture reassessments, duty time limitation shifts, pilot replacements by automation, and... the eventual grounding of the Max if there's another accident."

"All the airlines will benefit from each of those issues," Darby said. "Except one airline will benefit more." John nodded and Darby said, "Global would benefit from another Max crash."

"They would," John said with concern.

"Then I don't understand why not ground it now?" she asked. "Global has power with the FAA to do that."

"They might just be waiting for the new FAA administrator," he said. "Someone who would keep it grounded as long as possible if there were a second crash."

Darby sipped her wine, her mind running through everything John had just said. "They're going to put George Wyatt into that position. He just retired from a two million-a-year job, and for what? To play with his grandkids?" Darby said. "No way in hell."

The busboy removed their plates. Then the waiter arrived with their meals and asked if they needed anything. Darby wanted to ask for a magic wand to fix everything, but instead she said, "No, thank you. I think we're good."

When alone, John said, "This is why we didn't bring noise to that bottle of wine Ray allegedly sent. We tracked the shipping point. Oklahoma City. We know who did it. We suspected how. That empty pill bottle you found was a prescription for the same drug within the wine. You would have been a suicide."

"Not only is Rich Clark a criminal, but he's stupid too," Darby said.

"If I'm correct, Global will spare no expense to have you discredited. They will do anything to ensure you are blackballed," John said. "They also don't want your books published. They don't want your research. They don't want you."

"They already got to my publisher," Darby said. "But I'm self-publishing."

"Good," he said. "But I'm not going to say it doesn't make me nervous."

Darby stuck a fork into her spaghetti and turned it slowly, rolling noodles around the tongs. "You know, if it's a battle they want, I'm going to give it to them." She stuck the pasta into her mouth.

"They're powerful, and they're vicious," John said, cutting into his filet.

"The only power they have over me is my job," Darby said. "If they take that away, they have no control. They won't have the social media policy to protect them. If they want to fight, my gloves are on." She lifted her glass and took another drink, this time for courage.

"Is putting your life at risk worth it?" John asked.

"I've wondered that often," Darby said, returning her glass to the table. "But the answer is always the same—yes. Each of us has a purpose. I know that I'm not going to save the world, solve the Iranian crisis, stop cancer, or fix climate change. But what I *can* do is keep our passengers safe. I'm not afraid to take one for the team of humanity, in the interest of aviation safety. Because the truth is, one of those lives that I save on my fight for aviation safety might just be the life that *will* save the world."

CHAPTER 83

NINETEEN DAYS AND counting, with absolutely no word from Dr. Hanover. Darby had half expected to receive a drop-dead notice on the Fourth of July to parallel Wood's Christmas Eve gift, but nothing had arrived. Kathryn and Linda told her he was probably on vacation for the Fourth of July weekend, and her report would be coming shortly thereafter. They assured her not to worry about the delay. It had been a week since that time. She was worried.

Darby climbed out of her car and headed into her house, closing the garage door behind her. She dropped her purse and gym bag onto the table. At least she was making it to the gym each day which was a mood enhancer. The waiting game was a struggle regardless. All she wanted to know was what her future would hold.

She wanted to fly. But now, flying up the stairs would have to do. She took them two at a time, stripping off her tank-top as she did. She tossed it into the hamper in her room and headed into the bathroom. She turned the shower faucet toward hot. She kicked off her shoes, removed her spandex leggings, and had just pulled off her sports bra when the doorbell rang.

"Dang," she said, grabbing a towel. Darby wrapped her body and ran down the stairs and peeked through the hole. Then she placed a hand to her heart, and opened the door a few inches and stuck her head out, "Hey, Dan."

"I have a letter for you, Darby," he said, glancing at her attire. "Shall I come back?"

"No!" she cried. "I've been waiting for this for almost three weeks."

He handed her a pen, and she signed for the letter, half in and half out the door, trying not to lose her towel.

"Thank you," she said, taking her envelope and closing the door. She leaned against the door and held the letter to her chest. Then she tipped her head back and closed her eyes. This was her moment of truth.

There was a quick knock at the door and she jumped. Darby turned and opened it.

"Are you cheating on me with the FedEx guy?" Tom asked, stepping inside and assessing her attire. He placed his palm on the door beside her head and then pushed it closed.

"Dan and I have had a long-term relationship," she said with a grin. "He delivers."

Tom chuckled. "I can deliver if you give me a chance."

"I think we could work on that," she said.

"Is this it?" he asked, taking the FedEx envelope from her.

"My death sentence. Yes."

He flung the envelope into the living room. "Then let's keep death at bay for a while longer," he said, unfolding her from the towel. "I have plans for you first, and I would prefer you were alive." He placed his lips onto hers, and pulled her into his arms.

Going to heaven before death sounded like an excellent plan. The outcome could wait a couple more hours.

CHAPTER 84

DARBY SAT INSIDE her car and glanced at the seat beside her. The unopened envelope was her passenger. Somehow time had flown by, and Tom would have been late for his shift if they had taken the time to open the letter, because he would have stayed to console her. Then one thing would lead to the next. She'd pushed him out the door, and he'd hurried off to work. Darby had called Kathryn, who decided to have a sanity revealing dinner party where they would open the letter together.

"You're the guest of honor," Darby said to the envelope and she patted it. She backed her car out of the driveway thinking about Tom Hanks talking to his volleyball. She grinned. Maybe she was going crazy. It was seriously hard not to with all that had transpired.

She pulled onto the street and drove down the block. Within minutes flashing lights glared in her rearview mirror. Chuckling, she pulled over.

Darby rolled down her window and said, "You're going to need handcuffs to keep me from dinner."

"We could probably arrange that," Tom said with a grin. "Did you open it?"

"Not yet. I'm heading to the opening party at Kat's."

"I'm sorry I threw it," he said. "I should have been more considerate of the situation."

"You're forgiven," Darby said with a huge smile. "If I had to choose between a career-ending letter or spending the afternoon in the shower with you, I'd do the same thing again."

"Will you call me as soon as you open it?" he asked.

"Of course."

He leaned down and kissed her gently, then walked back to his car. Darby pulled back onto the road and smiled. In no time, she was pulling into Kathryn's driveway.

Darby entered through the front door and Kathryn greeted her with a hug. She could hear Linda and Jackie talking in the kitchen.

"Something smells wonderful," Darby said, holding the envelope to her chest.

"Lasagna. Nothing says comfort like pasta. I hope you don't mind having it again," Kathryn said. "Have you looked, yet?"

Darby shook her head, and then said, "However, you could make me lasagna every week if you wanted to." They headed for the kitchen. She was greeted with warm hugs, followed by a glass of cabernet.

"Did you look?" Linda asked.

"Nope," Darby said, "and we are not opening it until *after* dinner." She set the envelope on the counter. "We are going to have a great dinner, where all hope is not lost, and there is a future of happiness. We can dream big. Then we'll open it."

"During dessert?" Jackie asked.

"Well, only if chocolate is involved."

Kathryn gave her a thumbs up and said. "We're eating in the dining room tonight." She handed Jackie a bowl filled with caesar salad. Linda picked up the french bread and dish of butter. Kathryn slipped on potholder mitts, and pulled the lasagna from the oven.

Darby lifted two bottles of wine into the air and said, "The party has begun."

They were all seated, plates filled, and wine glasses topped off, and Darby jumped up and said, "We forgot something." She ran into the kitchen.

When she returned, she held the envelope and set it on an empty chair.

"Do you want to explain?" Kathryn asked with a grin.

"This is going to be my new life," Darby said. "For better or worse. So, I decided we should become friends."

"Do you want my professional opinion?" Linda asked.

Darby grinned and said, "Of course."

"You're going to be just fine no matter what happens. Just don't ever give up your sense of humor."

"I'll toast to that," Jackie said.

"To keeping our sense of humor, while surviving life," Darby said raising her glass. "And afternoon showers with the local police officer."

Jackie's hand went to her mouth, Linda grinned wide, and Kathryn said, "Tom?"

"I'm not going to kiss and tell," she said. "But let's just say he's a really good bodyguard."

"You go, girl," Jackie said, giving Darby a high five.

"It's about time," Kathryn said.

"That explains why that wasn't opened, yet," Linda said, still smiling as she glanced at the envelope.

She and her friends raised their glasses and they all toasted. The one thing Darby knew was that with humor and friends she could survive anything, even the loss of her medical.

Dinner was incredible. The laughter was often. They didn't solve any world problems, because there were far too many, but they came up with a lot of ideas. They did make a promise that no matter what happened in life, they would always be there for each other.

Once the wine bottles were emptied and they had done significant damage to the lasagna, the ladies cleared the dishes into the kitchen, and then moved into the living room. Kathryn carried a plate of brownies and placed it onto the coffee table.

Darby carried the document of honor, holding it close to her chest. She sat on the couch, and Jackie and Linda sat on each side.

Kathryn pushed the brownies aside, and sat on the coffee table directly in front of Darby. She reached out and held a hand and squeezed. "Just like a Band-Aid, rip that sucker open."

Darby grabbed the strip on the back of the envelope, and ripped. She opened the FedEx envelope, and removed the letter. Darby handed the FedEx envelope to Kathryn, and took a deep breath, then opened the envelope within. She unfolded the letter and began to read, tears filling her eyes as she did.

CHAPTER **85**

D ARBY STARED AT the letter and looked up. She looked at each of her friends and said, "I'm cleared. I'm going to fly again."

"Oh my God!" Kathryn placed a hand to her heart. Then she began to cry. "I'm sorry. I promised myself I wouldn't cry, but I'm just so happy for you."

Linda tucked an arm in the crook of Darby's and squeezed. "Good for you, sweetie. Good for you. I've got to call Niman."

Jackie threw her arms around Darby. Hugging her tight, she cried, "I am so happy!" Then Jackie began crying, and said, "I have to call John. He's going to be so excited."

Darby found her purse and retrieved her phone, and then texted a thumbs up emoji to Tom. Kathryn rushed out of the room and returned with a bottle of champagne, and four fluted glasses. "We're celebrating properly."

Kathryn opened the bottle of champagne with a pop.

"Jackie, tell John you'll call him back," Kathryn said. "We have celebrating to do."

The glasses were filled, the ladies held their glasses out, and Kathryn said, "To never giving up, no matter what."

Darby added, "To my friends, who never gave up on me."

They touched their glasses and began talking about what would happen next. Linda, however, read the report with interest. Darby sipped her champagne and reached for a brownie. She wasn't sure if she was shocked or happy or both.

"I thought for sure he was going to say no," Darby said. "Why wouldn't he tell me at the time, instead of driving me nuts for almost three weeks?"

"Maybe he changed his mind," Jackie said. "Whatever, I don't care. I'm just so happy."

"Did Wood know Dr. Hanover?" Linda asked, after she finished reading his report.

"I think so," Darby said.

"This is the oddest report I have ever read," Linda said.

"How so?" Kathryn asked, topping off everyone's glasses.

"It appears he's more interested in defending Dr. Wood," Linda said, "than clearing Darby." She reached for her glass and sipped her champagne. "Can I read this out loud?"

"Please," Darby said with a grin. "Emphasize the part about my not having a problem."

Linda returned the smile and said, "The best part is the beginning." She began to read

> Based on my clinical interviews and the information sources detailed below, Darby Bradshaw does not have any psychiatric disorder, substance use disorder, or personality disorder. I have a very high degree of medical certainty that Ms. Bradshaw does not have bipolar disorder. Nobody, including Dr. Wood noted any episodic mania. I have a reasonable degree of medical certainty that Ms. Bradshaw does not have any other psychiatric disorder, including personality disorder [or neurosis) and substance use disorder...

"That is a good part," Jackie said with a thumbs up to Darby.

"The best part," Linda agreed. She continued reading.

Although Dr. Wood documented that Ms. Bradshaw displayed paranoia, his only evidence appeared to involve her employment, and was not part of a larger or more global paranoid personality disorder. Notably, Dr. Wood did not diagnose paranoid personality disorder. I found no evidence for any personality disorder. Lastly, there was no evidence for a substance use disorder. I determined that further evaluation would likely strengthen my opinion, and was unlikely to reveal compelling information leading to other diagnostic considerations, although it certainly could. I did not believe it would be reasonable to drive up the cost of the evaluation regardless of who would ultimately pay for it.

"The last couple sentences sounded odd," Kathryn said. "But the rest sounds professionally sound, and in Darby's favor."

"It's also my favorite part," Darby said, leaning back into the couch. She sipped her champagne, and grinned. She simply could not believe it. This had been such a long battle.

"I agree," Linda said. "It's the following section where he defends Dr. Wood that's off base."

"Why would he defend Dr. Wood?" Jackie asked.

"My question, too," Linda said, glancing Jackie's way and then back to the letter.

Because of the marked difference in psychiatric opinion with an esteemed colleague, I offer the following as a possible explanation for why Dr. Wood's impression was markedly different from mine. None of this detracts from my conclusions in the paragraphs above this one. Dr. Wood saw Ms. Bradshaw a few months after she got a "Section 8" letter, referring her for a psychiatric evaluation.

Tension had been building between First Officer Bradshaw and a few key personnel at Global, and at least some of this tension was related to Darby's perception that her ideas of how to improve the safety culture at the airline were undervalued, or worse, not appreciated at all...

"Wait a minute, this is an evaluation for Darby. Why is he justifying what Dr. Wood did?" Kathryn asked.

"That's my question, too," Linda said. "But it gets better."

This may have hurt and angered Ms. Bradshaw. She may have come to overvalue her ideas, to vigorously defend herself, and to vilify those who appeared to set aside her concerns. Clinically, this could appear as paranoid thoughts. Injury to the self-esteem of a high-achieving woman may have been hard for Darby to reckon with in a large airline. Her normally verbose speech may have appeared to be almost ranting (and pressured). She may have appeared to be grandiose as she was defending herself. She may have been inclined to be overly inclusive of details that weren't central to defending herself; she could have appeared distracted by these details. She may have appeared to be driven by her desire to set the record straight, at least in her mind.

Dr. Wood's very comprehensive report was, perhaps, a view of Ms. Bradshaw's mental health in a strained work environment, and not a comprehensive view across her entire life. There was no evidence that problems with others at work represented a repeated pattern of troubled relationships for Darby as would be the case if she had narcissistic personality disorder or any other personality disorder in which interpersonal relationships are affected.

"That's really weird that he's defending Wood," Jackie said. "But mostly I'm sorry about Darby's injured self-esteem." She winked at Darby.

"Thanks," Darby said with a grin. "I think it was my grandiosity in defending myself that could have caused it."

"But I thought your grandiosity was being on a first name basis with the CEO," Jackie countered. "Like he's your friend or something." Jackie and Darby clinked their glasses.

"This is nothing like anything I've ever read," Linda said ignoring Darby and Jackie's banter. "This report was supposed to be about Darby. Diagnosing Darby. Not dignifying, justifying or defending why Dr. Wood did what he did."

Kathryn reached for the report and scanned it, as she turned the pages. "Look at this page. He listed the time he spent talking to different people. He spoke to Dr. Sorenson for 10 minutes, but Dr. Wood for one hour." She shook her head. "Wow."

"I think the noose was around my neck," Darby said, more serious now, "and they spent an hour concocting that justification, together."

"I wish there was some way to prove what he said was wrong," Jackie said.

Darby grinned. "Oh, I could prove it, if I needed to."

"How so?" Linda asked.

"Hanover justified Wood's diagnosis because Wood saw me a few months after the Section 8, where Hanover said he assumed tensions were high," Darby said. "However, if you remember in Wood's medical report, he never once in his 366-page report mentioned anything about my behavior, or tension or anxiety, or anything that would be descriptive of Hanover's statement."

"That's right," Kathryn said. "His entire report was based on your safety report trying to discredit you from the authenticity."

"Exactly," Darby said.

"Why do you think he ruled in your favor then?" Jackie asked. "Since he was defending Wood."

"Good question, and I think I have the answer," Darby said. "Kat, do you have more champagne?"

"Kitchen fridge," Kathryn said, looking up from the report.

Darby found the champagne, and returned with the bottle feeling more than a little buzz. "Before I open this, will anyone join me?" All hands raised.

"I think Hanover had to clear me," Darby said as she unwrapped the foil off the bottle, "because of his plans for a career shift. Sorenson had told me he was doing these evaluations one or two days a month, with plans to get out of the military and do them full-time." She pulled the cork with a pop.

"Why would that make a difference?" Jackie asked, extending her glass.

Darby filled Jackie's glass and said, "The FAA medical appeals board ruled in my favor. Not to mention, the western division regional flight surgeon ruled in my favor. The Mayo Clinic ruled in my favor."

"I'm still not following," Jackie said.

"I am." Kathryn said, looking up from the report. "How in the hell would he be able to go against everyone, especially the FAA medical appeals board, in support of Wood's false medical report, and think he would be accepted as an aviation medical examiner for mental health?"

"Exactly," Darby said with a grin. "He was in a bind."

"He had to defend his buddy to soften the blow," Linda said. "Simply disgusting."

"Well, none of that matters now, because you're cleared," Jackie said.

"Truth prevailed." Linda extended her glass, and Darby filled it.

"To truth," Kathryn said, raising her glass.

"Truth," Darby said, "And to kicking their asses in court, and making sure they *never* do this to anyone ever again."

EPILOGUE

SUMMER HAD TURNED to fall, and not until all the leaves had dropped from the trees, did Darby receive her training materials. The company had delayed her yet another three months before she could begin. They would not allow her to receive her manuals until she was scheduled. But she learned there were no manuals. The training materials were answers to the electronic test she had to memorize on a flash drive.

There would be no ground school because now the pilots taught themselves. There would be no level of understanding assessed—simply whether or not she could regurgitate the information from the study guide electronically. She suspected they had delayed her training to ensure she would be paired up with a captain who only had a couple years remaining to fly. One of those holdover captains from Coastal Airways who had not been to training on a new aircraft for over twenty years. Rumor had it more than a dozen of those pilots had quit or failed training.

She wasn't worried about her simulator partner. He'd had his initial training from Coastal Airlines and had been a line check airman. Darby was happy to be paired with a professional. But it was the call she had received the night before which haunted her. She'd been so excited to return, but the reality of what she was about to face had smacked her hard.

The warning was that the Director of Training had advised her instructor to keep an extra eye on her. That was the message to fail her. She knew anyone could take down a pilot in the simulator if they wanted to. Those that began as perfectly good pilots, once the games began, could have their confidence shot so they couldn't do anything right.

Darby would not allow them to get her. The first step was to learn everything.

Now, she was curled up in front of a fire, sitting on the couch, memorizing her study guide. She would be headed to Oklahoma City in three days to take an electronic test to see if she could continue. They couldn't mess with her on that one. *One step a time,* she told herself.

The doorbell rang and Darby glanced at her watch. Tom was out of town, and she couldn't imagine who would be at her door on an early Sunday morning. She stood and stretched, before heading towards the door.

She opened it, and smiled.

"I thought you could use supplies while studying," Kathryn said. "Raspberry Mocha and a ham and egg sandwich."

"Thank you," Darby said, taking the coffee. She was mostly thankful there were two, and Kathryn would be joining her instead of it being a drop off.

"How's studying going?" Kathryn asked, sitting on the edge of the fireplace. She opened the bag and handed Darby a sandwich.

"Good," Darby said. She sat on the couch and removed the wrapper and took a bite. "This is delicious. Thank you. I kind of didn't eat dinner last night."

"I suspected as much."

They ate their breakfast and Darby told Kathryn about her phone call, and how they were after her in training.

"Are you nervous?" Kathryn asked.

"I don't think so. Maybe a little apprehensive." She sipped her coffee, thinking about it. "I was so excited about going back. All I wanted to do was get back to flying. I thought beating them at their own game would make me feel vindicated. But it just feels weird. I feel like I'm heading to the firing squad."

"I understand," Kathryn said, "More than you know."

Darby took another bite of her sandwich. Kathryn had been in a similar situation when she had been removed from her position at the FAA. It had been uncomfortable upon her return, but she survived.

"You know… we're all supposed to be the heroes of our stories called life. We're supposed to take charge, and make our lives happen. Do something important." Darby hesitated, trying to find her words. She took another sip of her coffee and thought about how to explain her feelings.

"Granted, sometimes bad shit happens and we have to deal with it. But… here I am," Darby said. "I saw a problem with our safety culture and training, and presented an internal report. I was warned they would do this to me. They did it. Then I went for a ride for the next two years. I simply got lucky. I accomplished absolutely nothing. My career was taken out of my hands and given to someone else. Dr. Hanover could have easily gone the other direction."

"But he didn't," Kathryn said. "You don't see how much control you had throughout this entire process, do you?"

"Control?" Darby said, and scoffed. "I don't think so."

"You made decisions that took you down the correct path." Kathryn moved to the couch beside Darby. "You did not listen to your union when they told you to take an unpaid leave. You didn't listen to them when they told you not to get your medical. You ignored your union's advice to not disclose you were seeing the psychiatrists on your medical application. You refused to go to Dr. Brody, who would have nailed you. You made the decision to go to the Mayo. You built a rapport with your AME, who knew and trusted you. He stood by you. You wrote the rebuttal to Dr. Wood's report and shipped it off to the FAA. Whatever you said to Dr. Hanover made him go against his *esteemed* colleague."

Darby grinned, and said, "Did you forget anything?"

"Yes," Kathryn said, "You passed that effing neuropsychological test with flying colors. Who does that on the first try?"

Darby laughed. "Okay. Maybe I did have something to do with the outcome. But this has been such an ordeal. Wyatt is gone, but not without his benefits. He received more in retirement than the highest paid pilot. I also think they are going to make him the next FAA administrator. Rich Clark was promoted. And I'm sure that it was Dr. Marsh who violated our contract and told the FAA about this, but nothing is going to happen to him, either. I now have a permanent medical record."

"You also have a record of standing up to these guys," Kathryn said. "I doubt they will ever do this to anyone again."

"I'm sure they won't," Darby said. "But my union really let me down. From what I can see, there were some really bad players who were part of this."

"What are you going to do about that?" Kathryn asked.

Darby grinned. "Maybe I'll run for the Seattle representative position and make sure every pilot is supported no matter what."

"Are you going to go back to the 757 as a captain?" Kathryn asked.

"I'm kind of frozen for a couple of years now," Darby said. "I probably shouldn't have bid off my plane, but at the time it sounded like a good idea."

"I think it was a good idea," Kathryn said. "Two years will go by quickly."

"You know, this is not the first time Global used this tactic," Darby said. "But I am the first pilot who has ever returned."

"You faced the worst possible experience a pilot could face, and you survived," Kathryn said. "I'm proud of you."

"Kat, thank you," Darby said. "I have been trying to figure out what's been bothering me and I think it's that they got away with this, and feeling like all the effort was for nothing. I'm still thinking about what John said, about another potential accident and how bad training is worldwide, and at Global."

"None of this was for nothing," Kathryn said.

Darby thought about that and then said, "No, it wasn't. And now that I have my job back, I don't have to rent my house and I can afford my attorney fees."

"How's the case going?" Kathryn asked.

"We've officially filed the appeal and we requested discovery from both the company and Dr. Wood. We're scheduling depositions to occur after my training's complete."

"That's going to be time consuming," Kathryn said.

"And there you have it," Darby said. "The reason that being a first officer on an international airplane works for me. Time and money will both be on my side."

"Do you think your case will make it all the way to court?" Kathryn asked.

"I hope not," Darby said. "I don't think they'll like what a judge will have to say about what they did. It probably won't be the best publicity."

"Do you think you will win the AIR 21?" Kathryn asked.

"From what Robert has told me of the law, absolutely," Darby said. "But at the end of the day there is truth, and there is justice. It all comes down to what you can prove in court."

"You prove the truth, and you'll get justice," Kathryn said.

Darby raised her coffee and said, "To truth and justice."

ACKNOWLEDGMENTS

BRINGING A BOOK to life takes a team. People often wonder how I do it all—I don't. I have people who help. My team is phenomenal in every way, and I am ever so grateful for them and their assistance. They are the reason this book made publication in 2020. Thank you all!

Nathan Everett is my go to guy for his final editing talent, with an eye for perfection. He is a master of publication, and is always willing to work my projects into his schedule. This time he said, "you are my priority." He can be found at elderroadbooks@outlook.com.

Captain Kathy McCullough is actively supporting female pilots and involved in many social groups. She is the author of Ups and Downs, To The Edges of the World, and Breakfast in Narita. In her busy schedule she took the time to do a detailed final line edit. I cannot thank her enough for stepping up in the final hour, and dedicating her attention to this book, and for the wonderful endorsement.

Trimbi Szabo is a pilot and passionate reader who loves Darby Bradshaw. She edited the first draft of this book while on vacation. I now think Trimbi is ready to write a novel of her own, and I'll be there for her support. While many of the passages have changed since her read, hopefully she will enjoy it the second time around as well.

Dick Petitt, my husband of 39 years, felt like he lived this story. He read, edited, and gave me great feedback throughout the entire process. There is no greater support system than my husband. He always places everyone else's priorities above his own, and never complains if I'm up late with a deadline. He also plays scrabble with me every night, too.

Captain John Nance, Captain Kathy McCullough, and Mike Lawson—I am honored to have these best-selling authors give me their valuable time to read and endorse *Flight For Truth*. Especially when they are all in the middle of projects of their own.

ADDITIONAL WRITINGS

NOVELS

Flight For Control
Flight For Safety
Flight For Survival
Flight for Sanity
Flight For Truth
Flight For Justice (February 2021)

NON-FICTION:

Normalization of Deviance, A Threat to Aviation Safety
Based on the dissertation
Safety Culture, Training, Understanding, Aviation Passion: The Impact on Manual Flight and Operational Performance
https://petittaviationresearch.com

Flight To Success Be the Captain of Your Life.
For everyone who wants to master their life and achieve their dreams

I am Awesome, the ABCs of being me
To inspire your little ones to find their passion and think of how passion can apply to a career

ABOUT KARLENE

KARLENE PETITT IS an international
airline pilot who is type-rated,
and has flown and/or instructed
on the B777, B747-400, B747-
200, B767, B757, B737, B727,
and A330 aircraft. She has been
a pilot for 41 years, holds MBA
and MHS degrees, and earned
her PhD in Aviation, with a focus on safety, from Embry Riddle
Aeronautical University. Petitt is a mother of three, grandmother
of eight, and author who has written numerous books in multiple
genres. Novels: *Flight For Control, Flight For Safety, Flight For Survival,
Flight for Sanity, and Flight For Truth. Motivation: Flight to Success:
Be the Captain of your Life. For the children: I am Awesome, the ABCs
of being me*

KARLENE IS AVAILABLE to host aviation discussion groups, join book
clubs, or speak at your meetings.

Please email her at Karlene.Petitt@gmail.com to schedule your next
event. And check out her blog for more writings at KarlenePetitt.com

www.ingramcontent.com/pod-product-compliance
Lightning Source LLC
Chambersburg PA
CBHW020637020726
47494CB00001B/234